PRAISE FOR MYKE COLE

*"A dark fantasy tale with sharp teeth and a hard punch.
Heloise is the hero we need, and Myke Cole is the writer to bring her
transformation to light."*
Chuck Wendig, New York Times Bestselling author

"Cross The Forever War *with* Witch World, *add in the real world
modern military of* Black Hawk Down, *and you get*
Control Point, *the mile-a-minute story of someone trying to find purpose
in a war he never asked for."*
Jack Campbell, New York Times Bestselling author of
The Lost Fleet series

*"Cole's managed to cover a hero's journey story, a quest story,
and now a running battle interspersed with a romance.
It works spectacularly."*
io9

*"A tense and action-packed ride... full of desperate,
back-against-the-wall combat scenes."*
Tor.com

*"Very entertaining... The best ride military fantasy has to offer...
The Magic 8 Ball says 'will enjoy.'"*
Mark Lawrence, international bestselling
author of *The Liar's Key*

"Hands down, the best military fantasy I've ever read."
Ann Aguirre, national bestselling author of *Endgame*

BY THE SAME AUTHOR

Myke Cole

SIXTEENTH WATCH

ANGRY
ROBOT

ANGRY ROBOT
An imprint of Watkins Media Ltd

Unit 11, Shepperton House
89 Shepperton Road
London N1 3DF
UK

angryrobotbooks.com
twitter.com/angryrobotbooks
Hold on to your hats…

An Angry Robot paperback original, 2020

Cover by Issac Hannaford
Edited by Simon Spanton-Walker and Paul Simpson
Set in Adobe Garamond

ISBN 978 0 85766 805 9
Ebook ISBN 978 0 85766 806 6

Printed and bound in the United Kingdom by TJ International Ltd.

9 8 7 6 5 4 3 2 1

FSC
www.fsc.org

MIX
Paper from
responsible sources
FSC® C013056

AUTHOR'S NOTE

This book relies heavily on military acronyms. In order to maintain authenticity and not interrupt the narrative, I will not always define those acronyms for the reader. I am including a glossary at the end of the book for those who need it.

For those of you familiar with radio argot and the structure and operational procedures of the United States military, and the Coast Guard in particular, you will doubtless notice deviations from your experience. This is a work of science fiction, and I have taken some liberties in evolving both the service and the military at large to fit the purpose of the narrative. Where I could, I have cleaved as closely as possible to my own experience in the guard. Any errors are entirely my own, and I beg your patience with them.

AUTHOR'S NOTE

PROLOGUE

…Live from the Moon's Lacus Doloris, the "Lake of Sorrows" where tensions between American and Chinese Helium-3 miners have just escalated into open violence. Now, technically, the 1967 Outer Space Treaty prevents exploitation of lunar resources for the benefit of any one country, but settlement here has outstripped the authorities' ability to do anything but keep groups of miners separate and keep the peace. Until now, that is.

JENNIFER HSU, REPORTING FOR THE LUNAR 6 NETWORK.

The Coast Guard Cutter *Aries* bucked as she fired attitude thrusters to keep herself in position, making her groan and creak like a wooden sailing ship. Below her, the Lake of Sorrows boiled, its surface rippling with knots of miners, hurling boulders in the lunar gravity.

Commander Jane Oliver didn't bother to look through the quartz-glass window in the cutter's underbelly. She also didn't bother to check the LADAR for the *Aries'* exact altitude above the Moon. Though her eyes were still sharp despite fifty years of hard use, she knew it was too far to see much with the naked eye. Instead, she turned her attention to the high-definition screen and its magnified view. Digital crosshairs swept over the mobs of dueling miners. She would have felt better if the rioters had formed some sort of battle-line, but the skirmish had become so intense that all sense of organization had vanished, with clots of people battling back and forth, swirling and mixing like droplets of oil on the surface of an agitated pond. In the chaos she was left to pick out the Chinese from the Americans by their suits, with her countrymen in their bulky hardshell models lumbering forward to scatter their more agile Chinese enemies in skintight biosuits. If it came to guns, the Americans would be glad of that thick, rigid material, but it hadn't come to guns yet.

Thank God.

Oliver had spent her career on the surface of the Earth, most of it saving drunk boaters from freezing water. The most violence she'd seen was when a bigger version of Willie Nelson decided to resist arrest after her boarding team had found a kilo of uncut heroin in the hold of his fishing vessel. She'd certainly never dealt with a riot in lunar-g. She rubbed her temples. "Somebody please tell me how this happened again?"

She could make out knots of police, American Lacus Doloris Police Department officers and Chinese People's Armed Police, watching from a distance, guns at the low ready. She didn't blame them for staying out of it. The melee was much too big for them to do any good without killing people. They were trying to keep it contained while they waited for orders, and backup, hopefully.

"Who knows?" Lieutenant Commander Wen Ho's voice was politician smooth, soft and calming. Her executive officer had been working with her since she'd pinned on field-grade rank, and was like a lung to her. She felt herself relax as soon as she heard the hint of humor that always rode his words. "Near as we can tell, a Chinese miner detonated a charge that resulted in an accidental American death. The Americans lynched the Chinese miner, and things just kind of played out from there."

Oliver nodded and looked back to the screen. Several of the habs were already demolished. She could see the miners bounding through the wreckage, stopping only long enough to scoop up huge chunks of structure, 3D-printed from the lunar soil. The debris would have weighed hundreds of pounds on Earth, but on the lunar-g surface of the Moon, the miners lifted the chunks easily, and with no atmosphere to slow them down once they were thrown... She watched in horror as an American miner threw a car-sized hunk at a fleeing Chinese man in a biosuit. She could almost hear the crunch as the debris impacted and he went down.

"This is out of control," she said. "We don't know anything else?"

"I already asked for clarification," Ho replied, and she smiled. Of course he had. "This is Navy intel we're talking to here."

Oliver increased the pressure on her temples. "Let me guess... you don't have a..."

"...Need-to-know, yes," Ho finished her sentence for her, "that is precisely what they said. I have already registered a complaint."

"Those fuckers will *never* learn that there are *five* armed services in the United States," Oliver said. "Have you reached out to the LDPD?"

Ho stepped over to the screen, moving with a dancer's grace despite the spin-gravity forcing a slight lean. His body was so long and thin he looked made of stretchable plastic. He tapped the monitor with a slender finger. "See that?"

"That..." Jane leaned closer, squinting at a jumble of twisted metal in the middle of the riot, "...is that another smashed hab? A vehicle park?"

"That's the regional communications array," Ho said, "they're bringing the backup online, but it'll be a minute."

She looked up at the radar just as the watchstander opened his mouth to speak. "Thanks, BM3," she cut him off, "I see."

A capsule-shaped wash of blue indicated the cutter *Volans* coming out of orbit and maneuvering in alongside. She took another look at the riot, and willed the fighting to stabilize before anyone else got hurt. "Give me a visual."

The screen flashed away from the rioting and showed the *Volans*, rocking as its reaction-control system engaged, attitude thrusters keeping its bulk from spinning. Whoever was at the helm was good, and she glided into a station keeping position alongside *Aries*. At 378 feet, the Constellation Class cutters were the biggest ships the Coast Guard had, but Oliver knew they would be dwarfed even by the smaller Navy frigates. The double triangle constellation Volans was painted on the ship's side, above a cartoonish image of a flying-fish.

The encrypted radio channel buzzed. "Coast Guard Cutter *Aries*, Coast Guard Cutter *Aries*, this is Coast Guard Cutter *Volans*, over."

Oliver waved off both Ho and her radio watchstander and grabbed the mic herself. "Hi Clare."

"Jane, sorry," Lieutenant Commander Clare Montaigne sounded frightened, "figured it was faster to ride out the orbit than try to burn all the way here."

"Don't sweat it, you're well in time."

"What the hell is going on?"

"Nobody knows, but LDPD aren't going to do anything about it, and people are dying down there. I need you to turn out your boarding teams. How many small boats you have on there?"

"I've got two longhorns, same as you."

"No, I mean are either of them charlie status?"

"No, they're ready to go, but are you sure this is the right move? I see the PAP on my screen here. What if we spook them? If shooting starts, people could die."

"If you see the PAP on the screen, then you also see the riot, and you know that people are dying right now while we sit here jaw-jacking. Turn out your crews, launch your boats, and let's get down there and stop this thing."

"Jane, I don't…" Montaigne began. Her voice was cut off by a priority hail on the encrypted channel.

"Hang on, Clare," Oliver said, hovering her finger over the button that would patch the priority hail through. "I've got an override."

"It's probably Ops, hopefully with orders."

So long as they're the right ones, Oliver thought, punching the button. "*Aries* Actual, go ahead."

Oliver felt herself automatically stiffen at the sound of Admiral Allen's voice. She'd only met the Coast Guard's head of operations once, when he'd spoken at the change-of-command ceremony that saw her installed as the CO of the *Aries*, and once had been enough to cement her impression. Save for a rare few, admirals were political animals, soft-handed smooth-operators long removed from the late-nights, bad coffee, and tense stand-offs that were the Coast Guard's daily fare. Allen was one of those rare few. "Jane, you wouldn't perhaps be thinking of launching your boats now, would you?" Allen had long mastered the trick of combining gentle, amused-sounding words with a tone of pure iron.

"I'm the operational commander on scene, admiral," Oliver said. "It's my call."

"Not anymore, it's not," Allen said. "The Navy is taking point on this. You and the *Volans* will deploy on their mark and according to their instructions."

Oliver felt the familiar frustration boiling up the back of her throat. The Navy. Always the goddamn Navy. "Sir, with all due respect... what the hell? This is a civilian riot. We need to *de*escalate. The Navy is a warfighting service. That sends the wrong message. We can't send them blazing in there to..."

Her voice cut off as Allen hit the override button and the buzz of his hail made her wince. He paused, letting the silence make its point before he spoke. "What's this 'we' business you're referencing, Commander? There is no *we* here. There is only *me*, receiving my orders from the Commandant, who got them from the Secretary of

Homeland Security. Just little old me, passing those orders along to little old you. That clear?"

Oliver could picture the Navy assault craft disgorging marines onto the surface, the frigates shadowing them overhead, bristling with deck guns and ball-turrets visible to anyone who cared to glance at a radar signature. This was going to be bad. But she was lucky Allen had been willing to indulge her even this far. She swallowed. "Aye aye, sir."

"Besides," Allen's tone softened, "we're keeping this in the family anyway."

"Excuse me, sir?"

"Ops out."

As soon as the click signaled that Allen had cut comms, the watchstander spoke. "Ma'am, we've got a contact coming out of orbit."

Oliver glanced at the radar and instantly identified it as a Perry Class Navy frigate. She tensed at the thought of its crenelated hull-signature showing up on Chinese radar. Missile pods, deck guns, extended launch bays crammed with assault craft.

The watchstander's voice cracked as he said, "It's… It's the *Coates*, ma'am."

Oliver's mouth went dry. She felt her heart speed up. The *Coates* was the frigate commanded by…

"Hello, Commander!" Thomas Oliver's voice sounded over the radio. "Sorry to steal your thunder."

…her husband.

She remembered them lying on the couch in their Brooklyn apartment, right after she'd pressed the assignment officer for a transfer to the Moon. *You realize what's inevitably going to happen if we're both out there on the 16th watch?* he'd asked.

We'll wind up running an op together, Oliver had said, nestling her head on his shoulder and burrowing her foot between his calves.

It's inevitable, Tom had said. The wine made her drowsy, and his voice was a pleasant buzz. The kids had been out of the house for years now, but they were well past the age where they'd rush to take advantage of the quiet time. A tendril of desire flickered somewhere between the bottom of her ribs and the tops of her thighs, but she'd been content to let it be for the moment.

I don't know, she'd said. *Nothing's inevitable.*

Tom ignored her, *So what do we do when it happens?*

Oliver had shrugged, kissed his neck. The tendril of desire was snaking down further, lighting up her crotch.

Our jobs.

Jane Oliver watched her husband's ship fire attitude thrusters to move in alongside her cutter, its launch bay doors locking open, and realized that the time for them to do their jobs had finally come.

She tried to say something professional, a greeting, a formality, anything. Instead what came out was, "Is this some kind of a joke?"

The encrypted channel made Tom's laugh into jovial static. "Don't think I can handle it?"

She glanced at the picture she kept taped to the corner of her desk monitor – the last family photo they'd taken at their daughter Alice's wedding. Alice in her white dress, dark-haired like her mother, her brother Adam smiling as much as he ever did. Oliver stood in front of them, shorter by a head than both her kids. Tom towered over them all, sandy-blonde hair and blue eyes sinking in a joyful sea of crow's feet, beaming as if he knew some happy secret that he couldn't wait to tell the world.

"Of course you can handle it," she spoke into the radio, wishing she could see his face. She briefly considered asking the watchstander to get her a video call, but that was a level of intimacy she didn't want to share with everyone on the bridge. This familiar talk over an encrypted radio channel was bad enough. "You can handle it better than anyone alive, but the Navy's the wrong tool for the job and you know it."

She could hear Tom's smile, the sad and serious one he wore to show the person he was talking to that he had heard their concern and was doing what he wanted anyway. "I also know that it isn't up to me. But I'd be lying if I didn't take some perverse pleasure from being in charge."

"Jesus Christ," Oliver breathed. "Talk about insult to injury." *Enough. Just be professional.* "You want me to hold position?"

"Nope. I want you planetside, ready to respond. Bring the *Aries* as low as you can and launch the small boats. Station keep back from the skirmish line but stay close. I want you ready to respond if there are civilian casualties."

"There are already casualties, and there's no skirmish line."

"I intend to make one. And I mean *more* casualties."

"I've already ordered the boats loaded for bear. I'm not taking the guns off the hardpoints and…"

"I'm not asking you to. If you need it and don't have it, then you'll never need it again."

She rubbed her temples harder, risked a sideways glance at Ho. Her XO was smiling at her, arms folded. Somehow, the look gave her strength. "OK. When do we jump?"

"ASAP," Tom said. "We're going now." Oliver could see the Navy boats streaming out of the launch bays, moving entirely on thrusters, their solar sails swept over their flanks. Like the frigate they'd left behind, they bristled with armament.

"We… Are you on one of those small boats?"

"Goddamn right I am. This is as delicate a thing as I've ever seen. I want hands-on personally."

"Then I'm coming down too. For the same reasons. This needs the skipper's touch."

"Hey, I'm not arguing. See you down there," Tom's voice had its smile back, the bigger one he wore most of the time. He toggled to a private channel, so that his voice was only audible to Oliver's ears. "And angel? I love you."

"Great," Oliver said, feeling her cheeks flush.

"Say it," Tom said, still on the private channel, "come on."

"I'm on the bridge, Tom," Oliver said as quietly as she could manage. "Jesus Christ." Ho laughed, and the watchstander suddenly became very busy with the work on his desk.

"Say it," Tom repeated. He sounded pouty.

Oliver couldn't help but snort a laugh. "I love you too."

"Oh, yeeeahhhh," Tom said and cut the connection.

The boat bay was outside the cutter's toroidal spin-gravity module, and Oliver stepped through the airlock with the queasy feeling of her stomach rising inside her abdomen. *Christ. I never get used to this.* She took a deep breath of stale, recycled air, and drifted toward where the longhorns waited.

Small boats were all named for beetles, on account of their hunched hulls. Nobody ever penetrated atmosphere in a small boat, and so there was no need for aerodynamics. Instead, they'd been designed to carry crews and to deploy solar sails to take advantage of surface maser-lanes, folded over their back like beetle-wings when they were not in use. The *Aries* carried two Longhorn Class boats, each just twenty-nine feet long. Oliver had ordered the 23mm autocannons mounted on the fore and aft hardpoints, which added to the squat insectile look, a single antennae and ovipositor. The guns were designed to breach the hulls of fleeing craft, exposing them to the vacuum of space. The massive rounds would turn even a human in a hardshell into red mist. If she had to use the guns, then something would have gone horribly wrong, but being responsible for people's safety meant *all* people's safety, and that included her crew.

That crew was mustering outside the longhorns now. A longhorn could run with a crew of four, but was rated to carry up to ten. The guard liked to run light, and so four sailors were doing boat checks now. Chief Brad Elgin was the first to look up at her. He was just a few years younger than her, short and blocky. Most coasties had calloused hands, but Chief had spent so much time underway that his entire being seemed calloused, roughed over and tested by salt-spray on Earth's oceans and radiation out here with no atmosphere to screen him from the sun. "Skipper," he nodded, "just finishing up boat checks here."

"Great," she said, "sorry I had to finish up a few other things on the bridge. Give me a minute to suit up and we can launch."

Linda Flecha, the crew's engineer, stiffened. She was taller than Chief, but not by much, and it was hard to tell, as she'd already put on her suit's hardshell, the huge articulating plates making her look like some giant, rigid balloon animal. Her long black hair was braided and wound into a bun on top of her head, barely clearing the hardshell's massive shoulders. "You're coming with us?"

Chief shot Flecha a glare and she hastily tacked on a "ma'am."

"If you don't mind," Oliver said. "Thought this was important enough to warrant a personal touch." Her habit of asking her subordinates' opinions rattled them, she knew, as did her insistence on performing menial tasks below her pay grade, but she wasn't about to stop. Treating her people like *people* was the only way she wanted to lead, and though it had likely held her back on the climb up the promotional chain, she slept just fine at night.

"Come on," Andraste Kariawasm's inability to control his mouth was mitigated by his unmatched skill at piloting the longhorn, "her husband's skipper on the Navy detail. He's down there so..."

"So, I'm going too," Oliver finished for him. "Thanks, coxs'un. As always, I find your candor refreshing."

"Sorry, ma'am," Kariawasm grinned, "should have asked permission to speak freely."

"We'll discuss that mouth of yours when we debrief," Chief said. "Get your ass on the boat."

Kariawasm nodded and ducked through the hatch. His mother was Greek and his father Sri Lankan, and the combination had resulted in a man nearly as tall as Ho, but with more muscle, so big he had almost failed the physical to qualify on small boats. *Lucky for the guard that he passed*, Oliver thought as he made himself comfortable at the helm.

Connor McGrath had also almost failed the physical qualification for his size. The Irishman was so bull-necked his head seemed welded directly to his shoulders. His eyes were perpetually half-lidded, as if he were eternally ready for a nap. Oliver had always wondered if the guy was a little slow, but that was fine. He was a solid team-player, and as the crew's designated bruiser, she didn't want him overthinking things. Even with four long guns hanging around his stub of a neck, he managed to look unburdened. He slapped the butt of one, setting them all drifting on their slings. "You want me to grab another one for you, ma'am?"

"No, thanks," Oliver said, pushing off to drift behind the privacy screen just long enough to change into the skintight day-glow orange bodysuit that all coasties wore under their other suit layers. She came back around just in time to see Ho setting the plastic case containing her bunny suit and hardshell to float just above the deck.

"Ma'am, with respect, we could really use your help here, on the *Aries*," he said. His voice was a bland monotone that showed that he already knew what her response would be, was engaging in a pro-forma ritual out of familiarity.

"I appreciate that," Oliver said, slipping into her bunny suit and connecting the leads to her bodysuit. The base layer would monitor her heart rate, her breathing, sending information on her vitals to the Heads Up Display on the inside of her helmet visor. The thick layer of the bunny suit would have her sweating in a few minutes, but she'd be grateful for it once the unheated boat launched and departed the climate-controlled bay for the cold of space. "But there's no one who I have more faith in. Consider this a training exercise," she said as Ho helped her fit the hardshell torso over her head, testing the shoulder articulation by swinging her arms. "You need more experience running a bridge."

"Aye aye, ma'am," Ho said, locking the helmet in place and giving her a thumbs up as the seal indicator light flashed green. "I'll relay your orders to Commander Montaigne. Both longhorns launched and station keeping."

Oliver used her chin to toggle the button that piped her voice to the hardshell's external speaker. "Tell her to use her judgment if it gets hot, but otherwise wait for my mark."

She glanced over her shoulder to see if the rest of the crew had already boarded the longhorn, saw only white plastic. She would never get used to the hardshell's limitations. She checked again, turning her whole body this time, and saw the crew in position and waiting for her.

"I'll get the crew turned out for SAR-2," Ho said, motioning to the other longhorn, "just in case."

She set a hand on his shoulder, the hardshell's articulated gauntlet making her giant fingers eclipse his upper arm. "Wen. It's fine."

He sighed. "I know it is, ma'am. Just be careful out there."

She frowned through the clear plastic of the helmet's faceplate. "When am I not?"

"It's just… this is the first time you and Tom have done a joint op and it worries me."

"I'm delighted that you care, and horrified that you have so little faith in my professionalism."

"I do care, and even my judgment would be clouded if it were Ting-Wei down there."

She felt a lump in the back of her throat, swallowed it down. Wen

Ho loved his wife like he loved air and water. The only thing that came close were their two children, at home in New York City. "Wen, thanks, truly. But I've got this."

"I know you do, ma'am, and so do I. Don't worry about things up here, stay in the bubble."

"Always," Oliver said, and ducked through the hatch.

The longhorn's interior was cramped even by spacegoing standards. Where the Navy insisted on deck gray and black for camouflage, the search-and-rescue oriented Coast Guard insisted on white and the fluorescent orange of their suits. Oliver squinted against a riot of color. The longhorn could pressurize and heat its interior if needed, but it was a cumbersome process, and with the crew expecting to deploy to the Moon's surface, they'd be relying on their suits to handle that work.

"Everybody hold on," Chief said as the crane hauled the boat up and over the launch bay doors. The boat bay might not have had spin-gravity, but the Moon's gravity still exerted a pull, and Oliver reached out for one of the super-sized metal handgrips on the boat's roof. She gripped it just in time for the deck to pitch sickeningly under her feet as the crane adjusted, tilting the longhorn to point nose down at the bay doors.

She turned and looked out the starboard side window in time to see Ho closing the airlock behind him. A moment later, a red klaxon flashed. "Venting atmosphere in three, two, one…" His voice sounded in Oliver's helmet speakers. She knew Ho was using the crew-wide channel, and that everyone else on the boat was hearing him as well. "Opening bay doors."

Below them, the bay doors slid slowly open, and the Moon stretched out beneath them.

"Sound off," Chief called to the crew, the speakers in his helmet made his voice sound tinny. This was a ritual officers weren't supposed to hear, Oliver knew, but she had barged onto his boat and that meant she would have to shut up and pretend it wasn't happening.

"Honor, respect and devotion to duty, Chief!" the crew responded, casting worried glances at Oliver.

"Not that bullshit," Chief said, "sound off for real."

The crew's discomfort was palpable, and Oliver felt a pang of guilt for being the cause of it. Small boats just didn't get underway with the cutter's skipper on board. But the thought of Tom out there without her made her stomach do loops. If it was a weakness to want to go help him in person, it was one she would indulge. She used her chin to toggle the radio to the bridge's channel. Maybe if she were having a separate conversation, the crew would feel more privacy. "Coast Guard Cutter *Aries,* Coast Guard Cutter *Aries,* this is CG-23359 requesting designator."

"Sound off for *real!*" Chief said again.

"CG-23359, this is *Aries,*" Ho's voice came back over the commlink in Oliver's helmet, "CG-23359 is designated Search-And-Rescue-One for mission duration. I say again, 359 is SAR-1. Good luck, all."

"We have to go out," the crew said now, eyes locked on the bay doors, still sliding open, the velvet black of the void swirling below.

"But we don't have to come back," Chief said. "Let's go save some lives."

The Moon's surface glowed, swathed in blots of gray terrain that looked like mist to Oliver's naked eye. The sun's radiation bathed them, blocked by the shielding in the longhorn's hull and the armor of their hardshells. The wash of it made the Moon blink like a warning.

"Boat checks are green. Ops normal," Chief radioed to Ho on the bridge. "Go when ready."

"Roger that," Ho said as the bolts fired and the crane released them.

"SAR-1, launch."

They fell.

They dropped down into the middle of the fight.

Oliver swallowed the last of the sickening nausea of their free fall. Even in the Moon's low gravity the boat accelerated fast enough, until the plummet became wrenching and she was grateful when Kariawasm engaged the thrusters and the longhorn leveled off just above the Moon's surface.

The gray-white of the lunar regolith was scarred and stirred by buggy tires, boot prints, and the tread of the gardeners, the mobile 3D-printers leaving divots as they sucked up the regolith before pumping it full of bonding agents and plasticizer and putting it to use as construction material. The fruit of that labor was all around them – the low domes of the habs with their radiation shielding cowls; most of the structure underground where it could take advantage of the Moon's natural heat exchanging; the maser-pylons firing their invisible beams to create propulsion lanes for the solar sails; and the tall tubes of the Helium-3 furnaces, the shovel scoops funneling in regolith as fast as they could cook it down. The regolith, the Moon's soil, was the stuff of the surface itself, and Oliver marveled at how quickly humanity devoured it.

All around the structures, the miners fought, utterly careless how they were destroying what they had worked so hard to build. Oliver could see intertwined groups of miners spacing out, drawing back into two groups marked out by their different suits – hardshells on one side, biosuits on the other.

Tom had gotten his skirmish line after all.

She saw the Navy boats immediately, stag-beetles to the guard's longhorns, bristling with guns that had clearly given heart to the American miners.

"They think the cavalry's coming," Chief said.

"Yeah," Oliver agreed, "they think the cavalry's coming to help them take the fight to the enemy. That's not good."

Below the Navy boats, the American miners were surging forward with renewed aggression. There was still no shooting, but the melee had become tightly locked, urgent in a way that she knew could only get worse. But Tom's boats had forced a line of separation to open up as the Chinese miners fell back, standing shoulder-to-shoulder in an effort to prevent the Americans from advancing toward their habs, where their families were hiding.

"Get me a channel to the Navy's lead boat," she said.

"Thought you might want that," Kariawasm was already toggling the channels for her. "Go ahead."

"Tom, are you there? They think we're…"

"I know, babe." Her husband's voice had the same maddening smile as when they'd spoken on the bridge. It both frustrated and comforted her that he could be so relaxed in the midst of a crisis. "Calm things down back here. I'll establish a front and keep them separated."

As he spoke, Tom's boat fired its thrusters and executed a smart port-side turn, diving down between the fighting miners and running the skirmish line. The miners scrambled back from the boat's attitude thrusters, though Tom was careful not to fire them. The two sides parted, drew away from one another. Oliver was put in mind of the fable of the Red Sea.

She used her chin to activate the commlink once more, "Be careful."

Tom's response was a popping sound that she belatedly realized was a blown kiss. "Always."

"Orders, ma'am," Chief called to her.

"Wen, what's my SITREP?" Oliver spoke into her own commlink after chin-toggling back to the *Aries'* bridge.

"LDPD is finally on the move," Ho's voice came back. "We must have inspired them. Looks like most of the action in your zone is around the gardener repair facility. I sent the coords to your plotter. It's pretty hot over there, so don't take any chances."

"Roger that, thanks," Oliver cut the connection, "Chief…"

"One step ahead of you, skipper," Chief said, as Kariawasm executed a tight burn and the boat spun. He fired the aft thrusters and they rocketed over the heads of the miners. The curved domes of the habs dotted the lunar mare's surface, big bubbles of their radiation-shielding cowls interrupting the smaller bubbles of the miners' hardshell helmets. A few of them waved up at the small boat, or pumped fists. The idiots really did think SAR-1 was there to help them rout their neighbors. They'd be singing a different tune when the settlement was placed under martial law. One of the miners had pulled the stars-and-stripes off the roof of one of the government habs and was waving it madly overhead, the fabric billowing in the weak lunar gravity.

"That's it," Flecha pointed at the long, broad expanse of the gardener repair facility. Outside, at least five of the mobile 3D-printers were knocked on their sides. American miners boiled around the base, trying to reach two more Americans standing on the roof. She could tell by the make of their hardshells that they were a man and woman. The man was laying about him with a metal pole, and the woman hurling down chunks of debris. One collided with a miner's helmet, and Oliver could see the puff of atmosphere indicating the neck seal had been compromised. She prayed that the person inside was able to get on emergency oxygen quickly enough. *Why are Americans attacking Americans?*

Without atmosphere to carry the sound, there was no point in trying to shout a warning, and she didn't have time to negotiate with the LDPD for the public channel. "Put her down."

"Where, ma'am?" Kariawasm asked.

"Right in the middle of them. If they don't want to get squished, they'll get the hell out of the way."

Chief toggled the switch for the blue lights, and the crowd turned as the flashing strobe sent rays flickering across the structure's wall.

"Do we still need to…" Kariawasm began.

"Set this boat down right now," Oliver raised her voice, saw the crew wince as the speakers in their helmets relayed her impatience.

Kariawasm wasn't happy, but he was far too professional to let a stern order rattle him. He gave the attitude thrusters a nudge, just enough to pivot the longhorn sideways and send it drifting into the crowd. They fell back just as they had from Tom's boat, desperate to keep clear of the thruster nozzles, as potentially deadly as the muzzle of the autocannon. All Coast Guard longhorns were outfitted with an LED readout that scrolled along the hull collar. Stock messages were preset by switches right below the blue lights, and Chief hit one now as he motioned to McGrath to open the hatch. The glowing red words scrolled across the cabin's interior readout as they would appear moving along the outside of the craft. DISPERSE AND DEPART THE AREA OR WE WILL FIRE ON YOU – AUTH 14 USC 89.

McGrath was the first out, leveling a long gun. It was a duster, one of the big bore shotguns they used for boarding actions. They were meant to fire dust, a cloud of metal particles that would easily shred a human at close range, even through a hardshell, but would disperse too quickly to pierce a ship's thicker hull, exposing the boarding team to the vacuum of space. McGrath had likely loaded it with plastic frangible slugs, enough to put someone in a hardshell out of the fight without compromising the suit's integrity.

The crowd scattered as he raised the weapon. Oliver snatched one of the beanbag pistols from the arms rack above the seat and followed him out. She checked the boat's collar to ensure that the LED was scrolling correctly, and once she'd confirmed that it was, began making vigorous get-the-fuck-out-of-here motions with her hand to make sure the point was getting across.

There must have been at least thirty miners around her, and she was momentarily painfully aware of how surrounded her small team was.

She was reassured by the autocannon on its hardpoint, swiveling to track the crowd as Kariawasm worked the controls.

"Don't!" Chief's voice sounded in their commlinks, and Oliver turned, realized that he was shouting at the two on the roof, forgetting that they couldn't hear him in his excitement. Oliver looked up to see the woman lifting another chunk of debris just before Chief's plastic round caught her in the face. The bullet exploded, lifting her off her feet in the lunar gravity and sending her onto her back on the far side of the roof.

"Shit," Chief said.

"I got it," Oliver said, "just make sure the ones down here steer clear."

She ran to the utility ladder on the structure's side and began hauling herself up it. The weak lunar gravity meant she weighed little more than a car battery on Earth, and she flew up the rungs, barely having to use her arms.

"Sorry, skipper," Flecha said, racing to climb up behind her, "can't let you run this alone."

Oliver crested the ladder top and pointed her gun at the man, who was raising his hands and backing away. Once Oliver was on the roof, he began gesturing frantically at the woman. At this distance, Oliver was able to bridge directly to his radio. She looked at her helmet's interior HUD and saw the blinking icon that indicated the man, chin-toggled to select it. "I'll check on her. You will remain here until instructed otherwise. You will not move, and you will not interfere with myself or any of the other officers, do you understand?"

"I'm American!" he shouted back to her in slightly accented English. "I'm not Chinese!"

He unsmoked his faceplate and Oliver could make out his Asian features, his eyes wide and panicked. "I believe you, sir. Just follow my instructions and you'll be fine."

"I have my passport!" the man shouted at her, but made no move to interfere.

Oliver made her way to the woman, who was getting to her feet. Chief's round had knocked off her radio antenna and her suit's camera, but it hadn't compromised her visor. She was fine.

"She OK?" Flecha asked.

"Suit's damaged, but she'll be fine."

Flecha scanned the Quick Response Code on the man's suit and checked the readout in her helmet's HUD. "They're Americans."

"Chinese-Americans," Oliver said. "I'm guessing that gang of idiots down there felt it was a distinction in search of a difference."

"Uh, ma'am," McGrath's voice crackled over the commlink.

Oliver raced to the roof's edge as McGrath spoke. "PLAN's here."

The Chinese People's Liberation Army Navy small boats looked nearly identical to Tom's, save the antennae array and the aft mounted ball turrets, and of course, the huge red and yellow stars blazoned on their hulls, the numbers 8-1 written in Chinese below the anchor symbol.

"Well, that's not good," Oliver muttered as the small boats touched down. One of them came alongside Tom's vessel, running the skirmish line, and the Chinese miners moved forward to just outside the range of its attitude thrusters, emboldened by their own cavalry's arrival. Two more set down just behind the crowd, and Oliver winced as they disgorged fire-teams of Chinese marines. They were armed with hornet guns, compensating for the recoil by firing tiny smart munitions at low velocity, which in turn would fire their own rockets after they'd exited the muzzle to bring them up to lethal speed.

Hornet guns weren't less-lethal munitions for crowd control. They were weapons of war.

Oliver winced watching Tom's small boat and the PLAN boat matching speed and direction, just meters apart, turrets swiveled to train their guns on one another. She swallowed a sudden desperate need to radio him. She didn't want to risk breaking his concentration. She hoped to God it wouldn't matter.

"Skipper," Flecha's voice sounded unusually calm, which worried Oliver even more. "I may have two contacts off our starboard beam, two hundred yards out."

They weren't on a boat, but Flecha communicated by instinct, using the nautical parlance all coasties knew by heart. Oliver turned to follow her directions, looking off to Flecha's right, then using her chin to toggle the magnification lenses in her helmet. They slid down with a click audible inside the pressurized suit and dialed their focus in at two hundred yards.

Oliver could see two figures scrambling over something long and low. They were wearing skintight suits, which likely marked them as Chinese, but Oliver couldn't be certain. An American could buy a biosuit same as anyone else. She squinted in spite of the magnification, painfully aware that her focus was off the chaos around her, and stared at the figures. They were removing the cover from something long and gray, pulling it up onto... what looked like a...

"All-hands," Oliver worked to keep the panic out of her voice, "two contacts right, two hundred yards. Crew-served weapon. They're finishing assembly. Ready to fire in thirty seconds."

"What?" Chief asked. "Sorry, skipper, where?"

Oliver extended an arm, "Two hundred yards that way."

"Jesus," she heard Kariawasm breathe as she used the small boat's camera. "I see them. Yeah, that's an anti-materiel gun."

"Is it the PLAN?" Chief asked.

"Looks like civilians," Oliver said, coming off magnification and scanning to make sure the rioters weren't closing back in. They'd lost interest for the most part, joining the crowd on the skirmish line, waiting for the American and Chinese navies to start shooting at one another.

"What the hell are civilians doing with a crew-served anti-materiel gun?" Kariawasm asked.

Trying to start a shooting war, Oliver thought.

She went back to the mag-lenses. The flared muzzle confirmed her estimate, it was an anti-materiel gun. It would cut through civilians in hardshells without losing velocity or even changing direction, but it was made for penetrating vehicle armor. As she watched, one of the gunners lifted a pair of binoculars to their faceplate, and the other swiveled the weapon toward the skirmish line.

It was too far to make it on foot, not in a hardshell. Quicker to use the longhorn.

"All-hands!" Oliver was shouting now. "Back to the boat. Do it right now!" She toggled channels to the *Aries*. "Wen! Launch SAR-2 and get them down here right now! Call the *Volans*! Get them scrambled!"

She didn't bother with the ladder, leaping off the roof and relying on the weak gravity to soften the impact of her fall. She still landed hard enough to make her teeth click together, the silicon dioxide soil crunching under her boots with the same consistency as snow. She shook her head to clear it, ignored the groaning in her knees and bounded toward the small boat, deliberately pushing off in the lunar gravity and launching herself in long leaps toward the craft. She could hear the grunting breaths of her crew as they accidentally chin-toggled the radios in their struggle to keep up with her.

A few miners didn't move quickly enough and she lowered her shoulder to shove them out of the way. They would likely be launched some distance, but she couldn't worry about that now. There was no time to get a private channel with each of them and warn them to disperse. She toggled to Tom's channel as she reached the longhorn and hauled herself through the hatch. "Babe! There's a big gun setting up off your stern! Two hundred yards out! I'm heading there now!"

"Where?" Tom's voice sounded calm, but perplexed. "I don't

see anything?" The turret on his small boat swiveled, tracking to his stern. The PLAN small boat alongside him jerked sharply away, misinterpreting his movements, but they didn't fire. Yet. *Jesus. This is way too close.*

She threw herself into her chair, grabbing the overhand handhold just as McGrath came in behind her, followed by Chief and Flecha. "Get us underway!" she called to Kariawasm. "All ahead full!"

Her mind spun with possibilities. It could be a clandestine group sent by the Chinese disguised as civilians, or Americans bent on turning this standoff into a shooting match. She went back to the mag-lenses and saw the gunner drawing a bead, finger tensing along the upper receiver.

They wouldn't reach it in time.

Tom was much closer. "Go for the Navy head-boat!" she ordered. "Shoulder it!"

"Ma'am…" Kariawasm began. Oliver knew she should listen to her coxswain, but her head was ablaze with the knowledge that Tom was on that boat. She had to do something.

Kariawasm fired the thrusters and wrenched the helm joysticks and the small boat lurched, miners scattering at the sudden movement. The bow rose briefly and it leapt, gliding smoothly toward the skirmish line, gathering speed. The crowd parted again, this time to admit the longhorn as it accelerated toward the Navy vessel.

"Don't worry, ma'am," Chief said over a private channel, "we'll get him."

He might have said more, but the channel was overridden by the coxswain of SAR-2. "Skipper, SAR-2 is on station. Put us where you want us."

She glanced at the plotter and saw that Kariawasm had already marked the gun crew's position. Damn, but that man was good. Like Ho, he knew what she would want before she wanted it. "Grab the mark from our plotter and get on top of it!"

"Roger that," SAR-2 radioed back, "we're on our way."

McGrath had punched up the gunnery computer, was manipulating the autocannon's controls. Targeting data began scrolling across the plotter, feeding distance angle and hit probability.

"Don't," Oliver said, "way too many civilians in the path." The miners were dashing about, jostling one another now, trying to be as close as possible to both SAR-1 and Tom's boat while simultaneously staying clear of the attitude thrusters of either.

Why the hell isn't that gun firing? She shot a nervous glance at the gun crew. Surely, they had a clear shot at Tom's boat by now. SAR-1 were almost to him. They could shoulder the Navy boat out of the way, and then…

"Ma'am," Flecha said.

"Throttle!" Oliver yelled to Kariawasm. She could almost feel the gun firing, the hair on the back of her neck prickling in anticipation. She had to get there first. "Pour it on!"

"Ma'am!" Flecha was shouting now.

But Oliver's vision had shrunk to a gray tunnel, the world vanishing save the distance between her and Tom's boat. "Shut the hell up and give me more throttle!"

"Ma'am!" Flecha did not shut up. "Goddamnit we have another contact on our starboard side!"

Oliver sawed her head to the right.

The habs were whipping by, big domes dragged into a rounded blur. She caught a flash of something long and gray.

A second gun crew. Setting up on a hab roof closer to the skirmish line. That's why the first crew was waiting.

She saw the gray line of the second crew's gun swivel, shortening in length as its profile changed, dissolving into a point as it locked on its target.

Her.

There was a flash, and all directions changed places. Oliver had felt this sense of losing direction before, but only in zero-g, when the space elevator carrying her to the *Aries* had finally breached Earth's atmosphere and she reached orbit. The freefall had left her disoriented, unsure of which way was up as her mind tried to reconcile the relative position of bulkheads, gear lockers and display panels. She felt it now. Only gravity was stronger if anything, as centrifugal force whipped her against the chair. *We're spinning. The round must have hit one of our thrusters.*

Which meant the shooter was very good.

A jarring crash and Oliver lurched forward, her helmet banging off the back of the helmsman's chair. The horizon suddenly stopped spinning, leveled. She could tell up from down again. There was a pounding on the cabin roof as if a giant were drumming on it, gradually tapering off to gentle patters. Debris, falling on them. They'd crashed into one of the habs.

She took mental inventory of her own body, realized she was OK. "Is everyone all right?"

Silence. Chief was stirring weakly, but he didn't answer. Kariawasm was still. Oliver sawed her head to the left to try and see McGrath and Flecha and was rewarded by a view of the inside of her hardshell helmet. "Sound off!" she yelled into the commlink. No answer.

She tried to move, realized that something in the cabin had shifted, pinning her to the back of the helmsman's chair. She tried to turn her body, couldn't. The only view was straight ahead, out through the cracked windscreen in front.

"Tom!" she toggled channels, "Tom! We're down, watch out for..."

No sound. Not even static. No wonder her crew wasn't answering her. The radio was dead.

She winched her arms down to her sides, felt resistance as they came in contact with whatever was pinning her. She pressed, felt the resistance give, wedged her arms in and pushed. The resistance was strong initially, but she felt herself lean back first by inches, and then finally she was free in a rush as whatever was behind her gave way. She spun, saw that her chair had been crushed beneath the dented metal of the cabin roof, staved in by some of the hab debris, most likely.

She was free and unharmed, she turned to check on her crew.

And froze.

Outside the starboard hatch, she could see the miners fleeing like fish in a pond when a stone is thrown, bursting out from a central point. That point was occupied by the PLAN boats and the US Navy boats. Two were flipped on their sides, hulls rent by autocannon fire. In the distance, she could see the Chinese marines bounding toward the action.

Tom's boat was frantically firing attitude thrusters, bouncing to making itself a harder target. Below it, the PLAN boat that had been holding alongside juked port and starboard, turrets swiveling to track her husband's vessel.

They were firing on each other.

Tom.

She raced to the hatch, yanked on the handle. It didn't budge. The joint was frozen solid, as if handle and door were made of a single piece of metal. She strained to look out through the hatch window at what might be jamming the handle, but between her helmet and the metal of the hatch door, she couldn't make it out. She pulled harder, dimly aware of a whine rising in the back of her throat, knowing the pulling was useless, but powerless to stop herself.

"Somebody help me!" she shouted into the commlink, then remembered the radio was dead. She turned back to her crew now, saw Chief was up, his arm around Kariawasm's shoulders, shaking him. McGrath was up, too, his eyes wide and stunned behind his cracked faceplate. The emergency failsafe in his hardshell had fired, shrinkwrapping him so tightly that only a thin film of emergency oxygen inflated the plastic. Blood trickled from a shallow cut on his forehead. "Help me!" she shouted again, hoping he could read her lips.

She turned back to the hatch and tried the handle again, but by then Tom's boat was already spinning in the air, riddled with autocannon rounds. She could see the crew inside being flung like clothes inside a dryer, slamming into the cabin walls hard enough to shatter their hardshells.

She was still screaming when one of the Chinese marines fired something shoulder mounted and her husband's boat was ripped in two.

CHAPTER 1

"The top story tonight – military sports continue to dominate ratings for the twentieth straight week, with the Army's World's Best Ranger Competition capturing over 100 million viewers in the coveted prime time slot. Even bigger is this year's Boarding Action, which pits space-based crews in a simulated boarding of a hostile vessel in zero-gravity. The highest rated civilian sport is still the American NFL, but it doesn't even come close, with less than fifty percent of military sports' audience share in that coveted 18-39 demographic. It truly looks like the new age of military training competitions as a civilian spectator sport is here to stay."

JENNIFER SALVATORE, MEDIA MIX

"Now this," Captain Jane Oliver said, gesturing through the hatch of the Defiant Class response boat, "is a really bad place to put your shotgun."

The students in the boat maintenance class crowded closer, squinting through the fluorescent overhead lights at the weapons clasps. Then they stood back, looking at her with blank expressions, nobody wanting to question the wisdom of such a high-ranking officer. The instructor was used to Oliver pausing in her daily rounds to take over the class, and had patiently stood aside, but he spoke now. "Ma'am, that's the *proper* place for long guns. That's why the clasps are there."

"That's real nice," Oliver replied, "but you try getting it out of those rubber bands in four-foot swells when you need it in a hurry. In the clasps for inspection. In the seat-sleeve for ops. Trust me on this."

She smiled and the students smiled with her. To them, a captain was akin to a god, and she knew the reminder that their leaders rode the same rough seas they'd be tackling went a long way. She also knew there were precious few officers at her level that still did.

"That's gear adrift, captain," one of the students ventured. The rest glanced from his face to Oliver's in shock, and then with admiration once they realized that she wasn't annoyed by being challenged.

"New rule," she said, "unless there's water on the deck, gear isn't adrift. You can quote me on that. Now, are you insulting your coxs'un? Saying he can't keep water off the deck?"

She gestured to the two students with coxswain qualification badges, and the class laughed. "No, ma'am."

"Thought so!" She grinned. In the years since they'd assigned her here, she only ever smiled when she succumbed to the temptation to take over the classes and give them the real scoop on what life was like in the boat forces. And as the commanding officer of the training center, she could only do that once in a blue moon. The rest of the time was a video on repeat in her head – her shouting to Kariawasm to pour on the throttle, Tom's boat coming apart under a hail of autocannon fire.

The instructor exchanged a look with Commander Ho. Her XO only smiled. If Oliver was frustrated with being pulled off operational duty, then Ho was thrilled. The sterile halls and quiet contemplation of the schoolhouse suited him just fine. She felt a pang of jealousy at his obvious contentment and squashed it an instant later. She had promised herself that she wouldn't let Tom's death make her bitter. She would be happy for the happiness of others, and if she couldn't feel it, then she would damn well fake it.

She turned back the class and paused. Captain Sean Elias was walking through the maintenance bay doors. Behind him, the York River twinkled in the Virginia sun. He was wearing his "tropical" blue uniform, the hard shoulder boards and pressed shirt that he only wore for important business. That he'd come to find her in the boat maintenance facility instead of waiting in her office was troubling.

"OK, Chief," she said to the instructor, "I think I've stolen enough of the class's time, you have the conn. Thanks for indulging an old lady."

"It's our pleasure ma'am," the instructor said, but she saw his shoulders relax as he returned to the lesson.

Ho was at her side as she shook Elias' hand. "Hey Sean, you clean up nice."

Elias glanced down at his crisp uniform as if he were surprised to be wearing it. "Sorry to interrupt, you looked like you were on a tear there."

"Nah," Oliver said, "I was just wrapping up."

"That's a lie," Ho smiled.

Elias laughed. "Yeah, I don't believe that for a minute. Jane, do you mind if we do this in your office?"

Oliver cocked an eyebrow. "Depends on what we're doing. You look like you're about to summon me to a court martial."

"No, nothing like that. Just something best done in private."

Oliver's office was just plush enough to convey her authority to subordinates, but not so well appointed that Oliver might start thinking she was an admiral. A long, glass-surfaced cherry-wood desk dominated the blue and gold rug, emblazoned with the crossed anchors of the Coast Guard. Behind the desk, a broad oil painting depicted the Coast Guard's sole Medal of Honor winner evacuating marines off Guadalcanal in a hail of machine gun fire. The same family picture she'd had on the *Aries* occupied the credenza beside her challenge coin display, Tom smiling out at the camera as if he would be waiting for her when she got off duty.

Ho's office was adjacent, but she motioned for him to stay, and he leaned against the credenza as Elias took his seat in the chair she reserved for students who were in her office for an ass chewing. She'd deliberately chosen chairs with short legs in order to make her charges smaller than her. She hadn't intended the effect for Elias, but she was glad of it anyway. If she didn't know what he was here to do, let him be intimidated while he did it.

"OK," she said, "what's this all about?"

"You want the good news or the great news?" Elias spread his hands.

"How about the cut-the-bullshit-news?"

Elias bit back his smile, "Well, there's a star for you, if you want it."

She saw Ho stir out of the corner of her eye. He was normally as still as a crocodile until he had to move. This was as much of a tell as a man like him gave. Oliver didn't move, but it was a long moment before she answered. Whatever she'd expected Elias to say, it wasn't this.

"I'm pushing thirty years in," Oliver said. "I can't take a star."

"Yeah, well. They're willing to make an exception in this case. We can get you a waiver, and in this command, you'll… uh… well, you'll age more slowly."

"What the hell are you talking about?"

"The 16th Watch, Rear Admiral Select," Elias leaned forward, grinning, "the Moon."

Oliver felt her stomach turn over. The image of Tom's small boat ripped in two swamped her. She was there again, wrenching the frozen handle as she watched the wreckage of her husband's ship settle into the snow-like surface.

"I'm a blue water coastie." Oliver had to speak slowly to keep the tremor out of her voice. "I've been on the Moon exactly once. This has to be some kind of mistake."

Elias shook his head. "No mistake, Jane. They want you on SAR-1."

"You can't want an O6 kissing retirement to run search-and-rescue in a domain she isn't familiar with."

"SAR-1 is now part of the Tactical Law Enforcement Detachment on Mons Pico."

"SPACETACLET," Oliver said. "The lunar head shed. What's SAR-1 doing attached there?"

"SPACETACLET is the command element now. The Commandant wants a unified presence for all lunar ops. Law enforcement and SAR are one body. Putting SAR-1 front and center sends the right message."

"And what does the old man want me to do with SAR-1?"

Elias gestured at the silver eagles stitched to her collar. "You're a leader. He wants you to lead it."

Oliver stared at him so long that Elias began to talk to fill the silence. "Look, Jane. SPACETACLET was the main responding element at Lacus Doloris after you were knocked out of the fight. They lost people."

Before she knew what she was doing, Oliver had leaned forward, covering her face with her hands. She remembered the Quick Reaction Force prying the hatch open, dragging her out. She remembered them cracking the hardshells of Flecha and Kariawasm's suits, laying them out on silver blankets on the regolith despite the lack of atmosphere. It didn't matter, they didn't need air anymore. Somewhere less than a hundred yards away, she knew the Navy corpsmen were going through the same ritual with her husband's body.

When she looked up again, Elias' face was inscrutable. "Morale is low on Pico, Jane."

She stumbled over the next words, desperately searching for something to say. "Chief Elgin and Petty Officer McGrath… are they still attached?"

Elias nodded. "Both of them were due to rotate out last year. They requested extensions. Chief pulled in every card he had to stay put."

Elias looked uncomfortably at Ho. "Jane, maybe it would be best if…"

"Commander Ho has been with me for my entire career. Anything you can't say in front of him can't be said."

Elias shrugged. "Look, Jane. We both know you've been… adrift since Tom died. Are you sure you're ready to retire?"

"That's condescending as fuck. I've made it through worse."

Elias' position in the sunken chair didn't intimidate him at all. "We're all worried about you."

"Who is?"

"I am, everyone in the C-suite is. The boss is."

Oliver swallowed the anger that rose in the back of her throat. Tom's death was *hers*. Her loss. Her fault. It wasn't for Sean or any of the top brass or even the goddamn Commandant himself to be deciding what that meant to her. She paused, steadying her breathing before she answered. "The Commandant doesn't know who I am."

Elias sighed. "You're the legendary 'Widow Jane.' Of course he knows who you are."

Oliver remembered an interrogation she'd done of the head of a metal theft ring, stealing copper wire out of offshore buoys. The man had an odd tic – whenever he was hiding something, he would lick his lower lip, darting just the tip of his tongue out to barely sweep it before reeling it back in. Elias did that now. Oliver's eyes narrowed. "Look, I appreciate the routine to make it seem like it's in my own best interests, but you're not here because you're worried I'll wilt in retirement. You want something. The Commandant wants something. I don't know a damn thing about space, Elias. I've been a blue-water coastie my whole career. The one tour I had out there was cut short after… what happened."

Elias ignored the reference to Lacus Doloris. He laced his fingers behind his head and leaned back in his chair, as if they were only talking about where to go for lunch. "Space-schmace. It's just another unforgiving environment, think of it like the dunk tank. You can't tell which way is up, only, it's all the time."

"You're not exactly selling it," Oliver stifled a smile.

"Yeah, well. The old man doesn't want you for space stuff. He wants you to teach." Elias leaned forward again.

"To teach what? I've been doing boarding actions all my life."

"That's what he wants you to teach."

"You want me to teach water-surface boardings to lunar SAR operators? What is wrong with you?"

Ho cleared his throat so softly it would have gone missed had it been anyone else. "In all fairness, ma'am," he said, "you could teach fish to walk."

"Thank you, Commander Kiss-Ass." Oliver slapped her palms on the desk and turned to glare at him. Ho tugged his forelock, inclined his head and smiled.

"Here's the thing," Elias said. "Navy is making a big push to remove us from lunar operations. They want the Coast Guard earthbound, for space to be declared 'universal high seas.'"

Oliver sucked in her breath as she thought of the Navy small boats torquing into position over Lacus Doloris. She thought of their flat-gray, gun-studded hulls. She thought of the way the miners surged to the attack at the sight of them. "What? That's a terrible idea. We need less militarization of space, not more. The Navy's the wrong tool for the job."

"That's what they're saying about us, and the President is listening. Jane, I can't stress this enough, we're on the brink of war here. The Commandant has met with the Secretary of the Navy three times in the past month, and he can't convince him. You don't need me to tell you how bad this is. We're not going to bring peace to the Moon if the American and Chinese navies are skirmishing every time a quarantine-runner strays into the Chinese Exclusive Economic Zone."

"So what do you want me to do about it from Mons Pico? Shouldn't you make me Navy Liaison Officer or something?"

"That's not how the Commandant wants to handle it. Look, we've pretty much lost the argument that this is a law enforcement or customs issue. The government is sold that it's a military one. If the Coast Guard wants to take the helm here, we can't keep showing the President that we're the right SAR element to keep space safe, we have to show him we're the right *military* element to beat the Chinese."

Oliver felt the first touch of a headache behind her eyes. None of this made any sense. "Sean. We're the *Coast Guard*. We're not the right military element to beat anybody."

Elias laughed. "Well, you've got me there. Fortunately, politicians are easily impressed."

"What do you want me to teach these guys to do?"

"We need you to get them in shape for this year's Boarding Action. Commandant thinks if we win, it'll give us the hand we need. It's a major media event, watched by millions of Americans. If we win it, that'll give us the leverage we need to stay on, and if we stay on, we can keep the Navy from turning quarantine-runners into a pretext for war. SPACETACLET came close last year…"

Oliver blinked. "We're going to stop a war… by winning a game show?"

Elias smiled. "I know it sounds odd, Jane…"

"You're goddamn right it sounds odd!"

Elias passed over his phone. "Here, let me show you something."

"Look, I like baby pictures as much as the next gal, but if you're hoping to soften me up, you're going to have to…"

Elias laughed. "My daughter is a junior in high school and my son starts college this year. I've queued up two videos for you in my camera roll."

Oliver arched a skeptical eyebrow. "Should I be careful scrolling here? I don't want to accidentally run into…"

Elias waved a hand. "Jane, please. Humor me here."

Oliver thumbed through and played the first video. It was well familiar to anyone from hundreds of social media ads. Vice Admiral Augusta Donahugh, commanding officer of the Navy's 11th Fleet – in charge of the service's operations on the 16th Watch. The vice admiral was a small woman, lean and healthy looking, her defiantly undyed hair and the wrinkles around her eyes the only hints that she was either north of sixty, or very close to it. She leaned into the camera, her eyes burning with passion for her mission, her solid gold shoulder boards bunching toward her neck. The video must have been shot in front of a green screen, washed out now and replaced with 11th Fleet's flagship – the USS *Obama*, its thousand-foot length stretching past the borders of the screen, toroidal chambers slowly rotating to bring spin-gravity to its sickbays and ops center. The film's producers had highlighted the ship's batteries, lightening them to make them stand out to the audience – ball turrets projecting autocannon barrels, missile pods with gleaming orange piezo-electric fuses. Navy small boats swarmed around it like a cloud of gnats, guns run out, a few flying American flags from their antennae mastheads.

"As a little girl, I dreamed of visiting the Moon," Donahugh said. "I never imagined the day would come when I'd stand at the helm of the one force that is making life there possible. The United States Navy has led the way to new frontiers for the entirety of our nation's history, projecting American power into the farthest reaches of our oceans, a truly global force for good. And now we're the tip of the spear, bringing justice and peace to that same Moon I dreamed of visiting when I was growing up. You don't need me to tell you how important this is. As the main source of Helium-3, the Moon is the future of clean energy for the entire world. It's imperative that the United States remain at the forefront of the fight to secure this critical resource."

Oliver had seen this video so many times that she knew the next bit by heart. The screen cut away from Donahugh to a scene of last year's winners of Boarding Action, the US Marine Forces Special Operations Command – 16th Watch team, moving and covering as they breached and cleared a large range tanker held by the second-place finishers, the State Department's Diplomatic Security team. The MARSOC16 team moved like they were flying, gliding through the micro-gravity like they were born in it, making the incredibly skilled DIPSEC operators look like kindergartners. The cameras cut to the studio audience for the show, cheering themselves hoarse as the show's announcers blinked in disbelief at the speed and skill with which MARSOC16 swept the opposition. "11th Fleet is proud of our marines, who've won Boarding Action for the third year running, a testament to the dedication and skill our people bring to the fight. The Navy is the right tool for this job, because we're the best there is. We train harder, work harder, and fight harder than anyone on Earth, or beyond it."

The camera cut back to Donahugh, standing now, surrounded by flint-eyed sailors and marines, all in their hardshells, helmets held under their arms. The American flag waved in the background, translucent, the surface of the Moon shining through it. "The 16th Watch is America's most important fight. And we can't win it without your help. Join us."

The video ended with the Navy's recruitment hotline number, email address, and chat handle, flashing yellow across the bottom of the screen.

Oliver looked up, met Elias' expectant gaze. "Sean, I've seen this a hundred times already. Everybody has. It's good."

"It's better than good," Elias said. "Navy is over 400 percent past their recruitment quota thanks to that, with the majority of the applicants pushing for contracts guaranteeing them tours on the 16th Watch."

"So? We're a smaller service. We don't run ads because we don't have to."

"Yeah, but nobody signing on with us wants to go to the Moon, and that's part of the why. Folks see it as a military matter. Well, that and they don't want to piss into a vacuum tube for a four-year stretch. Anyway, my point is that the Navy is winning the messaging war here. They are convincing the public that the Moon is a war zone already. This video is part of that."

"Don't you think you're being a little bit dramatic, Sean? It's just dick-measuring bullshit. Their target audience is boys about to graduate high school. Of course they're pumping the rah-rah it's a war stuff."

Elias shook his head. "It's worse than that. Watch the next video."

This video was wasn't familiar – a group of serious-faced men and women in sober suits sat around a horseshoe-shaped panel table of rich, golden wood. Oliver noted the regal, overblown red leather and green felt upholstery, the somber classical tones in the columns behind them. "Is… this the capitol?"

"Yup," Elias said. "That's the Armed Services Committee."

She'd have figured it out in another instant, anyway. The camera pulled back to show the service chiefs in their dress uniforms around a smaller table. Donahugh was standing beside Admiral Perea, the Chief of Naval Operations. Perea was seated, a look of performative concentration on his face as Donahugh gestured to the same recruiting video Oliver had just watched, finishing its last few seconds on a flat-screen monitor wheeled into the chamber.

Admiral Zhukov, the Coast Guard Commandant, was shaking his head. "That is a recruiting video. Senators, I will caution you against making decisions based on marketing materials."

"Admiral Zhukov is absolutely right," Donahugh said, "and it is equally important that this committee keep in mind that these marketing materials are built on *facts*. Nothing I say in that video deviates from the strictest truth. The Navy is leading the fight on the Moon, and it's imperative we continue to do so."

Oliver tried to read the expressions of the senators, but they were studiously game-faced, wearing the same gravitas-laden performative looks.

"This presumes that this is a fight at all," Zhukov countered. "It currently isn't, and it doesn't have to be. This is a customs and border control matter, and the issue at hand is quarantine and evasion of vessel-inspections. That is something that the Coast Guard is uniquely equipped to do, and the reason this service was chartered."

"I'm not certain the families of those sailors killed at Lacus Doloris would agree with you, admiral," Donahugh countered.

"Jesus," Oliver whispered. "That fucking bitch."

"Yup," Elias agreed.

If Zhukov was rattled by the comment, he didn't show it. "The Chinese can tell the difference between a light-armed law enforcement vessel and a warship. They are well familiar with the difference between the Coast Guard and the Navy's authorities here. I grieve for the lives lost at Lacus Doloris as much as the rest of you, but that was *nothing* like a full-scale war. If we want to avoid the potential for that degree of conflict, we need to be showing good faith efforts to deescalate the situation. It has to be the Coast Guard."

"And if we were talking about the waters off Baja California or Miami, I'd agree," Donahugh said, "but China isn't Mexico or Haiti, and the stakes on the Moon are worlds higher. The national security implications of losing ground in our ability to exploit Helium-3 are several orders of magnitude more grave than our ability to keep recreational boaters from harming manatees."

"It's official," Oliver said, "I fucking hate this woman."

"So long as you respect her hustle," Elias said. "Because she's currently cleaning our clocks."

Now Zhukov appeared rattled. "That's a gross mischaracterization of the Coast Guard's mission. And it only distracts from the fact that I am not the one laying out the lanes in the road here. They are clearly expressed by the titles 10 and 14 of the United States Code. This is *our* job!"

"The US Code," Donahugh said, "has always been interpreted. US law is governed by precedent, admiral. And with the stakes so high, our interpretation here is critical. Let me ask you, do you agree with the position that noncooperative dockings, boardings, are the key to enforcement of customs controls on the 16th Watch?"

"Don't do it," Oliver said to the video. "Don't walk right into it." She looked up at Elias. "Tell me he doesn't walk right into it."

Elias sighed. "Watch."

"Of course they are," Zhukov said. "They're the main tool in our arsenal right now, at least until we can establish a culture of compliance. But that takes time."

"It does," Donahugh agreed. "It's impossible to say for sure, but the Naval Innovation Advisory Council is currently estimating at least a five-year horizon to turn the current culture of quarantine evasion around. Five years is a long time, admiral."

"We can do it much faster than that," Zhukov said. "We're making headway every day, and I don't see what this has to do with…"

"Oh man," Oliver said. "This is bad."

"The worst," Elias agreed.

Donahugh had already turned to the monitor, clicked the remote, replaying the last section again – showing the MARSOC16 team's almost superhuman performance, the DIPSEC operators going down hard, the cheering crowd. "The Navy has proven, for *four* years running now, in the highest-pressure and most public forum available, that we are the best equipped, the best trained, the overall best at boarding actions on the 16th Watch."

Zhukov sputtered, his military bearing slipping. "You can't be serious. That's a game show!"

Donahugh looked at the senators now, still speaking to Zhukov. "If it's just a game show, admiral, why can't you win?"

Oliver stopped the video, unwittingly repeated the Commandant's words. "You can't be serious."

"As a heart attack," Elias said. "Ask me if that video has leaked to the public."

"I refuse."

"It's been trending on three social media platforms for a *week*, Jane. That's what we call a coup."

"Sean, this is reality TV! The SASC can't possibly…"

"This is the reality TV generation, Jane. The SASC is composed of senators, and senators care about getting reelected. This just became a platform issue. And the presidential election is right behind it. So, guess which way he's leaning?"

"Fuck."

"We have to win this thing, Jane. We have to prove the Navy wrong."

"And you think SAR-1 is how we win it?"

"With you pushing them, yes."

"Sean, they came in fifth last year. Behind the Mare Anguis Police Department."

"That's top ten. We need you to bump them up the other four slots."

Oliver's head spun with the inanity of the request. "Have you looked at my file? I don't know anything about non-cooperative dockings in space!"

Sean's face went serious. "I have, in fact, looked at your file. Hell, I've memorized it. You've done over two thousand contested boardings in your career."

"Those were on Earth! On the water!"

Elias was unfazed. "Every one of them is the equivalent of a non-cooperative docking in space, Rear Admiral Select."

"Stop calling me that!"

"Over 2,300, actually," Ho said.

Oliver turned to him slowly. She blinked, trying to make sense of his sudden interjection. "What?"

"Contested boardings, ma'am," her XO was smiling, "you've done over 2,300 in your career. I can double check the Personnel Records System if you want, but I'm pretty sure I've got the number right."

"Whose side are you on!?" Oliver slapped the desk again.

Ho shrugged.

"The issue isn't technical knowledge," Elias went on. "The acting commander out there says it's… morale holding them back."

Oliver's stomach turned over. "Morale how?" she asked, though she already knew the answer.

"They blame themselves for Tom," Elias said, "and for Kariawasm and Flecha. They feel like they failed you."

It can't be their fault. Because it's mine. She cursed herself for what seemed like the thousandth time. If only she hadn't insisted on going on the boat personally. If only she'd… *No. That way lies madness.* She had replayed what happened on that day over and over again ceaselessly for years now. There was nothing to be gained from it. Her thoughts were poisonous loops. They held no answers, only whispers that all pointed to her as the culprit for everything that had gone wrong.

But she hadn't been able to spare the emotional energy to think that the same toxic lines would be repeating in Elgin and McGrath's minds. "Oh, come on, Sean," she tried to sound nonchalant, but her voice broke. "I don't blame them for what happened. I know they did the best they could. I wrote to Chief and told him as mu–"

"No, Jane," Elias said. "You know that's bullshit. It's one thing to hear that you forgive them. It's another to believe it."

The grief rose so suddenly and she only barely choked back the tears in time. "Sean, why are you doing this? Bench 'em. Get another team."

"You're not reading me, Jane," Elias' voice went hard. "They're the best we've got. There is no other team."

It took Oliver a full thirty seconds to gather herself. She sighed, cradled her head in her hands. "And you think that if I work with them…"

Elias finished for her, "That you might be able to help them figure it out, yes."

"Sean," and she let herself cry now, not caring if they saw. "I don't know that *I've* figured it out."

A hand squeezed her shoulder, but with her eyes closed, she couldn't tell if it was Ho's or Elias'.

But it was Elias who spoke, his voice soft now. "Well, of course you don't. The good ones never do. But, you have, Jane. Ask anyone in this school. Ask anyone who works with you."

Ho passed her a tissue and she nodded thanks, blotted her eyes, blew her nose. "You don't want a leader, you want a therapist."

"We want the whole package, Jane," Elias said. "That's why it has to be you."

She tried to answer, but the tears were back. She waved a weak hand at him. "Message received, captain. Just… just give me some time to think it over, OK?"

Elias stood, tucking his cover under his arm. The gold oak leaves on the brim reflected against the glass surface of the desk. "Take as long as you need, so long as that isn't more than three days. I look forward to making your transport arrangements, Jane. And I look forward to saluting you as a rear admiral."

She signaled Ho for another tissue as Elias left, closing the door behind him. She kept her eyes tightly shut, but she could hear him make his way to the credenza, take out a bottle of the bourbon she'd kept there ever since Tom had died. She finally opened her eyes and saw the label as Ho sloshed the brown liquid into two glasses. In a turn of gallows humor that surprised even her, the brand he'd chosen was Widow Jane.

He passed her a glass. "You OK?"

She stared into the liquor. "You know when they promoted me to captain and parked me out here, I figured it was because after what happened, they… didn't trust me to lead, but they felt bad about Tom, so they wanted me to retire on captain's pay."

Ho took a swallow and crossed his arms, swirling his drink and looking at her. "I'd say that's exactly what they did."

"So, why the fuck is this happening?"

Ho laughed. "You're good at stuff. They parked you here to grieve and wash out. And you went ahead and produced the best and brightest crop of boarding team members the guard has ever seen."

She finally took a sip, closing her eyes and relishing the burning as the liquid slid down her throat. "You are such a fucking suck-up that I can't stand it sometimes."

"You don't want compliments," Ho said, "stop being good at shit."

"It's just… I'm not just good at stuff. I'm good at taking care of people. I took care of the kids, and after Adam moved out I took care of Alice. Then I had to take care of her again when she left Matt. I guess I'm still taking care of her now, only it's over the phone. Then I was taking care of Tom."

"Tom didn't need taking care of."

"No, he didn't, and that was why I was so happy to do it. And now that he's gone, all I have to take care of," she waved a hand to the school outside her door, "are these people."

"Well, you're doing one hell of a job."

"Christ, Wen."

"It'll get you to Alice," Ho looked at her from under his eyebrows. "You said she still needs taking care of."

"Good luck getting her to admit that. She went to the Moon to get away from…"

"She went to the Moon to get away from the memory of Matt, and the embarrassment that she'd made a hash of her marriage, and for the illusion of a new start."

"She told you this?"

Ho shook his head. "You know I'm not wrong."

"No, you're not." She pounded the desk at the memory of Alice handing her the phone with the email announcing her selection for the space elevator's next open running. "I still can't believe she won that fucking lottery. I still can't believe she left."

"Well, you do this thing, boss, you'll get to be up there with her. That's not nothing."

"No," Oliver admitted. "It's not."

They drank in companionable silence for a while, and when Ho was done, he turned to put the bottle back, but Oliver held out her glass for a refill. "Think this one's a two-banger."

Ho cocked an eyebrow. The Widow Jane was not known for having more than just one. "Wow," was all he said.

She waved her glass, sloshing a little over the side. "Man, I was really looking forward to retirement."

Ho laughed out loud. "Like hell you were. I've never seen anyone more frightened of anything in my entire life."

She downed the second drink in a single swallow, set the glass down with a click, met her XO's eyes. "So, what do I do?"

Ho leaned forward, and the intensity in his gaze reminded her so much of her husband that it frightened her. "Your job."

CHAPTER 2

"Sir, the quarantine is ridiculous. There is no such thing as 'space diseases,' and this administration's insistence on abandoning evidence-based policy in favor of pandering to public fear is bringing us to the brink of war with China. American miners lose money in the quarantine queues, and when they seek to evade them, they inevitably violate the Chinese Exclusive Economic Zone. This forces us to intervene to protect American lives, which in turn puts the US Navy into constant conflict with the PLAN. Allowing the Coast Guard, a law enforcement entity, to pursue quarantine runners as a SAR mission will deescalate the situation, showing the Chinese we are not exercising military force over portions of the Moon they consider to be critical to their continued security."

CONFIDENTIAL STATEMENT BY ADMIRAL ZHUKOV, COMMANDANT, UNITED STATES COAST GUARD, TO THE CHAIRMAN OF THE ARMED SERVICES COMMITTEE OF THE UNITED STATES SENATE

The Moon was at its orbital apogee when Alice finally called back, giving the conversation the maddening one-second delay that had the two of them constantly tripping over one another as they tried to talk. That alone made Oliver desperate to get up there, if for no other reason than to talk with her daughter without unintentionally interrupting.

"Mom, are you serious?" Delay or not, her daughter's voice was crystal clear, so much like Tom's that it made Oliver's heart clench.

"As a heart attack. They need my decision in three days, which means they need it tomorrow."

"I can't believe it." There was a slight warble in her daughter's voice, one Oliver had heard all too often of late.

"You drunk, honey?"

"You know me, mom. Always."

"I hate it when you joke like that."

"Then don't ask me if I'm drunk."

"I just… I worry that…"

"Mom, my marriage blew up and my dad died. That warrants a drink or two, wouldn't you say?"

Oliver thought of the belts of Widow Jane she'd had just a few hours before, and sighed. "Yeah, I guess I would." The cold plastic of the phone against her face was maddening. She wanted to *hold* Alice. She couldn't shake the idea that if she could just touch her daughter, she could somehow fix her sadness. She knew that wasn't how sadness worked, how comforting worked, but that was the way with some thoughts – they took root in your brain and no amount of reason could shake them loose.

"Are you going to take it?" Alice asked.

"Try not to sound so thrilled."

"No, no. I'm sorry, mom. I didn't mean it like that. It's just…"

"You went to the Moon to get the hell away from all of us on Earth and you don't need us coming to you?"

"You know that's not it. I wanted a fresh start, and I think that with a little more time to get my feet under me, I'll figure it out. I'm starting to make friends. Sort of."

"Really?"

"No, not really. I don't know. It just seems that in a lot of ways nothing has changed. Sinus Medii isn't any warmer than Minneapolis and it's almost as flat. Christ, mom. I would love to have you out here.

You know I would. I just don't want the responsibility of uprooting your whole life. It's not a small ask."

"You're my daughter. There is no limit to any ask you might have. You should know that."

"You have a son."

"Adam could give a flying fuck. I'll probably see him just as often if I'm on the Moon as if I'm in Virginia."

"Yeah. Sorry, mom. He just… He always wanted to make his own way. And after what happened with dad… well, that didn't help."

Oliver couldn't think about it now. "How's the mining operation?"

"Still not breaking even. I've got no problem running the drones and production is solid, but I think my issue is the deals I'm cutting with my distributors. I just… Negotiating isn't my strong suit."

Oliver fought against the urge to reach through the phone and grab her daughter by the shoulders. "You're running a business, honey. You can't be nice to these people."

"I know." Alice sounded very young.

"What if I pitched in? What if I handled the books while you handled the ops? I mean, after the tour."

"I could never ask that of you, mom," Alice said, but Oliver could hear the faint ring of hope in her daughter's voice.

"Listen, you are *never* a burden to me, do you hear? You're my own."

"OK, just promise me that if you do take the gig, it won't be just for me."

"It won't be, and I really do have to think it over. I just… it's…"

"I mean, are you so happy running TRACEN Yorktown?"

"No. Hell, no. I mean, it's a good job, but… it isn't enough, Alice. Now that Tom's gone, there's just you and Adam. And we already talked about Adam."

"Then just say yes. Take the gig."

At those words, Oliver felt her stomach clench in spite of her near physical need to throw herself across the quarter of a million odd miles to the Moon to hold her daughter. Her throat closed and she found herself unable to answer.

"Is it because of dad?" Alice spoke into the silence. "Because of what happened at Doloris?"

"No. Yes. I don't know. I mean, they're only picking me…"

"They're only picking you because you're the right woman for the job, mom. You remember the old Indian proverb you told me when I fucked up in college? The one about the chasm you come across in life? What did you tell me to do?"

"Jump." Oliver sandwiched the phone in between her shoulder and her cheek and covered her eyes with a hand.

"It's not as wide as you think," Alice finished for her.

"God. I wish I'd never taught you that now."

"Come on, mom. When things started to go south with Matt, I thought… I thought I was going crazy. Do you know what I was most scared of? What I really believed would happen?"

"I've got a feeling you're going to tell me."

"I was afraid you'd take his side. I was afraid you'd reject me. You'd stop speaking to me. Shit like that."

It took Oliver a moment to realize that her daughter couldn't see the look of horror on her face. "Oh, honey. How could you ever think that? You're my own."

"I know! It's crazy. But I really thought it. And I jumped the chasm anyway. And yeah, it's hard now, but I'm happy that at least I didn't stay stuck."

"You sure didn't. Now you're prospecting on a Moon on the brink of war."

"Uh, mom. I mean, you're the military lady and all, and I don't want to tell you your business, but I'm pretty sure if war breaks out here, it's not exactly going to spare the Earth. And anyway, my tough old mom would never let anything happen to me, right?"

"You're goddamn right," Oliver said with a fierce heat.

"Look, if you're serious, I won't say no. I could…" Oliver could hear her daughter trying to keep her voice even, trying to be strong for her mother. "I could use you out here. I won't lie. I thought getting away would make a difference and it has, just… not like I hoped it would. Maybe dad dying made me go a little crazy. Maybe I'm not totally over it yet."

"I don't know that it's a thing you ever get over, sweetheart."

"Look at it this way, mom. You take the star and come out here and run things. Do it through the next Boarding Action. If we win, great. If we don't, great."

"On what planet is that great?"

"The Moon!"

"The Moon's not a planet, sweetheart. It's a…"

"What I'm saying is, either way, after Boarding Action, win or lose, you hang it up. You retire on that sweet admiral's pay and if you're serious about helping me…"

Oliver felt a strange feeling in her gut. It took her thirty seconds to realize it was hope. "Honey, you live in a closet."

"Nope. Just bought my own gardener last week. I can 3D-print on extra rooms by the time you're ready to move in. The grandma suite."

"I'm your mother."

"It'll be like a slumber party, only every night!"

Oliver fought the grin that stretched her face. "You're ridiculous."

"Look, mom," Alice's voice went serious. "All kidding aside. I lost dad, and I know it was my choice to go, but… I lost Matt, too. I don't have kids. I miss you every day. I know we'd get on each other's nerves, but it'd be worth it. Maybe this will be good for you *and* for your crew. Maybe, working together, you can help each other heal. Either way, it'll get you out here, and that's a start."

Oliver didn't realize she was sobbing until the tears made the receiver slick against her mouth. "Oh God," she managed.

"You OK?" Alice asked.

"Yeah… I'm all right. I just realized… I was just thinking I wanted to ask your father what to do. But he's not here."

"No mom," Alice's voice broke on the other end of the phone, "he's not. But I'm out here, and I'm waiting for you."

Oliver sat in silence for a long time after she hung up, her mind whirling. At last, she gave herself permission to take a belt of the Widow Jane. She'd been slugging directly from the bottle a bit more than she was entirely comfortable with lately, and made a mental note to knock it off. *But not yet. For now, you have permission to be weak.*

She tried her son, Adam, next. It went to voicemail as she expected. If Alice had reacted to Tom's death by reinventing her entire life, Adam had doubled down on his. He was probably in his office, or on a date with any of a string of girls he'd lined up out west.

And what do you expect from him? she thought, *Permission? He's sure as fuck not going to invite you to come live with him.*

The thought sent a spasm of fear up her spine. She realized with a start that she hadn't given any consideration to what her life after the guard might look like, now that Tom wasn't there to share it with her. She turned to the family picture on the corner of her desk, spoke to his broad smile. "I always thought we'd get a yacht. Be snowbirds. Maine in the summer and down the waterway to Florida in the winter."

Alice's Helium-3 stake was a far cry from that, but at least there was someone who loved her in that picture. *It's not just love. Alice is someone who needs you.*

She let her finger hover over the keypad for a full minute before she punched Elias' number. After ten rings, she figured she'd missed her chance to wake him up, but then the receiver clicked.

"Jane," he sounded exhausted. That was good.

"OK," Oliver said, "we go year to year. I can resign at any time."

It took Elias' sleep-fogged brain a moment to process what she was saying. "That's just standard policy."

"How much time do I have?"

"Jane, you just woke me out of a deep sleep. Do not ask me to do math."

"How much time?"

"Fuck... Three months? Next Boarding Action is in three months."

Oliver sighed. "That's... less time than I hoped."

"If anyone can make it work, you can, Jane."

"Fine, I accept. Make it happen before I change my mind."

"Congratulations, admiral. We'll launch you..."

"You'll launch me *after* I've had basic non-cooperative docking training and zero-G ops coursework completed."

"Jane, we're bringing you in to lead, and you've already done time in zero-G. You don't need..."

"If I'm going to lead, I need to understand what I'm asking my people to do, *intimately*. I graduate NCD/0G or I don't go."

She could hear the rumble through the speaker that was Elias running his hand through his hair.

"That's a three-week course. Boarding Action is in three months. You're burning a lot of time to make a show."

"It's no show. Slow is smooth, smooth is fast. I do the job right, or I don't do it."

"OK," Elias said. "Christ I need to set up your promotion, your change-of-command. I'll send you over a prep sheet. If you're going to make the right entrance at SPACETACLET, we need it to make kind of a splash, you..."

"No. I promote on the Moon. Not on Earth."

"Jane, we need you to show up *already* an admiral. Why are you breaking my balls here?"

"Because if you were so damn smart, they'd be pinning a star on you and sending you up there. I want Alice to pin on one of the boards, and she's on the Moon."

"So? We'll fly her to DC for your damn promotion!" Elias was surely awake now.

"She's prospecting H3 on Sinus Medii! You think she can spare a week away from the operation? Especially now? We do this on the Moon."

"Jane, the Commandant is watching this whole thing. You know that, right?"

Oliver smiled into the receiver. "Outstanding. We're going to give him one hell of a show. One more thing. I want the option to retire on the Moon."

Elias sighed. "Jane. You know that's not regs. Everybody retires on Earth. The Moon isn't a place for you to live as a private individual without a business purpose."

"It is for rich fuckers."

"You're not a rich fucker. Even retired admirals don't make that kind of money."

"Alice is hurting, Sean. She needs help running her mining stake. I want that option."

"Christ, Jane, I…"

"Get me a waiver to retire on the Moon or the answer is no."

"Fine! I'll get it done. You want anything else? A robot to massage your feet three times a day? A new Porsche?"

"Don't give me any ideas, Sean."

"OK, Jane. I'll get it all done."

Oliver had one more call to make before she packed her things. Ho was awake, despite the late hour. "What are you doing up?"

Her XO laughed into the receiver. "Hui-Yin had a nightmare."

Oliver nearly accepted the answer, but something bit at the back of her mind. "Wen, I have known your kids since they were born. You have never once said they had a nightmare."

Ho laughed again. "First time for everything, and… I guess you could say I had a premonition."

"Did you bug my phone or something?"

"You're doing this, aren't you?"

"Yeah. I just got off the phone with Elias."

"Shit. I have to be honest, ma'am, I wasn't sure you would. I guess I need to prep for your change-of-command."

"Make sure you prep your whites while you're at it, because you're changing commands with me."

Ho was silent for a moment. "You want me to move my family to the Moon?"

Oliver's laugh sounded harsh in her own ears. "You're goddamn right I do. You wanted me to do this, so now we're doing it."

For once, Ho didn't laugh. She could almost hear the wheels of his mind churning.

"Look, Wen," she said, serious now, "I can surely do this without you, but man, I have to be honest. I… I really don't want to."

The silence stretched, and Oliver could have sworn her heart stopped beating for fear she would miss his reply.

"Yeah," he finally said.

"Yeah, what?"

"Yeah, OK. I'll uproot my whole family and move them to Mons Pico."

"You're sure."

"Yes, ma'am," he said. "I can surely have a career without you too, and I really don't want to either."

"Ting-Wei…"

"Has been through six PCS moves already. She'll be fine."

"16th Watch is a bit different, though."

She could hear Ho's shrug. "She'll live, and the kids will flip. And it's super-promotable, right?"

"Operational hardship tour. XO at a critical command. You'll make captain for sure."

"I will or I won't, but the…"

"No, Wen. You will. Because I'll make damn sure you will."

She broke the connection and stared at her own reflection in the glasslike surface of her desk. It lengthened her features, smoothing the wrinkles, sapping the gray from her hair. She looked like the commander she needed to be, even though she knew a real mirror would be less kind.

Her mind tried to turn the decision over, pick it apart. She quashed it. She had made her choice. *If anything, it brings me closer to Tom.* The Moon was where he'd died, and they'd jettisoned his casket on a straight trajectory to the sun. But that was all nonsense. The Moon was no closer to Tom than Earth or Saturn or Alpha Centauri. Her husband was gone. He had ceased to be the moment the PLAN kinetic round had struck his boat.

But she couldn't shake the feeling that closer was somehow better, and after a few minutes of wrestling with it, she stopped trying. She'd have enough on her plate in the days to come.

CHAPTER 3

Service members in all five branches commonly refer to any tour of duty in space, whether assigned to a space station or to the Moon, as "the 16th Watch." The term comes from the sixteen sunrises and sunsets witnessed by inhabitants of the original International Space Station. You don't see that many from the Moon, but the term stuck, and is uttered with reverence or dread, depending on whether you see space as a new frontier, or a wilderness.

"THE FINAL FRONTIER? THE MILITARY STRUGGLES TO ADAPT TO THE DEMANDS OF OPERATING IN SPACE." *GQ MAGAZINE*

The space elevator's lift schedule was watertight for a month, so the Coast Guard shelled out the outrageous fee for a heavy lift rocket. It was Oliver's second time on propellant lift.

Well, the third time, if she was being fully honest, but escaping the Moon's non-atmosphere and weak gravity had made the ride back to Earth after the Lacus Doloris incident trivial. It felt about as bumpy as your typical airplane ride.

Breaking free from Earth was another matter, and she was sharply reminded of the stomach flattening, bone-rattling pressure of the acceleration as the hundreds of thousands of gallons of propellant forced her up, ripping her from the planet's grip. The whole structure trembled and her back ached from the mule-kick of the initial acceleration, but once the boosters separated and they eased into the final burn stage, she began to relax. Acceleration-gravity beat spin-gravity, she remembered. It was more comfortable to feel the pressure evenly rolling you back than wrenching you over to one side.

Oliver and Ho had hitched their ride on a payload delivery mission, redeploying the Coast Guard Cutter *Corvus* into lunar orbit after a complete refit at the Pascagoula shipyards, leaving Ho's family to follow later. The final stage of the trip was announced with a loud bang, as the heavy lift rocket fell away entirely, and the *Corvus* continued under her own thrust. The trip to the Moon would take three days, but they were bound for the Coast Guard's Orbital Training Center at the Lagrange point just a couple of hundred nautical miles off the Moon's surface. It would shorten the trip by a little, but not much.

She spent the intervening days with Ho, mostly playing cards and swapping sea stories. In her younger days, she'd have been afire with planning, setting up her command structure, building budgetary castles in the air. But she had been in the guard long enough now to know that commands were built on the people in them. Until she met them, her plans were dust. And besides, Elias had been clear – the Commandant expected her to run SPACETACLET *after* this year's Boarding Action was won. Until then, she was to let the acting CO handle affairs quietly, and focus one hundred percent of her time and attention on prepping the SAR-1 team to win.

She relished the break from responsibility, and was even a little disappointed when her small boat coxswain, a young Boatswain's Mate First Class with a thick southern accent and a nametape that read LEE, knocked on her stateroom door and told her it was time to suit up. Ho was, not surprisingly, already in the cutter's launch bay and into his hardshell by the time she arrived. "You're going to make us late ma'am," her XO quipped, handing his helmet off to one of the crewman to help him seal in.

But Oliver ignored him, looking at the hunched domes of the boat's furled solar sails. "This… is not a longhorn."

Lee looked surprised. "No, ma'am. Longhorns started phasing out the year after…" He paused awkwardly.

"It's OK," she said, "Lacus Doloris sure as hell isn't a secret to me. Just don't call me 'Widow Jane' to my face, and we'll get along fine."

"Yes, ma'am. Sorry, ma'am. Well, they started bringing the Rhino Class in. Right after the dustup. Stronger belly thrusters and a longer nose."

"For an extra hard point, am I right?" Oliver asked.

"You'd have to ask Northrop-Grumman, ma'am."

Ho was looking at the small boat's bow now. "Huh. You could put two autocannons on there."

"More guns," Oliver shook her head, as one of the crew helped her suit up, "exactly what we need."

Lee gave an embarrassed smile and stepped through the hatch, motioning her to follow.

The interior was different from the longhorn. They'd left the metal unpainted, and the wider space made her feel oddly agoraphobic, too far to reach the handholds she'd been used to in the past. The weapons and gear lockers seemed too far away, the windows too big, as if, once they launched, space might reach in and snatch her away. But there was enough of the familiar in the new model to make her eyes sting and her throat close. She realized with a start that this was the first time she'd been in a small boat since Lacus Doloris. Since Tom.

Ho kept his eyes resolutely forward, but Oliver had sailed with him long enough to know he was thinking the same thing. Lee was busy strapping himself into the helmsman's chair, which seemed a mile away. Oliver wrestled with the terror, grief and uselessness. *No. I am not going into my new life like this.*

She worked her way to his side, tapped him on the shoulder. "You conn. I'll run the helm."

His eyes went wide behind his visor. "Ma'am?"

"What, you think I can't figure it out? I qualified on the longhorn."
The two joysticks certainly looked the same, even if the plotter and the
radar were in different spots.

"I doubt your cert is current," the coxswain said.

Oliver shrugged. "I've logged thousands of hours on Defiance Class
gunboats back home. How different can it be?"

"Those are Earth boats, on water. This is space. It's pretty different,
ma'am," Lee looked like he wished the bulkhead would swallow him.

"Well, good thing I'll have a qualified coxs'un standing right next
to me." Oliver gave him her most winning smile, and belted herself
into the helmsman's chair, gave the thumbs up to the crane-operator
through the window.

"Jesus Christ," Lee muttered, strapping into the conning chair.
"Ma'am, respectfully, you have to let me take the stick when we tie up.
It's a lot less forgiving than…"

"I'll consider it," Oliver cut him off, "stand by for lift."

The hull shuddered as the crane hoisted them over the bay doors.

"Jesus Christ," Lee said again.

In the end, Oliver relented. The coxswain was right that the complex
series of maneuvers necessary to get a small boat to match the rotation
of an orbital dock was far less forgiving than in open space, and while
she had confidence in her ability to steer the vessel, she wasn't stupid.
Lee uttered a sigh so grand it was almost audible in the vacuum, and
gratefully slid into the helmsman's position for the last leg of their
journey.

OTRACEN was a giant spinning metal donut, festooned with solar
collectors and crowded with small boats chasing one another in what
Oliver assumed were training exercises. Here and there, two of them
were clamped together, looking nothing so much like beetles mating,

as their crews practiced contested boardings. A range drifted a few kilometers above it, floating targets riddled with 23mm diameter holes. Like all live-fire ranges in space, its backstop was the distant sun, on the presumption the rounds would travel until incinerated by the heat.

Their small boat was greeted by a man so tall and thin that he rivaled Ho. But where Ho's face was open and perpetually amused, this man looked like he'd just funneled a lemon. His pencil-thin mustache fought for purchase on an upper lip that was having none of it. The rest of his head had dispensed with hair long ago. "Captain Oliver," the man's voice was reed thin, and his nearly imperceptible lean spoke of a career spent in spin-gravity, "welcome to OTRACEN. I'm Captain Fullweiler. I command here."

Oliver shook his hand, suppressed a shudder at Fullweiler's dead fish grip and smiled. "Nice to meet you, captain. Thanks for having us."

"Well, it's very unusual for us to have an O6 enroll in NCD/0G, especially one who is about to make flag," Fullweiler said, his patchwork mustache dancing like a wispy caterpillar, "so of course we have to roll out the red carpet." His tone indicated he was none too happy about that fact. "If you'll follow me, we can talk more in my office."

"This," Oliver threw her arm around Petty Officer Lee as he exited the hatch and broke the seal on his hardshell helmet, "is BM1 Lee, off the *Corvus* and he is an outstanding coxs'un."

Fullweiler paused before dropping his eyes to the man, wrenching them down with an effort. "Welcome aboard, BM1."

Lee looked about as awkward as Fullweiler, "Sir."

"I haven't seen him fly all that much," Oliver went on, "but he's got the patience of a saint, and as we all know, that's the key to running any boat, big or small."

Fullweiler looked at her and said nothing. His formal half-smile seemed bolted on.

"Anyway," Oliver went on, "I'd be in your debt if you'd square Lee and his crew away with chow and a shower and a ready rack if you've got them before you turn them around. They just came off Earth and they've got to be beat to hell."

It took Fullweiler a few moments to answer, "Of course. I'm sure Master Chief will see to them."

"Much obliged," Oliver said. *And now we know that I don't like you either.* She gestured behind him, "ready when you are."

Fullweiler's office was as professional as they could make it, but it still spoke of life in orbit rather than on Earth. No cherry-wood or American flags, just the white paneled plastic and video screens that Oliver knew were standard in any room outside the Earth's atmosphere. Fullweiler slouched in a swivel backed chair that she assumed was supported on one side to counter the artificial gravity. The other two chairs in the room didn't have backs at all, which Oliver assumed was deliberate. Assholes were assholes on Earth or off, and their asshole tactics never changed.

"I'm sure your XO will be more comfortable in his quarters," Fullweiler began.

"I'm sure he would too," Oliver agreed, "but he doesn't get paid to be comfortable. He gets paid to be here when I need him, and I need him now."

Ho simply took his seat, elbows on his knees, looking up at Fullweiler expectantly, his ever-present slight-smile never faltering.

Fullweiler sat in silence for a full thirty seconds before shaking his head and giving an exaggerated shrug. He reached into his desk drawer and drew out a bottle of pills, thumping them down hard enough to make them rattle against the plastic. "These are for you."

Oliver took them, turning the plastic bottle over in her hands. It wasn't labeled.

"I wanted to give them to you personally," Fullweiler said, "rather than having them issued by one of our staff. You're going to have to command out here, and it won't help anyone if folks start off seeing you as…"

"As what?" Oliver asked. "As weak? As an old woman? Jesus. Anyone looking at me can see that I'm an old woman."

"Lunar coasties are a different breed," Fullweiler said.

"You forget that I did a tour out here."

"You did less than half a tour out here," Fullweiler corrected her, "otherwise you'd know that the pills in there are calcium supplements. You'll be spending a lot of time in micro-g. That's going to hit you particularly hard."

"It's not going to hit me any harder than…"

"It's going to hit you particularly hard because you are, as you just said, an older woman. You have early onset osteoporosis as it…"

"How the hell would you know…"

"…Which I know because I have read your medical file, which I am authorized to do because I command OTRACEN and while we are equal in rank, as long as you are *enrolled* here, you are a *student* and your care is my responsibility."

Oliver closed her mouth so hard her teeth clicked. Her mind raced to find a retort, but Fullweiler had it right. She was a student, he was the school chief, and that was that.

In the end, Ho broke the tension, coughing softly.

"You have something you'd like to add, commander?" Fullweiler asked.

"If you knew anything about Rear Admiral Select Oliver, sir," Ho replied, "you'd know she doesn't need me to add a thing."

Fullweiler turned back to Oliver. "Look, I know we're off on the wrong foot, and I get why you're doing this, but I want you to know that it isn't necessary, and I'm asking you to reconsider."

"Reconsider?" Oliver asked.

"That's right. Stay here for one day for a 'facility familiarization,'"

Fullweiler softened his tone and smiled, "then head on to Pico to take your command. NCD/0G school is not a game and it's not a joke. It's punishing work, and it's punishment that, with respect, I don't think you're up to just now, Jane. May I call you Jane?"

"Absolutely not."

"Well, Captain Oliver, I hope you understand that being out here could do real and lasting damage to your body."

Oliver had had enough. She stood. "Well, it's like you said, I'm an old woman. I won't be needing it much longer anyway. Just point me to my quarters, please."

Fullweiler sighed and spread his hands. "I'll take you personally—"

"Directions will be fine, thank you. I'm sure you have plenty to do."

Fullweiler pursed his lips. "All right. Two adjoining staterooms are waiting for you in O-country. Just turn spinward out the door and head straight down. The duty PO can show you your quarters."

Oliver nodded, and left. It wasn't until the door shut behind her that she turned to Ho. "Which fucking way is 'spinward?'"

Ho jerked a thumb to his left. "He means with the station's rotation."

"Of course," Oliver said, "I just wanted to see if you knew."

Ho grinned and they turned to make their way down the passage toward officer's country. "That man," he said, "is a special kind of asshole."

"He's not wrong," Oliver said. "I am an old woman."

Ho shrugged. "Way I see it, the guard allowed you to enroll here, and that means you're not the only one who thinks you can hack it."

"You don't think there's just a hint of pity driving that decision? The old man feeling bad for the poor Widow Jane?"

Ho stopped, looked at her, his expression horrified. "Absolutely not."

Oliver held his gaze for as long as she could. "Come on, Wen. I *am* an old woman. An old woman who's been running a school for years! I've been out of the game for so long. Am I ready to go back to operational command?"

"I hate to break this to you, Rear Admiral Select…"

"…Stop calling me that!"

"…Rear Admiral Select, but *I,* as your chief of staff, will be doing the commanding, in concert with whoever the acting CO happens to be. Your primary mission is to make the Boarding Action team ready to win."

"Jesus H. Christ on a crutch. Do you honestly think I'm going to let you run my shop, Wen? Have you met me?"

Ho sighed. "Yeah. Well, I was hoping that maybe once you got the bit in your teeth training this crew up, you'd let me help you out a little."

"Not a chance. This is my job."

"Ma'am, I've been working with you since God was a non-rate. I get the in-the-trenches-sharing-the-load mentality, but you're going to be an admiral, and you can't save the world all by yourself. You have to learn to delegate. You have to let someone else take care of you once in a while."

"Well, that's the one advantage of being an old lady. I don't have to change."

"Jesus Christ."

"It's true! My brain is a fossilized sponge. My personality is completely crystallized."

"Then what are we doing here?"

"Accommodating my irascible whims, as always. And my current whim is chow and a rack. Go forth and find the duty PO, grandma needs her nap."

CHAPTER 4

Muster at 0600 was no problem, but the makeup of the class certainly was.

The syllabus instructed Oliver and Ho to report in PTs, and the two stood in their short blue shorts and gray T-shirts, Oliver painfully conscious of the varicose veins in her legs and the love handles that bloomed over the sides of her elastic waistband. Ho looked like a toothpick with blue and gray tape stuck to it.

They were the only two officers in the class, and the only two people over thirty. The remainder were what looked like a scattering of children to Oliver, men and women just out of their teens. Every single one of them wore the tan and green PTs of the United States Marine Corps. The entire class had instinctively struck the pose that was common to

all training evolutions, dressed in ranks, at parade rest. Oliver and Ho
were fallen into one corner of the formation, in no special order, but
it seemed to her that the distance between her and the marines was
greater than the spaces they created between one another. They kept
casting quizzical glances over their shoulders at her, which didn't help
matters.

She thought of Tom. He'd have laughed himself into stitches seeing
this.

"They should have painted us hot pink," Oliver whispered to Ho,
"we would have blended in better."

"It's a joint training center, ma'am," Ho said. "Taking in everyone is
how the Coast Guard shows we're in charge."

"Then why are we the only coasties in here?"

Ho jerked his chin to the front of the classroom, as if that was
answer enough.

Fullweiler stood there, at parade rest, flanked by two instructors.
"Good morning! I'd like to welcome everyone to first platoon, alpha
company of NCD/0G. This course will teach you the fundamentals
of non-cooperative docking maneuvers, more commonly known as
'boarding actions,' in a micro-g environment. In a moment, we're going
to stop the rotation of this chamber, and you will begin to experience
orbital weightlessness. Before we begin, do you have any questions?"

No one spoke, but Oliver could see the question the marines wanted
to ask burning in their eyes. *Who the hell are these two and what are they
doing here?*

"All right," Fullweiler said as his instructors fanned out. "Here we go."

Oliver wasn't a stranger to micro-g, but neither was she a veteran.
She certainly had more experience than the marines who began to push
off as the chamber ceased its rotation and their bodies went into the
weightlessness of freefall. But sometimes, the sensation could catch you
flat-footed, and she couldn't deny the vertigo as her body lost all sense

of which way was up. She could feel the fluids in her stomach rising, her half-digested breakfast bar no longer held down.

Ho executed a neat flip, hugging his knees to his chest. "You OK, boss?"

She fought the urge to swallow, worried it would make the sickness worse, and shot Ho a thumbs-up, not trusting herself to speak. The marines were laughing, pushing one another, flipping off the walls, or the floor, or maybe the ceiling, Oliver wasn't sure which was which. One or two of them looked sick, but they were green recruits getting their bearings. She was a skipper who had already done time on the 16th Watch. *Must. Not. Puke.*

She forced herself to do a roll and immediately regretted it, covering her eyes with a hand as her head spun. Closing her eyes somehow only made the queasiness worse. "Oh, God," she managed. One of the marines barreled past. "Chin up, ma'am! You'll get the hang of it!"

God. Is it that obvious?

After what seemed hours of free play, during which Oliver desperately strove to will her inner-ears to orient her and decide which direction was up, Fullweiler called the class to order.

"Some of you," he paused just a hair and pointedly looked at Oliver, "look a little green. That is because you are fighting against the environment. You are insisting on reckoning the cardinal directions. You must not do this. In space, up and down no longer have meaning for you, and so long as you insist on trying to find them, you are going to be one miserable marine... service member. Let go, start thinking of space as multidimensional; you are relative to other surfaces or objects, nothing more. The more of you grasp this, the less puke I'm going to have to clean up."

Ho drifted next to her. "You going to be OK, ma'am?"

"I don't understand why this is so hard on me," she said. "This isn't my first time!"

Ho smiled, "Well, you're ancient for starters. And its been a long time. It's not like riding a bike, ma'am."

"We call the next exercise the waltz," Fullweiler called, "and its goal is to familiarize you with some core concepts. The first is closing with and grappling a hostile opponent. The second is what I just explained to you about directionality."

He divided the class into two halves, and sent them to opposite sides of the room, where Oliver saw handholds had been bolted to the walls. She clung there, her stomach gurgling, blood pounding in her veins. She could feel the pores of her forehead open, the first beads of sweat beginning to form there, even though the room was not hot. Fullweiler gestured for Ho to take up the position opposite her. It wouldn't do for a captain to be grappling with a private.

"On my mark, you will launch yourselves at one another, grasping your opponent's shoulders firmly, and letting momentum do the rest. This will be more like bumper-cars than an actual waltz, so let's keep those knees up and feet in. Ready? Mark!"

Oliver pushed off with her feet, saw Ho do the same, his narrow face growing larger as he sped toward her, arms outstretched. She heard grunts and laughing as some of the marines crashed head first into one another, leaned her own head to the side to prevent the same thing. She let her hands drift forward, felt Ho's slim shoulders and grabbed handfuls of his PT shirt just as his own hands found hers. Their momentum ran counter, and they began to whirl together, the walls and their classmates' faces turning into a spinning mass. Oliver felt her gorge rise and struggled not to inhale. The smell of Ho's breath was overwhelming.

"Ma'am," she heard her XO hiss, "do *not* puke on me!"

Her vision went gray, she felt her pores open fully, sweat sheeting down her face.

Ho's grip remained tight. "Ma'am!"

"I'm sorry," she said… except she hadn't spoken. When she'd opened her mouth, her stomach had seen its chance, and she failed Ho for the first time since they'd boarded the rocket from Earth.

Oliver wasn't the only student to lose her breakfast in that class, but she was the first. Fullweiler's smile was smug, but his words were decent at least. He nodded as she apologized for the mess and said, "That's why we train, captain. And you're sure as hell not the first student to puke in this classroom." *But you're sure as hell the first in this particular class*, her mind added for her.

She had miraculously gotten absolutely none of the contents of her stomach on herself, and her classmates had the presence of mind to steer clear of the cloud of vomit, which turned into a spray and finally a rain as the gravity came back on.

Ho was much less fortunate.

He sat next to her on the floor, wiping his head and shirt with a towel as some poor sailor on punishment detail finished mopping. "I don't know why you hate me so much, ma'am. I've only ever been nice to you."

"This is so humiliating," Oliver said.

Ho looked down at his shirt. "I am going to have to burn this, then invent a machine that burns things that have already been burned, and fucking burn it again."

"Who's that?" Oliver pointed to the glass windows of the observation deck, high above them. A man stood there, built like a linebacker, but without a linebacker's beer gut. He was too far away for her to be able to make out the name tape or rank on his crisp marine uniform. His head was shaved to reveal his dark pate; dark eyes and sharp features. He looked grim, and Oliver could tell even from this distance that he was beautiful.

"Some marine. Maybe another student?"

"No," Oliver said, "that's somebody special."

Ho shrugged, got to his feet. "Maybe he can get me a new PT uniform."

Oliver looked down at her own clothes, thoroughly soaked with the flop sweat she'd had just before she'd lost her breakfast.

"All right!" Fullweiler said, "fall out for the noon meal. Don't bother with showers." He didn't so much as glance at Oliver and Ho.

Oliver grabbed the corner of Ho's sleeve, wincing as she found it wet. "We are absolutely showering."

"Aye aye, ma'am," Ho said, helping her up.

They were late to the meal, but at least Fullweiler didn't ask questions or make a snide comment. The mess hall was alive with traffic, and Oliver felt more at home as she saw that the Coast Guard sailors outnumbered the small knots of service members from the other branches crowded around the tables. She headed over to the officer's mess and stopped short as a voice called to her.

"Captain Oliver?" It was a deep, singer's bass, smooth as polished mahogany, and she knew immediately who it belonged to.

She looked up to see the man from the observation window standing in the flag mess. His rolled sleeves strained to contain arms that were thick around as her thighs. His head was shaved as smooth as his face, but the dusting of white in his eyebrows and the hard lines of his eyes and mouth made him of an age with her. A single star was stitched to the velcro tab on his chest. His name tape read FRASER.

"Sir?" She turned.

He gestured her to his table, taking a seat. "There's no need for that. I hear we're going to be the same rank in a few weeks. I'm Demetrius Fraser. Why don't you and your aide join me?"

Fraser waited patiently while Ho and Oliver filled their trays at the cafeteria line.

"I really don't feel like eating," Ho said.

"Pile it on," Oliver hissed, "we're faking it till we make it today." She grabbed everything that looked starchy – bread, almonds, a banana, and a pile of saltines. Ho looked green but followed her lead.

Fraser ignored their odd choice of cuisine as they rejoined him, and they sat in awkward silence for a moment, neither party clear on how to start. Ho, as usual, saved her.

"I'm Wen Ho," he said, reaching across the table to shake Fraser's hand. "I'll be Mrs Oliver's XO when she assumes command."

Fraser smiled. "The real power behind the throne."

"Not the way Mrs Oliver runs things, sir."

Fraser laughed at that.

"So, what brings you here, Demetrius?" Oliver asked. "I'm surprised to see so many marines here. I figured you'd have your own facility."

"We do," Fraser said, "but it's not adequate to the training needs and the guard has been kind enough to assist here."

"Are you... training here, sir?" Ho asked.

"No," Fraser said, "though seeing you are, I've got to admit I feel more than a little showed-up. That's A+ leadership right there. I thought I was some kind of hero just for stopping by to check on my people. Those are my lambs you're training with. I command the 32nd Marine Expeditionary Unit. We're with 11th Fleet. MARSOC is attached to us for their ops out here."

"So, you're the Navy's boarding teams," Oliver said.

"In a pinch," Fraser said, his smile not reaching his eyes, "we're here to keep you coasties honest."

Oliver smiled back, genuinely liking him. But that didn't mean she trusted him. At his rank, everything was political. *Why is he talking to me?*

"So," Fraser said after another awkward silence, "do you mind if I ask why you decided to enroll in this course?"

"I'm taking charge of SAR-1," Oliver answered.

"Sure, but are you planning to personally go on boardings?" Fraser's smile broadened.

Oliver's dropped. "You're goddamn right I am. You can't lead people if you don't know what the hell they're doing."

Fraser's smile left his mouth and transferred to his eyes. "You should've been a marine. Look, I agree, but life in micro-g is hard on a body. Aren't you worried about the bone density loss?"

"Aren't you?"

Fraser frowned. "What makes you think I go on boardings?"

"You lead marines," *now* Oliver smiled, "so surely you're doing it by example."

The moment hung in the air until Fraser broke it with a bark of a laugh. "That I am."

Oliver punctuated the exchange by popping a saltine into her mouth and forcing herself to chew.

"Look," Fraser said, "I'm not dumb. You're the officer they brought in to make sure your team goes all the way in this year's Boarding Action."

"So, what if I am?"

"I hate to disappoint, but it's not going to happen."

"You're so sure?"

"I am," Fraser jerked his thumb at the table in the enlisted mess where Oliver's classmates were eating. "These are marines. We suck at losing."

"I dunno," Oliver said, "I've been training with marines all day. They're capable, but so are coasties."

"No doubt, but you're training with my ground pounders." Fraser pointed out the thick glass of the mess window at the stretching darkness of space. "What do you see?"

"Nothing," Oliver says.

"That's right," Fraser says, "because the Marines Spec Ops Command's Orbital Training Center is on the other side of the Moon. That's where we train the team your people will go up against. You won't see them until it's game time."

"Good," Oliver said, though she wasn't feeling good at all, "we like surprises."

"Not this one, you won't," Fraser's smile returned, feral.

CHAPTER 5

CHINA CLAIMS WEAPONS DISCHARGE THAT STRUCK NAVY PURSUIT CRAFT
DUE TO "TECHNICAL MALFUNCTION."

Mons Pico / Earth date – Wed, February 27 / 16:07 hours

*Chinese People's Liberation Army Navy spokesman Wu Peixin stated
yesterday that this morning's incident where a PLAN vessel fired on a US
Navy craft in pursuit of a US-flagged quarantine runner was "a regrettable
technical malfunction." Peixin added that, "it is not China's policy to
engage foreign flagged vessels in our Exclusive Economic Zone. However,
we remind the United States that the presence of military vessels in Chinese
space greatly increases the risk of regrettable accidents like these." 11th
Fleet's Vice Admiral Augusta Donahugh responded with a statement this
afternoon. "The United States Navy will not tolerate hostile fire while we
engage in legal hot pursuit operations authorized by extant maritime law.
Navy gunners are authorized to return fire and otherwise take whatever
measures are necessary to protect US sovereignty and ensure the safety of
their crews."*

LUNAR SHIPPING NEWS

"Soooo?" Alice's voice was so much clearer this close to the Moon's
surface. "You made it two whole weeks!"

"Well, it's like I always keep telling you."

"Don't date anyone in the military?"

"The other thing."

"The only way out is through."

"That's it! But I won't lie, it's just been hors d'oeuvres so far. We're starting the tacpro round."

"Mom, acronyms."

"It's the practical portion. We're doing simulated boardings."

"Cool! That sounds like fun."

"Yup, just me and a gaggle of fifteen year-old marines. Total blast. How are you holding up?"

"I'm OK. Nothing much changes here."

"Honey," Oliver said, "I'm your mother. You act like I don't know that 'I'm OK' is code for 'I am not OK.'"

"I don't want to go on about it, mom. I'm just still finding my feet here. Figuring things out. I'm a big girl. I'll get it done."

"Is it the distribution negotiations? Maybe I can…"

"No, mom, you can't. Even I know you're not allowed to do outside work, especially when you're about to become an admiral with responsibility for shipping in the lunar port."

Oliver felt her stomach do a loop. Alice was right, of course, but it did nothing to quell the involuntary response in her body – her revving heart, her tightening muscles. She remembered sleep-training Alice, having to lie awake in the next room and listen to her daughter cry out for her, Tom stroking her hair and telling her it would be OK, *Alice is fine, babe. She's really fine.* But her body didn't care. No matter what her mind believed, her body knew that Alice was *not* fine, that babies who were fine did not cry like that, that she had to save her daughter now now now now *now*.

It took Oliver a moment to be able to speak. "How long are you good for? Can you make it until I finish this tour?"

"I'll be OK, mom. Just focus on your promotion and winning this thing."

She is not OK. "I will finish this tour, and then I will come and help you. I promise."

"Love you, mom," Alice made a smooching sound. "Get this thing over with so we can get you promoted and I can see you."

"Love you, honey," Oliver said, turning off the connection and standing.

She opened the door to the communications booth, stepped out into the passageway, and was almost knocked over by three coasties running past. She heard shouts from further down the hall.

Oliver turned to look after them, felt a tap on her shoulder, and turned back to see Ho, panting. "You weren't in your stateroom. Where have you been?"

"I was talking to Alice. Jesus, Wen, you're scaring me. What's going on?"

"Come on!" Ho was not a man to get excited without cause, and Oliver felt dread curdle in her belly as she jogged after him down the passageway. Ho took a sharp right and led Oliver into the enlisted coffee mess, so crowded with marines and coasties that Oliver had to wedge herself in alongside a mountain of a marine who was himself wedged up against the wall of freeze-dried coffee packets. All eyes were glued to a flat-screen monitor spread across the upper corner of the room.

Oliver could see the logo of the Lunar 6 Network, the dominant English language channel across the Moon. She recognized Jennifer Hsu's voice, the channel's lead anchor, who Oliver had heard narrate her husband's death to thousands of strangers at least twenty times. Oliver could hear Hsu's training desperately trying to keep her voice even, to assert some kind of calm over the swirl of emotions she was clearly grappling with. "It appears both the US Navy and PLAN boats were pursuing the same quarantine runner." The screen displayed what looked to be a civilian six-pack, a short-range hauler named for its maximum capacity of six passengers, burning hard through empty space high above the surface. "I'm... The Captain of the Port reports that the Navy and PLAN boats were unaware of each other's position, and it is not clear why the vessel's instruments didn't pick up on the…"

As one body, the crowd leaned in toward the monitor. The six-pack's rear thrusters finally sputtered out, a sign that it had burned all its propellant and was flying on inertia now. An instant later, a US Navy small boat leapt into the frame, its own rear thruster burning bright, gaining on the fleeing vessel. AFT FLIR POD 6 – USS *OBAMA* appeared in the screen's lower right-hand corner, indicating the source of the camera feed. Oliver felt her stomach clench, the dread rising up her throat and sticking there, until she found it hard to breathe.

The Navy boat dipped its bow and dove toward the six-pack, skillfully pulling up as it closed, exposing its belly where the boarding "nipple" could latch on to the fleeing vessel's tow-fender. "Oh, Jesus," someone whispered.

An instant later, another boat flashed into view, moving so quickly it was little more than a blur. It took the Navy boat broadside and both vanished in a bright orange flash. Oliver felt her jaw drop as she watched the screen, her hands making helpless circles. The orange flash pooled and oozed the way explosions did in micro-g, and from the debris she saw tumbling out of it, Oliver could tell there was nothing left of either boat bigger than a softball.

Hsu was speaking again as the six-pack sped away from the wreckage, but it was so much buzzing in Oliver's ears, the magnitude of what she was seeing overwhelming the coordination of her senses, forcing her to focus on just her sight – watching the tape for any indication that the other boat had been… But then the feed was looping, replaying in slow motion – the blur of the intercepting boat slowed down enough for Oliver to clearly see the Chinese star and anchor, the numbers 8-1 on its side.

"Fuck this," one of the marines was saying.

"That's some kamikaze shit," another one added.

"Those are the Japanese," Oliver spoke before she could stop herself, "and it was also over a hundred years ago."

Heads swiveled to regard her, eyes narrowing.

"With all due respect, ma'am," one of the marines said, "that was fucking intentional."

"We don't know that," Oliver said, "there could have been an instrumentation issue. Maybe the PLAN boat was trying to herd them toward another vessel. There's a million things that…"

"Looked intentional to me," Oliver turned to see Fullweiler standing behind her. "I've been running this school for four years. All I see is boardings. I can't think of a single good reason for coming in that hot on a quarantine runner."

Oliver felt her stomach clench tighter. It was Fullweiler's school, but these were the people who would be conducting boardings across the Moon for years to come. They *had* to understand nuance. They *had* to get control of their emotions. They couldn't be getting out there spoiling for a fight. "I can think of a thousand," Oliver said. "The chief one being that Chinese people don't want to die any more than Americans do. A competent Chinese coxs'un isn't going to deliberately incinerate their boat and crew just to… I can't even think of what the reason could possibly be."

"China's different from us," Fullweiler shrugged.

"I want all my marines back in quarters." A deep, singer's bass sounded from beside her, and Oliver realized the Marine she was wedged against was Fraser. "I want gear checks done and watch your tablets for recall orders. Comms dark for everyone and no more watching the news. Let's go, people. Right now."

"Yes, sir," the marines said in one voice and began filing out of the room.

"Recall orders?" Oliver asked.

"This could blow up very quickly," Fraser said, "and if it does, I want my people ready. Please excuse me," he turned to go.

Oliver stopped him with a hand on his arm. "I'm sure you don't want to start a war with China, General Fraser."

"Of course not," Fraser said, "but it's my job to be ready to finish one."

He left, and Oliver turned to Ho, but her XO had his eyes locked on the screen which had switched away from the news channel and was now reeling off an emergency message from OTRACEN's watch floor. WARNING ORDER (WARNORD) 11FLT CO VADM DONAHUGH ALL HANDS GEAR CHECKS AND STAND BY TO DEPLOY. The words scrolled across the bottom of the screen in an endless loop, the room gone silent save for the sounds of thudding boots as the crew raced to comply.

Vice Admiral Donahugh could command her marines, and Fraser had clearly anticipated this, but she had no authority to order the Coast Guard to do anything. The Coast Guard wasn't subordinate to the Navy.

Except in time of war.

"Jesus," Oliver said, turned and nearly shoved Fullweiler out of the way as she raced back to the comms booth.

"Captain Oliver!" Fullweiler called after her. "We need to talk about getting the crew ready! I could use your help!"

Oliver ignored him, fumbling up the receiver and connecting to OTRACEN's watch floor. The watchstander had barely answered on the other end before she was speaking, using the full hammer of her impending rank, "This is Rear Admiral Select Oliver, I need USCG Ops Actual now, please."

"Aye aye, ma'am," said the watchstander, and there was a brief click and then a long pause while someone at the other end of the line hunted down Admiral Allen.

"Ops Actual," Allen finally came on the line, "go ahead."

"Sir, did you see the…"

"I see it, Jane. It's a WARNORD, do not do anything yet."

"Sir, we don't know what caused that collision, it could have been anything. We can't let the Navy use this an as excuse to…"

"No, we can't. But they're damn well going to try. I've got the old man on the other line, and he's going into session with the joint chiefs in a few minutes. If this thing can be unfucked, we'll unfuck it. Just sit tight and wait to hear from me."

"Jesus," Oliver could feel her pulse hammering in her temples. "We've got to talk to the Chinese. We've need to deescalate this. OTRACEN is rigging up to deploy."

Allen sighed. "Christ. We've got to get control of this thing. Tell Fullweiler to get our people stood down, at least."

"Not sure he'll listen to me, sir."

"If he doesn't, tell him to give me a call."

"Aye aye, sir," Oliver said, and hung up the receiver, turned to find Fullweiler standing in the hatch. He had his hardshell base layer tucked under one arm, his utility belt dangling from his fingers. "You should suit up, captain."

"Negative," Oliver said. "You should stow your gear and wait for an OPORD from your proper chain of command."

"Captain," Fullweiler sighed. "This isn't what any of us want, but…"

"Isn't it, though? Because for someone who doesn't want war, you seem awfully enthusiastic to get moving."

"We've got a WARNORD from–"

"From a service that you're not a member of. We fall under the Navy in a declared war and during no other time. I just got off the phone with Ops, and you are to stand down, *and* you are to stand down every coastie on this station until we have a better picture of how this thing is unfolding."

Fullweiler cocked an eyebrow. "Admiral Allen said this?"

"If you don't believe me, he told me you should give him a call."

Fullweiler's eyes narrowed. "That's exactly what I'll do," but he remained in the hatch, eyes locked with Oliver, until Ho appeared behind him, tapping him on the shoulder. "If you'll excuse us, sir, I'm sure Rear Admiral Select Oliver would like to confer with me in private."

Fullweiler glanced at him, shook his head, and moved on down the passageway toward his office.

"Jesus, that fucking guy," Oliver said.

"It's not just him," Ho said, "this whole station is a lit fuse. What the fuck is wrong with people?"

"Have you ever heard of the Chinese deliberately ramming a Navy vessel? For any reason?"

Ho shook his head. "No way, ma'am. That's not a thing they do. It's not a thing they've ever done."

"So this was accident."

"Of course it was. What the hell else could it be?"

"Christ," Oliver found herself echoing Allen's words. "We've got to get control of this thing."

"Yes," Ho nodded, shoulders slumping. "Yes, we do."

WARNORD CANX – ALL HANDS STAND DOWN SAY AGAIN ALL HANDS STAND DOWN scrolled across every monitor in the station roughly an hour later. Oliver sat beside Ho in the coffee mess when the message appeared, and both exhaled audibly. Ho let his head sink into his folded arms, tipping over his thankfully empty cup.

Two marines were in the room with them, and both cursed just as audibly, got up and stormed out.

"Who the hell," Ho asked, "actually *wants* to get into a shooting war?"

"People who've never been shot at," Oliver sighed, the feeling of her longhorn spinning as the anti-materiel round struck it rising so clearly in her mind that she felt a brief touch of vertigo.

"Thank God," she added. "I guess Zhukov was able to talk sense into the Joint Chiefs."

"This time," Ho said. "How long do you think we have until the next incident like this?"

"Hopefully it'll keep until after boarding action." Oliver stood, feeling some of the tension seep out of the knotted muscles in her back, and headed over to the coffee packets. "I need a refresh."

"Gonna have to wait, boss," Ho jerked his thumb at the monitor: WARNORD CANX RESUME SCHEDULE AT THIRD PERIOD ASSIGN. "Third period is back on. That's our tacpro round. Here's our chance to demonstrate that all the book learning stuck."

"It's a full-on boarding?"

"Yup," Ho said. "No holds barred. Instructors acting as a hostile enemy in a non-cooperative docking. Everything real except for the bullets."

"Christ, I am not ready to do a boarding right now," Oliver sighed.

"Were you ever ready when you actually had to do them?" Ho stood and headed for the passageway.

"No," Oliver admitted, and followed.

When Ho finally emerged from his stateroom to join her in heading toward the launch bay, Oliver had to stifle a chuckle. Her XO somehow managed to look more ridiculous in his hardshell's undersuit than he did in his PT uniform. He handed her a bright yellow paint gun. It was built to simulate the size, feel, and weight of a hornet pistol, but fired a lower velocity paint packet. "You ready?"

She holstered the pistol-sized weapon and picked up the pelican case that contained her hardshell. Fullweiler had offered to have it prepped for her in deference to her rank, but she'd come this far with the rest of the class. She'd walk into the launch bay, lugging the damn thing along with everyone else. Two weeks on OTRACEN had helped her to adjust to the spin-gravity, and she instinctively moved the case to her counter-spinward side.

The two marines launching with them were waiting in the launch bay and already in their hardshells, patterned with the digital camouflage white and gray worn by all marines who might deploy to the Moon's surface. The day-glow orange of Oliver and Ho's suits seemed even more garish in comparison. They'd been assigned Gonzalez and Catrona, two marines that Oliver would have called "fresh-faced," if she were being charitable.

Gonzalez waved a clipboard as Catrona put his helmet on and sealed it. "Crew assignments, ma'am." She could barely hear him through his faceplate.

She glanced at the sheet, not surprised in the least. GONZALEZ – BOARDING TEAM MBR CATRONA – BOARDING TEAM MBR HO – COXSWAIN OLIVER – HELM. Fullweiler wanted her front and center for the action, as she'd known he would.

"Looks like you're driving, ma'am," Gonzalez said, opening the rhino's hatch and heading inside.

"Color me shocked," Oliver went in behind him.

"Rank has its responsibilities, I guess," Ho said, "and it's certainly nice to have the shoe on the other foot for a change. The coxs'un calls the shots, and I know I can count on your prompt obedience to orders, ma'am."

"Absolutely," Oliver said, "right after I've removed this butcher knife from your eye-socket."

Ho grinned at her as she locked his helmet in place and the seal indicator flashed green. He gestured to the helm chair. "Mush, doggie."

The exercise was run in a four-person launch – a stripped down version of the small boats, used almost exclusively as escape craft. It was half the length of the rhino, and without the capacity to pressurize.

It had no hard points, and therefore no autocannons, a feature that made Oliver both concerned and pleased. Pleased because it meant this was strictly a SAR boat. Concerned because, well…

Ho took in the lack of hard points and said what she was thinking. "I wonder if we're going to regret not having guns."

The tiny launch felt cramped compared to a rhino, and groaned under their weight as they boarded. That groaning rose to an outright squeal as the crane lifted them, and Oliver could feel the rickety frame flexing. The onboard plotter lit up with the LMGRS coordinates of their "radio call," the simulated incident they were supposed to be investigating.

"That's… the range isn't it?" Oliver asked.

"Think so," Ho said, leaning in to look, "and us without a bow gun."

"They're not using live rounds, are they, ma'am?" Gonzalez asked.

"You think they intend to shoot at us. With live rounds. During a training exercise." Oliver arched an eyebrow she knew Gonzalez couldn't see through her hardshell helmet.

"Roger that, ma'am. Sorry."

"No need to apologize," Oliver said, "just trying to lower your temperature on this."

"Gonzalez could definitely stand lowering his temperature," Catrona laughed.

"As coxs'un, I ask that all members of my crew keep their temperatures low, thank you," Ho solemnly intoned.

"Well, if they do blow us up," Oliver said, "at least I won't have to put up with what you think passes for humor."

"My first order as your coxs'un," Ho's tone became even more formal, "is that you take us to the coordinates in such a manner that we do not get shot."

"Aye aye, sir," Oliver said as the crane let go.

The launch shuddered like a tin can in a storm, but steadied as she engaged the thruster and the craft began to glide smoothly under its own power.

The bow rose and OTRACEN loomed bright and blinking off their starboard beam as they pushed off toward the range. On her opposite side, the Moon glowed so brightly that she squinted.

"Contact, two hundred yards, constant bearing, decreasing range," Gonzalez said. Oliver could hear the question in his voice.

"You're the lookout spotting the contact, Gonzalez," Oliver said, "advise your coxs'un." She could certainly take over the mission by virtue of her rank, and that was surely what the young marine would have preferred, but he would never learn a thing that way.

"Roger that, ma'am," Gonzalez looked at the transponder data. "I've got them on AIS, now. US flagged. Mining rig, six-pack. Scenario says they're on the border of the Chinese EEZ. We need to push them back into US space."

Oliver squinted out the windscreen, and spotted their target vessel, roughly the same size as a rhino, patches welded over the hull where past boarding simulations had cut into her, all the glass removed and replaced with metal plate. It was built on the frame of a real American mining six-pack complete with pressurized cargo pods that would have been packed with liquid Helium-3 bound for markets planetside.

"I guess we hail them?" Gonzalez asked.

"Concur," Ho agreed. "Ma'am, if you'd do the honors?"

Oliver nodded, leaned down to check the transponder code, toggled the radio channel to reach them. "Mining vessel *Marlin*, mining vessel *Marlin*, this is the United States Coast Guard. You are on the border of the simulated Chinese EEZ. Bring your helm to two-seven-zero and make way at ten knots for two nautical miles. Acknowledge."

She held her breath as the silence stretched without a response. She was just about to take another one as the radio crackled into life, and a voice answered in a southern drawl so thick that she could barely understand the words. "Well, hello there, coast guard! Sure thing, we'll turn her around right away. Our plotter's using an old chart. That's probably why we missed it. Sorry about that."

"Huh," Ho said, as the six-pack fired its attitude thrusters and pointed its bow to the heading Oliver had specified, "that was easy."

"There's no way in hell it's that easy," Oliver said, "stay frosty."

"Let's light 'em up so they don't forget we're here, Gonzalez," Ho said.

Gonzalez looked up uncertainly. Marine small boats didn't have blue lights.

"It's here," Ho said, reaching up and toggling the rhino's light bar, sending a cascade of blue dancing down bow as Oliver maneuvered them in. She felt goosebumps rising on the backs of her arms as the azure shimmer washed over her. She'd been lighting up on ops for nearly her entire adult life. It never got old.

The six-pack cut its thrusters and let itself drift gently until Oliver could see inside the slit in one of the port-side plates, made out the helmets of the boat's coxswain and helmsman, the white and gray digital patterns sweeping over the hardshell's shoulders. She could see them flailing their arms, the articulated joints of the hardshells making them look like nothing so much as the Michelin Man doing a backstroke.

Ho squinted past her. "What the hell are they doing?"

Oliver puffed their port side attitude thrusters to keep their bow pointed at the slit. "I can't... They're messing with something..." At last the coxswain found what he was reaching for, and yanked a long polyester strap across his chest.

"Shit! They're strapping in!" Oliver realized too late that they were station keeping much too far from the six-pack to do anything now.

The six-pack's hull and aft thrusters fired at the same time, making the boat execute a neat somersault. Oliver was still fumbling for her own throttle when the aft thrusters lit up again, and the six-pack was rocketing away from them – into the fictional Chinese EEZ.

"Shit!" Gonzalez nearly yelled into his radio.

"Calm down, Gonzalez. I can't fly if you make my ears bleed," Oliver said, finally getting the launch burning.

"Can they outrun us?"

After a few seconds of burn, the six-pack grew in her vision, but only slightly. "No," she said, "the launch is lighter, smaller. They've got more ass, but we've got more sass."

Ho chuckled. "How long until we can intercept?"

Oliver glanced at the radar. "We should catch them sometime next week."

Ho's radio crackled as he began to respond, then cut off abruptly as two gray dots detached themselves from the blue-white burn of the six-pack's aft thrusters and drifted toward them. "What the heck is…" Catrona began.

But Oliver was already yanking the helm, punching the starboard attitude thrusters, whipping the launch past the first of the dots, growing to a frightening size so quickly that it was if it had materialized in front of them – a light pod of compressed garbage, ejected from one of the six-pack's cargo pods. She felt it streak past them, close enough to sweep a shadow over the starboard side.

"Jesus," Oliver said. "These fuckers are not kidding."

"Well, they did say that quarantine runners will frequently launch garbage to slow pursuit," Ho said.

"When did they say that?" Oliver asked on a private channel.

"Somebody hasn't been paying attention in intercept tactics class," Ho said.

The six-pack shrank in their vision again, until Oliver had to squint as it swept over the gray-white expanse of OTRACEN.

"Damnit, we'll never catch them now," Gonzalez said.

"No, they're slowing," Oliver said, as the blue-white dot of the six-pack began to grow into a broader circle of gray. "I guess they burned all their propellant."

"Or enough of it, anyway. We can't get out in front of them. They're much too bigger than we are, they'd blow right through us."

"We don't need do," Oliver said to Ho back on the private channel, touching the throttle to give them just enough speed to come up alongside. "We can shoulder them."

"Shoulder them into what?" Ho asked. "This is a deep space simulation. There wouldn't be anything out here to shoulder them into."

"Sure there would," Oliver said, cutting the thrust and letting the launch's greater velocity pull it ahead of the six-pack. "There's that big planet right there."

"OTRACEN?" Oliver could see the horror on Ho's face. "Jesus Christ, boss. That's… That's goddamn unforgiving is what that is. This is supposed to be a deep-space simulation!"

"If they wanted it to be a deep-space simulation," Oliver grunted as she goosed the throttle and yanked the control sticks hard to starboard, "then they shouldn't have put a simulated planet right in the middle of it."

The launch bucked, canted and drove hard at the six-pack. She could see the coxswain waving his arms and shouting at the helmsman, the six-pack's bow thrusters burning hard as it desperately sought to slow itself. OTRACEN stretched across Oliver's vision with astonishing speed. The six-pack managed to slow so quickly that Oliver missed it entirely and raced past its bow, so close that the launch's collar nearly brushed the six-pack's bow lift-point.

She could see Gonzalez shouting into his radio, made sure to keep his channel muted. She didn't want him flattening her ear drums while she was trying to concentrate. Catrona was silent, at least, but she felt her seat shifting as he braced himself hard against it.

"What the hell do you think you're doing?" the southern accent barked over the radio.

"Back it off, boss. Back it off!" Ho's former calm was a memory.

But Oliver was as placid as still water on a hot summer day. She cut the aft thrusters, yanked the control sticks hard to port and burned the starboard thrusters. Her stomach lurched as the launch spun like a penny turned on its side. She watched the six-pack appear and disappear twice before she compensated, firing the port side thrusters. The spinning gradually stopped, and she was already giving the launch aft thrust as the six-pack rotated into her vision just off the launch's bow. One hundred yards, fifty, thirty. She miscalculated the distance slightly, and was surprised by the gentle nudge as the launch's belly slid over the six-pack's tow-fender.

Ho had braced himself against the plotter with a shaking arm. "Dear God," he said, still on the private channel, "my poor beleaguered guts. Ma'am, as long as we sail together, I swear I will never forgive you…"

"XO," Oliver cut him off. "Get us soft dock."

"Jesus Christ," Ho shook his head. "Catrona, soft dock, please."

Catrona punched out of his restraints and raced to the control lever of the launch's grasping "nipple" – the long, flexible gangway that would latch on to the other vessel's tow fender. Oliver felt the launch tremble and stop moving as it locked together with the six-pack. "I have soft dock," Catrona said.

"Gonzalez," Oliver said, hoping a task would calm the marine, "call it in. Get us permission to board."

"OTRACEN, OTRACEN, this is training vessel 199," Gonzalez did sound calmer, "we have soft-dock with non-compliant vessel. US flagged, unknown status, ops normal at SMGRS 39952. Positive control. Request permission to board."

"TV-199, this is OTRACEN," Oliver could hear the irritation in Fullweiler's voice, presumably at her aggressive maneuver. "Permission granted. Go when ready."

"Cut in, sir!" Gonzalez said.

"You heard him," Oliver said. "XO, make the cut."

"Why am I cutting?" Ho radioed on the private channel.

"Because the assignment sheet didn't list an engineer," Oliver responded on the same channel, "and I want the kids to train getting eyes-on, now start cutting."

"I'm the goddamn coxs'un," Ho said, digging the torch-assembly out of the gear locker. "I'm supposed to be telling myself to start cutting."

Catrona pulled another lever, securing the nipple. "Hard dock. Venting atmosphere." It was a formality. Performance for Fullweiler and the instructors listening on the radio. Both vessels were in vacuum. There was no atmosphere to vent. Ho threw open the belly doors and pushed off, floating down the nipple. A moment later, the sparks of the cutting torch came leaping up.

The six-pack was hailing them, but Oliver overrode them with her own priority hail. "Fugitive vessel *Marlin*, this is United States Coast Guard. Prepare to be boarded. Muster all crew on the bow behind the helm. Do you have any weapons aboard?"

There was a long silence before the southern accent replied with an angry, "Yes!"

"That's nice," Oliver said, "steer clear of them if you don't want to get shot. XO! How's that cut coming?"

"Cutting a hatch is an art. You can't rush art."

"Catrona! On me!" Oliver drew her paint gun and took position behind Ho. The exterior hatch had been unlocked, as was customary, and Ho was inside the six-pack's airlock, carving into the sealed inner hatch. He finished cutting and rolled aside, dropping the cutting torch.

"Stack up," she told Catrona, kicking her spider boots down on the nipple, feeling the thousands of setules digging in and holding her in place. Walking in spider boots took some getting used to, breaking the Van der Waals force with each step, then the setules re-adhering with each new one. It was, she imagined, what walking through glue might be like.

"Christ," Ho radioed her over the private channel. "I still can't believe you did that."

"Guess they know who they're dealing with now," Oliver said.

"Yeah," Ho said, "a lunatic."

"Guns up, Wen."

"Aye aye, ma'am, go when ready."

"Ready?" she radioed the whole team.

"Ready," they sounded off.

"Here we go, buttonhook right." She grunted as she pulled up one boot, snap kicking the cut section of bulkhead hard enough to send it spinning inward and keep her spider boot from adhering.

She leveled her paint gun and rolled into the space beyond, bridging to the six-pack's open channel. "United States Coast Guard!" Her vision expanded just as it always did in a crisis, her peripheral zone growing, details going blurry. She could feel her heart slowing, the world slowing with her, giving her the room she needed to make decisions.

The vessel's interior was completely stripped save for a dummy helm and console, bare of instrumentation. There were only four occupants, all in marine white-gray camouflage hardshells, and all making an exaggerated show of being surprised.

Oliver held her weapon at the low ready. "Identify yourselves, explain why you didn't comply with our directions."

"Bork bork bork," one of the men in the hardshells said, the pre-agreed code for passengers and crew who did not speak English.

"Back away, move behind the helm, keep your hands where I can see them!" Oliver knew the scenario called for the role-players to not understand her words, and so she made her intentions abundantly clear with her tone and hand motions. But she was careful to keep her weapon pointed at the deck. Nothing escalated tensions faster than having a gun pointed at you.

The role-players complied, moving behind the helm console, hands above their heads. Oliver saw no visible weapons in reach, and was satisfied the role-players were shepherded into the vessel's small nose.

"On your knees!" she shouted, motioning down with a single hand. Two of the four role-players knelt immediately. Two remained standing, and only one raised his hands over his head.

Oliver opened her mouth to order him down when Gonzalez's voice vibrated in her helmet speakers. "Motherfucker, did you not just hear her!? Get the fuck down now!"

The kid was so amped up, he'd forgotten to pipe his voice to the six-pack's channel and was instead yelling at his own team.

Oliver tried to radio him on the private channel, but he overrode her again. "Asshole, do you want to get shot!? I said get the fuck down right now!"

She knew she shouldn't look away from the role-players, but she also had to be sure of Gonzalez's position in case he…

…She had just begun to turn as Gonzalez's paint gun kicked, the paint packet rocketing across the intervening space and thunking solidly against the standing role-player's face plate.

It was an amazing shot. Had it been a hornet gun, the rocket munition would have blown the man's head apart. Had it been a duster, it would have sheared off his entire upper torso.

Either way, this unarmed man, hands above his head, would have been dead.

Oliver opened her mouth to yell at Gonzalez, but the remaining standing role-player advanced on her. He was still outside her twenty-one foot zone, so she was not authorized to shoot, but she swept her weapon up. "Don't! Get down right now!"

Oliver checked to make sure Ho and Catrona had everyone covered. The role-player Gonzalez had shot angrily wiped the paint off his face plate with one gauntleted hand, and lay face down on the deck. "I'm dead."

The remaining role-player stopped his advance and put his hands in the air.

"I need you to put your arms out at your sides, palms up. Do it now!" Oliver bridged directly to his radio. She could feel her arms trembling, her pulse racing. *That marine just killed an unarmed man. No! It's just a simulation.*

The man, and it was a man, Oliver could tell by the size and shape of his suit, complied with her order. "Now," she said, "turn around until I tell you to stop. Go!"

The man complied, giving her a full view of his entire suit. No visible weapons, no breaches in the suit's integrity. He'd kept his faceplate smoked, and she couldn't see who was under the helmet. "Stop!" she said when his back was to her, "Take a wider stance! Bend over at the waist! Do not move! Do not resist me!"

"XO," she radioed Ho on the private channel, "you got the other three?"

"One of them is out of the fight thanks to the Punisher over here, ma'am," he radioed back. "I think the three of us can cover the other two."

"OK," Oliver said, reached back and removed the restraints from her waist. They looked like normal handcuffs, with supersized bails designed to cinch tight around a hardshell's thick wrists.

"Cross your wrists!" she radioed, heard the tension in her own voice. Gonzalez's lapse had rattled her.

Oliver waited a few seconds both to center herself and to throw him off, half expecting him to run, but he only crossed his wrists and waited for her next order. Oliver stepped in, pushing one bail down over his wrist. Once she had it locked on, she would effectively have a metal handle attached to him, one she could use to fling him around in the micro-g, or even break his suit's integrity if she had to.

As if he'd known she were coming, the man turned his wrist.

Suddenly, the narrow portion of the hardshell's articulated wrist was replaced with the wide. Oliver saw what was coming and tried to pull back her hand, but she was already committed to the movement, the restraints coming down, the metal bail colliding with the man's hardshell, the clasp swinging around and rebounding, hanging open.

The man ripped the restraints from Oliver's hands and turned, spinning the metal circles on the short chain between them. The metal ring crashed into Oliver's faceplate hard enough to crack it. Oliver felt the puffing cold of the emergency oxygen billowing around her face, the suit's failsafe coating shrinkwrapping her, trapping the precious oxygen. It made her eyes water, and she lost her view of her adversary for a brief moment.

A brief moment was more than enough.

Oliver felt something strike her back hard enough to knock the wind out of her even through the hardshell. *The deck. I'm on the deck.* She tried to rise, found she was pinned in place. She blinked the tears from her eyes and saw the man kneeling on her chest. He had her pinned on her back, his hand spread across the seal between the hardshell's helmet and body. She could feel the edge of his gauntlet on the seal, and knew that with enough pressure, he could rupture it. His other hand was outstretched, and Oliver just knew that even though she couldn't see it, he held a gun.

"Ho!" she radioed her XO, "did they get you?"

"Right in the dick," Ho confirmed. "Christ this is embarrassing."

"ENDEX ENDEX ENDEX. End exercise," Fullweiler's voice on their radios sounded almost cheerful. "Evolution complete. Secure from exercise and RTB. I say again, return to base."

Red lights strobed through the cabin interior and the man stood, extending his hand to help Oliver to her feet. She took it grudgingly, the hot flush of humiliation making her cheeks burn against the cold touch of the emergency oxygen. "You could have killed me."

"Sure could have," the man replied in a deep, singer's bass, "but really, it would have been because of that royal fuck-up you called a 'cuff.' So, if we're being fair, you'd have killed yourself."

He unsmoked his faceplate and Oliver found herself face to face with the gorgeous, hard-edges of Demetrius Fraser. "Besides," he added, "I have a lot of faith in these suits. You'll have to rely on that when you go on boardings yourself."

Oliver knew he was being gracious, that she should answer in kind, but the ease with which he had beaten her was still too fresh. "I've been on thousands of boardings."

"Could have fooled me," Fraser said. "I'm guessing maybe those were blue-water boardings? Out here on the 16th Watch, we do things different. You run by the numbers like that, try to play nice, this kind of thing can happen." He jerked a thumb at Gonzalez, knocked on his back where one of the other role-players had charged him. Catrona was wiping paint off his faceplate. "I know you're not a fan of this sort of thing, but my marine there had the right idea."

Oliver felt a sudden heat rising in the back of her throat. "Like hell he did. Shooting an unarmed suspect with their hands up is never the right thing."

Fraser patted her on the shoulder. "Look, it's been a real pleasure to meet you, and I know you're going to do a great job leading SPACETACLET. But I think now's a good time to remind you about the MARSOC marines I told you about in the chow hall. I'm an old man, Jane, and look at what I just did to you. The marines I'll be sending to Boarding Action are all trained harder and meaner'n me, and they're in the prime of their lives."

Oliver thought of Chief Elgin. He was already on the SAR-1 crew selected for this year's Boarding Action. How old was he? Fifty? Fifty-five?

"I don't doubt you're ready to lead," Fraser said, "but you better remember that you're not ready to *fight*."

Oliver gave a shrug exaggerated enough to be visible through her hardshell, felt the shrinkwrapping of the internal failsafe hugging the chilly oxygen to her body. She struggled to keep her voice nonchalant, but she felt the humiliation heat her cheeks. "Botched a cuff. Could have happened to anyone."

Fraser grinned, shook his head. "Well, I guess it could have." His faster pace carried him a few steps away from her before he stopped, turned back. "But it didn't happen to anyone, Admiral Oliver. It happened to you."

As they moved back through the cut in the six-pack's hull. Oliver radioed Ho on the private channel. "That kid," she seethed, "is never to pick up a weapon again in his life."

"Roger that," was Ho's only reply. She had no idea how she would make good on that threat. Rank aside, Gonzalez wasn't in her chain of command, and she hadn't exactly made a great showing herself on this boarding.

The enormity of it dawned on her. It wasn't just what Gonzalez had done, it was that they had failed the training evolution. What would this mean for her course status? She couldn't afford to roll back and take it again, and she certainly couldn't afford to wash out now that she had so publicly committed to going the distance. *Christ*. Her mind whirled with potential consequences.

They were silent the whole way to their staterooms, where Ho finally got the nerve up to ask her. "You going to be OK?"

Oliver spun on him, realized the rage must have been visible on her face. It was bad military bearing and she swallowed it at once. "Fraser said what Gonzalez did was the right move. Said that was the way things are out here."

Ho didn't hesitate. "I actually like General Fraser, but that's some high-test bullshit right there."

"Good," Oliver nodded. "That's my thinking too. I need to think about this. Figure out a way forward."

"Aye aye, ma'am," Ho said.

He was still showering in his room when the email arrived with the class scores.

Oliver had to read it twice before she could believe the grade they'd received.

PASS.

"What the hell is this?" Oliver attempted to slam the printout on Fullweiler's desk, failed to account for the fact that his office wasn't currently spinning, and succeeded only in making it drift erratically between them. *Well done,* she thought, *he's surely intimidated now.*

"That's your notice of passing," Fullweiler answered calmly. "I'm sorry, did you want to fail?"

"How can you pass us after what happened?"

"What happened? Are you referring to your fancy flying?"

Oliver felt herself getting hotter. "Your fancy pursuit evasion maneuvers required fancy flying," she answered more quickly than she'd intended. "I wonder what would have happened if we'd hit that garbage in a rickety launch."

Fullweiler shrugged. "We pride ourselves on preparing our students for real-life conditions."

Oliver mimicked his tone. "And I pride myself on training the same way. Nothing I did exceeded safe speed or thruster application per the manual."

"Uh-huh," Fullweiler said. "Just a friendly warning not to try that in a rhino."

"I wasn't in a rhino."

"I'm trying to give you advice. I have some experience with this stuff."

"It's appreciated. You'll forgive me if I think it lacks conviction coming from a guy who was fine with a marine whose balls had barely dropped shooting an unarmed civilian in the face."

Fullweiler's smug expression finally dropped. "Look, if you want to have a professional conversation in respectful tones, then I'm more than willing, but I'm not going to sit here while you unload on me. Gonzalez shot a *role-player* and instructor in the face, and then only after that role-player failed to comply with his order to get down."

"He never gave an audible order! Kid was so amped up he forgot to bridge into the vessel's radio! He was screaming at *us*."

Fullweiler shrugged. "Video shows a hand motion, first from you, and then from him. Plus, there were two other men on their knees, which is direction-by-context per the manual. This isn't Earth, captain. You know how unreliable audio is in space-ops." He knew she did, and it was why he was reinforcing the point. He might as well have said, *you don't know what it takes to command out here.*

"I do know. I also know that shooting an unarmed civilian in the face because they don't comply with an order that they didn't even hear in the split-second you wanted them to will *not* fly when it goes to trial. And it *will* go to trial."

"No, captain, it won't," Fullweiler said. "Because when Gonzalez graduates here, he will not be going out on SAR runs with *us*. He will be going on boardings with marine crews who are breaching and clearing. They won't be police actions. They'll be meat grinders."

"Not if the guard takes the lead. Then that kid will be part of a joint operation led by someone coming out of *my* command, and *you'll* have taught him it's OK to go in there and mow down anybody who doesn't heave-to quickly enough."

"No," Fullweiler growled, "far better to have a botched-cuff scenario like what just played out on that boat, with the bad guys all fine, and your boarding team dead."

"Far better a botched cuff than a murder. This is the Navy. They've packed this place with marines. They've poisoned the whole process. If you're such a bleeds-blue coastie, then why are you letting their belligerent shit infect our training pipeline? We don't want a war with China? This has to be a SAR mission, not a military one. Gonzalez has to fail out. Shit, captain, *I* have to fail out for letting him do that."

"The Navy hasn't…"

"Oh, horseshit. I saw you drooling over that collision. You couldn't wait to get in the fight, Fullweiler. You want to get out there and show China who's boss. Maybe you should transfer services, because in this one we *save* lives first."

For the first time since she'd met him, Fullweiler utterly lost his cool, punching his desktop and leaning over it, as the rebound caused him to float slowly up. "Don't presume to tell me what we do or do not do in this service, *captain*. I may not be pinning a star on in a week, but I have given my life to the guard and I bleed blue same as you. Now, I am doing you a favor here. If you *want* me to fail you, I'm sure I can arrange it, but if you're just going to come in here and question my commitment to my life's calling, then I'll thank you to see yourself out."

Oliver swallowed at least half-a-dozen biting responses, turned on her heel, and nearly sent herself rocketing toward the ceiling before she remembered the micro-g environment and slowed her roll. "There's still a week left for you to screw something else up!" Fullweiler shouted at the back of her head.

Their final exam took place on the last three days of class. The practical was far less challenging than their run with Gonzalez, a mere formality focused on safety. Oliver realized that her run-in with Fraser had been the real test, to see if she would drop when they threw everything at her.

The practical was followed by a comprehensive oral board, followed by the graduation ceremony. Once she'd reached the realization that Fullweiler wouldn't fail her, she could suddenly see it in his smile, read it in the faces of every instructor in the school. *They think I'm going out to pasture. They think the Navy already has this in the bag.*

She shook the thoughts from her mind as she entered the boardroom. The oral examination was a joint board, with a member of each of the five branches seated behind the horseshoe shaped table. Fullweiler represented the Coast Guard, and her eyes swept the other Air Force, Army and Navy representatives without recognition. She froze when she came to the representative of the Marine Corps and took in Fraser's shaved head and strong jaw.

The questions were easy, mostly confined to points of salvage law, the Outer Space Treaty that existed now only in name, the useless specifics of the rhino – length nose to stern, length trailered on Earth, weight in Earth-gravity, loaded and unloaded, weight in micro-gravity, loaded and unloaded. The questioning came rapid-fire and in the style of all military boards, her examiners stone-faced and making notes while nodding. All to give the appearance of paying close attention. Oliver had sat on enough of these boards herself to know that they were probably doodling with their pens, scratching reminders of tasks they'd have to do when this formality was over.

Which is why Fraser's question took her completely off guard.

"Let us suppose," Fraser steepled his fingers, resting his chin atop them, "that you're coxs'un of a Rhino Class small boat. You have what you believe to be a quarantine runner inbound to Chinese-held space, but you are on an intercept course at a distance of half a nautical mile and closing, with both vessels moving at approximately thirty knots. You have an autocannon fixed to the boat's hard point, and you have target lock on the unknown vessel. It has no transponder code and you cannot determine its port-of-origin, port-of-call, flag or status."

"And I'm assuming that it doesn't respond to hails," Oliver had a sickening feeling she knew where Fraser was going.

"That's right," he said.

"And you want to know if I have the guts to open fire? Is that it, general?"

"The *board*," General Fraser smiled, "would like to know how you would respond to this particular contingency."

Oliver swallowed, willed the flush that was rising to her cheeks away. *He wants me to pick a side. This question isn't about my competence to graduate this class, it's about how I'll run my unit when I get to Pico.* "I would accelerate to towing range, and get a visual on the unknown vessel's hull markings, or I would look to see if I could get a visual ID on the vessel master through a window."

The Navy board member coughed to cover his surprise. "A… visual? With your naked eyes?"

"That's right," Oliver said. "General Fraser said I couldn't get a transponder signal and couldn't determine anything about the vessel or its occupants through sensors. That leaves me with my eyes."

Fraser smiled. "It also leaves you with your weapon, captain."

"That's right, it does," Oliver said, "and I'll go to the weapon, if and when the safety of my crew is in danger. Not before."

"And risk allowing a quarantine-runner to penetrate Chinese-held space?" Fullweiler at least did her the courtesy of looking genuinely curious.

"What do you think will bug the Chinese more?" Oliver answered. "An unarmed miner violating their EEZ? Or an American warship pursuing it into that same space?"

"Small boats," Fraser said, "are hardly warships."

"Did you, or did you not, say there was an autocannon mounted on the hard point?" Oliver asked. "Not sure what else you use an autocannon for."

"I'll remind you," Fullweiler said, "that this is an examination board. You will treat your examiners with professional respect."

Oliver fought against the rising flush again. "My apologies, Captain Fullweiler."

"Captain Oliver," the Navy examiner, a captain whose nameplate read HUNTER, leaned forward on his elbows. "I find this line of thought concerning. The Moon is on a war footing. The Chinese are aggressively testing territorial boundaries and your people are going to look to you to lead them. If you are unwilling to use deterrent force to enforce US rights on the 16th Watch, how can you expect your people to?"

"With respect, Captain Hunter," Oliver said, "the Moon is *not* on a war footing. But we certainly *will* be if we go around waving guns in everyone's face. It will be my policy, as it is the Commandant's policy, to deescalate at every opportunity. That is what I will order my people to do, it is what I will expect them to do."

Hunter frowned, his gray speckled brows practically meeting. "Captain Oliver, how much time do you have out here?"

"I don't see how that's releva–"

"I've been out here for four years on just *this* tour. And every minute of my time has been spent 'waving guns in people's faces.' I do this because I have learned in my vast experience that is how you command the respect of the PLAN. The moment we show weakness, we are going to have border incursions that are eventually going to turn into de facto annexations. Helium-3 is a critical resource for the United States. We cannot afford to cede it to a hostile power."

"They *aren't* a hostile power, Captain Hunter," Oliver worked to keep the heat out of her voice. "But they are damn well going to be if we keep stoking the fire here. Deescalation doesn't cede anything, it just finds a way to get things done that doesn't involve shooting people."

Hunter started to roll his eyes, caught himself. "You are a member of the United States military, Captain Oliver. Are you prepared to fight if it comes to war?"

"Are you?"

"This board is examining *you*, captain."

"Then my answer is this: it doesn't matter if I'm prepared. Because I will be a cloud of radioactive dust faster than you can blink. And not just me, you. You and everyone you know and love. A lunar war won't stay lunar, and it sure as hell won't stay conventional. If I'm asked to fight I will do my duty, but it won't matter once the nukes start flying here *and* on Earth."

"It won't come to that," Hunter's voice was even, but he looked unsure. "The Chinese don't want a nuclear war anymore than we do."

"Are you prepared to stake your life on that, Captain Hunter? Are you prepared to stake *everyone's* lives on that?"

"That's enough," Fullweiller cut in again. "This board is questioning you, not the other way around. Limit your words to answering questions, please."

"Apologies again, Captain Fullweiller," Oliver ground out the words.

But while her mouth limited her words, her mind reeled off a few more choice ones. And though it took superhuman effort, she did not utter them.

Her notice of passing the orals came via email in her stateroom, while she and Ho prepped for the maneuvering practical. She'd piped her email to the wall screen on Ho's insistence, and she saw his eyes twitch toward it as the new-mail chime sounded, in what passed for excitement in a man as reserved as her XO.

She sighed, closed the lid on her pelican case, began checking the leads on her undersuit.

"Aren't you going to read the email?" Ho asked.

She shrugged. "We passed. I could have gone in there and foamed at the mouth and we'd still pass. We're like Gonzalez to them. No, we're worse. At least Gonzalez is a known quantity."

"Does it matter that I care if we passed?" Ho asked.

Oliver rolled her eyes. "We passed. This is just them figuring out who we are and how we're going to run SPACETACLET. They want to know what they're up against."

"Ma'am, with respect—"

"Nothing after the words 'with respect' is ever entirely respectful, Wen."

"With respect," Ho carefully enunciated each word as he stood, walking to her keyboard. "It's possible you're being a little paranoid here. You're the one who insisted on this school in the first place."

"With no damn respect, I'm around a hundred years older than you and I have been at this game for my entire life. I am not misreading the situation here."

Ho clicked the mouse to open the email. "Well, you're right. You passed."

Oliver gave an exasperated sigh. "I told you I was smart."

"No, ma'am," Ho said, "you told me you were old."

CHAPTER 6

SUBMERSIBLE PRESSURIZED POD WAREHOUSE HAS
BEEN DISCOVERED OFF SABA COAST
CNN DIGITAL EXPANSION CLARE TOPAN
BY CLARE TOPAN, CNN

The Royal Netherlands Navy (RNLN) reported the discovery of a network of submersible pressurized pods approximately a kilometer off the coast of the Dutch Caribbean island of Saba Thursday. Luitenant Michiel Tromp, commanding officer of the Offshore Patrol Vessel Zeeland, stated the pods were likely meant as "splashdown" transfer points for storing smuggled Helium-3 in evasion of US-imposed quarantine. The contraband would then likely be loaded onto fishing vessels or aircraft bound for the global gray market.

LATEST "SPLASHDOWN" TRANSFER POINT DISCOVERED, CNN.

Graduation was held in OTRACEN's auditorium. It was expansive by lunar standards, but still tighter than a small high-school gymnasium back on Earth. As was the tradition, the facility had no bleachers, and the spin-gravity was stopped for the occasion. Few family members could manage the trip to space to attend from Earth or afford the expense of long-haul lunar surface transport, and nearly all of the bodies floating in the micro-g were graduating students, staff, and their friends already on the station. Oliver scanned the few people gathered against the audience's wall, and immediately spotted Fraser, his handsome face proud as he observed the marines gathering on the opposite wall, ready to graduate. He caught her looking, flashed her a grin, inclined his head. Oliver swallowed her anger, nodded back, doing her best to channel a duelist greeting a worthy opponent. So many fights were won or lost in the mind, before opponents ever took the field. The memory of her practical exam was still fresh, but she'd be damned if she would let him see that.

She looked away, back to Ho, then back at the audience. She could feel Fraser's presence like the heat of a close fire, and wished she could have just one other friendly face to focus on out there.

While they were still milling about waiting for the ceremony to start, one floated in through the hatch and sent Oliver's heart into her throat.

Alice looked exactly as Oliver remembered her the day she'd kissed her tear-streaked cheeks and seen her to the space elevator. The same dark hair, done up in the same careless bun, held in place by a single pencil high on her head to accommodate a hardshell helmet. She even wore the same sky-blue suit of coveralls she'd worn that day, the same steel-toed work boots. As she floated closer, Oliver could just make out the faint laugh lines radiating up from the corners of her mouth, reaching out for the crow's feet beside her daughter's sad eyes. Oliver was surprised to find that wrinkles could make a person look even younger, but in Alice's case, it was true.

Oliver pushed off from the wall and launched herself at her daughter. She knew right away that she'd put too much force into the push, and kicked uselessly toward a floor that was much too far below her as she barreled toward Alice. The kicking threw her even further off balance, and her charge became a tumble. Alice's smile turned to laughing surprise, and she spread her arms to catch her mother, sending the two of them into the same whirling pirouette that had made her lose her breakfast during her first day of training.

Oliver didn't care. She was holding her precious baby girl. They could spin until the end of time as far as she was concerned. She could hear laughter rising around her, but it quickly receded into a background buzz, drowning in the tickle of Alice's hair against her nose, the grunt of her daughter's breath as she flailed with an arm, seeking purchase to steady them.

The walls, ceiling and floor all switched places again and again, until Alice finally found the wall and they slowly spun to a stop. At last, they drifted apart to arm's length.

"Welp," Alice grinned, "I guess the training didn't take, huh?"

Oliver shot a glance over her shoulder to the graduates at the far end of the room, most of whom were doing their best to control their laughter and failing miserably. "So embarrassing. Watch, they'll rescind my graduation now."

Alice shrugged, sending the wisps of hair that had escaped her bun floating. "Works for me, you can come move in now. So? How do you feel?"

"Like I burned three weeks to learn that I can't tangle with marines."

Alice looked over her shoulder at the proportion of olive uniforms to coast guard blue. She arched an eyebrow. "That is... surprising. I thought this was a Coast Guard training center?"

"So did I. Apparently tensions with China have adjusted the... sense of urgency among senior decision makers."

Alice paused, then shrugged again. "All right, well, I guess you'll just have to kick their asses then."

"Yeah, they were non-cooperative in that department."

"Well, they're marines. Cooperation isn't their strong suit."

"I'm not a big, tough Helium-3 miner like you."

Alice's smile faltered. "Not exactly kicking ass in that department."

"I'm going to help you fix that. All you have to do is hang on long enough for me to wrap things up here."

"I'll be OK. Your big concern should be me dying of congestive heart failure. Helium-3 mining is ninety percent sitting on my couch using my phone to control my drones. If I didn't hit the gym, I'd probably be eight hundred pounds right now."

"Christ, honey. You sound so much like your father."

Alice lit up, squeezed her mother's hand. "You think? Thanks mom. Hey, where's Wen?"

"Yoo hoo!" Ho called, drifting past posed as if he were lying on a divan, with his head propped up on one hand, the other resting on a cocked hip. He waggled his fingers at them as he slid past.

"Jesus Christ, Ho," Oliver muttered.

Alice detached herself to give him a hug, babbling questions about his family. Ho answered them, then drifted back over to Oliver. "I was super nervous command wouldn't agree to your mom's request to fly you in! They don't always do this, you know."

"I know," Alice said. "I shudder to think of the taxpayer fuel cost to pick me up and bring me here. And I get to come to the promotion!"

"I've given my entire adult life to the guard," Oliver said. "The taxpayers owe me this much."

Ho rolled his eyes. "So, has your mom started complaining yet?"

"She's fine," Alice said. "Apparently she needs to knock some marines around until they learn respect."

"She's already made a good start," Ho said.

"Dad would have been proud," Alice said. "And since I'm channeling him apparently, I'll also say what he would have said if he were here. You didn't have to do this. You could have gone straight to your command and let the rank do the talking. Instead, you'll arrive showing your people you won't ask anything of them you aren't willing to do yourself, and that will pay off big time."

Alice placed a gentle hand on the back of Oliver's neck, drew her back into a tight embrace. "I know this was rough on you, mom, and I'm proud as hell that you saw it through."

Oliver inhaled the light scent of her daughter's hair, somewhere between the jasmine of her perfume and the tang of acetone from her work. She crushed her to her chest. "Ah, honey. You always know just what to say."

"Argh," Alice grunted, "I'm not going… to be able to say anything… if you crush me to death."

Oliver released her hold, held Alice back at arms length, trying to focus on her daughter's face, and to ignore the nagging feeling that the three weeks she'd just poured out of the hourglass had been wasted. Alice was right, of course, it would inspire the folks at her new command, but it also had given her valuable intel. She tried to review it in her mind, then dismissed it, focusing on the best summary she had, Fraser's extended hand, shrouded by the pale-white mist of her emergency oxygen refracted in her cracked faceplate. *I don't doubt you're ready to lead, but you better remember that you're not ready to fight.*

Fullweiler called the assembly to order and Oliver reluctantly detached from her daughter and took her place on the podium. The school chief droned on about the complex and dynamic environment on the new frontier, and the challenges the Coast Guard faced moving into the future. "Complex and dynamic," Oliver whispered to Ho, "he means keyed-up and spoiling for a fight."

"Yup," Ho whispered back, "he sure does."

"Christ, Ho, we have to fix this."

We will, Ho mouthed back, gently jerked his chin toward Fullweiler in a gesture clearly meant to convey, *now, shut up*.

As Fullweiler went on, a man drifted in through the hatch and floated to Alice's side. He was bull-necked and barrel-chested, his spiky gray hair cropped longer than a marine, at least, a point in his favor. He wore a Coast Guard uniform with a commander's stripes on the shoulder boards. Oliver could see the qualification pin over his ribbon rack, crossed gold sabers behind a silver shield bearing the Stars and Stripes. Though she couldn't make them out at this distance, she knew the words beneath would read TACTICAL LAW ENFORCEMENT.

Ho noticed too, "Looks like the welcoming committee is here."

Most graduations ended with families flooding the stage, and devolved into impromptu social events that took some time to clear the auditorium. But out here on the 16th Watch, with no real families present, it was simply over, and the graduates just drifted out as soon as Fullweiler handed them their folders with the graduate certificates and assignments inside. Oliver floated for a moment watching the graduates disperse, before Ho chucked her shoulder and made his way toward the new arrival. Oliver finally sighed and followed him, drifting close enough to make out the nameplate.

"Rear Admiral Select, I'm Eric Avitable, I'm acting CO while we waited for your assignment." His voice was warm, with the slightest touch of a former-smoker's rasp. He gripped her hand firmly, but without the bone-grinding power of the insecure types who wanted to establish who was boss at first meeting. Oliver decided she liked him.

"I assume Admiral Allen told you that you'll pretty much remain the acting CO for the first couple of months of my command, with assistance from my XO," Oliver said. "I'm here to prep SAR-1 for Boarding Action. I've been instructed to leave the day-to-day to you until we get past that."

"Yes, ma'am," Avitable said. "Admiral Allen also said he'd rather that not be common knowledge, and I figured it was best to do a full change-of-command and get the crew used to having a new skipper. I hope you're OK with that."

"I'm perfectly fine with that, thanks. Are *you* OK with that is the real question."

Avitable gave a pained smile. "SPACETACLET has a lot of moving parts, ma'am, and now that SAR-1 is rolled up into it, there's the whole SAR element which is mostly new to me. But, I've been doing OK so far, and I guess a few more months won't kill me. I'm grateful for the opportunity to lead at this level. Good training for when I make O6." He raised an eyebrow at that last comment, noting the presumption. Oliver liked his honesty, and her opinion of him rose.

"Sorry it took me so long," she chuckled. "I know this was an additional three weeks you hadn't planned for."

Avitable shrugged, floating up a few inches. Oliver took comfort in noting that even what must be a seasoned micro-g operator wasn't in full control of his position. "I think it was a good call, ma'am. You're leading from the front, and I find that inspiring."

"Oops," Ho smiled at him.

Avitable's face fell. "Commander?"

Alice put a hand on his arm. "Don't compliment mom, she can't stand it."

Avitable turned to Oliver. "I don't understand, ma'am. Are they serious?"

"No," Oliver smiled.

"Yes," Ho and Alice said at exactly the same time.

"This is very confusing," Avitable said.

"Well, I'm the boss," Oliver said. "Alice isn't staying on Pico, and Ho has to do what I tell him. I say they're not serious, and I beg your patience for putting up with my insufferable inner-circle. Anyway, thanks for the kind words. It's appreciated."

"Wow," Alice stared at her in exaggerated surprise. "Who are you and what have you done with my mom?"

Oliver pursed her lips. "May I recommend, commander, that you never try to meet a commander in the company of her family? At least I can have Ho here court martialed."

"If I remember correctly," Ho said, "you tried to spank Alice exactly once. You said you chased her around the house for five solid minutes and gave up when you couldn't catch her."

Avitable blinked. "Duly noted."

"So, you brought a ride?" Oliver smiled.

"Yes, ma'am. Got an executive shuttle docked and waiting. Brought an extra hardshell for your daughter."

"Aw, man, I hate wearing those things," Alice said. "I thought the shuttles had atmosphere?"

"They do," Avitable said, "but it's policy to suit up just in case there's an emergency, though I guess your mother has the authority to grant an exception if she wants."

"I can't very well lead a unit and expect them to uphold rules that I break myself," Oliver said, "but because I need my XO, I'll let him wear the hardshell inside the shuttle, and overcome my strong inclination to put him in it and tow him from the engine cowling."

The executive shuttle wasn't much bigger than a rhino but featured a finished interior, pressurized, with white plastic paneling and swivel mounted chairs upholstered in a fairly convincing approximation of cream-colored leather. The weapons-racks were replaced with video screens and slots for binders, each held in place with a tiny rubber strap to keep it from drifting away in micro-g.

A slim blue folder lay on a round table nested between the four chairs. COMMANDER'S INTRODUCTORY BRIEFING was written on a yellow stickie note stuck to the front. Avitable knelt beside his hardshell. "I have that memorized," he said. "I've actually worked with people who can leaf through papers in a hardshell, but you don't have to. I just brought it along in case you were one of those… enthusiastic types."

"She is absolutely one of those enthusiastic types," Ho said, putting on his bunny-suit, "and I would pay money to see her try to page through a briefing while wearing a hardshell."

"What my XO means," Oliver said, "is that I prefer to talk turkey with my staff. How much of that is fluff?"

Avitable froze for a moment, and Oliver could practically see the wheels turning in his head as he tried to figure out how direct he could be with her. After a moment, he shrugged. "Honestly, ma'am? Ninety percent. A lot of it is housekeeping. Unit history. Stuff you can Google on your downtime."

Oliver arched an eyebrow. "I'm going to have downtime?"

Avitable spread his hands and smiled. "No, ma'am."

"So, screw the briefing then. Let's suit up, strap in, and you can tell me what I really need to know."

Oliver ignored the irony of being strapped into what looked like the first truly comfortable chair since she'd left Earth, prevented from enjoying the experience by the hardshell, or more accurately, by the hyper-safety-conscious Coast Guard policy that forced her to wear it. *Pick your battles,* she thought to herself. *You're coming into a new command. Go slow, listen more than you talk, and make changes slowly.*

The shuttle launched like a small boat, dropped by crane out of the bay doors. Oliver tensed her muscles in expectation of the acceleration into a gut-wrenching drop, but the shuttle's helmsman knew their business, and there was only the slightest sensation before the belly thrusters compensated, gently floating the shuttle along below OTRACEN and down towards the Moon's surface below. The shuttle banked as it descended, the windows near her dipping to give her a clear view of the landscape in what was probably a deliberate action on the part of the pilot.

If the helmsman was trying to suck up to the new boss, it worked. Oliver caught her breath as she realized that over the past three weeks, she'd been so focused on getting through NCD/0G that she had almost forgotten this incredible landscape slowly rising up to meet her, silver-gray and shining, the wash of radiation and the combined refraction of her helmet and the window making it waver like a mirage. Of all the analogies for the Moon's surface, the food ones had always suited Oliver the best, the whorls of impact craters melting into the trails of ancient lava flows amidst the slopes of long dead volcanoes like the crannies of crusty bread.

It would have been far more economical to just let the shuttle drop, but the helmsman was happy to burn propellant keeping them under thrust the whole way. This gave Oliver the chance to see the landscape materialize before her slowly, the ridges and plains slowly sprouting the bubble-fields of the habs, some still glinting from the binding agents the gardeners used in the 3D printing process. Some of them were bigger than she remembered. When she'd last been on the Moon, even big municipal buildings were little more than simple, sprawling domes, the lobes of their curving roofs the only indicator of the partitioned rooms inside. Now, Oliver spotted towers, tallish cylinders that looked a lot like old style rocket ships without their fins, bubbling around their bases with support structures. As they drew closer, Oliver could pick up the maser-lanes, bounded by the huge towers firing their invisible microwave beams. The ship traffic had increased too, and in places she could see actual traffic jams as shuttles, regolith-haulers and government vehicles dipped their solar sails into the beams, gathering thrust as the ablative surface cooked off, leaving tiny clouds of dust behind them. "Wow," she said on the open channel. "Business has picked up since I was last here."

The silence that followed jerked her head up, and she took in the awkward looks on her companions' faces. "Guys," Oliver said, "it's fine. We're not going to tiptoe around what happened the last time I was here. I plan to hit it head on, so there's no need to walk on eggshells."

Avitable nodded, relaxed, but not much. "Thanks, ma'am. That is definitely top of the list of things I think you need to know."

"Hit me," Oliver said.

"Morale is low, ma'am," Avitable said. "You know the SAR element just got folded into SPACETACLET, and a lot of the SAR operators are seeing it as a punishment, like they need adult supervision from our folks."

"Because of what happened at Lacus Doloris," Oliver said.

"Yeah," Avitable agreed. "Because of that."

"That was over three years ago," Oliver said, "there's been no improvement?"

Avitable only shrugged.

"And is their impression correct, commander?" Oliver asked. "Have you received any directive from Ops or someone else on high directing you to babysit the SAR staff?"

Avitable met her eyes, "No, ma'am."

"So, what have you done to combat this impression?" Oliver asked.

Avitable looked at his lap. "Well, now I feel like an idiot, to be honest, ma'am, but I was working on the assumption that if I tried to tackle it, I'd just throw gasoline on this thing. I figured the best move was to give it time. When sailors are in tight together, doing the work every day, well, they get past differences. They tighten up. I was hoping to let that machine just run. But listening to you, I–"

"It's all right," Oliver interrupted him. "Your instincts are good, and you're absolutely right. A lot of the time, you don't want to draw attention to something like this. You pick the scab off too soon, and things don't heal. But sometimes things aren't like a cut with a scab. They're like a broken bone that's set wrong, and you have to get under the surface and fix it if you ever want it to heal right. Even though digging down into the old injury hurts worse at first."

"No disrespect, ma'am," Avitable said, "but what makes you sure this is that kind of… wound? The digging-down kind?"

"Because it's *my* wound," Oliver said, feeling her heart speed up, tears pricking at the corners of her eyes, "and because I didn't realize until now, just now while I'm talking to you, that I'd been treating it like the scab would hold. That if I just sat tight for long enough, I would get better. But it won't and I won't."

She turned, met Alice's eyes, toggled her radio to a private channel. "I needed to be up here to handle this. I can't wait for Tom to give up real estate in my heart. That won't ever happen. I need to honor the spot he's carved out there. I need to do what he would he would have wanted me to. I was out to pasture running TRACEN back on Earth. I was trying to make up for the family I'd lost. I was trying to take care of a family by proxy. It wasn't enough. Training isn't enough. I need to do the job. I need to take care of things for real. I couldn't save Tom, so maybe I'll save the world instead. Does that sound crazy?"

"It absolutely does," Alice said, "and it's exactly right."

"I need to... I know this sounds stupid, but I need to make your father proud again. One last time."

Alice reached across and placed her hand on her mother's knee. "He already is, mom. I know it."

They sat in silence for a while after that, Oliver holding her daughter's hand through the hardshell gauntlet, imagining she could feel the pulse through the layers of plastic as the landscape rose up around them.

Pico meant "peak," but Oliver was struck by how squat the mountain looked as the shuttle closed in and the SPACETACLET complex came into view. The broad expanse of the mountain was almost entirely obscured by the concrete pads and 3D-printed structures around it, rising in a rash of gray-white bubbles that made the peak look like a pill-case or some kind of insect-hive. Not far to the north, she could make out the icy lip of a vast ghost crater, the faint imprint of some tectonic event long past. Sometime back, they'd assigned the gardeners to 3D-print directly onto the surface at the mountain's base using some kind of reflective material visible from above. She could make out the crossed anchors and shield, the American flag above it.

UNITED STATES COAST GUARD, was printed in letters Oliver assumed had to be twenty feet across, SPACE AREA – TACTICAL LAW ENFORCEMENT DETACHMENT.

Just below it was a massive concrete pad clustered with small boats, almost entirely rhinos, but here and there a longhorn or two which had yet to be mothballed. There'd be no more sickening crane-drops here. SPACETACLET, and now SAR-1, launched straight up into the Moon's tiny shred of atmosphere using their belly thrusters. Beside the pad, Oliver could make out a massive tower, far too big to have been built by gardeners, a structure of concrete, rebar and steel most of which had probably been shipped from Earth or made in one of the Moon's few industrial plants. It rose up to support a huge ball of habs, all bolted and welded together until they looked like nothing so much as a giant white fist atop an extended gray arm. Clenched in that fist were massive metal gangways, each sturdy enough to act as berthing for the command's two assigned Constellation Class cutters.

The first, Oliver knew, was the *Volans*. She thought she'd be prepared to see that ship again, the last one she'd seen before the Lacus Doloris dustup, but the sight of the flying fish painted on the side made her tear up. She'd known that everything she'd see from the moment she left OTRACEN would be a stark reminder of Tom, and she'd thought she'd been prepared, but the actual sight of it brought the memories flooding back. She could taste the panic in her throat as she wrenched at the frozen door handle, see the gray-white landscape blurring into a solid gray line as she raced to shoulder Tom's boat out of the way.

She closed her eyes, resisted the urge to shake her head. She was confident she could show that kind of weakness in front of Ho and Alice, but Avitable was new to her. He was one of the people she was here to lead. She blinked hard, then flicked her eyes up again, taking in the other cutter. It was identical to the *Volans* but in better repair, freshly painted, with some kind of refit featuring a taller antennae boom, and bigger shoulder pods port and starboard, that Oliver assumed covered the cutter's massive solar sails. For a moment, she dared to hope it was the *Aries,* but she already knew that had been assigned to quarantine enforcement duties on the Moon's far side. She squinted until she could make out the logo painted on the side, a stiff wooden board cutting through storm-churned waters. *Carina* – the keel.

Oliver wasn't a superstitious type, but she couldn't help but view it as a good omen. *Steady as she goes*, she thought, *exactly what I need.*

She turned and glanced through the opposite window as the shuttle leveled off, affording her a view of what looked like an unbroken gray-white expanse of lunar regolith – the Mare Imbrium, the Sea of Rains. It did look like a sea from this distance, albeit an unnaturally calm one. It arced out of view, the black void of space descending until the glowing albedo swallowed it, but Oliver could see the jagged boundary where the American habs began to peter out and finally stop, and the bigger structures of the Chinese EEZ control posts began. They were squat, black structures, sprouting concrete small boat pads like toadstools, each emblazoned in the center with the red and yellow logo of the PLAN. Here and there, above the endless gray plain, she could see the firefly glimmer of the PLAN small boats' running lights, the white-blue plumes of their thrusters. She wondered if some of those lights came not from PLAN boats but from American quarantine runners, trying their luck launching through the Chinese EEZ in an effort to save days and dollars. Perhaps there were Coast Guard or Navy boats in pursuit, guns fixed to their hard points, all just one bullet away from sending the whole mess over the edge and into war.

OTRACEN had been... a ship of sorts, so the kind of cramped opulence that was O-country berthing on sea-going vessels had made sense. But her stateroom on the landlocked SPACETACLET campus made her realize this was simply the way people lived on the surface of the Moon. Oliver's quarters befit her status as the incoming commanding officer: blue carpet, two rooms, not including the head, a wide quartz-glass window with a view of the small boat pads, and the broad basalt sweep of the Sinus Iridum, the Bay of Rainbows, beyond.

They'd tried to assign her an orderly, but she'd immediately shut the idea down. "I'm not going to have junior enlisted washing my feet for me," she said, cocking an eyebrow at Ho. "I've got an XO for that."

Alice was enthralled by the view. "This is amazing!"

"I thought you were the old lunar hand," Oliver said.

Alice shook her head. "Are you kidding me? Sinus Medii is worse than Nebraska. You stand on a beer can and you can see the whole thing."

"The Apennines aren't too far away," Oliver said.

"I wish I had time. I'm burning money just to have the operation covered while I'm here."

"Are you trying to make me feel bad?"

Alice looked horrified. "Sorry, mom. I didn't mean it that way, it's just that..."

"I get it, honey. And I appreciate you taking the hit."

"Oh, you know I wouldn't have missed it. I needed to be here as much as you needed me here. I'm grateful you invited me."

Now it was Oliver's turn to look horrified. "You cannot seriously think I would have done this on the Moon and not had you present."

Alice shrugged, looked back out the window. "I've never been up this high. Not on the Moon, anyway."

"This is nothing," Avitable said. "If you want, I can take you up to the cutter launches. That's the highest point here. Can't swear if it's exactly accurate, but I think the cutter antennae booms are higher than the top of Pico."

"You OK with that, mom?"

Oliver waved a hand, and Avitable led her daughter out.

Ho made to follow, but Oliver stopped him with a touch on his elbow. "I thought you were my orderly now."

Ho rolled his eyes, but he waited with her as she unpacked her sea bag, hung her uniforms in the closet, one of the few ones made of real wood on the whole installation. She stepped back, smoothing the settling clothing as it rippled in the lunar-g, and sighed. "This will need ironing."

Ho folded his arms. "I don't iron. Or do windows. You should have taken the orderly."

"Relax. I can walk them down to the laundry same as... Shit. Where's the laundry?"

"This is why you have an orderly, *Rear Admiral Select*."

"Never mind. I'll figure it out eventually."

Ho took a seat at the room's expansive desk, carved from the same glass topped reflective cherry wood that decorated most high-ranking government offices on Earth. "Nice digs, anyway."

"Needs decorating. We can get that sorted out once we're settled in. For now, all we need is this." She plunked down the same picture she'd kept taped to her desk monitor on the *Aries*. It was protected by a silver frame now, and she misjudged its weight in the lunar gravity, and watched it bounce a millimeter before settling back down again.

"All you need, as far as I'm concerned," Ho jerked his chin toward the picture. "Really ties the room together."

Oliver grunted and gestured at the far edge of the view of Bay of Rainbows, where the Sea of Rains stretched out like a portent under the invisible shadow of Chinese EEZ. "What do you make of that view?"

"I'm... less enthusiastic than your daughter, ma'am."

"How so?"

"It's... scary," he said.

"Because of the EEZ?"

Ho shook his head, stood, came to stand beside her before the broad quartz-glass window. He tapped the thick glass, his slender finger indicating the far distance where the albedo's glare sucked up the darkness and the horizon curved out of view. "That's the northern edge of Oceanus Procellarum, right?"

"The Ocean of Storms," Oliver nodded, "and at its heart the Aristarchus crater. I flew over it once while I was on area familiarization. Makes the Grand Canyon look like a dimple."

"And that's where the PLAN HQ is, right?" Ho asked.

Oliver nodded. "Sure is. Crater's got a mountain at the bottom. It's on top of it. All their frigates, destroyers, the lion's share of their small boats. Most of their IR and EW gear. Belly of the beast."

Ho swallowed. "And it's right on the far side of their EEZ, like they're just waiting for one of our boat coxs'uns or frigate skippers to get hotheaded and chase a quarantine runner in too deep."

"And then they'll come out shooting."

Ho met her eyes. "You think they really will?"

"Yeah," Oliver sighed. "I do. We got lucky with that collision, Wen. We're not going to survive another 'misunderstanding' like that. We're past saber-rattling now. The swords are drawn."

"Well, that's what's scary. I mean, look at that, it's so... samey. All that flat gray. It's... peaceful, you know?"

"Yeah," Oliver said again. "It is. It's kind of nice."

"Yeah," Ho agreed, but she could hear the worry in his voice.

Oliver scanned the distant horizon, as if she could somehow bring the Aristarchus crater into view. She imagined the central peak in that crater's bottom, the PLAN headquarters squatting atop it, its massive arrays ever trained on the EEZ, alert for the faintest electro-chemical signature that might suggest Chinese space was being violated, its gigantic fleet ready to spring into action.

Lacus Doloris was out of sight to the southeast, blocked by the long ridge of the Montes Appeninus. That had been first blood for

Oliver, but as much as she hated to admit it, Tom had lost his life in a mere dustup, easily defused and papered over. A *real* war would start somewhere out in that featureless gray expanse before her, lit only by the running lights of distant PLAN patrols.

It took her at least an hour to get the promotion script pared down to something she could stand. Avitable had stuffed the script into the back of Oliver's briefing folder, but she had known immediately what it was by the thickness of the papers, and the almost embarrassed looking miniature binder clip in the upper right-hand corner.

Ho had looked at the first three pages as Oliver stripped them out and tossed them on her rack. The lunar-g caused them to float a bit, and Ho reached out with deft fingers to snatch the drifting pages out of the air. "This," her XO said, arching an eyebrow as he paged through them, "is the history of the United States Coast Guard."

"Which everyone at this ceremony already has had drilled into their skulls a hundred times already in shitty ceremonies just like this one. And they still don't care."

"I care," Ho folded his arms.

"You," Oliver snatched the pages from his hand and set them back on her rack, but she misjudged the force and they drifted up again, floating out over the edge and seesawing their way down to the floor, "are a giant nerd."

"You take that back, ma'am."

"I will do no such thing. You are the biggest Coast Guard dork I have ever met in my life."

"I am not."

"In what year did Ida Lewis make her first rescue?"

"1854. She was twelve."

"Where was DC3 Bruckenthal born?"

"Stony Brook, New York, but he grew up in Hawaii."

Oliver turned to the mirror, straightened her tie. "You didn't even have to look that up."

"You know that stuff too!"

She turned, brushed a speck of imagined lint off his whites. "Not without Google."

She checked the hang of her saber one last time, drew a deep breath and walked out.

"I use Google!" Ho hurried after her.

"You *are* Google." Oliver turned down the passageway and headed toward the facility's expansive Morale, Welfare, and Recreation Center.

"Your face is Google!" Ho panted as he hurried to catch up.

Avitable had done his level best to turn the MWR into some dignified semblance of an auditorium, but Oliver was pleased to see that he wasn't entirely successful. The couches had been stacked at the big room's far end, covered with a SPACETACLET banner. He'd disconnected all of the video game consoles, but he'd left the flat screen monitors in place, now displaying looping videos of Coast Guard operations on terrestrial water and the Moon alike.

The room wasn't big enough for all the assigned personnel. The windowed passageways that ran to either side of the MWR were crammed with bodies, and Oliver knew there were even more in the overflow spaces, watching on monitors. It gave the impression of a concert spilling out into the street, a must-see event, which was exactly what she wanted. She'd arranged to have senior enlisted get the front row seats, with officers on the edges and in the back. She hoped it sent the message she intended – that the non-commissioned officers would be the real drivers of this unit under her command.

She glanced up at the door she'd entered through, and caught her breath. Hanging over the door were two portraits, each framed in black ribbons. She recognized the faces instantly – Linda Flecha's coiled black braid, and Andraste Kariawasm's broad forehead and dimpled chin. She nodded toward the pictures, drawing Ho's attention. "Bet you anything Chief Elgin had those put up when they folded SAR-1 into the command."

"Sounds like Chief," Ho nodded. "Man, that's a bucket of cold water."

"It's good," Oliver swallowed. "Reminds us why we're here."

Somewhere in the crowd Oliver knew were the two survivors of her boat on Lacus Doloris – Elgin and McGrath. She had directed they be included in those seated up front, but when she scanned the audience, all the faces bobbing above the starched sky blue collars ran together, and she could hardly distinguish one person from another.

It was her second time seeing Admiral Allen. He'd aged visibly over the last few years, but his eyes were every bit as hard as they had been the last time she'd met him, taking command of the *Aries* before Tom's death had sent everything to hell. Her shook her hand, reaching out with his free one to grip her elbow. "Jane, it's good to see you again. Thank you for inviting me."

I had to invite you. You're the only one with rank out here to make an admiral, Oliver thought, but she said, "It's an honor to have you, sir."

"I know it was a tough decision to come out here, but I'm glad you made it. You're doing a great service not only to me, but to the whole guard. I know the Commandant feels the same way."

"I don't think it was my decision to make, sir. My XO here would have had my head if I'd said no, and that doesn't even count my daughter."

Allen shook hands with Alice, standing beside her folding chair in the front row. "It's a pleasure to meet you, thanks for your help in convincing your mom to come out."

"Well, it's good for me too," Alice shook his hand and grinned. "Mom's going to give me a hand with some things when she's wrapped this up."

Allen cocked an eyebrow, "You're planning on becoming a miner?"

Oliver shrugged, "Let's see if I survive this first."

"If anyone can," Allen said, "it's you."

Avitable approached, smoothing wrinkles out of a uniform clearly much too small for him. "Sorry," he said, "we just don't wear these very often. I'm afraid the last time was… some time ago."

He handed Allen the ceremony script and shook his hand. Allen leafed through it, a frown deepening with each page. "This appears… shortened."

"It is, sir," Oliver said, "I'm allowed some latitude for my own promotion, and I thought it best to keep things brief."

"You've removed the section on our history and traditions."

"That's right, sir."

"May I ask why?"

"Because nobody cares, sir."

"I beg your pardon?"

"Let me rephrase that, sir. They do care, but they don't need to be reminded of it at length while they're standing at attention in uniforms," she gestured at Avitable, "that they only wear once a year if that. What people want out of a promotion is to get the measure of the new boss, and then get back to whatever it is they were doing before they were voluntold to attend a non-mandatory all-hands event."

Allen was quiet for a moment, and Oliver wondered if he would burst out laughing or yell at her, but in the end he only shook his head slightly. "Well, I guess it's your call."

He gave a speech anyway, extemporizing with what Oliver thought was troubling accuracy most of the material that Oliver had stripped out. She caught Ho out of the corner of her eye, his smug smile staying with her even when she looked away. At last Allen called her up to the podium, read her promotion scroll, and slipped on one of her shoulder boards while Alice slipped on the other. The four gold stripes of a coast guard captain were stripped away, replaced by the admiral's solid gold. Oliver knew this was a singular moment. Almost no one in any service ever made flag rank. It was a career high point that should have made her tingle.

But as she looked out over the audience, she only felt the enormity of the task before her, her mind repeating her defeat at Fraser's hands over and over again. She felt like an old woman in a costume, who had somehow hoodwinked all these otherwise smart people into believing that she could be the answer to their prayers. *Knock it off. This is toxic thinking.*

And then she glanced to her left and saw her daughter there, slipping the gold shoulder board in place, buttoning it down. Her daughter's mouth was open in a tiny O of concentration, tears beginning to well at the corners of her eyes. She looked like nothing so much as a little girl, and the fear and doubt vanished, and for a moment Oliver felt the same awe Alice did. Pride swelled up her spine, did cartwheels in her head, making her shoulders lift. *This is how my daughter sees me*, she thought as Alice finished buttoning the board down, and stepped back, her eyes shining as she looked at her mother.

It mattered to Alice that her mother was an admiral. *Well,* Oliver thought, *then I suppose it matters to me too.*

She felt the pride then, as she turned, rendering her salute to Allen, her first as an admiral. Allen returned it, shook her hand firmly. "Congratulations, Jane. This is well-deserved. You've got your work cut out for you, but I want you to know there is no one else in any branch of service I trust more to get it done."

"Thank you, sir," she said, "let's see if you feel the same way after you hear this bit."

She left Allen, still smiling, the surprise only registering in his eyes, and stepped up to the podium. As the applause died and the audience quieted, Jane scanned the faces again for Elgin and McGrath, and again was defeated by the uniforms and the closely packed crowd. Just a sea of faces, each blending into the next. *They're in the crowd. Have a little faith.*

"Thank you." Avitable had set out a small monitor on the floor, angled up at her, and Oliver could hear the tinny echo of her voice through the speakers in the overflow rooms outside. "I appreciate you all taking time out of your busy days, completely without any coercion whatsoever, to greet your new commander on an entirely voluntary basis."

Smiles, and scattering of chuckles. Sarcasm and honesty worked with this crowd.

"Since you've been kind enough to give me your time, I'll be kind enough to respect it. I'll keep this as brief as I can. If I were sitting out in that audience, I'd want to know what I could expect from my new skipper, and how she was going to impact my life. Am I right?"

Nods, a few faces frozen in surprise. Here and there, an NCO leaned forward, forearms on their knees in the universal *you have my attention* posture that Oliver had come to associate with enlisted sailors in operational roles. "You've probably heard the term 'servant leadership' before, and I want you to know that a) I believe in it, and b) what it means to me is that you work *for* the people you lead. They have to render courtesy and obedience. You have to put their interests before your own. Last in line for chow, last off the shop floor, first into the thick of things, first to accept responsibility for failure. This is the standard I hold for myself, and it is the standard I will hold for every single officer and NCO in this command. The fastest way to make me into an intractable enemy is to let me catch you throwing your own people under the bus. The fastest way to make me your staunchest ally is to show me you are putting your people before yourself. That scan for all of you?"

More nods. More grunts of approval. Here and there, clapping hands. "If you've read anything from my bio, you know that I come out of the SAR community. I'm a career lifesaver, always in the small boat world. That means I've done some law enforcement, but not the kind of heavy-hitting law-dogging you do at SPACETACLET. I imagine that might make some of the pipe-hitters in the audience nervous that I'm going to come in here with peace signs and bouquets of flowers, making everybody talk about their feelings."

Laughter erupted from the entire audience at that. She could see shoulders relaxing. *You're killing it, Jane,* she thought, *let's hope you just bought enough good will for this next part.*

"Well, you're not wrong. I am a firm believer that the Coast Guard is a unique institution, empowered by Title Fourteen of the US Code to act with a flexibility that no other branch of the military can, and I intend to use that flexibility to accomplish our mission here."

OK, Admiral Allen, she thought. *Here's the part you're not going to like.* "And there's something else we've got to tackle before we can accomplish anything. There's a pink elephant sitting in the middle of this room." She pointed to the middle of the audience and a few heads swiveled to look as if they expected to see the creature sitting there.

"How many of you call me 'Widow Jane'? It's OK. I won't hold it against you." A scattering of hands went up. Then, a few more. "Come on," Oliver said, "I'm playing it straight with you. Play it straight with me." More hands went up at that, until nearly every one in the audience was raised.

"OK, that's what I thought," Oliver said, "and that's fine. Just don't call me it to my face, OK? The reason I asked if you called me this is because it confirms what I already knew, that what happened at Lacus Doloris is fresh in all of your minds. And that's the thing we're going to have to tackle.

"I'm not going to mince words. I know we took some licks at Lacus Doloris, and I know that's left scars. There are commanders who would try to put that behind us, as if silence could somehow erase the pain. That's not how I operate and it's not how this unit will operate under my command. We will tackle problems head on, and that means morale. I believe the surest way to do that is to remember why we signed up to be here. Every other branch of the military has a primary mission – to kill people and destroy property. Nothing wrong with that, necessary evil. But not us, not the Guard. We are here to *save* lives. We are here to *protect* property. That is why we are the smallest, the most elite and yes, the *best* of all five branches of the armed service. Because of our mission, and starting today, we're going to recommit to that mission."

She looked up at the portraits of Flecha and Kariawasm, and pointed at them. "I want everybody to look up at our two shipmates there. The ones we lost. The ones we must never forget."

Heads swiveled, and chairs creaked as the audience turned to take the pictures in. Oliver could feel the mood in the room dropping precipitously. Her stomach clenched at the risk she was taking. *If you lose your audience now, you'll have sunk this unit's morale and your own authority for nothing.* She swallowed the fear and pressed ahead. "Confronting things head on means we confront them head on, and that means we don't pretend that I didn't lose someone at Doloris, too. We don't pretend that you don't know why they call me 'Widow Jane.' Tom went down doing the job he loved, surrounded and protected by people he honored. He didn't blame you, and I don't either. Those we've lost are gone, and it's not for us to waste time looking in the rear-view mirror, rehashing what we might have done differently. Everyone here knows what all sailors say, 'the sea doesn't care about you.' Yelling at the ocean won't make it bring our loved ones back to us. Now, I was lucky enough to get to run that fateful mission in the company of Petty Officers Kariawasm and Flecha, but that's not the same as knowing them. I can't tell you how they honored their dead. But I can tell you what Tom would have told you. He'd have…"

She could see Alice out of the corner of her eye, could tell her daughter was crying openly. The sight almost set Oliver off herself, and she paused for a moment to maintain her composure. She wanted her command to see her vulnerable and open to them, but not *that* vulnerable. "Tom would have told you that the best way to honor the dead is to honor the living, to share the example of our loved ones with others, through our actions. My husband was brave, and kind, and patient, and he lived for others. And that's what SPACETACLET is going to do. What is our motto?"

"Honor! Respect! Devotion to Duty!" the audience roared.

"Oh, horseshit," Oliver said. "You think I just got out of academy? What is our *real* motto? The one we're not allowed to put on T-shirts?"

There was a long uncomfortable silence. Oliver could almost feel Admiral Allen's eyes burning into the back of her neck. *I told you you wouldn't like this part, sir.* The silence stretched on, and Oliver's stomach sank with every passing second. *Come on, people. Work with me here.*

"So others might live," a familiar voice said. Oliver looked up, saw a man standing at the back of the room. His thick arms were folded across his broad chest, his deep-set eyes sad. Chief Elgin had grown in a tight iron-gray mustache since Oliver had last seen him, and what little hair left to him had retreated to the point where he'd given up and shaved his head. But there was something so familiar to him, something that evoked that day on Lacus Doloris so strongly that she had to swallow hard to keep the tears from coming.

It took Oliver a long moment to find her words. "That's right. So *others* might live. *Others*. It's not about us, and it never was. Retreating into ourselves isn't the way. If we are going to move past Lacus Doloris, we're going to do it aggressively, by going out there and showing what our loved ones have taught us, by *living* it for others. We will save their lives, we will protect their goods, and those we've left behind will meet us on the other side someday, and thank us for shining their light for just a little longer.

"Lord knows, out here," Oliver gestured to the window, a sweeping vista of the deep black of space stark against the gray lunar landscape, "we could use a little more light."

The silence was total as she finished speaking. She stepped back from the podium, and suddenly the audience's faces were plain to her. More than a few were white with shock. She spotted a few red-rimmed eyes, faces pressed into hands before shaking shoulders. *Christ, I made these people cry.* She had hoped that being straight with them would set the right tone, would shake them out of their stupor and galvanize them to tackle the challenge straight on. *I've miscalculated. I picked the scab when it was still too fresh. I've crushed their morale.*

She turned to Alice, more to not have to face the reactions of her audience than for any other reason. Her daughter was still crying, a hand held to her mouth. *Oh, angel. I'm so sorry*, Oliver thought. *First NCD/0G, and now this. I've made such a goddamn hash of things. My first steps as an admiral, and they're right off a cliff. I swear to…*

And then three things happened.

Alice rushed into her arms, hugging her so hard that the breath was blown from her lungs.

Admiral Allen's hand settled on her shoulder, squeezing gently. Oliver could hear the low murmur of his voice. She couldn't make out the words, but the support in his tone was unmistakable.

Chief Elgin began clapping, his thickly calloused hands thundering against one another, shockingly loud at first, but gradually dissolving into the ocean of applause that spread out from him through the audience, as if the Chief's clapping hands catalyzed a chain reaction, sending the sailors in the room to their feet.

Oliver broke away from her daughter long enough to face the cheering room. The looks of shock were still there, as were the tears, but now Oliver could see they drowned in the inspiration burning in the eyes of everyone present.

"We should take you on the road," she heard Ho say, his voice thick. "You missed your calling, boss."

"Well, I'll be damned," Oliver said. Then, because she couldn't think of what else to say, she said it again.

CHAPTER 7

"Sure, it's weird switching between worlds," Petty Officer Almond's grin is self-deprecating, and she appears uncomfortable with her newfound fame, "but the Navy has my contract, and I was raised to do what I said I would." Still, PO Almond privately admits that being the spotlight of a Boarding Action finalist initially impacted her duties for the brief period before her command opted to transfer her to train full time – a billet the Navy describes as "Public Affairs." She's up for reenlistment in two months, and says she plans to process out, a decision that isn't surprising given the many lucrative private sponsorships awaiting her in civilian life.

BOARDING ACTION FINALIST STRUGGLES WITH A LIFE SUDDENLY ON
STAGE
STARS AND STRIPES SPECIAL FEATURE

SAR-1's training evolution began at 0600, so Oliver made sure she was up at 0400. She allowed herself a few minutes in the rack, staring at the ceiling, as she did each morning. In these few stolen moments she was not a commander, Tom was not dead, and the world was not on the brink of a lunar war. There was only her, and the foam of the mattress pad beneath her, the dull soft throb of her shoulder where it had gently pushed her into it as she slept. She savored the moment, trying to be grateful for what she had – a daughter who loved her and a son who probably did, though he didn't know how to show it, and a career that had, as of yesterday, officially exceeded her wildest dreams.

She sat up, blinked sleep from her eyes, kissed her fingers, and then touched Tom's face where it smiled out at her from Alice's wedding photo. "Made flag, babe," she whispered to him, "wish you could have seen it. Man, I'd have given my left tit to make you salute me."

Tom's face was frozen in joy, as it had been for all these years. "Well," Oliver said, "you look happy. Guess I'll take it."

She swung her feet onto the deck, grabbed her calcium pills and swallowed two of them dry. It would have been charitable to call them horse-pills, and her throat worked against them, but she managed to get them down without water. If her traitor body was going to go all wobbly with age out on the 16th Watch, then she wasn't going to do it any favors.

SPACETACLET didn't have a private gym for senior staff, and Oliver had had enough of being the old woman working out in the company of babies who were made entirely of stretchable plastic at OTRACEN. She changed into her PTs and hit the deck at the foot of her bed, grunting her way through pushups and sit-ups, rowers and burpees, one eye on the LED clock above the mirror.

The door chimed and opened even as Oliver was in the process of saying "Come!".

She knew it was Ho before she even saw his boots lightly push the door open and step to her small desk. She heard a clattering of plastic as he set something down. "You did not just bring me breakfast."

"I'm starting to think, ma'am," he sighed, "that you'd complain if I paid off your mortgage."

"Nope," she said, standing up and surveying the tray of food – exactly what she liked, yogurt with fruit and granola and a mug of black coffee, "but the ethics committee investigating improper gifts from a subordinate would be furious."

"Figured I'd save you some time."

"Well, thanks, Wen, but I need to show my face in the mess sooner or later."

"You need to show your face in the gym sooner or later. When I didn't see you there this morning, I figured it was later. Eat, ma'am, today's the first day as boss. You'll need your strength."

Thank God for you, Wen, she thought as she crunched down the granola, still standing. *I don't know what I'd do without you.*

"Alice get out OK?" Oliver asked as she grabbed a fresh utility uniform and stepped into the head to change.

"She texted me last night that she'd landed back at Sinus Medii. She seems... she seems adrift, ma'am."

"I know it." Oliver grabbed her tablet computer and opened the stateroom door. "Well? I can't get down to Medii to help my daughter until we win this stupid contest. So, let's hurry the hell up and get it done."

SAR-1's first training evolution was the zero-g "dunk tank," a space variant of the one back on Earth. Oliver remembered her dunking days fondly when she'd still had to stay certified – the metal simulation chamber mimicked the inside of a small boat perfectly. The crew had strapped in, and held their breath as the chamber spun upside down and plunged into a swimming pool. Oliver had remembered the disorientation, her lungs crying out for air, the sounds of her seat-harness groaning with the dull echo that being underwater added to everything. She'd been shocked at how calm she'd felt, even as the pressure built in her chest and ears, even as the need for air became more frantic. *Chaos is contagious, and so is calm.* She'd taken her time, made sure she was clear on which way was up, punched out of her restraints, and swam to the surface, gulping air that tasted like sunshine.

This "dunk tank" didn't use water, but the idea was the same. The simulator was a mocked up longhorn cabin suspended between four metal poles, which would simulate a loss of control from impact, whirling the crew as they would be in space, giving them the same wild disorientation, testing their ability to recover and exit the craft according to mission parameters.

It was one of the events at the Boarding Action.

Elgin and McGrath were suiting up into their hardshells when Oliver arrived, speaking with the simulator operator, a short, broad-shouldered woman whose nametape read ENGLE. Suiting up with them were two more coasties, a southwest Asian woman with hard eyes and a long black braid coiled around her neck, and an African man so tiny that Oliver wondered if he'd gotten a height waiver to join up.

"Those are the replacements for Kariawasm and Flecha," Ho said.

Oliver nodded, looking down at her tablet. "BM1 Naeemah Pervez and MK3 Everistus Okonkwo. She's coxs'un, and he's engineer."

"Pervez. Okonkwo," Ho tried the names out. "Pervez. Okonkwo. Holy shit. I can actually pronounce these."

"What do we know about them?"

"Okonkwo's solid. Two comms is pretty unheard of for an MK3. They're operational awards, before you ask."

Oliver grunted. "OK, so he's good at his job. Anything else?"

"Nope, pretty unremarkable otherwise."

"And Pervez?"

"She got the Coast Guard Medal for stopping an attempted rape. The attacker was another coastie. He shot her, she sucked it up and beat him half to death. He was planning to kill the victim after he was done, so they ruled it risking her own life to save another's."

Oliver swallowed. "My God. That's awful. Was the victim…"

"She's fine. Pervez intervened before the attacker could do any real damage."

"Well, that's incredible. I look forward to–"

"She's also been NJP'd, boss. Twice."

"Twice? For what?"

"Fighting, the first time. Mouthing off to an officer the second."

"That should have washed her out. Even with the Coast Guard Medal."

"It should have," Ho agreed. "She'll certainly never make Chief."

"So, why is she still in the guard?"

"Because," Ho said, "and I am quoting from her last FITREP here, she is finest small boat coxs'un in living memory."

Oliver watched Pervez give the thumbs up as Okonkwo locked her hardshell helmet in place and Chief Elgin checked the seal, giving his own thumbs up. The woman was barely bigger than Okonkwo, but the ferocity visible even through the helmet's clear plastic made her appear bigger somehow. "Well, I've dealt with attitude before. I can't make someone into a stellar coxs'un in two months."

"Can you make someone into a grownup in two months?" Ho asked.

"We both raised two kids, Ho. You tell me."

"No. It took me nearly that long to potty train Hui-Yin."

Oliver sighed. "Maybe it's different when they're already grown up."

Elgin shot Engle a thumbs up, and the operator returned to her control booth beside the dunking machine. As the SAR-1 crew turned to enter the simulated boat hatch, Oliver saw that all four of them wore a black mourning stripe over their nameplates. She doubted Pervez and Okonkwo had ever even met Flecha and Kariawasm, but clearly the legend of their loss loomed large enough in the unit's culture that everyone was expected to be in official mourning. Oliver made a mental note. *If they're going to perform their best as a team, they can't be laboring under the shadow of the dead.* She would have to find a way to break them out of it without making them feel as if they were being disrespectful.

"Ready in the cabin?" Engle's voice sounded on the PA.

Elgin flashed a thumbs-up through the simulator's window.

"Stopping spin," Engle announced, followed by a loud clunk and whirring shudder as the chamber's braking mechanism engaged and the spin began to slow. Oliver felt the familiar queasiness as her stomach rose, but she was much better with it now, and simply relaxed and enjoyed the gentle feeling of lift as the room normalized to lunar gravity. It wasn't the micro-gravity she experienced further from the Moon's surface, but it was still a fraction of what they'd had while the chamber spun.

"Contact right, fifty yards, CBDR," Engle called over the PA. Oliver watched as the crew braced themselves, warned that the exercise would simulate the impact of a vessel coming in hot from fifty yards out – constant bearing, decreasing range.

"Bang," Engle said and punched a button in her booth.

The simulator shuddered, then spun like a dropped penny, whirling so quickly that Oliver lost any sense of front and back, up and down, and she wasn't even inside the thing. She couldn't imagine how much worse it must be for the crew. It spun for a long moment before Oliver could see air puffs as the simulated port side thrusters fired. That was good. Even the best coxswains could mix up the cardinal directions in a spin like that. If Pervez had fired the starboard side thrusters, she'd have made the spin worse. But she hadn't, and the simulator slowed the spin, bow and aft coming into focus and the day-glow orange of the crew's hardshells becoming visible through the windows.

"Gunfire right," Engle said, letting the crew know they would be taking fire from their starboard side, and needed to bail to port to get the vessel between themselves and the enemy. Even as the spin slowed to a near stop, it bucked on its right side as the metal rods suspending it simulated the impact of autocannon rounds.

The port side hatch blew open with a puff of gas, swinging out from the simulator. Elgin hauled himself through, using the lunar-gravity to launch himself behind the simulated longhorn's stern, where the thickness of the engine would provide some cover from gunfire. He had his long gun dangling from its sling from his elbow, was fumbling it into his grip as he let the momentum carry him into position. It looked clumsy, but Oliver knew it was a display of incredible skill. Anyone else would have bailed on the wrong side, or not been able to find the hatch at all, let alone being able to get their long gun out of the rack-restraints on the way out the hatch.

Behind him came Pervez, her small frame clearing the hatch easily. She hadn't bothered with a long gun, but she carried the small boat's survival kit, which would be critical if the crew was stranded in space for any period of time. She drew her handgun as she pushed off to join chief, so smooth and graceful that Oliver could almost believe she hadn't just been in the middle of a skull-shaking, stomach churning spin.

Okonkwo came next, even smaller than Pervez, flailing one hand back into the cabin, presumably to get his long gun from McGrath. The act forced him to pause for a moment, and Oliver's throat tightened. They would be timed in the actual Boarding Action, and these kinds of delays would be as fatal to their chances of victory as they would to their odds of survival in a real ramming scenario. At last Okonkwo kicked off. *Good,* Oliver thought, *they didn't lose more than a second or two at...*

Okonkwo's drift abruptly halted, his feet shooting out in front of him as his back hung fast to the hatch.

"Shit," Oliver's stomach clenched. "What's..."

"It's the drag handle on his hardshell," Ho said. "It's hung up on the hatch."

And sure enough it was. Oliver could see the tiny loop of nylon hooked on one of the hatch's fastening tabs. If Okonkwo could simply pull himself up an inch, he would be free. But the engineer was pulling straight ahead. As Oliver watched, Okonkwo swung his feet behind him and pushed hard against the hatch interior, trying to break himself free by pure force. But the hardshell drag handles might be the last resort for a coast guard reaching out to stop a shipmate from drifting beyond help. The ripstop fabric was made to be strong, and all Okonkwo succeeded in doing was making his hardshell stutter and jerk as his feet slipped and kicked out in front of him again.

Oliver caught her breath, "No, this is not good, where's…"

McGrath appeared a moment later. Or, his fist did, the hardshell gauntlet slicing upward to punch Okonkwo's drag handle free. As bad as his start had been, Okonkwo rallied magnificently, kicking off and sending himself gliding smoothly to his shipmates behind the simulated engine housing, his gun stock already nestled against the sweet spot of the hardshell's articulated shoulder. McGrath followed behind him, ducking low to ensure his much bigger bulk cleared the hatch without a similar issue.

When all four of the crew were behind the engine housing, Engle punched a button in her booth and red strobes above the simulator began to flash. "ENDEX, ENDEX, ENDEX," she called into the PA. There was a low whirring as the chamber spun up again, and Oliver felt her feet slowly pushing back down into the deck, the slight lean in her posture as the spin gravity took hold.

Elgin popped his hardshell helmet, turned to look at his crew. Pervez already had hers off and was turning to Okonkwo, cheeks puffing out as she prepared what Oliver assumed was a robust criticism of his exit.

"Do *not* speak," Chief said before she could get the words out.

Pervez spun on him, looking as if she might say something, stopped as Chief stabbed a finger in Oliver's direction. "The skipper is watching!"

Pervez's eyes widened as she followed the direction of Chief's finger and saw Oliver and Ho, but they narrowed again nearly as quickly. *This one will be a tough nut to crack.*

The rest of the crew looked up at her. McGrath stood at ease, acknowledging her with a nod and smile. Okonkwo came to attention for a moment before an elbow from Chief snapped him out of it.

Oliver couldn't suppress a laugh at the crestfallen look on Okonkwo's face. "It's all right, MK3," she said, "you did right. You should always stray on the side of formality until you get the lay of the land."

"The lay of the land," Ho added, "is that the skipper doesn't stand on formality. Don't go calling her by her first name, but no 'attention on deck.'"

"Got it, sir," Okonkwo sounded rattled, "sorry."

"Are you apologizing for standing on protocol," Pervez drawled, "or for hanging up on the simulator hatch?"

Okonkwo flushed and looked at his feet.

"He's not apologizing at all," Oliver frowned at Pervez, "because he has nothing to be sorry for. That's what training is for, to iron out the mistakes so that we don't make them during the real thing."

"That's right, admiral," Chief said, sounding painfully uncomfortable.

"Great speech yesterday," Okonkwo added, then flushed again.

"Jesus," Pervez rolled her eyes, "wipe some of that shit off your nose."

"Can you please," Chief sounded exasperated, "let our new CO get her boots on the damn ground before you start embarrassing us? Christ, you are not just filling a role here. You are living up to a legacy!"

He means Kariawasm, Oliver thought. *No, Chief. That's not going to work on this one.*

"Sorry, Chief," Pervez didn't look sorry at all, "just kidding around."

Chief opened his mouth to reply, and Oliver spoke over him. "That's a good choice of words – 'kidding around.'"

"Ma'am?" Pervez's smirk straightened out.

"Look, I'm not asking any of you to apologize for your performance just now, but you're the select team to represent the guard at Boarding Action. Millions of viewers. Primetime TV. The reputation of the service. Possible fame for all of you. Now, I don't know about you, but *I'm* fixing to win this thing. Which is why, while you don't have to apologize, you do have to do better. Because I watched that evolution stem to stern. And that's what it looked like – like you were kidding around."

All trace of humor vanished, and the entire team snapped their eyes to her.

Oliver took a small step toward them, raising her chin just a fraction. She hated this brand of intimidation, but the dynamic Pervez had set had to be countered and fast. They had to know that the Widow Jane was not to be fucked with. "Just out of curiosity," Oliver kept her voice soft, "do you think the Navy is kidding around right now? How about the marines? Because I just came from NCD/0G school, and they sure as hell didn't look like they were kidding around to me. There's just two months until Boarding Action, and that's one hell of an unforgiving timeline."

Pervez flushed, forced a ghost of a smile onto her face. Chief almost snapped to attention before stopping himself. Okonkwo looked like he wished he could melt into the deck, and McGrath was as expressionless and placid as ever.

"No excuses, ma'am," Chief said, "it's just… We've been trying to adjust. We're still getting used to one another. After… well, after what happened we had to reform the team. We lost some people. I mean, I know that you lost someone too…" He stammered, running a hand over his shaved head. "Ah, hell, ma'am. I'm making an awful mess of this. I'm real sorry."

The man looked so hurt that Oliver had to stifle the urge to bundle him into her arms and tell him everything would be all right. *He lost Tom, too.* She softened her voice, lowered her chin. "Look," she kept her voice firm, professional, but took the edge out of it. "Did you not read the email I sent after I got back to Earth?"

Chief flushed. "Of course I did, ma'am. I'm sorry I didn't reply, it's just…"

Oliver cut him off with a shake of her head. "I don't blame you for Tom. Nobody blames you. This is the job we signed up for, and nobody knows how rough it is out there better than I do. You did what you could. Looking over your shoulder won't fix things."

"Yes, ma'am," Chief said, "thank you, ma'am," but he glanced down at the mourning band on his chestplate before he could stop himself.

"You have nothing to make up to me," Oliver says, "but if you feel like you want to do something for me, then win this year's Boarding Action."

"We'll do it for your husband," Chief said, "and for Kariawasm and Flecha, too."

"We will, ma'am," Okonkwo said, "we just need some time to come together."

Pervez rolled her eyes, the move just unsubtle enough to attract Oliver's attention, but she ignored it for now.

"I'd like to accelerate that timeline, if I can," Oliver said. "Any of you ever heard of a *contubernium*?"

"A con-tube-what?" Pervez asked.

Chief turned to upbraid her for not adding "ma'am," but Oliver spoke first. "The contubernium was the basic tactical unit in the army of ancient Rome. A contubernium ate together, bunked together, ran ops together. Everything – together. In my experience, that's the best way to make a team gel. You down with that?"

Pervez blanched, it was the first time Oliver had seen the woman looking something other than smug. "With respect, ma'am, it took me a long time to get my berthing ironed out. I'm not in a hurry to switch it up again if I don't have to."

"Noted," Oliver put on her own smug smile. "You have to."

"Ma'am," Chief stammered, "may I have a word?"

"You may," Oliver replied, "but since we're a contubernium now, you can have it here and now, in front of your shipmates."

Chief looked deeply uncomfortable, "Ma'am, are you sure this is a good idea?"

Not really, Oliver thought, *but I've been leading by instinct my entire career and it's steered me… mostly right so far.* "If you've got something to say, best get saying it."

"Ma'am, I've been leading sailors for over twenty years. This crew needs time to gel before we start living on top of each other like that."

"I have also been leading sailors for over twenty years."

"Ma'am, they'll be at each other's throats."

"No, they won't, because they will have an admiral on top of them, 24-7."

The crew all looked at her with stunned surprise. Even Ho's eyes snapped up at that. "I am forgoing a stateroom," Oliver said, "and berthing with you for the foreseeable future, we are all going to be one big, happy family."

SAR-1 berthed dormitory style, in a converted bay which had once stored SPACETACLET's gardener repair shop. The deck and bulkheads had all been scrubbed clean and repainted, but Oliver could still faintly smell the lingering oil and the high chemical tang of the plasticizers the machines used to 3D print structures. There were two bunk beds opposite a pair of cheap pressboard wardrobes and dressers, college campus style desks with shelving. A stateroom stood to either side, separated by a partition so thin it could only charitably be called a wall. The crew's nameplates were affixed to the side of their racks, and Chief's occupied the door to one of the staterooms.

Kariawasm and Flecha's portraits, draped in black, hung just below the American flag on the back wall.

"No bunk for you," Chief looked so uncomfortable that he was on the verge of crawling out of his own skin, "but you can take the opposite stateroom. You'll still… be part of the… I'm sorry ma'am, I forgot the word."

"Contubernium," Oliver said. "That will do nicely, Chief, thanks."

"Where do I sleep?" asked Ho.

Oliver looked at him. "You're my XO. You don't."

"Seriously, ma'am," Ho said, "there's no room for me here."

"There doesn't need to be. You can remain in your stateroom. If you really want, you can use mine."

"Ma'am, I should be with you." Ho folded his arms across his chest.

"To bring me a glass of water if I wake up thirsty in the middle of the night? To be on hand if I run out of toilet paper in the head? Come on, Wen. I'll ping you when I need you. O-country is just down the p-way."

Ho shook his head. "This isn't right, ma'am."

Chief nodded agreement. "Are you sure you want to do this, ma'am? I have to say it's… unusual having an admiral bunking right next door to a bunch of junior petty officers."

"Not junior petty officers," Oliver said. "This is SAR-1. This is the best the guard has to offer. These are the people who are going to bring us our first Boarding Action victory since we joined the 16th Watch."

Chief still looked uncomfortable. "Aye aye, ma'am."

"I know it's a little unusual, Chief," Oliver made sure to speak loudly enough to be heard by the rest of the crew, milling about uncomfortably by their bunks. "But you're going to be glad that the old Widow Jane is on the scene when you get to Boarding Action."

"I thought we weren't supposed to call you that, ma'am," Pervez said.

"You're not," Ho said. "The skipper can call herself whatever she likes."

"We're already glad you're here, ma'am," Chief said.

"You're not reading me," Oliver said. "It's not just the stellar cut of my jib that's going to benefit you here."

"What then, ma'am?" Okonkwo asked.

"I went through NCD/0G because I wanted to learn what it was you were going to be doing out here, to make sure I knew intimately what your jobs would be like."

"We appreciate that, ma'am. It's good leadership," Chief said. "A lot of officers wouldn't have done that."

Oliver had to fight to keep from rolling her eyes. "Chief, Christ. I'm not fishing for compliments here. I'm trying to tell you that going to NCD/0G had an unexpected benefit."

Chief folded his arms across his chest. "All right, ma'am, I wasn't blowing sunshine. I really do appreciate that you went through the trouble, is all. What's the unexpected benefit?"

"The school is all marines," she said. "Well, mostly marines. Did you guys know that? XO and I were the only two coasties in our class."

Elgin and McGrath exchanged a look. "We'd heard some talk, but that school was a long time ago for us."

"I got to see how they train," Oliver said. "I got to see how they fight. I've got the intel, and I'm going to use it to help train you to face them."

"You sure those marines are the same ones they're going to be fielding at Boarding Action, ma'am?" Okonkwo asked.

"There's a only one surefire way to find out," Oliver answered. "Follow me into the ready-room, folks."

The duty section ready room was adjacent to the crew quarters. It was spare and functional – a flat concrete pad, desks with terminals and chairs. Cheap metal lockers for hardshells and gear, a dry erase board for making diagrams during pre-mission briefs. A huge plasma screen monitor dominated the room temporarily cleared of the scrolling data on radio calls, vessel status, and surface conditions that normally covered its surface.

"OK," Oliver gestured to the monitor, "everybody take a seat. It's my experience that nothing intimidates more than the unknown. They say familiarity breeds contempt, and we're going to work to breed a little of that here. But *just* a little, mind you. We're going to respect our opponents, but we're also not going to fear them. So, starting now, we'll be watching video of Boarding Action's past winners, in every single event, and making sure we know what we're up against."

Oliver gestured to Ho, who clicked a remote, washing the screen with video of Boarding Action's familiar logo – two stylized small boats closing with one another against a field of stars, the American flag translucent in the background. TV network logos crowded together in the lower right hand corner. Oliver felt her heart rev a little at the sight. All her life, she'd avoided the public eye. The banner in her first ready-room on Earth had read "SUCCESS IS INVISIBLE, FAILURE UNFORGETTABLE." Even when ops she ran made the news, it was always the *Coast Guard* that was credited. That would be the same here too, but the individuals involved in Boarding Action could become stars in their own right, and the TV network logos reminded her of the millions that would be watching.

The screen then jumped with a slight crackle of static, the product of the hasty editing Oliver had asked Ho to do. It flashed and resolved into what Oliver could only charitably describe as a "glamour shot" of four marines standing, arms folded across their chests in a parody of tough-guy posture. They stood on a reflective black floor, backlit by colored gels, the marine corps logo emblazoned on the wall behind them. UNITED STATES MARINE CORPS FORCES SPECIAL OPERATIONS COMMAND – 16TH WATCH (MARSOC16). "Last year's winners," Oliver said.

"And the year before that," Ho added.

"And the year before that," Oliver echoed.

"And the year before that, too," Ho added again.

"Shut up, Wen," Oliver said.

The black reflective material of the floor must have been a green screen, because it resolved now into red letters, edged with gold, each "O" the globe-and-anchor of the marine corps' logo. The letters formed the ranks and names of the four members. 1LT DAVID KOENIG below a broad-shouldered man with a dimpled chin and a craggy forehead that made him look like a Hollywood action hero. "Check out Buzz Lightyear," Oliver said, "I'm flagging the name, sounds like 'conehead.'"

"Pretty sure it's German for 'king,' ma'am," Chief said.

"Not while I'm in charge, it isn't," Oliver quipped as the letters formed beneath the next team member, a lean Asian woman whose muscles still strained the digital camouflage of her operational uniform – GYSGT MARIA FUJIMORI. The camera panned across her face, showing a placid, almost bored variant of the thousand yard stare.

"Is she wearing makeup?" Oliver asked.

"I think they do that for everyone," Pervez said.

"Not for you. I am not having my team go out there with eyeshadow on. Absolutely not."

"Fine by me," McGrath said, and Oliver was grateful for the smile she heard in his voice. This was what they needed – to laugh not at their opponents, but at their mystique. She needed the coming event, and its participants, demystified.

PFC FARAH ABADI. Private First Class Abadi was a hulking monster, easily the biggest woman Oliver had ever seen, dwarfing the other three members of her team to a comical degree. Her uniform included a digital camouflage hijab and niqab, leaving only her eyes visible, threatening slits that glinted under the stage lights. "They feed them well in the Marine Corps," Ho's awed voice was barely above a whisper.

"It's entirely possible they don't," Oliver said, "and she resorted to eating slower marines. I'm going to go out on a limb and guess she's their boarding officer."

"I'd say that's a safe bet," Chief agreed.

"Jesus Christ," Okonkwo said.

"Secure that," Oliver said, "I've taken down plenty of people bigger than her on boardings."

Okonkwo turned to look at her. "Really, ma'am?"

Oliver thought for a moment. "No, not really," she admitted, "but size is only an advantage to a certain degree."

"The degree in this case is fucking gigantic, ma'am," Pervez said.

"Language," Oliver said as the words formed under the final member of the crew: PFC DAVID SLOMOWICZ. The video paused.

He was cartoonishly contrasted with the hulking Abadi, small and gangly thin, his uniform almost hanging on his lean frame. His amused smile matched his eyes, looking huge behind a pair of bottle-thick wrap-around glasses. He held his arms-folded, tough-guy posture ironically. "That has to be their engineer," Pervez mused.

"I wouldn't bet on it," said Chief.

"I would," Okonkwo said, jerking his chin at Abadi. "No way that beast is going to be able to scramble under an engine cowling."

"Could be Fujimori," Chief said.

"Nope," Pervez said. "She's the coxs'un."

"How can you tell?" Oliver asked.

"Eyes, facial expression, swagger, ma'am. She's great and she knows it." Pervez's mouth quirked slightly.

Oliver smiled back. "Sounds like someone I know."

"They look pretty badass," Okonkwo said, and McGrath grunted assent.

"Looks can be deceiving." Chief didn't sound convinced.

"Well, we don't have to make assumptions here," Oliver said. "Let's see what they can do."

"This is from the year before last's final evolution," Ho said, clicking the remote and setting the video playing again. The screen jumped once more, bright lines of static where Ho had cut the video resolving into a glittering field of stars with the Boarding Action logo, and the words FINAL EVOLUTION – EVASION, PURSUIT, NON-COOPERATIVE DOCKING – USMC MARSOC16 VS USAF 30TH SPACE WING – SECURITY OPERATIONS. "Oh, wow. I forgot the chair force made it to the finals that year."

"The zoomies are surprisingly forgettable," Oliver agreed. "Let's see how they did."

The screen cut to the two announcers, thick-necked men in suits that Oliver knew only as Don and John – collectively "the Donjohn" – who had been announcing the show for the past five years at least. She knew nothing about them beyond their names, though she could tell by their buzzcuts and parade ground voices that they were veterans. "And here we are," Don was saying, "the final evolution, and I have to say I'm at the point where I'm yawning at the thought of the marines going all the way for the third straight year."

John looked surprised. "Seriously? Surely, they deserve it."

"Surely, they do. A stellar performance this year as always, but you've got to admit that when a team delivers performances this stellar year after year, it all starts to run together after awhile."

"No doubt, but you've got to hand it to the corps, Don, they know how to deliver. I feel sorry for the bad guys who go up against them on the 16th Watch."

"Well, it's not bad guys this time, John. It's the United States Air Force with their incredible upset victory over this year's favorites, the FBI's Hostage Rescue Team, in the 'Large Hauler Breach and Clear' evolution."

"Just incredible stealth from a team known for going in guns blazing," Don agreed. "The Air Force has absolutely upped their game this year, and shown themselves to be a force to be reckoned with. But can they hold their own against the reigning champion for the last two years?"

"We're about to find out, and I couldn't be more excited. The Air Force has drawn the short straw, and will be the 'bad guys' for this evolution."

"Some think this is a considerable advantage," Don said. "A static defense is always easier than a dynamic offense."

"Under normal circumstances, I'd agree with you, but this is MARSOC16 we're talking about. Here's their commander, Brigadier General Demetrius Fraser, talking about his team's winning strategy."

The video cut to Fraser's handsome face, at ease and smiling. He chuckled at some question that had not been aired, looked at his hands. "Well, Sarah, I'm afraid I can't answer that question without disclosing classified tactics, but I will say this – we're marines. We attack. I was trained that offense is the best defense, and I impart the same ethic to my team. In any combat scenario, the attacker controls the flow of the battle. The defender is necessarily reactive, and that's not a posture marines like to be in."

"Sure," Ho said to the screen, "but this isn't combat."

"Goddamn right it's not," Oliver agreed.

The screen flashed to a view of the interior cabin of what looked to Oliver like a six-pack. The Air Force team was already in their hardshells, paint guns held at the ready.

"And we'll have camera views both inside the cabin and on the MARSOC16 boat," John said, "so you won't miss a thing! Let's go live now to outside the US Navy's Orbital Training Center's range to watch the action!"

The view switched to an interior cabin shot from the marines' rhino, looking over the digital pattern camouflage of the marine crews' hardshells and out through the front window. "For the life of me," Ho said, "I will never understand why they still use camouflage. You're either in a vessel, or EVAing in the blackness of space. What are you blending in with?"

"Old habits die hard," Oliver said.

"There's something to be said for tradition," Chief mused, looked sheepish as the rest of the crew shot him skeptical glances.

The video panned to show the four marines standing in a circle, arms around one another's shoulders, helmets pressed together. Oliver could see Koenig's lips moving through his visor, and knew he was speaking to them on a private radio channel that the show was being kind enough not to broadcast. She didn't need to hear him to know he was speaking words of encouragement. She could see the emotion clearly on his face, on Fujimori's and Slomowicz's as well. Abadi's face was covered by her niqab, but Oliver could see the creasing at the corners of her eyes. *These four people love each other. They trust each other implicitly.*

The MARSOC16 broke with a fist bump and the video panned again, showed that Oliver had guessed right – it was a six-pack, the small hauler floating into view through the marine boat's front window as they came closer. "VBSS Control, VBSS Control," Lieutenant Koenig's voice was self-assured almost to the point of smugness, "this is BA-1, we have a visual on unflagged vessel DIW outside shipping lane. They are not responding to hails. Request SNO for possible engagement."

"That's bold," John said. "The marines are asking for a peremptory 'statement of no objection'; this will basically give Koenig, who's just a lieutenant, the authority to conduct his boarding however he sees fit."

"That's unusual, right?" Don asked.

"Extremely," John said, "and not usually–"

Fraser's voice came back before John could finish speaking, "SNO granted, BA-1. Get it done your way."

"Roger that, sir, thank you," Koenig responded.

"Oh! Well, I guess that's…" John began again.

"Guns up," Koenig said. "Gunner, you are cleared hot. Target: propellant housing and feed left of engine cowling."

"Target aye, sir," Abadi's voice was dark, commanding, and utterly calm. "I have it."

"Jesus," Chief whispered. "Guns up, just for not answering a hail? How is that even OK?"

But Oliver could hear the cheering of the live audience in the studio around the announcers, and knew exactly why it was OK. "We have got to get control of this thing."

"Very well," Koenig said. "Let's hail them again, gunny, make sure they understand they're about to get shot."

"Aye aye, sir." Oliver matched the concentration in Fujimori's voice to the gentle goosing of the control sticks, and guessed she was at the helm. The six-pack grew in the marine boat's front window as she brought them in closer, the propellant lines growing in their vision.

"Isn't that risky?" Oliver asked.

"It sure is, ma'am," Okonkwo said. "They don't hit it right on the money, you could have a fire, or an explosion, or…"

"They're going to hit it right on the money," Oliver said, dread blossoming in her belly.

Fujimori had just opened the hailing channel when the six-pack's aft thrusters fired and the vessel jumped away from them. The audience gasped.

"Commence firing," Koenig said.

"Firing, aye, sir," Abadi answered as the guns lit up, "watch my tracer." The first round was bright white, the phosphorous coating streaking out from the autocannon's muzzle and arrowing straight into the propellant line coupling. Three more rounds followed, their explosive charges inert and replaced with paint packets for the exercise. The audience roared as the camera zoomed in on the impact, showing the propellant line painted in fluorescent pink, not so much as a speck of color outside the coupling where it met the engine intake.

"My God," McGrath was bent over his elbows, shoulders pinching together. "MK3, how big is that target?"

"The coupling… the intake's a little bigger, but maybe… six inches," Okonkwo sounded awed.

"A six-inch target," McGrath shook his head, "moving at what? Thirty knots? And they have to be more than a hundred meters out."

"Closer to two hundred," Chief said, squinting at the range readout below the guns' instrument panel.

"Jesus," McGrath said.

"Oh, come on," Oliver said, "you telling me you couldn't make that shot?"

McGrath turned to look at her, blinked. "No, ma'am, I'm not telling you that."

Oliver nodded, turned back to the video.

"I'm just telling you in all my years behind a console," McGrath continued, "and that's a lot of years, I have never made a shot like that before," he turned back to the video, eyes wide, "nor have I seen anyone else make a shot like that."

The six-pack abruptly cut thrust, began drifting forward. "Oh my God!" Don was yelling over the audiences' cheers. "Did you see that? What a shot! And the referee has fired the kill switch stopping the engines. The Air Force is dead in the water!"

"Gunny, get us in contact," Koenig said. "Slomowicz, I want soft dock instantly."

"Aye aye, sir," Slomowicz was indeed the team's engineer, and the camera rotated to show him slinging his cutting torch and rushing down into the nipple gangway.

"Soft dock only," Koenig's voice was as relaxed as if he were reciting a shopping list. "Don't start your cut until my mark. Gunny, vent atmosphere."

"Venting, aye, sir," Fujimori said, followed by the brief hiss of the oxygen and pressure puffing out into space. The video briefly toggled to a backward facing camera mounted on the six-pack, and Oliver could see the puff of the venting gas around the marine boat's windows.

"Yet another unusual move," John was saying. "I wonder what Koenig's got planned."

The camera toggled back to the marine boat's interior as Koenig bent to a gear locker and lifted up another cutting torch. The vessel trembled as Fujimori guided it gently into the six-pack's tow-fender, followed almost immediately by Slomowicz's triumphant call of "soft dock!".

"Kid's quick," Don said. *That's a gross understatement,* Oliver thought. *Jesus Christ, these people are good.*

Koenig clipped one end of an EVA cable to the front of his hardshell, locking the other end to a metal loop just beside the marine boat's exit hatch. "OK, going out. Wait for my signal."

"Aye aye, sir," the marine team answered at once as Koenig threw the hatch open and pushed his way out.

"He's... EVAing?" Pervez asked.

"Why is he..." Okonkwo added.

"What the fuck..." Ho finished.

The risk of tumbling on the end of the EVA tether made Oliver's stomach clench. With nothing to push off against in the emptiness around him, Koenig risked losing control of his movements, and right as his team had soft-dock with the Air Force vessel. *What the hell is he thinking?*

"Does he have a maneuvering unit on?" Chief asked.

"Nope," Ho's voice was flat.

"What the hell is he..." Chief said, his voice trailing off as Koenig choked his grip up on the EVA tether, grasping it close to the hatch. He pushed off with his boots, sending himself somersaulting out of the marine boat. The cable jerked taut, forcing Koenig into a tight arc, his feet kicking up over his head before swinging back down and slamming into the hull of the marine boat, where he engaged the setules on his boots with perfect timing. Locked in place, he bent his legs, and prepared to push off toward the six-pack.

The audience cheered themselves hoarse.

"That's some goddamn acrobatics," Chief said.

"Oh, how hard can it be?" Oliver asked as the video showed Koenig detaching himself from the MARSOC boat and executing a flawless leap that carried him across to the six-pack's hull where he landed so lightly that she was certain the Air Force crew inside didn't even know he was there.

When no one answered, she looked around. The crew was staring at her. "Pretty damn hard, ma'am. EVAs are tricky as hell," Chief said.

"I'm sure you could do that in a pinch," Oliver forced a smile.

Chief was looking back at the screen. "Let's just say I haven't before."

"First time for everything," Oliver said as the video showed Koenig disengaging the setules on a single boot, to permit himself to kneel, bringing the cutting torch around to press it against the six-pack's hull. "Slomowicz, wait until you see my sparks before you start your cut."

"Aye aye, sir," Slomowicz replied.

"Let me guess," Oliver said, "balancing on a drifting ship with only one boot engaged is hard."

"That's something of an understatement, ma'am," McGrath said.

"Like you said, ma'am," Chief offered, "first time for everything."

No sooner had Chief spoken than Don chimed in from the studio. "In all my years of doing this, I have never seen that kind of grace on an EVA before. Just one boot engaged on the exterior of the hull, and he's as steady as a rock!"

"Amazing," John agreed, "but what's the MARSOC team's plan here?"

"To show off," Oliver said.

"Cutting," Koenig radioed as sparks began to fly from his torch.

"Cutting, aye, sir," Slomowicz radioed back, the crackle of his own torch barely visible from the camera's angle.

The video then cut to the camera in the six pack's interior. The Air Force team was backing away as two cuts appeared, the expected one on their tow fender, and another one beside their access hatch. Oliver could see their weapons trembling as they tried to decide which entryway to cover. They clearly weren't prepared for this.

Oliver leaned forward in her seat. "Brilliant." She'd said the word before she realized she'd spoken.

"Brilliant!" John echoed, as the camera toggled back to show the MARSOC team stacked in the nipple gangway and ready for Slomowicz to finish his cut. Back inside the six-pack, the Air Force team had split in half, two guns on Koenig's cut, and two on Slomowicz's.

"Oh, man," Ho said, "that's not good."

"For the Air Force," Oliver agreed. "Now they've only got two guns on the right breach."

"The LT will still come through the other one," Chief said.

"Twenty bucks says he doesn't," Pervez said.

"You're on," Chief said.

"Not if you win, Chief," Oliver said. "No monetary gifts up the rank chain. Skipper's orders."

"Aye aye, ma'am," Chief and Pervez said at the same time.

Oliver found herself holding her breath as the twin cuts neared completion. The audience was shouting so loud that Don and John were raising their voices despite their microphones as they narrated the action. "Jesus," she breathed, "I can see why this show is so damn popular."

At last the cuts were almost done, the cut sections held in place by just a slim tab of metal waiting to be severed with a strong kick. "Hold what you've got," Koenig said. "Go on my mark. Three… two…"

The camera showed Slomowicz stepping to the side of the breach. He dropped his torch, raised his paint gun, aiming the butt at the cut segment, waiting for Koenig to finish counting down.

"Mark!" Koenig called, slammed his paint gun into his section. The plate broke away and spun into the six-pack's cabin. Both of the Air Force team members covering down on his section fired just as Koenig rolled aside, their paint packets firing off into the darkness of space outside the hull.

At the same instant, Slomowicz slammed his paint gun into the side of his cut plate, instead of the center. The motion caused the section to pop sideways, sending it spinning back toward his own crew. Oliver watched in amazement as Abadi moved with a speed that was shocking in someone so big, catching the plate with an outstretched hand, letting the force of its inertia make it hang there, a handleless shield.

At that precise moment, both of the remaining Air Force crew discharged their weapons. The paint packets shot out and collided with the cut plate, still quivering against Abadi's hand.

"Holy fucking *God*," Okonkwo said.

"That is some straight up ninja shit," Pervez agreed.

Abadi let the plate drop and raised her own paint gun as the Air Force team scrambled for cover. Koenig executed another breathtaking somersault, shortening his grip on his tether to send him swinging perfectly into the six-pack's cabin and setting him gently on his feet. He was raising his paint gun and firing even as he undid the carabiner with his free hand. The shot caught one of the Air Force crew in the face, sending him onto his back. "And that's one down!" Don was bellowing over the shouting of the crowd, an ecstatic roar which dissolved into chants of *Semper fi! Do or die!*

The rest of the Air Force crew didn't bother with their paint guns. They charged, the first at Koenig, the remaining two at Abadi.

"This should be interesting," McGrath grunted. An instant later, the video showed Fujimori leaning at the waist, bending past Slomowicz and shooting the airman charging Koenig in the side of their head. "Another one down!" Don called.

Abadi dropped her paint gun and spread her arms out as the two remaining Air Force crew dove into her, tackling her about the waist. Even with her spider boots engaged, the force of both men should have knocked her off her feet.

They didn't. Oliver watched Abadi make some small changes to her center of gravity, bending her knees, leaning forward. It looked like nothing, but Oliver could see the expertise in the movement, the veteran's economy.

The airmen slammed into her sides as if they had tackled a boulder. She trembled slightly as they bounced away in the micro-g, but not before Abadi slammed her fists down, smashing the backs of their helmets and sending their visors rebounding off the six-pack's deck hard enough to turn the audience's cheers into a pained gasp. "Owww!" John said. "That's gotta hurt!"

Whether it hurt or not, the two airmen were disoriented. They drifted, limbs flailing, unable to find the floor. *They can't tell which way is up,* Oliver thought. *She knocked the tar out of them.*

Slomowicz and Fujimori swung smoothly in behind her, paint guns holstered and forgotten now. They no longer needed them. The two marines produced hardshell restraints and secured the two stunned airmen before they could even arrest their drift. Neither offered any real resistance, with one breaking a hand free of Fujimori's grip for a brief moment before the marine grunted and slammed it into the restraint.

Koenig's sangfroid momentarily broke, the triumph sounding in his voice. "VBSS Control, this is BA-1. MARSOC16 has the vessel secured."

Red klaxons whirled both in the six-pack's cabin and back on the soundstage, washing the cheering audience in flashing red and making their celebration into a horror show parody. Don and John were bouncing in their announcers' chairs, babbling semi-coherently about the beauty of the final seconds of that engagement.

"Well," Oliver gestured at the two apoplectic announcers, as Ho killed the video, "that's just downright unprofessional. Where's the military bearing, I ask you?"

The crew, who had been leaning forward in their seats, turned as one person to regard her as if she'd grown a third head. "Ma'am," Chief said, "in all my years on the 16th Watch, I have never seen anything like that."

Oliver fought against the churning of her stomach, the feeling that she'd been set at the foot of a mountain – impossibly high, impossibly steep. "Oh, sure you have. I've gone up against teams tougher than that back on Earth."

Ho blinked at her. "We have?"

"Sure we have," Oliver forced a smile. "It was probably one of the ones you weren't on."

"I mean," Ho said, "I've been on most of them with you."

"Most isn't all."

"As you say, boss."

Oliver looked at the expressions on the faces of her crew and realized that humor wasn't going to work here. "Look, I know they seem tough, but you just watched *people* in action there, same as you."

"Abadi is considerably larger than me, ma'am," Okonkwo pointed out.

"Still a human," Oliver said. "She poops and farts just like you do. Anyway, you've all heard of imposter syndrome, right?"

The looks on their faces told her they hadn't.

Oliver sighed. "OK, imposter syndrome is the idea that you're not good enough to do great things. We're all raised to be self-effacing, so when we accomplish something extraordinary, our brains short circuit. We can't let ourselves acknowledge the possibility that we actually did it, because our brains interpret that as egotistical. So, we feel like imposters. Like it couldn't possibly be *us* who did this amazing thing, and we keep waiting for everyone around us to realize that we're actually frauds and take away whatever accolades we've earned. What's that Mandela quote, XO?"

Ho answered with a speed born of constant repetition. "You mean the one you use in pretty much every graduation speech? 'Our deepest fear is not that we are inadequate. Our deepest fear is that we are powerful beyond measure. It is our light, not our darkness that most frightens us. We ask ourselves, Who am I to be brilliant, gorgeous, talented, fabulous?'"

"Thank you. This is my point. You're asking yourselves right now – 'who am I to go up against a crew of such dedicated professionals, such obvious *naturals*, and actually *win*?' Well, I am telling you that you are the best the United States Coast Guard has to offer. I've run ops with two of you, and I can already tell the other two are up to snuff. You *can* beat these people. And once you have beaten them, I'll send you off to see the wizard to help get you through the imposter syndrome. But first, we beat them. So, we're going to watch this video again. And again. And again. And we're going to keep watching it until it no longer impresses us, until we are able to see the mistakes in their TTPs. And once we do, we're going to start training on ways to exploit them."

"Aye aye, ma'am," Chief breathed. "So, when do we start?"

"Right now," Oliver said. "XO, let's run it again."

The team loosened up their shoulders and settled into their chairs as the video rolled again. Oliver could tell they were less impressed by the third run through, and by the fifth they had the bored look of concentration she had come to expect in those handling a routine task. That was good, the awe was mostly gone at least. Chief had produced an old school scratch-pad and was taking notes with a pen.

Oliver turned back to the video, watching Koenig make his acrobat's leap to the six-pack for the sixth time. She prayed that Chief was spotting those flaws she'd just mentioned, and would highlight them to the rest of the crew.

Because after watching the video as carefully as she could six times in a row, Oliver could find none. It was the most flawless, matchless, perfect boarding, executed by the most gifted, dedicated crew she'd ever seen, in all her years on Earth and the Moon combined.

CHAPTER 8

The Peter Principle is insidious in any environment, but it is particularly pronounced in the military due to our organizational culture. We naturally promote those who are most competent in core operational roles. The problem is that all promotions eventually lead to staff, administrative and instructor positions, which are the polar opposite of operational – tying officers and senior-NCOs to desks, and the stage. There is a statistically significant correlation to increased instances of depression and anxiety in many of these cases, usually beginning at around O5 and E7 respectively. A lifelong ship captain or infantry commander isn't always the best candidate to run purchasing or write training manuals for a service. It's a persistent problem in the armed services, and one that urgently needs to be addressed.

MAJOR WENDELL MARCHEAUX
"THE PETER PRINCIPLE AND MENTAL HEALTH"
PROCEEDINGS OF THE UNITED STATES NAVAL INSTITUTE (USNI)

The following Earth day, Oliver ran them through their first simulated boarding since she'd taken over. Ho's eyebrows continued to rise as she told him her plan until they were in danger of crowding onto the top of his head. He was still arguing as they both suited up to run it.

"Boss," Ho said as he lifted his helmet out of the hardshell case. "This was dangerous as hell when you did it."

"That's right," Oliver nodded, "and I'm a withered old lady without a fraction of the sea time as this crew."

"That's not true," Ho shook his head. "Christ, ma'am. You know that's not remotely true."

Oliver waved the objection away. "OK, whatever. I didn't really mean sea time. I meant *space* time. I'll go toe-to-toe with any sailor on blue water boardings. I'll give you that. But there isn't any damn water out here. They're the best we have. They'll be fine. Just run it by the numbers. I need to see how this crew comes together under real stress conditions on an actual boarding. I can't get the measure of them watching them run simulations all day."

"This is still a simulation," Ho said. "Heck, Boarding Action is a simulation."

"A more realistic simulation. Wen, you watched that video same as I. You know what we're up against here. I've got less than two months to make sure this crew is ready. We need to push them hard, and that means I have to figure out just how hard I can push them."

Ho sighed. "You want it just as it ran with us. Garbage ejection and everything?"

"Wen. I did not stutter. In all your years working for me, have I ever backed off an idea once it was fixed in my head?"

"I was kind of hoping old age would mellow you."

"Death. You're describing death."

"That's an extreme interpretation of what I was describing."

"Just shut up and get it done, XO."

"Aye aye, admiral." Ho slapped his helmet on his head and nodded to his crew, climbing into the battered longhorn that would serve as the simulated quarantine evader.

Oliver waved, then turned and ducked through the hatch that led her to the adjoining bay. SAR-1's vessel was visible through a window in the opposite airlock. The duty crew had relocated it to the executive pad on her orders, the one closest to the Boat Maintenance Facility's airlock, and usually intended for shuttles carrying VIPs like... well, her actually.

The SAR-1 crew was already suited up into their hardshells, Chief checking the seal indicator lights on each one before waving them into the longhorn's open hatch.

Oliver faced the airlock as the duty crewman sealed her helmet in place, checked the indicator lights and flashed her a thumbs-up. She stepped into the narrow chamber, just big enough to accommodate a crew of four with hardshells and gear, and flashed a thumbs up of her own. Her radio was set to external audio, and she heard the thud of the door behind her, the whoosh of the venting atmosphere, and then the eerie silence as the far portal swung soundlessly open. She stepped out onto the regolith dusting the concrete pad, marveling at the crunching feeling, like freshly fallen snow.

She allowed herself a quick glance overhead, a move she knew would mark her as a newbie to the 16th Watch, but was powerless to stop. The towering jetties for the Constellation Class Cutters rose above her, looking so thin from the surface that Oliver wondered how they could possibly support such massive ships. Beyond them there was only the sprawling emptiness of space, stars spraying across it like a field of ground glass. She felt a brief sense of vertigo, as she had beneath the big sky driving Interstate-15 from Utah to Nevada in Tom's Jeep, her hand resting gently on his over the gear shift, on their way to let an Elvis impersonator do the honors at the Graceland Chapel. The wrenching sense of unmooredness, of her seatbelt being the only thing keeping her from tumbling out of her seat and into that vast open blue had been so overwhelming she'd had to rip her eyes away and fix them on Tom's reassuring smile. Space was black, not blue, but the sensation was almost exactly the same. Oliver wrenched her eyes away, ignoring the fluttering in her stomach as she met the faces of the crew, turning at the crackle in their comms units as Oliver bridged to their radios.

"Good morning, everyone."

"Morning, ma'am," Chief said, "you're suited up."

"Sure am. Figured I'd bop along."

"You're... joining us? Ma'am, our OPlan is based on a crew of four."

"Just as an observer. I want to see how my best and brightest perform. You won't even notice me. I'll just be your garden variety admiral and commander of this entire facility just sitting right behind you, staring at the back of your heads."

Pervez actually chuckled at that, but the others just stared.

She swept her glance past them and settled on the boat they were prepping for launch. She noted its old, familiar angles, comfortable in dear to her...

Too old. Too familiar.

"Hey, why are we in a longhorn?" she asked. "I thought this platform is deprecated. Why aren't we flying the rhino?"

"It's the platform I came up on," Pervez said, adding a quick "ma'am" even as Chief turned toward her. "Figured I'd play to my strengths."

"It's also the platform we ran at Lacus Doloris, ma'am," Chief added. "There's a compelling legacy there."

McGrath grunted approval. "Boarding Action rules don't specify the boat class, ma'am."

"Sure, but the rhino is faster and handles better," she said.

"Not for me, it doesn't," Pervez said. "Ma'am," she added after a pause.

"Look," Oliver said, "I appreciate the need for comfort and familiarity, but you're going to fight like you train."

"That's right, ma'am," Pervez said, "and this is the boat I've trained on."

"It's not so different that you can't get used to the newer platform," Oliver said.

"I don't need fancy bells and whistles," Pervez raised her chin. "I know the longhorn. It's an extension of me."

"Ma'am," Chief's voice sounded pained. "You don't understand. This is the boat we were in on Lacus Doloris." As if that explained everything.

Oliver knew she could simply order them to change platforms right then and there, but she could also feel the tension rising in the crew. Even McGrath's normally solid and quiet presence felt roiled, and he looked at her from beneath his brow, jaw tight.

She could sense the morale crisis and mentally filed the question. She was coming in new to a team that had been working together for some time. She didn't want to start out by moving the goal posts on their first run out together. Pervez had a point. She radioed Ho on a private channel. "XO, make a note for us to talk about SAR-1's choice of the longhorn. Not sure how I feel about that."

"I'll add it to the docket, ma'am," Ho replied.

Oliver turned back to Chief. "Well, both the longhorn and the rhino are rated for ten. One more body won't slow you down. Let's get moving."

"Aye aye, ma'am," Chief said, motioning them all into the hatch.

Inside, Oliver positioned herself on the "casualty" bench where the crew would lay out the injured so they could perform emergency medical care. It put her between the two rear seats, McGrath occupying one, and Okonkwo the other. Both men kept their eyes forward, and Oliver could tell they were grateful for the hardshell's limited peripheral vision.

She listened to the radio as the crew performed boat checks, McGrath inventorying the weapons, Okonkwo the engines, and Pervez everything else. Elgin supervised it all, finally turning to the crew – "Operating conditions are near perfect. Radiation report is low, traffic normal. Crew fitness is high. GAR score is well within green. Pervez, call it in."

"Just a sec, Chief," Pervez said, "there's a few factors you haven't accounted for."

Chief sucked in his breath, unsuccessfully kept the frustration out of his voice. He outranked Pervez, but as the boat's coxswain, she had a right to question the GAR score, and a good leader listened to their subordinates. "What's up?"

"We've got two factors here. One impacts crew fitness, and the other our operational planning," she raised one gauntleted fist, counting off on the articulated fingers. "For planning – this is an unknown training evolution. We won't get orders until we're underway. We don't know what's going to happen to us up there. For crew fitness," she jerked a thumb at Oliver, "we have the skipper sitting two feet away from us. Now, I don't know about you, but that makes me nervous as hell. That's going to impact performance for sure. I move to submit an amber score to account for these discrepancies."

"BM1," Chief's eyes were steady, but his tone rolled them plenty, "if we submit amber, we're going to have another thirty minutes of checks before we can launch, and another hour when we tie back up. I agree those are discrepancies, but they're minor."

Pervez's shrug was exaggerated enough to be clearly visible through her hardshell. "You're the one who always says we operate safe or we don't operate."

Chief turned to Oliver, but she spoke before he could open his mouth. "I'm here as an observer, Chief. Make the call."

"Sorry, ma'am," Chief said. "I'm used to a bit more flexibility in my crew." *He means Kariawasm.* Her eyes flashed to Pervez and saw the split second of a shadow across her features.

Chief turned to Okonkwo and McGrath. "Any thoughts on this?"

Okonkwo visibly blanched. "I'm good with whatever you decide, Chief."

McGrath only shrugged. "Let's get going."

"OK," Chief couldn't resist an uncomfortable glance at Oliver. "Call it in green and take us up."

"Aye aye, Chief," Pervez made no effort to keep the irritation out of her voice. "Control, control, this is CG-31118 requesting designator."

"CG-31118, this is control," came buzzing back, "31118 is designated Search-And-Rescue-One for mission duration. I say again, 118 is SAR-1. Skipper's orders, whatever boat your duty section is on is designated SAR-1 until further notice. No need to request future designator, SAR-1. Request GAR score and status for launch."

The crew all turned to look at Oliver.

"That's right," she said, "you all are the great hope for this organization. And I want everyone in this command to know it. While you're working together as a crew, you, and only you, will be SAR-1."

The crew looked briefly at one another before facing forward again. Oliver couldn't tell if the move had stiffened their spines, but she guessed time would tell.

"Boat checks are green. Ops normal," Pervez radioed back to control. "Go when ready."

"You might want to hang on to something, ma'am," Chief radioed Oliver on a private channel, "we're practicing contingency launching. We're going to jump hard."

Oliver just had time to grab the handles over her head before control radioed back, "SAR-1, launch."

Pervez punched the belly thrusters so hard that Oliver felt the longhorn flex as it rocketed straight up. Oliver felt her stomach pressing into the bottom of her abdominal cavity, her vision momentarily blurring with the rattling of the small boat's frame. The radio crackled as it desperately toggled between antennae arrays, trying to keep pace with the vessel's sudden acceleration. The altimeter spun desperately, finally flipping past its maximum range before it switched over to "range-to-target" measurement.

Oliver knew enough about the longhorn's controls to understand that this much belly thrust should have made the boat unwieldy, as likely to flip over on its back as to roll uncontrollably to either side. But Pervez's control over the lateral thrusters was masterful. Oliver could see the contrails of controlled burns to either side in her peripheral vision, and the boat balanced perfectly, rising straight up, bow slightly tucked to give Pervez and Chief a clear view of what was in front of them. *Holy shit, this woman is good.*

At last, the boat leveled and Oliver's stomach settled, and she opened a private channel to Ho in the training boat, which had launched at much more measured pace, and was only now slowly rising to its station keeping position just below them. "All right, Wen. Call the tune when you're ready."

"I don't like this, ma'am."

"If you know a better way to get us ready to take on Fraser's MARSOC bubbas in less than two months, you be sure to let me know. We fight like we train."

"Aye aye, ma'am," there was a click as Ho toggled over to SAR-1's shipwide channel. "SAR-1, SAR-1, this is head boat. STARTEX. I say again, STARTEX. Check your transponder for orders."

Chief glanced down at the transponder. "OK, BM1 – Chinese-flagged vessel DIW in US territorial space. Distance – one nautical mile, azimuth six degrees, elevation 22 degrees. Come right to heading two-two-zero. Come to elevation -22 degrees."

"Heading two-two-zero, elevation -22 degrees aye," Pervez said, her hands gently twitching the joysticks, the small boat spinning smoothly until it was pointed directly at the head boat. The boat had killed its thrust, was drifting slowly on its x-axis, twirling in a gentle circle. Ho had even gone so far as to kill the interior cabin lights. The effect was eerie, the craft a pale white and orange blot against the pocked gray surface of the Moon below.

"McGrath," Chief said, "guns up."

"Aye aye, Chief." McGrath had transferred the gunsights to the monitor mounted in the back of Chief's seat, and brought up the controls now, the targeting reticle blossoming on the screen. Through the front glass, Oliver could see the autocannon barrel swiveling to track the head boat. Oliver's stomach clenched as she realized she hadn't checked to see if they'd loaded live rounds for the exercise. *How have they been training out here?*

"Hail 'em," Chief said.

"Chinese-flagged vessel," Okonkwo's voice crackled over the shipboard hail, "Chinese-flagged vessel, this is the United States Coast Guard. You are DIW in US territorial space. Bring your engines online, station keep and state your intention."

"Don't answer," Oliver radioed Ho.

"I do speak Chinese, ma'am, if you want to make this realistic," her XO radioed back.

"You keeping quiet is extremely unrealistic, I'll admit," she replied, "but indulge me for now."

Ho responded with something in Chinese that Oliver thought sounded like *gǔn dàn*. The tone definitely indicated it was a curse.

The head boat's aft thrusters lit up.

"Chinese-flagged vessel," Okonkwo said, "your engines have come online. Maintain station keeping and state your intentions. Do not get underway or we will fire upon you."

"Not with a field of habs as a backstop," Chief said.

"I know, Chief," Okonkwo said, "just following protocol."

"Well, now you said it," Chief chided. "BM1, get to that elevation fast. I want the sun for a backstop."

"Roger that, Chief. Everybody hold on." The smile was evident in Pervez's voice as she punched the top thrusters and the small boat dropped. Oliver's stomach lurched as the bow swept up, and she was suddenly seeing the distant sun where the Moon's hab-studded surface had once been. The autocannon lost track, the barrel wrenching down as McGrath swung it back to its target – the head boat, rising up into view once more as Pervez fired the belly thrusters and arrested their descent so suddenly that Oliver felt her hardshell jerk hard against her restraints.

"There you go, Chief," Pervez said.

"Very well," Chief said, toggling to the hailing channel personally. "Chinese-flagged vessel, you have failed to respond to multiple hails by the United States Coast Guard. Heave to and prepare to be boarded."

"Here we go," Ho radioed Oliver.

The head boat's aft thrusters engaged with a sudden flash of blue-white and the head boat leapt forward.

"Hot pursuit!" The tiniest hint of excitement crept into Pervez' voice. "Engaging." The longhorn leapt after the head boat, accelerating fast enough to press Oliver back in her seat. Oliver glanced at the instrument panel – thirty knots and accelerating.

Chief scanned the radar. "Negative contacts, clear space. Do what you need to do, BM1."

Pervez didn't respond, and Oliver knew it was because the woman was already doing it. She felt the vessel buck as Pervez punched the throttle and the longhorn surged forward. Oliver had been hoping to put the crew in the same position she and Ho had been in when they'd pursued the six-pack in their rickety launch, but the longhorn was a far more capable boat than the launch, and Pervez immediately began to gain on the head boat. "Shit," Oliver radioed Ho, "they're gonna fucking catch you. Have you got any more juice in that thing?"

"It's a longhorn, ma'am," Ho's voice was mildly tense with excitement. "It's not like it has a nitrous tank."

"OK. Well, let them have the garbage now."

"You sure? They're a lot closer than we were back at…"

"They're not going to get any farther away!"

"Aye aye, ma'am." No sooner had Ho spoken than Oliver saw the head boat's gear pods flash, discharging what appeared to be a flickering silver pebble at this distance, but that Oliver knew was the same compressed garbage pod that Fraser's boat had launched at her back outside OTRACEN.

Oliver had been stunned at the time, but Chief didn't bat an eyelash, recognizing the radar signature immediately. "Deploying trash pods."

Oliver glanced at the instrument panel again. They were making forty-five knots now right at the top of the longhorn's safe operating parameters. Being hit by the trash pods would surely damage the boat. She swallowed sour panic at the thought of all that could go wrong.

But her crew wasn't fazed. "I see them," Pervez said. "McGrath, scatter them."

"Negative, maneuver to evade them. I don't want you shooting in…" Chief began.

"I'm operational commander on scene, it's my call," Pervez said. "I'm not losing speed. McGrath!"

"I got you BM1," McGrath said. The autocannon swiveled, kicked silently on the bow. Oliver could feel Pervez executing perfectly timed controlled burns to compensate for the recoil. Oliver knew the longhorn's Target Acquisition System made the shooting easier, but the speed with which he acquired and drew down on the pods was still impressive. Two shots for two pods – the steadily growing silver balls flashed orange and burst apart into a scattering of what looked like silver foil.

Chief opened his mouth to say something, but the head boat was growing rapidly in the longhorn's front window, and Pervez yanked on the joystick. "Hold on! I'm gonna bring her in hot!"

"Jesus!" Chief reached up and grabbed the handle as the longhorn's bow rose and they lost visual on the head boat.

"Uh, boss?" Ho radioed. "I think you guys are about to crash into us."

"I know," Oliver said.

"You going to say something?" Ho sounded worried.

"Nope. I'm observing... ugh," Oliver said as Pervez hit the topside thrusters and the longhorn sped forward with its bow still raised. Oliver could see her eyes flashing to the radar and the plotter, flying entirely on instruments. She was grinning like a wolf.

"Okonkwo! Get ready on the nipple! Hang on!" Pervez called. "We're gonna give 'em a little bit of a bump!"

Okonkwo grabbed the controller for the longhorn's nipple and Oliver could feel the deck vibrating as the motor extended it from the longhorn's belly. "Fifteen yards!" Chief called. "Ten! Two!" The longhorn collided with a boom that shook the boat, sending Oliver rattling in her restraints again.

"Okonkwo!" Pervez called.

"I've got it!" he called back just as the boat shuddered as the nipple gained traction on the head boat's tow fender. "Soft dock!"

"I can feel that!" Pervez growled. "Get your ass down there and start cutting!"

Okonkwo shot her an irritated glance, punched out of his restraints, and reached under his seat for the cutting gear.

"Check our drift," Chief said. "We hit them pretty hard. Mark your head and let me know our speed and course."

But Pervez was already out of her restraints and drawing her paint gun. "We're going to have hard dock in a second, Chief," she raced to follow Okonkwo as he dragged the cutting gear down into the longhorn's belly.

"That's OK," Chief's voice was petulant, sarcastic as he bent over the plotter. "I'll do it."

McGrath had grabbed a duster off the rack and was falling in behind Pervez. The boat shuddered again, and Okonkwo pulled the nipple's manual lever and locked them on. "Hard dock!" he radioed. "Venting atmosphere." There was no atmosphere to vent, but Oliver made a mental note that the engineer was going by the book. "Outer hatch is open." A moment later, Oliver could see the sparks of Okonkwo's torch cutting into the head boat's inner hatch. She unbuckled her restraints and pushed off the bench, letting the micro-g take her gently down onto the nipple behind McGrath.

Okonkwo's cut was near perfect, a long rectangle just big enough to admit a single boarder in their hardshell. He slowed as he made the final, descending cut. "You guys ready?"

"We're stacked," Pervez said, not looking behind her. *That either means she implicitly trusts her team,* Oliver thought, *or she's not paying attention.*

"They're coming through, Wen," Oliver radioed. "You ready?"

"Yeah. They better not kill me."

"They'll just hurt you real bad, most likely," Oliver radioed back. "You should be able to see the final cut now."

"I see it. Here we come."

As Okonkwo made the last cut, Ho kicked the section from the opposite side, shearing it off the hatch and sending it tumbling into the boarding team. Okonkwo shouted, thankfully with his radio toggled off, and dropped the cutting torch, stumbling back into Pervez. Oliver could see Ho and one of the head boat crew leveling their paint guns at the newly created opening, lining up their sights to fire on the...

Oliver could feel the deck shudder as McGrath stomped down his spider boots to give himself a stable platform and let loose with the duster. With the TAS, McGrath had easily nailed the garbage pods. Without it, he did just as well. Two targets, two shots. Ho caught the first one full in the face, went reeling into his shipmate. McGrath racked the duster's slide and fired again, this time at the tiny glimpse of the crewman's helmet not covered by Ho's tumbling body. He hit the target square on. The training beanbags were loaded with half-charges. A full charge would risk damaging a hardshell's integrity. But even with half the powder, the beanbags packed enough punch to send both Ho and the crewman on their backs. Oliver could see the remaining two crew inside the longhorn backing away with their hands up.

"Ow," Ho radioed to Oliver, "that was unpleasant."

"Kid can shoot," Oliver radioed back. She could see the remaining crewman behind Ho raising his hands, getting on his knees. "OK, looks like your guy is compliant."

"Yes, ma'am," Ho said. "Your team has the vessel secured."

"Outstanding. Call the ENDEX."

A moment later, the klaxons began whirling, washing the tight confines of the nipple-gangway in shimmering red. "ENDEX ENDEX ENDEX," crackled through their radios.

Oliver turned to head back to her seat and saw Chief holstering his paint gun. "In case anyone is interested, we were clear on our drift."

"Save it," Oliver said, "we'll discuss it in the hot wash."

"Absolutely, ma'am. Just give me a word in private with BM1 first."

"Negative," Oliver said, "we're a contubernium. We are going to air the dirty laundry together."

Chief kept his eyes straight ahead as he turned back to his chair, but not before Oliver saw his mustache twitching through his helmet. *Sorry, Chief,* she thought. *This is too important to let you do it your way.*

The silence on the road back was so uncomfortable that Oliver was grateful when Ho radioed her on a private channel. "So? What do you think?"

"I think we've got a problem," she said.

"Seriously? I've never seen flying like that in my life. Shooting either. MK3 cut through the tow fender like he was carving hot margarine."

"No argument. As individuals, they're best-in-class."

Ho paused before replying. "I see what you're getting at here."

"They're going to have to get the hell out of each other's way if we want to win this thing, Wen."

"And that's the impetus behind your whole contubernium schtick?"

"Something like that."

"Guess you've got your work cut out for you then."

"What's this 'you' business, XO? You're on the hook for this, too."

Ho's sigh was audible as he cut the connection.

They hot-washed in the BMF just beside the executive pad. Chief insisted on doing post-run boat checks, even though Oliver would have preferred to let the incoming duty crew handle it. Oliver guessed he needed the familiar routine to clear his head, and decided it was best to leave him to it, though the waiting frustrated her.

When they were finally done, the crew gathered around a work bench. Someone had clearly been checking autocannon loads, judging by the smell of propellant and the pooled stains of gun oil still faintly visible on the plastic. "OK," Oliver said, "hot-wash. How does everybody think we did?"

Pervez smiled. "We caught the fleeing vessel, neutralized a hostile crew, all without a single casualty or any damage to the longhorn. I'd call that a big win."

Oliver nodded, biting back a retort. "Everyone agree with that?"

Chief shook his head. "No way. We discharged rounds when we could have evaded. Crew abandoned the helm without checking drift. We weren't properly stacked on entry. All of that would have cost us points."

"I guess," Pervez countered, "but in a real evolution, we would have all come home safe. Isn't that what matters?"

"Not when we're training to win Boarding Action," Oliver said.

"With respect, ma'am," Pervez said, "Boarding Action is about seeing who is the best at conducting boardings. Why should we heave-to on their arbitrary rules? That isn't how things get done on the 16th Watch."

"Do you know what's at stake here?" Oliver asked.

"The guard's never won a Boarding Action before..." Chief began.

Oliver shook her head. "This isn't about bragging rights, Chief. The Navy is pushing to edge us out of ops on the 16th Watch. They want the Moon on a war footing. They want to be the executive element for things like quarantine runners and scraps between miners. They want Lacus Doloris again. And again. And again. And the President is listening to them."

"How is winning Boarding Action supposed to help with that?" Okonkwo asked.

"How is Boarding Action supposed to help with that, *ma'am*," Chief corrected him.

Oliver gave an exaggerated shrug. "Boarding Action is, in a development that none of us could ever have predicted, *big* TV. Twenty million viewers in the US alone last year, I think? People pay attention to it."

"So, ma'am?" Pervez accented the honorific ever so slightly with a glance at Chief.

"Come on. Don't pretend you haven't seen the viral videos of Admiral Donahugh wiping the floor with the old man."

"I don't use social media, ma'am," McGrath said. "Shit's bad for you."

"Concur," Oliver said, "but we also can't ignore it. And public affairs will probably require you to create accounts on every major service once we get closer to Boarding Action.

"Christ," McGrath muttered to himself.

"Look," Oliver went on. "Nobody knows who the hell the Coast Guard is, and those that do don't even think we're a branch of the military. The President doesn't pay attention to us because the public doesn't pay attention to us. And now our Commandant has been directly and publicly called out. A win at Boarding Action could change that perception overnight. It would give the Commandant leverage. It could help us stay at the helm of domestic ops out here. You remember Lacus Doloris. You remember what happened when they put Tom and his gunboats into the game. It turned a squabble into a massacre. You remember that boat collision just before I got out here?"

Everyone around the table nodded. "That was an accident, ma'am," Okonkwo said.

"It surely was, but it came this close to being a deployment order with us folding under 11th Fleet. I was there with the marines training in NCD/0G – they were ready for a fight. They *wanted* a fight. We came this close. And make no mistake, war with China here won't stay here. It'll come home. It'll be in the South China Sea and the Alaskan shore. If we're lucky it won't go nuclear, but I don't want to take that bet. Boarding Action isn't just about a win for the service. It could be the thing that helps us literally save the world."

"Jesus," Pervez breathed. "No pressure."

"This, right there, is the thing we have to overcome. This is what we're going to be working on."

"What?" Pervez looked up, "Pressure?"

"No, that attitude. You're bemoaning the pressure on *you*. But it's not about you. Chief–"

"So others might live," Chief said, "*others*. Not us."

Oliver blinked. "How did you know that was what I was going to ask you?"

"Ma'am, I didn't sail with you for long, but I sailed with you for long enough," Chief wasn't smiling, but Oliver could hear it in his voice.

She turned back to the crew, crossed her arms across her chest. "Forget the pressure on you. Let's start thinking of the pressure on everyone else. We're not doing this for ourselves, or even for the guard. We're doing it for the future of everyone. There isn't a human being on the Earth or out here who won't be impacted if this little cold war turns hot."

"Respectfully ma'am," Okonkwo said, "this isn't taking the pressure off."

"Not meant to," Oliver said. "The stakes are what they are. But it should help in one small way. A burden that affects all is shouldered by all, and many shoulders carry a load far more easily than one pair. What I saw out there today blew my mind. BM1, you are the greatest pilot I have ever had the privilege to observe on the sea or in space. ME3, I have never seen shooting like that in my entire life. XO didn't have a chance to get on his sights before you put one through his eye."

Ho pursed his lips. "Thanks for that."

Oliver waved his comment away, went on talking to McGrath. "And the second shot was even more breathtaking than the first. You had maybe a two inch target zone and you planted it standing on a nipple-gangway between two drifting boats. MK3, I have never seen a cut that precise and that fast. And Chief, you kept your hand on the tiller no matter what. You made sure things were run by the numbers, and when your people pushed back in a contingency, you didn't pull rank and turn into an asshole. You rolled with it, and gave your people the rope they needed to get the job done. That is what good leaders do."

"But," Chief said.

"But," Oliver agreed, "it wasn't good enough. And you all know that."

"Good enough to get the job done," Pervez said.

"The job is to win Boarding Action," Oliver replied, "and that means you run completely by the numbers. It means you hit every reg in the book, while *still* performing at the same outstanding level you demonstrated today."

"And how do you suggest we do that, ma'am?" McGrath asked.

"I'm not *suggesting* anything, ME3. I'm *telling* you that you will stop getting in one another's way, that you will come together as a team. BM1, I understand that you are the operational commander on scene, but we both know that is reserved for serious contingencies when Chief is clearly fucking up something major. And that was absolutely not the case here.

When Chief calls a shot, you are going to take it as called. Each time, every time. And Chief, you are going to put the hammer down when that doesn't happen. We're going to get all the butthurt that results from that out of the way in training so we don't have to deal with it when we go live. ME3 and MK3, you are going to be part of that, managing up when BM1 tells you to open fire on garbage pods, for Christ's sake. What the hell were you thinking?"

"I was thinking," McGrath's voice was low, "that the operational commander had given me a task."

"I'm sorry, ME3, is BM1 Pervez a Gunner's Mate?" Oliver asked.

McGrath folded his hands on the table and looked down at them. "No, ma'am."

"And are you not a Maritime Enforcement Specialist 3rd Class Petty Officer, and this team's weapons and tactics expert?"

"I am," McGrath answered.

"Then why on earth are you deferring to a fire decision from a woman whose expertise is flying small boats? Especially when Chief expressed reservations?"

McGrath kept his eyes down and didn't answer.

"MK3, are you ever going to stand up for yourself? Or are you content to take BM1's sniping all day long? Chief clearly isn't wading in there to put the kibosch on that shit, were you waiting for me to do it?"

"Now hold on, ma'am–" Chief began.

"No, you hold on," Oliver interrupted him. "Getting out of the way of your people is a fine leadership skill and I meant it when I commended you for it. But you wouldn't *have* to be getting out of the way if you hadn't let things get away from you. You've been in longer than any of us. You know damn well that you aren't on this crew to be friends with anyone.

"Why do you think I have all of us bunking up together? Do you think it's because I like it? Because I think it somehow builds character?

No. It's because from the second I met you all together I knew that this was going to be the heart of the problem. I've got four top-of-the-line thoroughbreds here, and all of you are trying to run out front. But that's not how we win this thing, people. We cross the finish line *together*, all at the same time, or not at all."

The silence as she finished was total. She looked at each of the crew, but their eyes were fixed firmly down at their hands, their laps, anywhere but at her. Oliver let the silence drag out, swallowing to stop herself from babbling to fill it. She'd made her point. It would either be enough, or it wouldn't.

At last, Chief cleared his throat, and all eyes snapped to him.

"Yes, Chief?" Oliver asked. "You want to tell me what you think?"

"I think," Chief stood, picking up his cover from where he'd left it on the table, "that maybe it's time for me to retire. By your leave ma'am?" He jerked his head toward the hatch leading back into the facility.

Oliver nodded, letting him go. She'd pushed them all far enough for one day.

CHAPTER 9

It can be tempting to run in guns-blazing when you see a problem. Leaders, by their very nature, tend to be proactive personalities that want to address problems quickly. But the ability to sit with discomfort can be one of the most important skills a leader can develop. Developing strong teams means accepting their faults, and understanding that sometimes people change slowly. Relentless, gradual pressure is often more effective than bringing the hammer down. Judging when to do which, of course, is the hard part.

HARVARD LEADERSHIP CERTIFICATE COURSE MANUAL
CHAPTER 3. MANAGING DYSFUNCTIONAL TEAMS

"This," Oliver splashed the Widow Jane into the tumbler, sloshing a tiny bit over the side, "is completely fucked."

"Don't let it get to you." Ho crossed his arms over his narrow chest and leaned against the wardrobe. After the tension of the meeting, Oliver had decided to let the contubernium pretense drop for a moment, and give the crew some space while she and Ho conferred in her stateroom.

"It is *not* getting to me," Oliver groused, paused. "Why do you think it's getting to me? Because I cursed? I curse all the time."

"Because you spilled on your desk." Ho gestured to the tiny dots of bourbon still glinting from the reflective plastic surface. "You never spill, and if by some miracle you do, you sure as hell don't let it sit there."

Oliver stared at the glass. "Holy shit. You're right. Am I drinking too much?"

Ho smiled. "I won't let you fall, boss. You've uprooted your whole life and carted your ass all the way to the Moon to take over a training mission in the hopes that it'll have the welcome side-effect of preventing the first lunar war. You're entitled to a drink now and then."

"Fuck," Oliver pushed the tumbler away, then fetched it back. "Keep an eye on me, Wen."

"Always, boss."

"Chief walking out... I'll admit that threw me."

Ho nodded. "Me too."

"But we have got to fix this shit. I have seen this problem a hundred times before when I was running TRACEN Yorktown. And it's the worst kind of problem. It's easy when you're just dealing with fuckups. They know they're fuckups. And every fuckup wants to do better, deep down. But virtuosos are the fucking worst, Wen. They all think they're God's gift to the service and that if things would just run their way... you know? Problem children, individually brilliant, unable to get out of their own way. And *of course* that's the situation here. It couldn't possibly be *easy*, now could it?"

Ho laughed. "You'll figure it out, boss."

"You know, it was like this with Adam when he was little. Alice developed... She wasn't a kid genius. She just wanted to make Tom and I happy. Tom, mostly. But Adam, that kid was so much *smarter* than anyone around him. By the time he was eight I couldn't help him with his math homework anymore, and I'm an astronaut. Sort of."

"It's post SpaceX, boss. Everyone's an astronaut."

Oliver took a sip of the whiskey and pointed a finger at him over the top of the glass. "Don't you fucking ruin this for me, Wen."

"So, what did you do with Adam? I assume he refused to obey you?"

"Christ, everything was a negotiation. From bedtime to every bite of food. But I somehow managed to raise that boy, and turn him into a…"

"A tech baron who never calls his mom."

"At least he's not selling his ass for drugs."

"Yet."

The word caught Oliver mid-sip and she almost spit the liquor out as the laughter bubbled up her throat. "Gah! That burns, Wen. I am racking my brain trying to remember how I did it, but it was so long ago it's like it happened to someone else. My kids are all grown up, but yours are still little."

"They are," Ho said, "and they're both like Adam was."

"How do you handle them?"

Ho was quiet for a moment. "Well, I'd caution you against treating skilled adults like kids, but I tell them to play nice and when they don't, I punish them. I take away privileges, or I make them do extra chores."

"Incentive training."

"Something like that, yeah."

"Here's the problem," she gestured at him with her tumbler, "it's that it's an exercise. These are real world coasties, they live for the *job*, Wen."

Ho thought about it for a moment, then nodded. "Yeah, I can see that."

Oliver blinked. "You're agreeing with me? Who are you and what have you done with Wen Ho?"

"Look, boss, running TRACEN Yorktown was a dream gig for me. I loved being there, but I wasn't blind to what it was doing to you. I watched you… wither, even as you ran the hell out of that place."

"You said I produced the best crop of boarding teams the guard has ever seen."

"And I meant it. You absolutely did, but it cost you. You're a natural-born leader and an outstanding teacher, boss, but you're also an *operator* first and foremost. You joined up to actually do the job. Do it in the

worst conditions on the roughest shifts with the hardest cases life had
to throw at you. That's what made you amazing. Ironically, I think it's
what made you a great teacher, too."

Oliver felt her cheeks flush at the praise. "Thanks."

"The job, the *real* job of getting out on the water and saving lives is
what made you great, ma'am. But it's also what made you *motivated*.
And after that was gone…"

He looked embarrassed as he trailed off.

"Ah, it's OK, Wen," Oliver said, "you can say it. After I was no
longer in the field, it was Tom's ghost that kept me going. I worked
hard to avoid facing that he was gone, and I also worked hard because
the work felt like I was keeping him alive somehow. Because it was a
shred of the life we'd had together."

"Not just that, boss. You were bereft. Adam drifted away, and then
– bam. Alice to the Moon. That was the real blow. I think a part of you
was always hoping you'd find a way to get back to her."

"Or that she'd strike it rich and come back to me. I didn't have
anyone to… take care of except my students. And that wasn't enough.
Yeah, Alice was a big piece. And also… because I just didn't know what
else to do."

"I'd say that's about right," Ho said. "But now you do know what
else to do. You're here to do it."

"We have to get them on the job, Wen. The *real* job."

Ho blinked. "We're supposed to be prepping them for a game show."

But as soon as she said the words, Oliver felt the flush creeping up
the back of her neck, burning at the base of her skull with a certainty
she knew from experience was useless to resist. This was the right call,
she knew it in her bones. "Christ, I need to take my own advice. I
said it in my change-of-command speech, Wen. We're all hurting over
Lacus Doloris. We get past that by doing the *job*, by remembering why
we signed up to do it in the first place. No exercise, no matter how

significant, is going to convey that. These people aren't going to gel in a simulator. They have to be running ops."

Ho was silent.

"You think I'm wrong?"

"It doesn't matter what I think," Ho said, "Admiral Allen isn't going to like that. You have less than two months to train this crew for a contest and you're proposing... not training them."

"No," Oliver said. "I'm proposing training them *differently*. I'm proposing training them *correctly*. Wen, I nearly died locked behind that desk in TRACEN. I nearly wasted away. That's what we're doing to these people here. There isn't anything wrong with their skill. We just saw that firsthand. The problem is their morale. This is how we fix it. I know it is."

Ho was silent for a long time, and when he finally opened his mouth to answer, the door chime sounded. Ho went to get it, stepping aside to admit Chief. "Ma'am, I know you've got your contubernium thing, but I was hoping we could have a word, just the two of us."

Oliver exchanged glances with Ho, then nodded. "Sure thing, Chief. Wen, I'll see you in a bit."

Ho nodded and stepped out, closing the door behind him.

"I just wanted to apologize, ma'am," Chief said, "for earlier. I got upset, and I shouldn't have."

"We all get hot from time to time, Chief. I pushed you all pretty hard there, and I'm not surprised it ruffled some feathers. But I appreciate you coming around to let me know."

"That's kind of you, ma'am. I just... Well, I wanted to let you know that as the senior NCO on the team, I feel like their performance is my responsibility. So that whole shitshow was my fault, and I want you to know I'm going to be working doubletime to get it fixed."

Oliver waved the statement away. "This team is going to rise or fall *together*. It's all of our responsibility, and that includes me, too. And this is nothing that we can't get fixed. I appreciate the accountability, Chief, but you're not responsible. Well, not any more than any of us are."

She expected him to turn and go at that, but he only stood, looking at his feet. "Respectfully, ma'am, that's not how I feel. And I wanted to say that to you... that I do feel responsible."

The realization rose suddenly in her gut. "You're not talking about the team."

Chief shrugged. "I just wanted to say... I never got to say to your face, with just the two of us, that I'm sorry."

Oliver was suddenly two people. One wanted to burst into tears and hug this hard-bitten man who was standing before her wringing his hands like a schoolboy. The other part wanted to smack him. This was over and done, she had made it clear to all of them again and again and again... *Easy there, Widow Jane. You're not the only one who lost Tom, remember that.*

She took a moment to gather her thoughts, leaned across her desk, propping herself up on her fists. "Chief, I am only saying this one more time. You are *not* responsible. This self-indulgence isn't helping anyone. Not me, not you, and certainly not Tom, Kariawasm, or Flecha. And you are also *not* responsible for how this whole team performs. On a mission, operational rank trumps organizational rank. And on a small boat, the coxs'un is king."

She fought a moment of panic as she finished. Had she pushed him too hard again? Should she have been gentler? *If he really does retire what am I going to do? I can't replace him with another NCO this crew doesn't know at this stage. We'll be sunk.* She watched Chief's face, utterly without guile, the emotions plain. Pride and grief warred with duty across his heavy brows, his hard mouth. At long last, Oliver could see his chin coming up, his eyes focusing as duty won out.

"You're right, ma'am, but it's the coxs'un that's the problem," he said. "Pervez is out of control. When it was Kariawasm, we were a well-oiled machine, but after Doloris…" he looked stricken, "…it just isn't the same. I'm not sure she has the right temperament to do this."

Oliver swallowed her anger and disappointment. *You're better than this, Chief.* "I believe there's nothing wrong with Pervez that, working together, we can't fix. I need you to believe that, too."

Chief sighed, nodded. "I hope you're right."

"I am right. Look, Pervez isn't Kariawasm, and she never will be. It's time we stopped asking everyone to labor under the shadow of the dead. I think we should upgrade boats to the rhino, Chief. I think the symbolism of that move is important."

Chief's eyes snapped up, trembling. He took a long, deep breath before he answered.

"Ma'am, with respect, I don't think it's a good call."

"You've made that clear, Chief, but rhino is a technically better boat."

"Not so much better that it's worth putting Pervez out of her element."

"Oh, horseshit, Chief. You know as well as I do that Pervez is good enough that she'd fly the hell out of a tin can with only three days to qualify on it if you asked her to. This is about honoring the dead for you. And I'm not proposing we don't do that, I'm just saying we don't have to labor in their shadow. I think that's part of Pervez's problem, trying to live up to that expectation."

"Please, ma'am," Chief said, "don't ask us to do this. It matters to this crew."

"Matters to this crew or matters to you, Chief?" Oliver asked.

Chief shook his head. "You heard Pervez's objections. Look, ma'am, it's your ship. If you order me to mothball the longhorn and put us in a rhino, then that's what I'll do. Are those your orders?"

He looked up, and Oliver could see the wash of grief and anger behind his eyes. She had seen the same look when he'd gotten up from the table just a little while ago. When he'd threatened to retire. *Slow is smooth, smooth is fast.* It was hard to repeat those words to herself, to feel like they mattered when the clock was ticking away toward Boarding Action, but they had never failed her before.

"No, Chief," she said finally. "We'll stay in the longhorn for now."

Oliver had the flag mess converted for her contubernium – the small round table reserved for her and her staff replaced by a long rectangular one big enough to accommodate the whole team. She pointedly made sure that no chairs were placed at either end, and that those ends were marked with black and yellow – CRIME SCENE – DO NOT CROSS tape she had Ho requisition from the logs officer. The crowd in the mess were polite enough not to stare directly, but she caught the sidelong glances and could overhear the whispered conversations. *That's OK, let them talk. I was sent here to win this, and the whole command has to be on board with that.*

She was already at the table as the crew arrived, filled their trays and sat silently. Okonkwo smiled at her and gave her a polite dip of his head. Chief smiled as well, but made no attempt at conversation. McGrath was blank-faced as always, and Pervez sullen and petulant. Oliver almost started eating before she noticed Okonkwo bowing his head in prayer. Pervez rolled her eyes and was about to lift her fork to her mouth when a glare from Oliver caught her up short. She set it down and looked at the table until he was finished.

"How's everyone doing?" Oliver asked as they set to work on their food. "Anything interesting happen on watch duty?"

"No, ma'am," they all answered in unison, not looking up.

"That's surprising," Oliver said. "We had at least one SAR alarm every day in Yorktown, and that's in the middle of nowhere, relatively-speaking."

"Yorktown's not nowhere," Ho offered. *He's trying, at least.*

"In terms of shipping traffic it is, compared to say, New York or Baltimore. Surely we have more traffic out here so close to the Chinese EEZ."

Heads remained down, forks continued moving. Silence.

Oliver bit back her frustration and crossed her arms over her chest. "All right. Out with it."

That brought the heads up, but did not get mouths moving.

"What's going on, guys?" Oliver asked. "We had a bad day. Teams have bad days."

"I think you're right, ma'am," Pervez said, her tone just barely respectful, "maybe we've 'lost touch with the mission.' Maybe we need to 'honor our lost loved ones.'"

Alice had briefly gone through what Tom had called 'her independent phase' when she was sixteen. She'd tried sassing Oliver then a few times, with limited success, until Oliver had finally dropped the hammer and put a stop to it. Pervez sounded so much like the adolescent Alice that Oliver had to swallow the urge to laugh.

Still, she couldn't allow even borderline insubordination. *Don't jump down her throat. That isn't going to work with her. You want to bring her around, you're going to have to meet her where she is. She doesn't get how important this training is. She's a racehorse set to pulling kids in a wagon. She wants to be out in the world doing the real thing.*

Her conversation with Ho pricked at the back of her mind. *They don't understand why this is important. They don't understand why I'm leaning on them. Why it matters. I have to get them back doing the job.* She thought of Ho's warning that Admiral Allen wouldn't like her plan. *Fuck it, he's not the one who has to make sure they win Boarding Action.*

Oliver relaxed her posture with an effort, leaned back in her chair, made a great show of thinking about Pervez' comment. The crew sat around the table, forks frozen half way to their mouths, waiting for her reaction. Oliver let the moment drag out, then brightened, tapping her chin. "You know what? You're right, Petty Officer Pervez. You're absolutely, one thousand percent right."

Whatever Pervez had expected, it surely wasn't this. "I am?"

"She is?" Chief echoed, his eyebrows doing their damnedest to meet in the center of his forehead.

"Yes. Pervez has identified the problem perfectly; that is you've lost touch with the mission, just like you said. In a simulator, training for a contest, the stakes aren't high enough. You need to be out there doing the real thing."

"But it's Boarding Action, ma'am," Okonkwo said, "The reputation of our service is at stake. There's millions of people watching on TV. That's pretty high stakes."

"Look, if we're going to win this thing, we're going to win it because we are the absolute best at what we do, stem to stern. Training is only going to take us so far, we have to get it right each and every time. The regs, the operational details, the results. It all has to be absolutely on point. And that means we have to be able to react to the unpredictable environment of real operations. So, Pervez is right. We need to get back in touch with the mission. The *real* mission. We're going to get good at this thing by doing the job, every day. We're going to run radio calls starting now."

"The stakes are higher running radio calls?" Pervez asked in disbelief.

"You're goddamn right they are," Oliver answered. "Radio calls mean *lives*. You fuck up at Boarding Action and we grit our teeth and say 'we'll get 'em next year.' You fuck up on a radio call and someone dies. So, yes, Petty Officer Pervez, you are absolutely right. I haven't been taking my own advice and I mean to start, effective immediately."

She pushed back from the table. "If you'll excuse me."

"Where are you going?" Okonkwo asked.

"To talk to the ops boss," Oliver said. "I want SAR-1 on alert status starting now. Finish up your chow and start gear checks. I'll meet you in the ready room."

She turned and walked out, conscious first of the heads of her own crew, and then those of the entire DFAC swiveling to track her movement. She heard another chair scrape back and knew it was Ho even before her XO fell into step beside her as she exited the DFAC and paced down the hall toward the airlock that would connect them to the ladderwell leading up to the ops floor. Out of tradition, grit, or a desire to sympathize with operational units, the ops section was never in spin gravity, and Oliver was steeling herself for the stomach-lurching shift when Ho finally spoke. "So," he sounded worried, "we're really doing this. You know this isn't just a normal Boarding Action. You know what's at stake here—"

"I know that," she cut him off. "Don't think I'd forget that for a minute. I know this is important and I know why they asked me to do this. And I'm doing it, OK?"

"OK," Ho breathed as the airlock cycled and Oliver felt her stomach rise. She pushed off, letting the drifting sensation take her, launching herself up the ladderwell, tapping the rungs only when she felt her momentum begin to spend itself, climbing with her eyes closed as if she were surfacing from the bottom of some hidden water.

The ops boss simply nodded as she relayed her orders. A magnetized board was bolted to the bulkhead just to the left of the control tower's massive quartz-glass windows. He went immediately to what looked to Oliver like a bewildering array of magnets on a board beside it, and instantly selected one in the shape of a longhorn that read "SAR-1." Oliver watched in frank awe. If she'd had an hour to dig through all of the magnets, she'd never have found it.

He then turned and slapped the magnet in the box labeled "ALERT STATUS," turned to her and said, "Let me know when your people are ready to launch, ma'am."

"They're ready now," she said with a conviction she didn't feel. *Please don't make a liar out of me.*

When she reached the bottom of the ladderwell, however, Ho plucked at her elbow, glancing down at the screen on his wrist. "Uh, boss. You've got a call."

"Is it Alice? I'll talk to her after…"

Ho looked up. "It's ops."

"Ops?" She turned back to the ladderwell. "He could have just come down and got me."

"No. Big ops. Admiral Allen."

Oliver blinked. "Oh."

"I'll send it to your stateroom," Ho said, tapping at his wrist. "You want me there?"

"Thanks, but no. Go make sure the crew is hopping to. I'm also going to chat with him about Fullweiler. See if I can't get some movement there."

"Could be a long call," Ho said.

"Not if I have anything to do with it," Oliver smiled and headed for her door.

She paused as it shut behind her, taking in the view through the massive window looking out over the Sea of Rains. The sight of the empty blackness cooled her, and she realized she'd been running hot, consumed with worry and almost never alone since the moment Elias had walked into the BMF at Yorktown. She took a second to draw in a breath, let it out. She looked at her reflection in the quartz-glass – the strong line of her jaw, her broad shoulders and straight spine. The silver thread of her admiral's stars glinted from her lapels. *This is a rough ride, for sure. But you are on the back of this horse and your hands are on the reins.*

She nodded to her reflection, and picked up the receiver. "SPACETACLET actual."

"Jane, hope I didn't catch you at a bad time." Allen's voice clearly indicated that he didn't give a flying fuck when he'd caught her.

"No, sir. Just about to head to the ready room for the next phase of SAR-1's training."

"That's what I'm calling about. I've got your control logs here and I see the team's been assigned to duty crew."

"Wow, sir. That's... fast."

Allen didn't sound amused. "Jane, I run ops for this service. I see the ops control data from every operational command in the fleet."

And you have time to consider them all? Oliver didn't ask. Maybe she'd just gotten lucky, or maybe Allen had singled her out for special scrutiny. It didn't matter either way.

"OK, sir. Well, yes. I'm going to have SAR-1 run radio calls for now."

"Out of the simulator."

"Yes, sir."

"Out of training."

"Sir, I'd argue this is the most effective training they could possibly be doing."

Allen sighed, and Oliver could hear the dull scrape of him rubbing a hand across the stubble of his head. "Jane, you were sent to Pico to prep this team to win Boarding Action. That's literally the reason you're there."

"Yes, sir. And that's exactly what I'm doing."

"How does *not* training your crew for the upcoming contest prepare them to win the upcoming contest?"

"SAR-1 doesn't have a skill problem, sir. They've got a morale problem. Individually, they are clearly the most competent operators I've seen possibly in my entire career. But they aren't gelling as a team because they are still messed up over Lacus Doloris. These are hard operators, sir. These are people who joined the guard to do the job, and we have to let them do it and do it *together*, or they are never going to come together as a cohesive unit with the capacity to win this thing. You were there when I made my speech, sir. I meant it. We have to recommit to our jobs if we're ever going to get past Lacus Doloris. We have to remember why we're here. And we're not here to win a goddamn game show, no matter how high the stakes might be this particular time around."

"Jane, this doesn't make sense."

"No, sir. It's *counterintuitive*, but it makes absolute and perfect sense. You sent me out here to do a job, and with respect you now have to get the hell out of my way and let me do it. It's my call to make, and it's the right call. I've seen them train, I've run a ops evolution with them. I know what's happening here and I know how to fix it."

"I could order you to rewrite that training plan, damnit."

"No, sir. But you can send me back to Earth and find someone else to do the job your way if you want. I will submit my resignation if that's what you're asking for. No harm, no foul." The words made her stomach churn. If Allen took her up on it and actually sent her back to Earth... Her daughter's face filled her mind, accompanied by Ho's words – *she seems adrift, ma'am.*

Allen was quiet for a long time. "Jesus Christ, Jane. You've got my balls in a vise here. You know damn well I don't have time to find someone else to finish this thing."

Oliver breathed an internal sigh of relief. "Do you expect me to feel bad about that, sir? You brought me out here to do this my way, and that means you either trust my judgment or you don't. If you do, then I'll get back to my ready room and get this team moving on radio calls. If not, you have my resignation, and you have whomever replaces me put them back in the simulator. But I can promise you this: if they stay in a simulated environment, they will lose this thing. We all know MARSOC16 is going to go all the way again this year, and the reason they're going to do that is not because they outmatch SAR-1 in any individual skill. McGrath is every bit as good a gunner as Abadi, and Pervez could fly rings around Fujimori in a small boat. But the marines *love* each other. They *trust* each other. And *that* is why they're winning out there, sir. I've got less than two months to build that same family here. And it's only going to get built one way."

Allen was quiet again for a long time. "You'd better be right."

Oliver shrugged before remembering that Allen was on the other end of a phone line and couldn't see her. "Either I am or I'm not. We won't have to wait long to find out either way."

"OK, well..."

"One more thing, sir, so long as I have you on the line."

She could almost hear Allen blinking in shock at the other end. "You are about to ask me for something...?"

"Sure am, sir. If that's OK."

"I can't believe this," Allen said. "It's like I work for you."

Oliver laughed. "It's Fullweiler, sir."

"Full... Captain Fullweiler?"

"Yes, sir. The training pipeline at OTRACEN is poisoned. It's lousy with marines and worse, Marine Corps culture. They are using our school to turn out shooters prepped and ready for close-combat missions, not for SAR runs. That's a systemic, deckplate level problem, and it needs to be fixed."

"What does this have to do with Fullweiler?"

"It's his ship, sir. And he's running it into the ground. He needs to be relieved. You saw how he reacted to that collision."

"I know, Jane, but he obeyed orders. It's hardly cause for such a drastic step. Let me guess, you have a specific replacement in mind?"

"No, sir, I do not. The only person I'd trust with the job apart from myself is Commander Ho, and he's busy right now. But it does need to be an actual coastie and not a wannabe marine. Someone who is onboard with the old man's vision for what we're trying to do out here."

Allen took a shuddering breath, and still failed to keep the anger out of his voice. "You are *way* out of your lane here, Jane. You are already trying my patience with your training methods, and now you want jurisdiction over our training pipeline which, you will recall, Captain Elias strenuously advised you *not* to enter. I said earlier in this conversation that you were sent to Pico for *one* reason, and that is to make sure SAR-1 goes the distance and–"

"No, sir. I was sent to Pico to help the old man in a broader effort to stop the Navy from dragging us into a war. Boarding Action is just a piece of that. Our training pipeline has *cancer*, sir. And in my experience, unless you cut cancer out, it spreads."

"Jane, that is *enough*. You are dangerously close to making me question your judgment to the point where I take you up on your offer of resignation and damn the consequences. You've said your piece and I've heard it and we are done with this conversation. Is that clear?"

She swallowed her anger with an effort. "Crystal clear, sir. Thank you for hearing me out."

"Ops out," Allen said, and cut the call.

Oliver sat for a long moment looking out the window, willing the sight of her reflection to instill some of the confidence back into her, but it was as if it were a resource she had spent to the last on that phone call. The reflection that had looked so competent before seemed old now, drained, the shoulders hunched. The tiniest hint of a paunch, that Jane had fought so hard to keep off with such success so late in her life was finally succumbing to the hints of age, beginning to show through the tightness of her uniform. She knew the worst thing a commander could do was waffle in the middle of a decision, but it was also true that the call had rattled her. Allen had at least as much experience as her. His opinion wasn't to be dismissed lightly. *No,* she thought firmly. *He's not here with these people. He's not seeing what I see.*

The thought was followed by another, which made her heart jerk in her chest. *If Tom were here, I could run it by him. He would have been the sounding board for my instincts.* Alice had good judgment, and so did Ho, but Ho was a subordinate and Alice had no military experience. Tom had always been the perfect person to talk these things through. She saw the family picture in her peripheral vision, deliberately avoided looking at it. She didn't need that right now. Not when she had to walk back into the ready room and face her team.

By the time she got back down to the ready room, she was relieved to see that the crew hadn't made a liar out of her after all. They were already in their bunny suits, their hardshells unpacked and arrayed on the floor before them to make them quicker to don when the alarm sounded.

Ho glanced up at her. "How'd it go?"

Oliver did her best to look unconcerned. "Well enough. We're good. I take it I didn't miss an alarm?"

"Not yet, ma'am," Okonkwo said. She heard the excitement in his voice and felt her confidence perk up a little.

"Good. You all ready to save some lives?" she asked.

"Yes, ma'am," the team answered in one voice, and she liked the look she saw on their faces. There was some excitement in those eyes as they checked over their gear again. *This was the right move, no matter how pissed off Allen is. This is what they needed.*

Oliver and Ho went to their own lockers, hurriedly donning their underlayers and bunny-suits, moving through gear checks to make sure they were ready, all the time casting nervous glances over their shoulders at the red klaxon attached to the ready room's ceiling, the monitor beneath, where they'd watched the video of the MARSOC16 team's winning evolution, now reeling out alarm calls.

She stared at it now that she was ready, feeling the adrenaline fade as the alarms scrolled by and were assigned to closer boats, those already out on patrol. After fifteen minutes, she heard the dull scraping of a chair as Ho took a seat. *Well, what did you expect? That something would blow up immediately?* She realized with a start that she did. *You've been in the business long enough to know that's not how this works.*

They were well staffed with a lot of boats on regular patrol, but surely something would exceed the usual capability eventually and they'd get scrambled. After another few minutes Oliver began to feel ridiculous, and took her seat at the same broad plastic table as Ho, busying herself with the training terminal there.

By the time the team had returned from the noon meal, the mood had stabilized, but SAR-1 was quiet. Chief kept them as busy as he could with desk-bound coursework, doing PQS sign-offs for boat specs, firearms handling, and space-borne hazards to navigation. The long lunar day dragged on, the sun bright enough outside to make them squint even against the glass' glare dampeners. The thermal collector-shields and solar panels spread over every available surface made the view below them look like glinting lake.

It had dragged on toward the evening meal when Chief finally sat down beside her. "Ma'am, could I have a wo... contubernium, sorry."

"You got it, Chief. What's up?"

"Ma'am, we're just starting the lunar day on this side of the Moon. It's got to be around 250 degrees out there."

"So? We live in an age of modern marvels. We can tackle that heat."

"Sure, but tackling that heat means burning more fuel and taking on more risk. It means traffic is going to be way down."

Oliver glanced back out the window. In the distance, she could still make out the occasional blinking of a vessel's running light, the pale-blue flare of thrusters firing. There was traffic out there. And where there was traffic, there would be an alarm. "People are out there."

"I know it, ma'am. I just... I wonder if we're going to learn anything by sitting here and waiting for the SAR alarm to sound. We don't want to waste time."

"We're not wasting time. We're training. We're learning patience. We're are learning to adapt to the mission, rather than the other way around. Right now, the mission means sitting around waiting for the flag to go up."

Chief cast a glance over his shoulder at the rest of the crew, who studiously avoided eye contact, heads bent on their training terminals. "OK, ma'am. If you say so."

"I do say so, but I appreciate your counsel regardless."

She turned back to the glass, satisfied, her own argument mollifying the churning worry in her stomach, but not by much.

When their next shift dragged on without an alarm, Chief kept his peace. Oliver guessed he knew he didn't have to say anything, and he was right. Her stomach was a clenched fist, her bolt of inspiration seemed a fool move. *You don't know enough about conditions out here. Maybe you should renege and get back in the simulator.* She'd lose face with the crew, and it would feed the rumor mill on post, but maybe it was for the best. But the spike of the idea remained firmly lodged. The team was not gelling in a training environment. The reality of radio calls and contested boardings had always worked in the past. No, she would trust her gut. Operations on Earth's blue water could not be so different than those on the 16th Watch. People were people, wherever they were.

She bit down on the discomfort, the sensation of the ticking clock, counting away the precious hours until Boarding Action was upon them.

The crew was practicing drawing and firing sidearms against a simulation screen when Oliver finally couldn't stand the boredom any longer. "You know Boarding Action is going to come with some fame," she said. "Bright lights, cameras. Magazine interviews. You psyched for that?"

The crew looked over at her, blinking.

"It's not a trap, guys," Oliver said. "I'm genuinely curious. I'm looking forward to a chance to tell the cameras about the guard and what we do. Counter some of the Navy's messaging."

The four of them were quiet for a bit, then to Oliver's surprise it was McGrath who cleared his throat. "Flecha had… has a husband, ma'am," he said. "Kariawasm was waiting for his parents to set up a marriage."

"Fuck that," Pervez said. "My mom wanted to do that for me, I told her to pound sand."

"Yeah, well," McGrath said, "Kariaswasm was into it. He wasn't like you."

"You got that right," Pervez said.

McGrath didn't take the bait. Looked at Oliver instead. "I'm really looking forward to telling the world about Flecha and Kariawasm, ma'am. Telling what they did and how they died. Telling everyone that we're out there for them. And I always pictured maybe Flecha's guy would see that. That would be pretty cool."

"That would be outstanding," Chief said.

"It certainly would," Oliver said. "How about you, Chief?"

"Oh, my family's back on Earth, ma'am. Kid's in college now. But she was over her old man a long time ago. I'm with McGrath. I want the world to know about our dead. Your husband, too, ma'am. I want to shine the spotlight on them."

"That's noble, Chief."

"Honestly," Pervez said, "I bet they're sick of the spotlight."

Chief turned an angry eye on Pervez, but she only straightened under his gaze. "They're heroes," he said.

"With all due respect, Chief, from everything you've told me, that's the *last* thing either of them would ever have wanted to be called."

Oliver had to stifle a laugh. *She's absolutely correct.*

Chief looked crestfallen, and Oliver could tell he knew Pervez was right. "It's different when… you die."

"I dunno," Pervez said. "I think it's like boss said when she came on board. It's who's alive that matters. I've got two little girls on Earth with my *ammi*. They'll be watching. I want them to see their *ammi* kick a hole in the world. Know that I left it wide open for them. If it turns into sponsorships or a sweet gig when I get out that I can use to pay for their college? I'll take it. But mostly I want them to know that they can win. You gonna tell me that Kariawasm and Flecha wouldn't have wanted that?"

Chief looked at his lap and said nothing, but Oliver could see the vein twitching at his temple.

"What about you, Okonkwo?" Oliver asked.

The engineer looked so panicked by the question that Oliver had to resist the strong temptation to let him off the hook, but she pushed it away and waited silently. At last he sighed, glanced over at Chief. "Of course I want to do it for the ones we lost, like McGrath said."

"Of course," Oliver said, "but you don't have any plans for after? Big thing like this could make some changes in your life."

Okonkwo shrugged, was quiet for so long that Oliver began to wonder if maybe he wasn't going to speak at all. "There's my *nne nne*. She raised me. She wanted me to become a priest. She 'bout killed me when I joined up here. I'm still not sure she understands what I do. Even if we lose, I wouldn't mind her seeing it. Just so she could understand."

"Understand what?" Oliver asked.

Okonkwo shrugged again. "Why it's worth it. Why once I got to do this, I could never be happy as a priest. I'm sorry those people died," Okonkwo continued speaking to Oliver, but his eyes were on Chief, "but in a way I'm happy for them. This is the greatest job in the world. If you have to go, what better way than this?"

CHAPTER 10

The President backed off a statement last Tuesday that he was considering using an executive order to limit the space elevator to military transport only for a period of five years. The move is widely seen as a reaction to China's completion of a second space elevator dedicated entirely to military transport. While succumbing to the backlash which included harsh criticism from tech titans including Apple, Tesla and IBM, the President warned the move would give China a significant military advantage on the Moon. "The ability to move troops and materiel into low-Earth orbit on a continual basis will put the US position on the lunar surface at risk long term, and weaken our position in ongoing negotiations to amend the 1967 Outer Space Treaty." Russia announced Thursday they are nearing completion of their first space elevator, though they have denied charges by both the US and the EU that it is primarily intended to move military equipment into low-Earth orbit with the ultimate goal of increasing their presence on the Moon.

PRESIDENT BACKS OFF MILITARY GRAB OF
SPACE ELEVATOR, ASSOCIATED PRESS

Alice called that night. "Hey, mom! Wanted to check in. Lunar day can be rough on people who aren't used to it."

"Please," Oliver snorted, "I did port security in Um Qasr. It was like 114 in the shade."

"Mom. It's over 250 outside."

"Same thing."

"That is not the same thing. That is 136 degrees of difference."

"I didn't realize my daughter was a math teacher."

"And I didn't realize my mom can't do simple subtraction."

"Not only does it not bother me, but I'm going to be getting out in it. I've got the team on radio calls."

"The *team,* mom."

"I am part of the team. I am leading from the front. I'm riding with them."

"You are? But you're an admiral."

"I am, and my primary responsibility is getting these people ready. Running radio calls is going to do that."

Alice didn't answer for so long that Oliver wondered if there was some problem with the line.

Maybe the extreme heat had more of an impact than she had thought. "Honey? You still there?"

"I dunno," Alice said, "you're a big girl, mom. I don't want to tell you what to do."

"Hell, Alice. You're a big girl, too. If you've got something to say, just come out and say it."

"You know I love you, but are you sure this isn't you just wanting to get back out there? Look, I know I went a little crazy when dad died. This worries me. What if you wind up mixing it up out there? You could get hurt."

"I'm with the best we have, honey," Oliver said, and immediately regretted the words. *Being with the best we have didn't help Tom.* She pushed the thought away. "Your old mom still has a few tricks up her sleeve."

"I know, and part of my motives are selfish. I'm really looking forward to you getting done and coming out here. I don't want you getting hurt… I'm sorry, it's selfish."

But Oliver's heart was revving at the naked need she heard in her daughter's voice. "Not selfish at all, honey. I'll be OK, and I'll be with you before you know it."

"I'd been thinking of maybe moving my stake to Lacus Odii. Some of my friends say the distribution line is cheaper if you're shipping from there."

"Honey," Oliver interrupted, "do you know what Lacus Odii means?"

Oliver could almost hear Alice roll her eyes on the other end of the line. "Lake of hate. I know, mom. I don't control the name. I assure you there's nothing hateful about it. It's one of the nicest stretches on the Moon. You should see how the soil glitters when it catches the starlight."

"Won't it be super expensive to move your stake?"

"Yeah, it will. But maybe it'll be worth it? I just need to sit down and crunch the numbers. I'm not... I'm not great with that kind of stuff."

"Not such a math teacher now, are you?"

"Mom, please don't."

"Just don't make any moves until I can get out there. This is one short tour. It won't be long."

"I won't mom. Just make sure you're doing this to get the team ready," Alice said, "and not being driven to it by..."

"By what?"

"By baggage. By demons. By dad dying, and you retiring and me breaking up with Matt and moving out here to start over. By Adam being a distant asshole. By being new to outer space. By... by everything, mom. I just want you to move deliberately."

Oliver felt her throat swell. *She's worried about you.* When you were in command as long as Oliver had been, it was easy to forget that people could still do that. "Thank you, sweetheart. I am. I promise you that I am."

But she thought about it after they said their goodbyes, and wondered if she was telling the truth.

When the alarm did finally sound, they were just walking into the ready room after the morning meal, their gear all safely stowed in their lockers. "*PIV reported at LMGRS coords in plotter. I say again PIV reported. SAR-1 launch.*"

Person-in-vacuum. The team exchanged a brief look before racing to the lockers, tearing out their gear, and throwing it on. "Slow is smooth, smooth is fast," Chief reminded them. "We're not going to help anyone if we go off half-cocked and get ourselves hurt. Take your time with your gear and boat checks."

In ten minutes, they were ready to go, and radioed their ops normal and green GAR status to the watchstander even as they were firing the longhorn's belly-thrusters and rising up into the lunar day.

The surface blazed with sunlight, the regolith gleaming. Earth was a glowing green-blue wedge off their port quarter, shining nearly as bright as a star. The longhorn's glass and their hardshell visors were all fully smoked, and Oliver still found herself squinting as Pervez ducked the boat's nose and got them moving to the plotter coordinates as fast as she could. "Easy, BM1," Chief cautioned.

"They're only calling PIV if there's a suit integrity issue, Chief," Pervez said, giving the aft thrusters a long burn. "We already lost ten minutes getting out the door."

"Got it," Chief said, "and we'll all have suit integrity issues if we crash into another vessel or hit a meteoroid too hot. I gave the same warning to your predecessor a hundred times, and it was always for a good reason. I'm not asking you to deploy sails. Just take her easy."

Oliver could hear the sucking sound over the radio as Pervez bit her lip, but she didn't add any more thrust.

Then the radio call's source came into view and Pervez cursed, firing their bow thrusters and slowing them to a drift. Oliver watched Chief pause as he presumably squinted through the quartz-glass. "Jesus Christ." A click as he toggled the radio to the SAR watchstander. "SAR control, SAR control, this is SAR-1."

"SAR control, go ahead."

"SAR-1 is on scene. Request call status change to BIV, DOA." Body in vacuum, dead on arrival.

The heat of the lunar day made the surface hot, but without an atmosphere to contain heat, the nude corpse was still frozen, draped across the thermal shield-collector atop what Oliver presumed was the person's hab. It was a newer model, half-sunk into the regolith, passive-cooling conductors ribbing the sides like retracted spider legs.

"Jesus," Okonkwo whispered. "You think he was murdered?"

"Probably a suicide," Chief said. "Happens out here."

They watched in silence for another moment. "I've tried hailing the hab's emergency channel. Nobody's home."

"Fuck," Chief breathed, toggled back over to the SAR controller. "We'll need a crime scene team. I'll mark the body's position and collect imagery."

"Roger that," came the controller's response. "MPPD has been contacted and are en route. They've requested you recover the body for transfer."

"Roger that, 1 PAX to EVA."

"1 PAX EVA, roger."

"Let me do it, Chief," Okonkwo said, already punching out of his restraints and moving to the longhorn's access hatch.

"I'll take lookout watch," McGrath unclipped the duster from over his seat and moved to stand in the open hatch with the weapon slung. Pervez brought the longhorn down to just above the surface, fired thrusters to keep the vessel steady as Okonkwo jumped out, bounded toward the corpse. They watched silently as he paused, the suit's camera photographing the area, feeding the imagery back to the longhorn's on-board evidence computer.

At last he hauled himself up the hab's side by the conductor tube, uncoiled the personal winch from the hardshell's waist and looped it around the corpse's waist. He gave an experimental tug, then got an arm around the corpse as it floated free, rigid as a marble statue. "Guy's frozen through."

"Any idea how he…" Chief began.

"It's suicide," Okonkwo said. "Guy wrote it on his chest."

They dragged him back through the hatch and strapped him down to the casualty couch. Oliver looked at his face, eyes open, expression blank. He'd either been high as a kite when he'd exited the hab's airlock, or else so bereft that there was no emotion left in him. Oliver had recovered hundreds of bodies back on Earth, and their expressions had been uniformly tortured. Something about the blankness, the dead-stare of the eyes beneath the thin skim of ice the freezing cold had made of his body's own moisture, was far more unsettling than anything she'd seen before. For the first time since she'd arrived on the Moon, she was left with the unsettling sense of the universe's vastness, and her own tiny insignificance in the face of the yawning void all around her.

The man had written on his chest and abdomen with what looked like spent mechanical lubricant, turned black from the filth of long use:

Too bright

Too dark

Too much

No job

No girl

No more

"Jesus," Chief breathed. "Poor bastard."

"The sea doesn't care about you."

"No," Chief agreed, "it sure doesn't."

MPPD met them halfway in two cruisers, one police interceptor and one ambulance, both clearly patterned off the Longhorn. They effected the transfer and were settling in to their questions when the SAR alarm fired again. "SAR-1, SAR-1, this is SAR control. Vessel DIW reported at coords in your plotter."

MPPD waved them off, and Pervez punched it hard again as they pivoted out toward the EEZ, looking for the vessel "dead in the water."

In turned out to be a commercial six-pack attached to a mining operation that had burned up all its propellant too far from a maser lane to get back underway. "Jesus, guys," Chief said over the hailing channel. "You have to be more careful about your fuel. Are your suits solid? It's not too far for you to get a couple of cans. Or you could just call surface-tow. You didn't have to put in distress hail. We're busy with…"

"Yeah, that's the thing," came the pilot's voice over the hail, thick with the wad of chewing tobacco they clearly had thrust into their cheek. "We got somebody real sick on board. Real, real sick."

"OK," Chief said, "I'll EVA to you with a first aid kit. Are they stable?"

"Nah," the pilot answered. "They're good. They're just… you know, real sick." Oliver could almost hear the smile in their voice.

"That's a bunch of bullshit," Pervez said on the longhorn's private channel.

"Yes," Oliver agreed, "it is. But the law is the same out here as it is on Earth. They say they're sick. We have to tow."

"Goddamnit," Chief muttered. "OK, Okonkwo, rig for side tow. Pervez, bring us up alongside. McGrath, get onboard with the skipper and find me a damn violation. If they're going to do this for us, we're going to damn well make them pay… Oh, sorry, ma'am. That is, if you're OK with going on a boarding…"

Oliver waved a hand as she punched out of her restraints. "It's fine, Chief, but you're not going to find any violations. I can promise you that."

"Yeah, well. Doesn't hurt to check."

As Oliver had predicted, they didn't find any violations, and the crew was silent as they gave the vessel the free tow they'd sought back to SPACETACLET to be refueled at government rate. The alarm was already firing again as they undid the towing straps – this time for an amber alert. Oliver knew it was a false alarm when the vessel made no attempt to evade them, and sure enough the call turned out to be from an angry ex-wife upset at the father legally taking his daughter to see his parents. They were barely back to base when their fourth alarm of the day went off, this time for an uncontrolled bleed that turn out to be mostly controlled after all.

By the time they were back at base for real, they'd missed both their afternoon and evening meal and the crew's mood was dark. Oliver surveyed them, unable to see their faces through the smoked glass of their helmet visors, but their posture was unmistakable. This wasn't working. SAR-1 needed to be SAR-1, responding to the worst disasters the Moon could throw at them. She was suddenly conscious of her time bleeding away again. This might be training them for patience and perseverance and acceptance of routine, but that would only make them better SAR operators, not more likely to win at Boarding Action.

She had to fix this.

She was still puzzling through the problem as the following Earth day and SAR-1's shift drew to a close without a single alarm. Chief dismissed the crew and got to his feet, beginning to strip out of his bunny suit. "Ready to eat, ma'am?"

She could hear Allen's words ringing in her ears. He was right, she had put his balls in a vise. And she knew he was watching the mission logs. He was watching her effectively keep the team idle. She was confirming his suspicion that she was wasting everyone's time. Chief had warned her. Heck, Alice had just warned her. There was barely six weeks to go to Boarding Action and she was just digging the hole deeper.

But the certainty in the back of her mind wouldn't let go. She knew in her bones this was the right move. Something was going wrong with it, and she had to figure out what.

"You go ahead," Oliver said, turning to leave without taking her bunny suit off.

"Where you headed, ma'am?" Chief said.

Oliver turned to him, anger rising at the presumption. Chief read her expression and smiled, spreading his hands. "Contubernium, ma'am."

She smiled back. "I'm going to go talk to the SAR controller. See if I can get this unstuck."

Chief looked over his shoulder at the crew changing back into their uniforms. "Give us a minute and we'll come with you."

"Thanks, Chief, but something tells me this is going to need... officer power. XO and I'll go."

Chief cocked an eyebrow. "If you say so, ma'am. Might be we could help."

"I appreciate it, but we officers have so precious little we're good for. Let us have this one thing."

Chief chuckled and turned back to his locker, and Oliver left, going faster and faster as she moved down the hallway until she was practically running.

Ho caught up to her after lengthening his stride so much Oliver thought he looked like a human protractor. "You're in a hurry boss."

Oliver bit out the words. "This is bullshit."

"What is?"

"Our radio calls. It's been three Earth days, Wen. So far it's either no alarms or bullshit alarms."

"So what? It's the lunar day. There isn't as much vessel…"

"Bullshit. It's bullshit. Something's up."

"Boss, you don't want to go storming in there and be wrong. Are you sure that—"

"Absolutely," Oliver said, the determination in her stride never slackening. Her mind checked in with her gut, as it always did when Ho counseled her, and as was usually the case, her gut won out in an instant. "This is fucking bullshit and I'm going to find out what the hell is going on, and you're going to cover my six because I'm fucking pissed and liable to say something stupid."

"So, just another day, is what you're getting at," Ho said.

"Yup," Oliver said as they reached the ladder and began hauling themselves up it.

The SAR controller looked up as Oliver crested the top of the ladder, snapped to attention. "Attention on deck!"

"At ease." Oliver was already waving everyone back to their posts before Ho had even exited the ladderwell. The SAR controller was a fresh-faced lieutenant junior grade whose nametape read BASKIN. He relaxed a fraction at Oliver's words, then tensed again as he saw the expression on her face. "How can I help you, ma'am?"

Oliver knew it wasn't his fault, that confronting the skipper and a flag officer besides was scary enough for him without putting any pepper on it, but she couldn't help herself. "Does this sector not have emergencies?"

Baskin blinked. "Ma'am?"

"Alarms! Crises! You know, radio calls? Do we not have them?"

"Ma'am, traffic is always slow during the lunar day, but of course we do. Your own crew ran…" he glanced over at the log, and Oliver could tell it was more of an excuse to busy his eyes, "four calls just the last shift."

"Yeah," Oliver said, strengthened by the sight of Ho moving up beside her in her peripheral vision, "but it's all bullshit. We're SAR-1 of the SPACETACLET and you've got us pulling over boats to count lifejackets."

Baskin cocked an eyebrow. "Ma'am, you're on the 16th Watch. People out here don't wear lifejackets."

"Sorry," Oliver said, grateful for the opportunity to back off some of the tension, "I've been working Earth missions for the past couple of decades."

"Ma'am, I assure you. I've been passing the calls down to you as the standby crew as we get them. Take a look at the log," he tapped his touchscreen and a list of radio calls scrolled out before her.

Oliver leaned over them, squinted. "These... these have a 'from' field. We don't take our own calls?"

"Of course we do, ma'am, but that's the minority. People don't know to call SPACETACLET directly. We only get the ones we pick up as an emergency hail. Have to be pretty close and pretty desperate."

"So, where do the majority of the calls come in from?" Oliver cursed herself internally for refusing Avitable's briefing back in the executive shuttle over from OTRACEN.

"Why, the main SAR controller at lunar 911, ma'am. Pipes to us via the Captain of the Port."

"The Captain of the Port." Oliver exchanged a glance with Ho.

"Yes, ma'am," Baskin said. "Admiral Santos."

"I know who the COTP is, lieutenant," Oliver turned back to Baskin. "What I don't know is why all these bullshit calls are being assigned to us. Show me last week's log, before SAR-1 got put on alert status."

Baskin turned back to the terminal, brought up the logs. Oliver ran her finger down the margins. "This is all... this is also all bullshit milk runs. What the hell is going on?"

Baskin shrugged. "This is what we get, ma'am. You'd have to take it up with Admiral Santos' staff."

She turned to Ho. "I was led to believe there are quarantine-runners on a *daily* basis. Even in the lunar day."

Ho nodded. "So was I, boss."

Oliver turned back to Baskin. "I don't see anything like that here."

"Oh, there are," Baskin said, "but 11th Fleet handles that."

It took Oliver a full thirty seconds to process what she was hearing. Ho touched her elbow, and the contact reminded her to take a deep breath and smile. "I'm sorry. *All* the quarantine runners? One hundred percent of them?"

"Yes, ma'am."

"Why is the Navy handling a border protection issue?"

"Navy and marines, ma'am," Baskin said. "It's a joint op. Captain of the Port has designated quarantine violations as a national security matter."

This is exactly what the Commandant wants to avoid, Oliver fought against the boiling feeling in her gut, *this is how we start a war.* The thought was followed by another. *Take it easy on the kid. It's not his fault.*

"It *is*," Oliver agreed, "so is hurricane relief, or a major oil spill. But you don't see the Navy responding to those."

Baskin shrugged. "Sorry, ma'am. I thought you knew. Been like that as long as I've been here."

Oliver took a long breath, proud of herself for keeping it from shuddering. "You have CGMS access on here, lieutenant?"

Baskin punched up the input screen for the Coast Guard's official messaging system. "Yes, ma'am, right here."

"Outstanding," Oliver said, staring at the blinking cursor. "Jesus Christ. I can't remember the last time I used this dinosaur to send a cable."

"That's because I've been drafting them for you since God was a non-rate, ma'am," Ho said, walking to stand beside Baskin, his fingertips hovering over the virtual keyboard.

"I knew there was a reason I made you my XO," Oliver said.

"Commander Ho, please draft a cable to the Captain of the Port. Instruct him that all, and I do mean *all – one hundred percent –* of alarms are to come through Coast Guard channels until further notice. SPACETACLET will assume authority for referring incidents under the jurisdiction of Title 10 to the Navy."

Baskin blanched, "Ma'am, you can't–"

"Excuse me," Oliver spun on him, "were you just about to tell me what I can't do?"

"No, ma'am," Baskin swallowed, taking a step back, "I wouldn't dream of it."

"I thought so," Oliver nodded as Ho finished typing and hit send.

"Care to make a friendly wager, ma'am?" Ho asked.

"What'd you have in mind?"

"Over-under on the phone call from the COTP. I like thirty minutes."

"Fifteen," Oliver said, heading back to the ladder.

"You're on," Ho said as he followed her.

The COTP called in ten. Okonkwo took the call, since Oliver had refused an orderly, and was standing holding the receiver as Oliver and Ho returned to the ready room. "It's… it's Admiral Santos, ma'am. He says he wants to talk to you. He's been holding for at least five minutes."

"XO," Oliver motioned to Ho and took a seat at the table, arms folded across her chest.

Ho picked up the phone, ignoring the confused looks of the crew gathered around. Oliver saw Pervez mouth to Chief *what the hell is going on?* Chief shook his head in reply.

"SPACETACLET – Commander Wen Ho, Executive Officer," Ho said.

"Yes, admiral. No, sir, I'm sorry. Admiral Oliver isn't available to speak with you right now. It'll be some time before she can take a call, but I'd be happy to get you on her calend… Yes, sir. Yes, sir. No, sir, she was very clear. I'm afraid not, sir, Admiral Oliver was extremely specific. Yes, sir. She told me to tell you that the SAR Watchstander has been instructed to scan all alarms, and that if any are referred to the Navy by any other authority than ours, she will have you court-martialed."

Ho jerked the receiver away from his head for a moment, worked a finger in his ear. "I'm sorry, sir? I didn't get that. Yes, well that's our view of the matter. Admiral Oliver was clear. Yes, I'll let her know, admiral. You do what you think is right, but we've made our position clear. Yes, sir. Thanks for your time."

He handed the receiver back to Okonkwo, who hung it back in its cradle as Ho turned to Oliver. "He's got a colorful vocabulary."

Oliver waved a hand. "Will he do as he's told?"

"In my experience, ma'am, people only blow up like that when they're terrified. He knows he's exceeded his authority. He'll play ball."

"I hope you're right," Oliver said.

Ho paused, stroking his chin.

"What?" Oliver asked.

"Sorry, ma'am, just trying to think."

"Well, don't strain yourself. What are you trying to think of?"

"The last time I was wrong about something."

"Very funny," Oliver said. "We can't assume he's going to do what's right. We need to be ready with charges if he doesn't cooperate. We don't have time to–"

But the klaxon was already blaring overhead with the latest alarm. The LED readout below was already scrolling off the description of the radio call – words Oliver hadn't seen even once since she'd had SAR-1 put on alert status.

Quarantine evasion. Unknown flag. Unknown status. Hot pursuit.

CHAPTER 11

We are completely confident that the People's Liberation Army Navy possesses sufficient capability to engage and defeat the United States in either a conventional or nuclear war on both the Earth and the Moon, simultaneously.

VICE ADMIRAL QIN JIANLONG. POLITICAL COMMISSAR,
PEOPLE'S LIBERATION ARMY NAVY

SAR-3 was on alert status for that call, and there was no time to get the crew scrambled, but there were two more quarantine runners that shift, so Oliver went to sleep confident that there would be ample opportunity to get after it once her crew was rested.

She was more right than she thought. The alarm sounded even as her crew was receiving the passdown from SAR-2. Another quarantine runner, this time US flagged, racing for the Chinese EEZ rather than submitting their cargo to inspection.

"OK," Oliver tried and failed to keep the joy from her voice. "Now, we're going to do our jobs."

The enthusiasm was systemic. The crew suited up and had boat checks completed in just a few minutes, and they were underway even as Chief radioed green status back to the controller. "SAR-1 is in pursuit. Expected intercept at course in plotter."

"Roger that," Oliver imitated Lieutenant Junior Grade Baskins' voice now. "Take her easy Chief. Slow is smooth, smooth is fast."

Oliver put her hand on Pervez's shoulder instinctively, knowing the woman wouldn't feel the touch through her hardshell. She bridged directly to her radio. "Drive it like you stole it, BM1. All you need to worry about right now is getting there before the Navy does."

Oliver could almost hear Pervez's grin as she responded, "Can do, ma'am."

The longhorn groaned as Pervez tucked the nose and kept the thrusters burning hard. Oliver bridged to Chief's radio before he could speak up. "Let her off the leash, Chief. Just this once."

Chief turned to look at her, but she could see nothing but the reflection of the sun's burning rays in his smoked glass visor.

"Safe speed, BM1," McGrath warned, stopping speaking as Oliver chopped one gauntleted hand across his vision.

The longhorn's frame groaned, rattled. The lunar surface below began to race past so quickly it was little more than a gray-white wash. "Contact! One hundred… no fifty…" Okonkwo finally gave up calling the contacts as they appeared on radar far too quickly for him to sound their relative position before they had zoomed past. *If just one of those changes direction suddenly, we are going to be pasted all over this rock.* A maser-pylon flashed past, just twenty-five yards off their port quarter, little more than a metal and plastic flash that would have ripped their boat in half if Pervez had tapped the control stick just an inch to the left. Oliver fought the instinct to seek reassurance, to remind Pervez to be careful. *No. She knows that. She knows the risk. Let her fly, Jane. Trust her to do what she's been trained to do.*

Oliver watched as the longhorn skillfully juked around a piece of debris settling down toward the surface from some load hauled by above them, and added, *What she was born to do.*

"I have a visual," Okonkwo said.

"Guns up," McGrath added, as the autocannon came online and began to track the target highlighted on the display.

"Make that two targets!" Okonkwo said.

"What?" Oliver asked, moving over to the binnacle to check the display.

The first vessel flashed red – the quarantine runner, burning aft thrusters hard as they futilely tried to accelerate away into the Chinese EEZ. The other vessel was tagged blue, with a stylized anchor and eagle splashed above a numerical designator "USN – 88126."

A Navy small boat, on an intercept course.

"Pervez, if you don't get us docked on that runner before the Navy can intercept, we are going to have a rather dynamic disagreement," Oliver said.

"Oh, ma'am," Pervez breathed, goosing the aft thrusters and making the longhorn shudder, "I do like negative reinforcement."

The hailer lit up on the encrypted channel – reading the Navy boat's designator. Chief reached across to patch it into their suit channels, but Oliver pushed his hand down. "Leave it, Chief."

"But it's a hail," McGrath said, "on encrypted. From the Navy. Regs say we have to…"

"Regs say you have to obey an admiral, right?" Oliver overrode him. "Leave it."

"OK," Chief exhaled slowly, making the radio crackle. "So, what do we do, ma'am?"

"What do you think we do?" Oliver didn't even try to keep the excitement out of her voice. "Hail that runner, and when they don't answer, have Pervez maneuver us in, and Okonkwo get us to hard dock."

"What are you going to do, ma'am?" McGrath asked.

"I'm going to turn things over to the coxs'un as the functional leader until we cut into the hull. Then Pervez will turn it over to you, boarding officer, and you will tell *me* what to do."

Oliver could feel McGrath staring at her through his smoked visor.

He knew the regs as well as anyone. As boarding officer, he would be in charge. But Oliver was an admiral. This had to be way beyond his comfort zone. *Good,* Oliver thought, *because nobody is going to give a fuck about making you comfortable at Boarding Action, either.*

Okonkwo stared out the front window as the runner drew closer, checked the vessel specs on the display. "It's a six-pack, ma'am. Standard short haul configuration."

"Hailing," Chief said, switching off the Navy attempt to contact them and opening a new channel. "US-flagged six-pack, this is the United States Coast Guard. Fire bow thrusters and bring speed to 00. Make your heading two-seven-zero and station keep. I say again, go DIW and await instructions."

The vessel did not respond, and there was no change in speed. "Well, that's a shock," Ho radioed her from his place in the control room. He had access to the boat's cameras, and could see pretty much everything Oliver did.

Chief chirped the hailer again. "US-flagged six-pack, this is the United States Coast Guard. We consider you in flight from lawful customs authority. Heave-to and be boarded. If you resist we will fire on you."

No response. The Navy boat was a growing dark-gray blotch in the corner of Oliver's eye, the blue-white plume of its aft thrusters leaving a smoking contrail behind it. "They're still trying to hail us, ma'am," Okonkwo said. "They're CBDR and gaining speed."

Constant bearing, decreasing range. In other words, on a collision course. *They want to play chicken.* "BM1, are they fast enough?"

"Not with me flying, ma'am," Pervez answered. The Navy boat was bigger, heavier, but that amounted for very little in the Moon's thread of exosphere. There was nothing to create drag. "Ma'am," Ho's voice on her private channel was shaking. "If she's wrong… we don't want to hit a Navy small boat going this fast."

Oliver wished she could see Pervez's face through the smoked glass visor. *Either you trust her or you don't. And if you don't, then what the hell are you even doing out here?*

"Light 'em up, Chief," Oliver said. Chief hesitated only for a moment before hitting the lights. Oliver could see the blue ripples washing across the Navy boat's hull markings, close enough now to read with the naked eye.

"That Navy boat is still CBDR, admiral," Okonkwo was working not to yell now. "They're not slowing. Still hailing us. Three hundred meters, two hundred meters."

Oliver could see Chief turning to look at the instrument panel, the Navy boat through the window, and then back to Pervez.

She would never be able to assert the Coast Guard's authority if she let the Navy shove her off her own intercept mission. But she sure as hell wouldn't be able to assert it if she had a collision either.

The risk was too great. She'd pushed the limit far enough.

"OK, BM1. Ease it back. I want to beat them, but not if it means risking a coll–"

"I've got this, ma'am," Pervez said. "I can get us docked." She gave them one more hard burn as they gained on the runner so rapidly, it looked as if a toy-vessel suddenly grew into a full-sized one before their eyes.

"BM1!" Oliver yelled.

"Hold on!" Pervez said, firing the bow thrusters. Oliver felt herself sink into her chair, as if she were pushed there by a giant hand, heavy on her chest.

"Navy's not slowing! CBDR!" Okonkwo practically shouted. "I say again, CBDR!"

"I got this!" Pervez answered, tapping the port side thrusters and nudging them to one side.

Oliver's heart was hammering so hard she felt it pressing back against the heavy hand of the inertia on her chest. The Navy boat was growing even faster than the runner. She could make out the masthead light in her peripheral vision, blinking so bright and close that it rivaled the distant Earth. The gun barrels projected from its ball turrets like massive insect limbs, casting shadows over the longhorn's cockpit. *Can we even avoid it now? It's coming too fast. It's much too late.*

"BM1!" Chief shouted, but Oliver could see Pervez's focus, her hands on the joysticks, her shoulders hunched forward over the longhorn's controls. The Navy boat wasn't catching her unawares. She believed she was making the right call. She believed she could get them docked safely. She didn't want to die any more than the rest of them. Oliver was a veteran of boarding after boarding... and she knew that experience still paled beside Pervez's. *But what if she's wrong?*

Pervez goosed the aft-thrusters one more time and the runner's tow fender filled their front window just before Pervez yanked the control stick back. "Okonkwo! Get the nipple on!"

The port side window rose, giving Oliver a perfect view of the Navy boat's bow. Her stomach leapt into her throat as it filled her vision, streaking toward them as quickly as a shooting star. They were so close she could see the boarding team of marines through the front window, on their feet, hanging onto handrails in the Navy boat's ceiling, clustered around the cockswain's seat. *Oh God we're dead we're fucking...*

And then there was a puff of blue-white, and the Navy boat was gone.

Oliver stared at the dissipating cloud of spent propellant before she realized she was looking at the exhaust of the Navy boat's starboard thrusters, burning hard to roll the vessel out of the way as it peeled off.

They'd won this game of chicken.

"Boss," Ho came through on her private channel. "Did you shit yourself? Because I'm pretty sure I shit myself."

"Jesus fucking Christ," Chief breathed.

"Okonkwo!" Pervez shouted again.

"On it!" Okonkwo sounded dazed. "Soft dock!"

"Outstanding," Oliver said, managing to keep her voice calm and even, her stomach still doing backflips. There was no time to deal with this now. "MK3, I want hard dock right now."

Okonkwo didn't respond, but Oliver felt the longhorn tremble slightly as he jumped down into the nipple gangway, cutting gear in hand.

"Did you see those marines?" Ho asked on the private channel.

"Yes, Wen, I did," Oliver answered as she punched out of her restraints and checked her boarding gear.

"They're going to be really unhappy about that, ma'am."

"Hard dock! Venting atmosphere!" Okonkwo called as he cranked the lever and the vacuum lock engaged. An instant later, sparks were spraying across the nipple gangway's entrance as Okonkwo cut into the inner hatch.

Oliver glanced hopefully up at McGrath, but the ME3 was simply sitting there, waiting for orders. "McGrath!" she said. "You're the boarding officer! It's your ship!"

He punched out of his restraints at last, stumbling over his words. "Aye aye, ma'am. Dusters only! Stack on me!"

McGrath dropped down into the nipple gangway.

Oliver snatched her duster from the clips over her head, and kept her voice even with an effort. "Orders, boarding officer?"

She could hear the tail end of McGrath's muttered curse as he toggled into the channel.

"Everybody on me, standard order. Ma'am, you stay in the ship."

"With all due respect, boarding officer," Oliver said, "I just graduated school for this. I'd like to come with."

"OK," McGrath swallowed, eyes on the growing seam from Okonkwo's cutting torch, "keep it tight."

Oliver raced along the nipple gangway, checked her momentum as her shoulder made contact with McGrath's. She could feel a nudge behind her, knew the next member of her stick was there, but resisted the urge to visually check who it was. *Keep your eyes on the breach, it could open at any second.*

Okonkwo completed his last cut, dropped his gear, dashed to take up the stick's anchor position. "Dusting first," McGrath sounded completely calm now. "Then crisscross by twos. Here we go."

Oliver saw his hand snake down and snatch a dust grenade off his waist. "On three, two…"

McGrath slammed the butt of his duster into the cut section, sending the metal plate toppling inward. Oliver resisted the urge to move, knowing she was out of the line of fire, the stick trailing off to the breach's side. "Fire in the hole!" McGrath shouted and threw the grenade into the open space.

"MUNITION DEPLOYED" flashed across Oliver's internal HUD, followed by a timer. The eerie silence of the vacuum implied a calm serenity she did not feel. An instant later there was a flash, and Oliver watched the metal dust spray out from the breach, rocketing past the stick and lodging in the nipple's protective cladding.

"Let's go!" McGrath shouted to the stick, then bridged over to the runner's radio. "United States Coast Guard! Get down on the deck! Let me see your hands right now!"

Oliver came after him, disengaging her spider boots' setules and high stepping. Okonkwo had cut the breach perfectly – not so large that the adversary would have a clean shot at the boarding team, but not so small that it would be impossible to get in. Still, in her rush Oliver caught the top of her hardshell's boot, felt herself stumble into the runner's cockpit. She let go of her duster to steady herself, her outstretched hand finding McGrath's back as he raised his own weapon to fire.

The grenade had done its work. Oliver could see the six-pack's interior riddled with the tiny impact craters left by the explosion of dust. The interior glass looked as if it were clouded, covered with thousands of minuscule scratches. Nylon strapping hung in tatters.

But the six-pack's binnacle was covered with an extra plate of what looked like ad-hoc armor, thick slats of metal crudely bolted over the instruments, swung down on a rough hinge probably just as soon as they had seen the sparks of Okonkwo's cut. *Only committed criminals would do something like that*, Oliver thought, feeling sick tendrils of fear slithering around her stomach. The metal plate had absorbed the lion's share of the dust, and the six-pack's four man crew were rising from behind it. One of them was lurching toward McGrath, a double-handed length of metal conduit pipe in his hands. Another was leveling a gun – the long barrel much too graceful to be a duster. She could see the extended magazine below it, long and wide enough to contain the rocket-propelled munitions that would allow the round to exit the barrel gently before igniting the thruster that would grant it lethal force.

A hornet gun. There would be no surviving a direct hit from it.

Sick panic bubbled in her throat. Tom's small boat flashed in her mind's eye, seeing the anti-materiel gun sighted in on him, powerless to do anything but yell a warning. She still shouted "McGrath!" on the team's channel, her hand scrambling to get her duster back up, knowing it was useless.

She saw the puff of propellant as the hornet gun ejected its munition, the flash as the munition's motor ignited.

She felt McGrath lean forward, his legs trembling slightly as his boots' setules engaged. His duster tracked a fraction to the right and fired. Oliver saw the man with the hornet gun fly backward, his hardshell venting oxygen from a thousand tiny holes.

But not before the munition launched for them.

The split second delay between the rocket munition ejecting and igniting allowed McGrath an instant of movement before it struck him. Oliver watched it slam into his hardshell's shoulder, saw the puff of oxygen blasting out as it penetrated, tore out the back, carrying clouds of polyester and fleece with it.

But no blood. Not yet, anyway.

McGrath flew backward, locked to the floor by his spider boots, bending so hard that his hardshell helmet rebounded off the deck. The boots emergency-disengaged, but not before Oliver heard his grunt across the channel and knew his knee had taken a hit from the sudden bend sideways. *So long as he's not shot through, I'll take it.*

She turned to him, scrambling to get her duster up. His autoseal should have engaged, closing off the suit, but she needed to be sure... *Idiot! You are still in a goddamn firefight! Get back to...*

Her head rocked to the side even as she turned back to the enemy. She disengaged her setules right as the floor raced up to meet her, her helmet colliding with it hard enough to crack the faceplate. But the suit's breach alarm was already sounding, the interior visor dropping and the shrink layer closing around her to contain the precious oxygen. She got her hands under her and launched herself upright, already knowing what had hit her – the length of conduit pipe had cracked her helmet's casing, and if she had to hazard a guess, her attacker was even now raising the weapon for the coup de grâce. She launched herself up, trusting to the suit's failsafe, hoping to sommersault over her attacker and...

The six-pack's low ceiling was not having it. She collided with it just as the pipe impacted her hardshell's shoulder, spinning her in place and bringing her into contact with her attacker. She fumbled, grappling with their hardshell, unable to even locate her duster, let alone raise it for an attack.

Whoever they were, they were ready. She saw the pipe floating away out of her peripheral vision, felt the enemy placing one gauntlet against her chest, trying to push her away to get enough space to throw a punch. She scrambled closer, clawing her way up her attacker's arm, trying to keep as close as she could. *And then what? If you're too close for him to hurt you, then you're too close to disable him.*

But she already knew. She wasn't alone on this op. She was with a team. *Trust them. You're the novice here. Just keep this motherfucker tied up long enough to let them get the rest of them wrapped up.*

She tried not to think about McGrath, his knee likely popped, his suit breached. *He's a pro. If anyone can fight through that, he can.*

She wrenched herself forward, felt her faceplate click against her assailant's. He had his visor smoked, but she could just make out his features through it – pale skin, thick lips disappearing into a thatching of matted beard. His eyes were narrowed, not in anger but concentration, a thinking opponent. The worst kind.

He pushed again, this time with both hands, but made no headway, tried to raise one of his arms. Oliver wasn't sure what he intended, but if he wanted to do it, then she passionately wanted the opposite. She scrambled for his free arm, felt her gauntlet's fingertips brush against it, scrape off. He lifted his arm and chopped down, the bottom of his fist colliding with her hardshell's elbow joint. Her arm slammed downward, losing purchase on him, and she felt the distance between them widen. He cocked his fist back for a haymaker she knew would crack her failsafe visor. *This is it. This is how I die.*

She exhaled sharply, expelling all the oxygen she could, silently grateful for insisting that she go through NCD/0G school. Asphyxiation would take a while, but the effects of depressurization would be near-instant. Her eyes scanned over his shoulder, desperately searching for a way to seal the coming breach as his gauntlet grew larger in her vision.

And then suddenly he rocked sideways and was gone.

Oliver drifted gently backward as Pervez tackled him into the binnacle, her duster wielded like a club. She bashed it into his helmet, once, twice, three times, puffs of oxygen venting as his faceplate stove in. *Shards of that have to be going into his face*, Oliver thought as she got her feet down on the deck and engaged her setules, fumbled for her duster.

Pervez had the man down on his back, smoothly reversed her duster to hover the barrel over his failsafe-sealed face. "Motherfucker, do you want to get shot?"

The man spread his hands in answer, making no move to counter.

Oliver raised her duster to the low ready and scanned the cabin. McGrath, shockingly, was standing, covering down on the remaining three bad guys. Two were on their knees, with Chief putting the restraints on the second of them. The third drifted on his stomach, blood misting from the wreckage of his hardshell's chest.

"Everybody OK?" Oliver radioed the team's channel. "Sound off!"

"Yeah," McGrath replied.

"Check," Chief said.

"Jesus Christ, I think I pissed myself," Ho groused from the control room.

"Good to go," said Okonkwo.

"ME3, are you sure?" Oliver asked.

"Yes, ma'am," McGrath answered. "It punched through the shell, but it didn't hit me."

"Will I go to jail if I shoot this fucker?" Pervez asked. "Because I really really *really* want to shoot him."

"Please do not shoot the helpless prisoner," Oliver said. "No saving that... clearly dead guy?"

"No way," Chief answered. "He kept fighting and I doubled-tapped him. Second shot must have shredded the failsafe."

"Christ," Oliver said.

"If he didn't want to die," Pervez said, "he shouldn't have picked a gunfight with the US Coast Guard."

Oliver felt the tremors rise in her, like they always did when the immediate danger was past. Sickness coiled in her belly, made her arms shake. She lowered her duster and clamped her arms to her side. "We sure we're clear?"

Pervez rolled her guy onto his stomach, wrenched him upright and began applying restraints. Chief had finished with the second of his captives and began making a circuit of the cabin. "We're clear, boss. Ready to call it in."

"No need," Okonkwo jerked a thumb at one of the scratched windows. "The Navy is here to save the day."

Oliver followed the direction of his gesture and saw the Navy small boat firing attitude thrusters as it drifted alongside, autocannons trained on the vessel. They'd surely have docked themselves if SAR-1's boat hadn't already been covering the sole tow-fender. But the boat's tiny shape was dwarfed by the massive shape of the Perry Class frigate moving into position just overhead.

"Wow," Oliver breathed, "cavalry has truly arrived."

"Good thing," Ho said, "never know when you'll need a Perry Class to... blow a small boat to smithereens with a Coast Guard boarding team still on board it, I guess."

"Logic definitely escaping me too," Oliver agreed.

"Boss," Chief said, "I don't want to speak for anyone here, but I know I sure don't want to get blown to smithereens personally. And it would really help with that anxiety if you'd answer their hail."

"Yeah, I guess I'd better," Oliver said, then bridged to the six-pack's comms array, silently grateful for the hinged armor-plating that had protected it from the gunfire in the cabin.

She saw the Navy's transponder signal flashing on her HUD, likely hailing both the six-pack and the longhorn at the same time. She took a deep breath, steadied herself, patched it in. "United States Coast Guard, Admiral Oliver."

The singer's base on the other end of the line sent a chill through her. She supposed she shouldn't have been surprised to find General Fraser responding to the incident, but she was.

"Admiral Oliver," he didn't bother to identify himself, his voice tight with anger, "you mind telling me what the hell just happened?"

"I don't mind telling you," Oliver said, acutely aware the hailing frequency was sounding in the helmets of every member of her boarding team, "but you should in no way misconstrue that to mean that I am in any way *obligated* to tell you. But, you know, since you asked nicely, SAR-1 just intercepted a six-pack evading quarantine. We have one KIA, three perps in custody, and we will now relay them to the Captain of the Port for booking."

"So, they're US persons," Fraser said after a moment, "which means you got lucky. If they'd been Chinese, you could have been sitting on an international incident. Tensions are high enough."

"If they were Chinese, they wouldn't have embarked via a US port."

"And this is why you don't have a homeland focused agency handling these things. Foreign nationals fake papers through US ports all the time."

She had known this very conversation would happen, though she admitted she hadn't expected it to be with Fraser, nor so soon. *You're taking apart the established process,* she thought, *that isn't going to happen unchallenged. Stick to your guns.* "If they do, that's a criminal-customs matter, and well within the guard's jurisdiction."

"Is it, now?" Fraser asked. "And are you prepared to explain the intricacies of jurisdiction to the skipper of the Chinese frigate that shows up to protect its citizens?"

This was becoming irritating. She wasn't a little girl to be patted on the head and scolded. Fraser might disagree with her, but her conduct was hardly egregious. "May I remind you, general, that the guard is an armed military service, same as yours?"

"You may, and it won't change the fact that our arms are bigger than yours, and if you wind up on the receiving end of a Chinese particle projection battery, the finer points of jurisdiction aren't going to count for a whole lot. Also, what the hell is an admiral doing on a boarding mission? A little below your pay grade wouldn't you say?"

"What's a brigadier general doing breaking my balls over a boarding? A little below your pay grade too, wouldn't you say?"

Fraser had to take a moment to master himself before responding. When he did, it was clear he was keeping his voice even only with the greatest effort. "Very cute. I'm not going to sit here and compare dicks with you. You are way out of your lane. Quarantine runners are a national defense matter. We don't answer SAR calls, and you don't do non-cooperative boardings that could potentially spark a war."

Oliver welcomed his anger, used it to fuel her own. "I appreciate your creative interpretation of Title 14 of the US Code. I have an entire JAG Corps that sees it differently. You'll forgive me if I rely on their view of the matter."

"You know I'm going to file a complaint through channels."

"I do, and I look forward to seeing it laughed off the Commandant's desk."

She could almost hear Fraser's smile. "Have you considered one more thing?"

"What's that?"

"You keep this up, you're going to need my guns eventually, admiral. You might want to play nice with me."

Oliver smiled back. "Haven't you been paying attention, General Fraser? I *am* playing nice."

CHAPTER 12

To fight and conquer in all your battles is not supreme excellence; supreme excellence consists in breaking the enemy's resistance without fighting.

SUN TZU, *THE ART OF WAR*

The Captain of the Port's municipal building looked surprisingly like SPACETACLET, nestled on the edge of the Plato crater, a knobbed tower of combined habs astride a massive concrete pad alive with commercial vessel traffic, their running lights and thruster blooms looking like nothing so much as a tacky Christmas show.

Oliver was grateful that the COTP didn't greet her personally. She knew she'd have a reckoning soon enough, but the conversation with Fraser had rattled her, and she wanted to put it off as long as she could. McGrath had merely grunted an affirmative when Oliver asked him how he was doing. Protocol forbid her from insisting he remove his hardshell to check, especially with the failsafes on both of their suits engaged. But she could tell from his voice that he was in pain, even as the instrument panel showed his vitals were stable. Okonkwo cycled atmosphere into the longhorn as a precautionary measure, the failsafes would see them safely back home, and he and Pervez handled turning the captives and the dead body over to MPPD reps who greeted them on the landing pad.

"You sure you're all right?" she asked McGrath for what had to be the tenth time.

"I've got it, ma'am. Just tweaked my knee a little. I've been through worse." He paused at that, probably regretting the words. Oliver had been there when he had been through worse. When people both of them cared about had died.

"Don't worry, skipper," McGrath spoke quickly, trying to cover up the clumsy words with new ones, "I'll be ready for Boarding Action."

"I could give a fuck about Boarding Action," Oliver said. "Just need to know my guy is OK." But it was a lie and they both knew it. She could feel the sour tug of anxiety roiling in her gut. She still firmly believed that pulling them out of the simulator and putting them on the job was the right move, but people got injured on the job, and if one of her prize horses broke his leg right before the big race...

It was a short jaunt back to SPACETACLET. A medical detail met them as they docked and gently worked McGrath out of his suit while Oliver hovered over him, impatiently complying with the HS3 who buzzed over her, removing her hardshell piece by broken piece.

McGrath's knee was bruised and swollen, but Oliver breathed easier when they cut into his underlayer and she finally confirmed that the hornet gun's munition had truly missed his body. A banged up knee would heal.

"I'll file the use-of-force," Chief said, sitting down at his terminal.

"Make sure I get to review it first," Oliver reminded him.

"Aye aye, ma'am," Chief said, "nobody will see it until you say so."

The HS3 finished her inspection, shining a light in Oliver's eyes and forcing her to track her moving finger. At last she nodded and removed the blood pressure cuff from Oliver's arm. "You're good, ma'am. You got lucky out there."

"Luck had nothing to do with it," Oliver said. *And here's hoping my luck holds.* "XO?"

"One step ahead of you," Ho said.

"One step... How do you know what I was going to ask?"

"You want the transcripts of the COTP's custodial debriefing. You want to know why those idiots were willing to take on the US Coast Guard. There's… like a ten percent chance I'm wrong, but I'll bet you they were career quarantine runners, either consignment agents for Helium-3 shipments or just miners who'd grown drunk on their own success evading us."

Okonkwo drummed his fingers on the table, stared at his knuckles. Oliver could see his jaw working. "Something on your mind, MK3?"

"Nothing, ma'am," he said, staring even harder at his hand.

"Contubernium, MK3. Out with it."

Okonkwo looked up, swallowed. "Ma'am, the Navy has been handling this for… well, forever. Every time these bad guys get run down, it's by a Navy boat, with a marine complement, and just guns for miles."

"And your point is?"

"Well, that's intimidating."

"Yes," Oliver said, "I'm sure it is. But that doesn't explain to me why you're looking like you're about to tell me you just borrowed my car and crashed it."

Okonkwo looked back at his hand, said nothing.

"What he means," Pervez offered, "is that the bad guys fought like that because they aren't scared of the Coast Guard. That if it had been the Navy, they would have complied."

"That what you meant?" Oliver asked Okonkwo. The engineer nodded.

"It's a fair point," Oliver said, "but it doesn't matter."

"Why doesn't it matter, ma'am?" Chief looked up.

"Because if it isn't true, then it isn't true. And if it is true, then it's good we broke the seal here. The Coast Guard *is* stepping into this role. This is a thing that is absolutely happening. And if it is happening, then I need the word to spread hot and fast that the Coast Guard is absolutely not to be fucked with, and that there will be KIAs if you take us on. The networks are going to be on this, and hopefully this boarding will be the bucket of cold water idiots need to keep them compliant in the future. We cannot let the Navy have the conn here. Not if there's anything we can do about it."

"Aye aye, ma'am," Okonkwo nodded, keeping his eyes down.

"I'm just sorry you had to get banged up over it, ME3," she said to McGrath.

"I'm good," McGrath grunted, waving a hand. "Banged up worse playing football."

"How's your head, ma'am?" Pervez asked.

"Thick as a brick," Oliver smiled, rapping her knuckles against her temple. "Thanks for saving my skin back there, BM1." *But we still need to talk.*

"Ma'am," Ho said.

"Let me guess," Oliver answered, "you were right about why those idiots resisted us."

"I mean, I know I am," Ho said, "but that's not it. In a development that I have no doubt will shock you, the Ops Boss wants to talk to you."

Oliver arched an eyebrow, swallowed against the nervous churning in her gut. "Put him on my calendar for tomorrow."

"No," Ho said, "the *big* Ops Boss. Admiral Allen."

Oliver exchanged a glance with Chief, the churning rising up into her throat. "Oh," she said.

"Yeah," Ho agreed, "good luck."

Oliver considered taking the call in her office, but she saw the eyes of her crew on her and knew that was the wrong decision. She had sold them on contubernium, on them all rising and falling together. She had to walk that walk. She picked up the receiver beside her terminal. "Sir."

"Jane." She had braced herself for anger, her muscles tensing as they did when she walked in a cold wind, but she wasn't prepared for the worried concern. "Are you OK?"

"I'm fine, sir, thanks for asking. Just took a pipe to the backside of my helmet. Failsafe covered me, and the bad guy wasn't able to get through all the layers."

"That's good to hear. I'm told your boarding officer took a hornet round."

"His hardshell took a hornet round. Exited over his shoulder. I'm more worried about his knee. The impact tossed him over sideways before his boots fully disengaged."

"Can he walk?"

"Nervous to test it yet, but once the HS is done with him, I promise to give you a full report."

"I'd appreciate that. Look, Jane... I'm in a really uncomfortable position here. I just got a call from..."

"Brigadier General Fraser, I know, sir."

Oliver could hear Allen swallowing his impatience on the other end of the connection. "No, Jane. I got the call from Vice Admiral Donahugh."

"The CO of 11th Fleet?" Oliver knew damn well who she was, she asked the question to give her spinning mind time to catch up.

"She's kind of a big deal around here, Jane."

"I know it, sir."

"Well, she's fit to be tied. Fraser is spinning her some yarn about you playing chicken with a Navy small boat and putting all the marines at risk. Then giving him a smart mouth when he tried to talk to you about jurisdiction. Fraser's telling it like you threw your people in there unprepared and nearly got everybody killed. Actually, I'm not being fair. Maybe Fraser isn't telling it like that, but that's sure as hell how Donahugh sees it. Meanwhile, I've got the COTP lighting up my other ear about you preempting his assignment authority. Jane, this is putting me in an impossible position. You tell me how to defend you here. We've given you a mighty free hand out there, and I warned you that taking SAR-1 out of the simulator and putting them into the field was risky."

"You did, sir. And we agreed that was the way we were going to play it anyway."

She heard Allen pause, the sharp intake of breath as he marshaled his patience. "Maybe. But we most certainly did *not* agree that you could get one of your crew injured *and* go to war with both the Navy and the Marine Corps at the same time. This is going to go all the way up the chain, Jane. The old man's probably reading a gist of it as we speak."

"Sir, respectfully, if he wants me to save him the trouble of reading it, patch me through. I'll explain it to him personally."

"Jane, please don't be…"

"Sir, again with all due respect, you know I am a team player, and I will follow your orders. But you have to make a decision. If the Coast Guard wants to be a homeland focused bit-player and accept a subordinate role on the 16th Watch, then that's fine, but you need to make that clear, at least to me. But if you agree with me that the Coast Guard is in its lane here, you have to back my play."

"We sent you out there to win Boarding Action."

"No, sir. You sent me out here to stop a war. We both know that's what happens if the Navy get their way here."

"Winning Boarding Action is how we do it, Jane. We win that prized media attention, we leverage it to change the public's mind."

"Boarding Action is the sizzle, sir. The *mission* is the steak. You don't get sizzle without steak. Admiral, this team is grieving." She could feel the crew stiffening around her, deliberately kept her eyes focused on the middle-distance. She wasn't saying anything they didn't already know. It wasn't a secret what was wrong, and what they needed to set it right. "These people need a reason to *fight*, and a simulation, an exercise, even an important one, isn't that reason. They can't go on like their life is what it was before. Things are *different* for them now. They will be different forever. They have to live for something more. Something else. The mission is that something. The *real* mission, not what the Navy says it is."

She held her breath, waiting for Allen to respond. She could feel her crew all around her, could feel their eyes on her like the pressure of the spin gravity, the gentle but constant push that tied her guts in knots. At last, she could hold her breath no longer, and inhaled loudly. Still Allen said nothing, and Oliver realized that she'd pushed him too far, said too much, not just in front of her crew, but to the head of operations for her service, whose favor she'd need to be successful in this mission.

She opened her mouth to say something when he finally broke the silence. "You sound so… sure."

"I am sure," she said, "because… I know. You know that I know." She choked off the words, swallowed. She allowed her eyes to drop, to meet the gazes of her crew. Ho watched her evenly. Chief's mouth hung open, and Okonkwo looked terrified, but Pervez's face was more open than Oliver had seen since she'd met her. She leaned back in her chair, folded her arms, raised her chin. *Go on,* her expression seemed to say.

"They want to make it right for me, sir," Oliver spoke to Allen, but held Pervez's eyes. "They feel like Tom, like Kariawasm and Flecha are… are their fault. Winning an exercise won't make good on that debt. They have to do something *real.* They have to save *real* lives."

"It's not their fault, Jane." The edge was gone from Allen's voice. He sounded bewildered. "They should know that. They did their jobs the best they could. It's not like they were investigated for dereliction. Sometimes people die in this business."

"Come on, sir. I know you made flag long before me, but surely you still remember what it's like to run ops. Escaping punishment doesn't stop them from blaming themselves."

"I do remember my ops days, thank you. And I've lost crew before. It doesn't always eat you. Maybe they're handling it better than you think. It's not like you can read their minds."

"I don't have to. *I* blame myself, so it's a pretty good guess they do, too."

"Jane," Allen said, "don't do that. You couldn't have saved them. I've watched the tapes, I've read the reports. You did absolutely everything you could, and probably a bit more than that. What were you supposed to, Jane? Take the round meant for Tom's boat?"

And now it was Oliver's turn to let the silence stretch. Allen tried to sit with it as long as she had, but at long last he sighed. "OK, Jane. I get it."

"Thank you, sir."

"Donahugh said she's going to put one of her Quick Reaction Force mobile boat launches out there on the edge of Sea of Rains."

"Right on top of us. She wants to be able to launch quickly and from the ground so she can beat us to radio calls."

"I can't stop her, Jane. It's not on SPACETACLET's footprint, and the COTP has assignment authority for unstaked territory so close to the Chinese EEZ. You know Admiral Santos won't say no."

"Sir, how do you think the Chinese are going to react to a warfighting unit, no matter how small, positioned right on top of their EEZ border? This is provocative as fuck."

Allen sighed. "To Donahugh's mind, I'd say that's a feature, not a bug."

"This is as risky as that collision when I was in NCD/0G, sir. Whatever favors you called in then, I'd call them in again now."

"Well, you certainly gave her the excuse she needed."

"No, sir. I'm not wearing that albatross. 11th Fleet has been looking for a fight since before Tom died. She'd have found another excuse."

"You're right, Jane. I'm sorry. I'll see what I can do about Donahugh.

Just… Well, I guess telling you to lie low for a bit isn't going to register, is it?"

"Not remotely, sir."

"You know, Jane, you're not alone on this. You need to remember that all of us in the head shed here are on your team. We're working our own angles. You have to trust us."

"I appreciate that, sir, but you know the view is always different when you're actually out on the water."

Allen sighed. "OK, Jane. Good luck."

Oliver set the receiver down, put her fists on the table, allowing the adrenaline to course through her and feeling the fatigue that inevitably came behind. She felt like she'd lived a lifetime in the past few hours. "I say anything there that anybody disagrees with?"

She looked up after no one answered, met their eyes. Each of them shook their head. "You've got it right, ma'am," Chief said.

"Good," Oliver said. "Hate to be a liar in front of Ops."

She rose, shaking off the fatigue, not wanting to deal with what had to come next. At last, she walked around the table, tapped Pervez on the shoulder. "Let's take a walk, BM1."

Pervez looked up, peeved, but not surprised. "Contubernium, ma'am?"

"You just watched me hang my ass out in front of the head of ops for the entire service," Oliver said, "that's contubernium enough for one day. This one's just for us girls."

Pervez shrugged and stood, followed her out into the corridor leading from the ready-room to the heads. Oliver walked far enough from the bulkhead that she knew they wouldn't be overheard, and turned, leaning against the wall. She deliberately kept her hands down, her shoulders slouched. *Non-threatening. You've got to get through to her. You can't have her shutting down.*

Pervez mimicked her posture, and Oliver saw the petulance in the stance, the statement, *whatever you do to me, I can do back*. She cursed inwardly. This wouldn't be easy.

"I know what you're going to say," Pervez said, "and I just want to say up front that I delivered on this mission. You specifically told me you wanted contact with that tow fender before the Navy boat could intercept, and that's what you got."

"That's true," Oliver said, "and I won't lie to you, Pervez. That was probably the best piloting I've ever seen on Earth and the 16th Watch combined."

Pervez looked surprised. "So what are we out here for?"

"Because you know even better than I do that it could have just as easily gone the other way. We collided with that Navy boat…"

"…and it would have been on the Navy," Pervez interrupted. "72 COLREGS for both international and inland give right-of-way to the starboard. We were the stand-on vessel, ma'am. It was for them to wave off."

"Oh, come on, Naeemah. I'm not going to argue the COLREGS with you. They haven't been updated significantly since 1972. We're still technically governed by the '67 Outer Space Treaty out here. Do you honestly think anybody is paying attention to that crap? You know better than that."

Pervez stiffened at the use of her first name. "Then what are we doing out here, ma'am? We're supposed to be the cops. If the law is meaningless, we might as well go home."

"Bullshit," Oliver said, "you know as well as I do that there's the law as it's written and the law when the rubber meets the road of real life. Cops have been living at that junction for as long as there've been cops. You know that better than anyone. Forget the gold on my shoulders, Naeemah. You need to remember you're talking to a thinking individual here. I may not be able to drive a boat like you can, but don't make the mistake of thinking I'm not as smart as you."

Pervez's cheeks colored, and she looked down for a moment. "You're right, ma'am, I'm sorry."

Oliver waved a hand. "Don't sweat it. I do shit like that all the time. You don't know who you're dealing with until you know who you're dealing with."

"Anyway, law aside, the job got done. And it got done the way you wanted it done. And you had your chance to knuckle your forehead to Ops, and you didn't, which tells me you're good with the result."

"That's the thing, Naeemah. I am and I'm also not. I'm good with the outcome, but you've got to dial it back anyway. Because this shit is killing us as a *team*. I can't have everyone else on the team thinking their safety is at the risk of your whims."

"That wasn't a whim, ma'am. That was me knowing my business. I *knew* the right-of-way rules. I *knew* the Navy coxs'un knew them too. I knew they would wave off. If you want me to deliver results, you have to trust me to know my business."

"Again, horseshit. You couldn't read that coxs'un's mind. What if he'd had a fight with his girlfriend that morning? What if he was fresh off leave and still feeling his way around the cockpit? What if he had a death wish? What if General Fraser was yelling in his ear that he'd better beat us to the tow fender no matter the cost? I know you know *your* business, Naeemah. But the fact is that you're not out here alone. It's everybody else's business that you seem to have a problem with. This is going to be an issue not just at Boarding Action, but out in the field in general, moving forward."

Pervez's mouth was moving before Oliver had even finished speaking. *She's not listening.* "Ma'am, I am following your orders to the–"

"Naeemah, I am not *ordering* you here. I am *asking* you. If we're ever going to fix…" she waved an arm, unable to find the word, "*this*, I need you to work with the team. And that means you wave off when Chief or I tell you too. Even when you're the operational leader on scene. Even when you think you know better."

"You want me to work with the team, then you need to make sure that the team understands that I'm not the guy I replaced. I will never be Kariawasm. I won't drive like he did, I won't navigate like he did. I do things differently."

"I know you do," Oliver said, "and that's what we need. The truth is that if I'd been one tenth as good as you are when I was back running ops, I'd have two more stars on my shoulder and the Coast Guard Medal by now. You have more natural talent for this than I could ever hope to have. But none of that is going to help you if you can't convince the people around you that when you put that talent to work, you're putting it to work for *everybody*, not just for yourself. We do dangerous work. We have to be able to believe that the person behind us is covering our six."

Pervez was quiet for a long time. "That's what Chief says your husband did."

"He really did." The memory of Tom, the knowledge that Oliver shared it with these veritable strangers, that Tom's essential *goodness* was so powerful that everyone who met him couldn't help but recognize it made her throat swell, and she blinked back tears. "It's what every good sailor does. Life is about leaning on other people."

"It is," Pervez said, "and that means you all have to lean on me too."

"We are. More than anyone else on the team, we're all leaning on you. You think I'm certain here? You think I came out here thinking it would be a cake walk to the finish? I'm *terrified*. I have no idea how we get this thing done, but I do know that if we're going to get it done it's because we all pull together." She paused, giving Pervez a moment to reply, and when she didn't she sighed. "Look, Kariawasm is irreplaceable. So, don't try to replace him. You don't have to be better than his shadow, Naeemah. You just have to do the job to the best of your ability, and part of that job is sticking with your team."

"You going to NJP me, boss?" Pervez asked.

"If I were going to have you NJP'd, Chief would be having this conversation with you, not me, and I sure as hell wouldn't be *asking* you to do anything, nor would I be calling you by your first name. I was sent here to do a job, and you are absolutely the coxs'un I need to get it done. You were the operational leader on scene. What you did was technically within the limits of your remit.

"But you've asked me to trust you, Naeemah. I'm telling you that I do trust you. I trust your years of experience, and I trust the skill you've displayed to me again and again. Now, I'm asking you to trust me, too. I know blue water boardings aren't the same as what we do on the 16th Watch, but they're not that different either. And more importantly than my time in the saddle is my time as a commander. I have been leading people for longer than you've been driving boats. I know how to make a team work together. It's my job to see the forest instead of the trees. I'm not telling you to back off believing in yourself, but I am asking you to believe in me. Can you do that?"

Pervez dropped her eyes. Her mouth worked, no words coming. Oliver's heart sped up, her mind racing. If Pervez shut down, if she doubled down on recalcitrance, she'd have no choice but to punish her, and she knew that would be the end of it. Pervez would retreat into sullen petulance, and the impact of the team's effectiveness, and morale would be devastating.

Come on, she thought, watching the corners of Pervez's mouth as she ground her teeth. *Come on. Come through for me here.*

At last, Pervez looked up. "OK."

OK, ma'am, Oliver thought, but didn't say. "Thank you. I'm going to hit the head. I'll meet you back in the ready room."

Pervez left without a word and Oliver turned toward the head that she didn't really have to use. She was less than surprised when Ho detached himself from the bulkhead. "Jesus, boss. That could have blown up in your face."

Oliver shrugged. "It didn't. If BM1 can play chicken with the Navy, then I can do it with my mission out here."

"Still, asking her? You're an admiral."

"This is why I'm the CO, and you're the XO. People have different learning styles, Wen. Pervez is a fighter in her bones. You come at her head on and she's going to dig in and scorch the Earth. She'll burn everything down – her career, the mission, everything, rather than give in. You can't tell people like that anything. You have to ask them, even in the military."

"I just hope she doesn't start thinking she runs SAR-1."

"Oh, don't you worry about that. You just saw the carrot. I've still got the stick. That was her free one. She's got the inch. She tries to take a mile, and I'll show my teeth and damn the consequences."

"I just hope you're right."

Oliver rubbed her temples, blinking back the headache that was beginning to form there. "Great leaping Christ, Wen, so do I."

SPACETACLET's sickbay had the latest regenerative medical tech on hand, and a stem-cell injection did the trick. McGrath's knee was better than Oliver could have hoped, and the team only lost a week back in the simulator before he was operationally capable with a brace. Oliver weighed ordering him to stand down longer, but the clock ticking down toward Boarding Action convinced her otherwise, as did the look on the big petty officer's face when he said, "I'm ready, ma'am, put me back in the fight." Oliver knew better than anyone the cost of refusal, both to his morale and the team's.

When he walked stiffly back into the ready room, the smiles on the team's faces set Oliver's heart at ease. She could see reflected in the eyes of all that she'd made the right decision. Chief clapped him on the shoulder, "Stop trying to get a Purple Heart."

"You dodge hornet rounds," Pervez added, "you don't block them."

McGrath grunted, embarrassed by the affection, and moved to inventory his gear.

He had just spread the pieces of his hardshell out on the deck and was sitting Indian-style, running his thumbs along the seals when Oliver heard a chirp from her terminal. It was a message from Baskin, and Oliver didn't bother to open it. The ops floor was close enough for her to check in person.

"Welcome back, McGrath," she said, gestured to Ho, and headed down the passageway and up the ladder, her stomach performing the customary acrobatics as she reached the central desk where Baskin stood awaiting her.

"What's up, ops? Get it? It's like what's up doc, only…" she trailed off.

"…Less funny?" Ho offered.

"Remind me to fire you the minute I need you less," Oliver said.

Baskin didn't smile, only tapped the plotter, which showed a blinking blue anchor just inside the Chinese EEZ. "You'd mentioned that 11th Fleet would be sending a mobile QRF launch, ma'am? I think they're here."

Oliver squinted at the map, countered lines showing the changes in elevation across the Sea of Rains. "That's… Is that inside the Chinese EEZ?"

Baskin nodded. "That's why I thought you'd want to know. They're well inside."

"And you have no indication that they're in hot pursuit of anyone?"

"No, ma'am," Baskin said.

"Have you hailed them?"

"No, ma'am," Baskin said again, "I figured I'd check with you first."

"Do you have a copy of their orders?" Oliver asked.

Baskin shook his head. "That's between them and the COTP, ma'am."

Oliver tapped her chin, hoping the motion would appear normal and settle the sudden churning in her gut and the roaring in her ears. "All right. SAR-1 will launch and see what the hell is going on. Any alarms to the next duty crew until we get back."

"Aye aye, ma'am," Baskin tried and failed to keep the excitement out of his voice.

Ho followed her down the ladder, silent and omnipresent as a shadow. "XO, if they are not in hot pursuit of a vessel, it is my understanding that they are in violation of international law. Do you have a different interpretation of the statute?"

"You're absolutely correct, ma'am."

"And they know this. They have to."

"They do."

"So what the fuck are they doing, Wen?"

"Well, I can't read their minds, ma'am, but I'd say they're trying to start a war."

They reached the bottom of the ladderwell and Oliver picked up the pace, moving toward the ready room. "Not on my watch, they're not."

The crew looked up as she entered, freezing in what appeared to be an exercise of stealing parts of McGrath's hardshell and forcing him to chase them around the ready room to get them back.

"Play time's over," Oliver said. "Hats and bats. We're launching now."

They immediately passed McGrath his gear and moved to their own lockers. "What's the alarm, ma'am?" Chief asked. "I didn't see any…"

"It's not an alarm. Navy set up their mobile QRF launch inside the Chinese EEZ. We are getting them the hell out of there before the PLAN decides to make an issue out of it. Okonkwo, what do you know about PLAN long-range sensors?"

The engineer looked up at her, hopping on one leg as he struggled into his bunny suit. "Not much, ma'am. I'm mostly boat systems, but we did learn a little…"

"If the Navy just set down a mobile launch inside the Chinese EEZ, how long until the Chinese see it?"

Okonkwo got his leg in, stopped hopping. "They knew the minute the Navy crossed the border."

"I figured, thanks. Light a fire under it, people!"

Pervez launched them hard, grimly silent as she angled the longhorn toward the blinking blue cursor in the plotter. Chief looked askance at Oliver more than once, but nobody on the crew asked the question she knew was foremost in their minds – *what are we going to do once we reach them?* Oliver wasn't sure herself, but she knew she couldn't allow this to happen unchecked. She strained to see through the front window, looking over the gray horizon for a sign of the Navy unit. "Chief, you see any contacts? PLAN inbound?"

Chief shook his head. "No, ma'am. Not so far. Their nearest launch is about two klicks out. It won't take them long to get here if they decide they want to get here."

"They're probably scratching their heads and wondering what the hell is going on," Oliver said. "Let's hope that condition holds until we can get this resolved. Sing out if you see anything."

"Wilco, ma'am," Chief kept his eyes on the plotter, silently yielding the helm lookout to Oliver.

The Navy had set down just outside SPACETACLET's footprint, and Pervez didn't have to drive them far before Oliver got a visual on the site. The mobile launch was a large wheeled rover, its thick, knobbed tires wide enough to give it strong traction in the lunar gravity. It hauled a single trailered small boat, the trailer itself a kind of flat-bed launch pad insulated to resist the pressure of the vessel's belly thrusters. The crew were already out, just four of them, setting up lighted wands to mark the corners of their position. Oliver could see by their hardshell markings that they were Navy personnel. No marines yet, but she didn't doubt those would be inbound soon.

They looked up as Oliver hit the blue lights and Pervez brought the longhorn down to settle gently just above the regolith beside them. Three of the sailors kept at their work, probably at a radio order from the fourth, who strode out to meet Oliver as she popped the starboard hatch and stepped out. She could see qualification pin of the Navy's construction battalion, the "SeaBee" with its grim smile and its tommy gun. A lieutenant junior grade's bars marked his shoulders. His name plaque read SCOTT.

"Lieutenant Junior Grade Scott," Oliver returned the young man's salute. He kept his visor smoked in the bright lunar day, so she was unable to read his facial expression. "I'm Admiral Jane Oliver, I run SPACETACLET."

"It's nice to meet you, Admiral Oliver," Scott said. "I'm surprised SPACETACLET's CO came all the way out here to greet us personally."

"Admiral Allen told me you'd be setting up out here."

"Well, we're almost done, ma'am. The launch is pretty self-sufficient. This is just the duty crew, the actual QRF operators should be here in…"

"What Admiral Allen didn't mention," Oliver cut him off, "was that you'd be setting up inside the Chinese EEZ."

Scott paused, and Oliver wished she could see the expression on his face. She was almost about to speak again when he said. "We're not inside the Chinese EEZ."

"Maybe your plotter is on the fritz, but mine is working fine. You'll find in the Coast Guard we live by the accuracy of our charts. You are outside US territory right now."

Scott looked back toward his crew, who were all paused in their work, watching their conversation. Whatever he was looking for, he didn't seem to have found it, and his voice shook a bit when he turned back. "We're on the LMGRS coordinates in my orders, ma'am. I triple checked before we started setting up."

"May I see your orders, please?"

"I don't see that I have to…"

"Lieutenant Scott, I am *asking* you nicely. These orders aren't classified, are they?"

"No, ma'am."

"Then there shouldn't be a problem bridging them to my boat so I can check your LMGRS coords. If this is a misunderstanding, this will clear it up."

Scott was silent for another long moment, then he finally grunted. "Just a moment, ma'am."

One of the other sailors bounded toward the launch, likely at a radio prompt from Scott, and hauled himself into the cabin. A moment later, Chief radioed Oliver on a private channel. "I'm looking at them now, ma'am. The coords are right. They're where they were ordered to go."

Oliver cursed inwardly. 11th Fleet had thrown this poor kid under the bus, but that didn't mean Oliver had to put up with it. "Well, you're not misinterpreting your orders, but you also can't stay here, lieutenant. I need you to move your position one klick south, right now. We'll accompany you in case you need assistance." *And to make sure you get where you need to go and stay there.*

"Ma'am," Scott said. "You are asking me to disobey an order from my CO."

"No," Oliver said, "I am telling you, as the service charged with maintaining border integrity on the Earth and the Moon that you need to adjust your position. I'll take the issue up with your CO once we've got you in the right–"

"Ma'am!" Chief radioed. "I've got two PLAN small boats launched and tearing ass for this position. I'm hailing but they're not responding. Not sure they speak English anyway, and I don't have a lick of Chinese."

"Ho?" Oliver radioed her XO on the ops floor. "You got them?"

"Yes, ma'am," Ho said. "I'll try to hail them now."

Oliver patched back to Scott, worked to keep the rising tension out of her voice. "OK, we are officially out of time, you need to relocate this launch right now, as in this very instant. That is a direct order. Let's go."

Scott bridled. "With all due respect, admiral, I don't take orders from you. I am accountable to my CO and my–"

"We don't have time for this! I have two PLAN boats inbound as we speak, and they are not going to–"

Ho overrode her channel. "Ma'am! I've got patrol drone footage from a quarter-klick out. Those PLAN boats are running out missile pods. You need to get off the X right now, please."

Scott was turning back to the launch's cab. "Are you sure? I haven't received any report of a–"

"Jesus Christ! Get your people in that bucket and drive the hell away from here right now!" Oliver resisted the impulse to shake the man.

Scott stopped, turned back to her. "Admiral, I respectfully decline. I have my orders and I am not abandoning my position without first consulting with my command, PLAN or no PLAN."

"Chief," Oliver switched channels. "What's the SITREP?"

"They're right on top of us, boss. They could fire if they wanted to, but I'm guessing they want to see what the hell is going on first. We need to–"

Oliver cut him off. "Leave Pervez at the helm and get out here with McGrath and Okonkwo right now. Bring dusters."

Chief was at her side a moment later, and she could feel Okonkwo and McGrath's presence behind him. He held his duster at the low ready. "Ma'am?"

She turned to him, unable to see his expression through his smoked visor, pointed at Scott, setting her radio to all-call, audible to all receivers in range. "Thanks, Chief, arrest this man."

"What?" Chief and Scott asked at the same time.

"Lieutenant Scott, you are violating Chinese territorial concerns without the exemption of hot pursuit. You have been advised that you've broken the law and been ordered to change position. You have refused to comply. You're under arrest."

"You can't arrest me!" Scott's voice rose to a squeak. "I'm an officer in the United States Navy!"

"And I'm an admiral of the United States Coast Guard. We have authority under Title 10, 14 and 18. It's like the royal flush of being able to arrest whoever we want. Turn around and put your hands behind your back."

Scott stared at her as two specks formed in Oliver's peripheral vision, became gray wedges growing in the distance. "XO," she toggled channels. "I need you to get through to those PLAN boats, we are arresting the officer in charge of the launch and forcibly removing them from the site. Can you…"

"Trying, boss. They're not picking up so far."

"Christ," Oliver toggled back to all-call. "Chief! I want this man in restraints yesterday."

Chief slung his duster and stepped toward Scott, raising a pair of hardshell restraints. "Sir, please comply. Let's not make a scene."

The other three sailors stood stunned. They were unarmed, and made no effort to intervene to save their commander. Scott also stood stunned, saying nothing, but also not turning around. The wedges grew in Oliver's peripheral vision, brick-sized now.

"Scott," Oliver bridged to his radio on a private channel, and now she made no effort to hide the panicked rage building in her as the PLAN boats drew nearer. "I am not fucking with you. You're going into those restraints. We can do this the easy way or the hard way, and I promise you that you will not like the hard way."

Scott said nothing, but he slowly turned, crossing his wrists behind him.

Chief stepped in and slapped the restraints in place, locking the bails down as the PLAN boats finally arrived, firing bow thrusters to slow their approach. Huge missile pods extended from behind their solar sails like insect antennae, each carrying a cluster of six warheads trained on the spot where Oliver now stood. They were too close to use them, of course, but the autocannons in their ball turrets would certainly do the trick.

Oliver swallowed the terror in her throat and gave them what she hoped was a casual wave. She grabbed Scott by the link in his restraints, thrust him roughly toward the longhorn. She made an exaggerated motion with her other hand toward the remaining sailors, who began to climb back in the cab of their rover.

The boats merely held position, weapons trained on her.

"XO," Oliver radioed. "Please for the love of God tell me you got through."

"I did," Ho came back. "They're aware of the arrest, and the pending reposition."

Oliver sighed relief as the sailors started up the launch and the vehicle cut a long arc, turning around and heading back the way it had come, leaving dented tire-tracks in the lunar soil.

She stood, watching them go, doing her best to ignore the firepower trained on her back. When at last the launch was completely out of sight, she turned, waved to the PLAN boats again, and got back in the longhorn.

"I can't believe you did that," Scott radioed her. "You just arrested your own countryman for following orders."

"I just kept all of us from being incinerated and possibly kicking off the first lunar war," Oliver radioed back. "Now, shut up while I get in touch with your Master-at-Arms."

Navy shore patrol was already waiting to pick up Scott by the time

SAR-1 returned to SPACETACLET. The Master-at-Arms signed the digital transfer paperwork Chief handed him, and passed the tablet back with a grunt. "I gotta say, this is the first time I've ever seen a transfer like this."

"Yeah, me too," Chief sounded embarrassed. "Me too."

When the Navy left with Scott, Oliver, still in her bunny suit, took a moment in her stateroom to sag into a chair and bolt down a bourbon. "Christ, Ho. What did I just do?"

"Exactly what you told Scott," her XO answered. "Staved off a possible lunar war and saved everyone's asses."

"You think Ops will see it that way? Or the old man?"

"If they don't they're fools. Look, boss. You were put in an impossible situation with no time to act. You did what commanders do in those situations. You made the call. It was a good one."

"I'm amazed Allen hasn't called me yet."

"Me too," Ho chuckled. "He's probably in quarters with his JAG trying to figure out what the hell to do with this mess."

"Donahugh is going to call for my head."

"Yup, she is. She'd created a perfect opportunity to spark hostilities and you sucked all the fun out of it."

Oliver chuckled in spite of herself. "Thank God for you, Wen. Seriously."

Ho shrugged, unzipping his bunny suit and fanning air onto his chest. "Sometimes you have to laugh to keep from crying, boss. Honestly, I think maybe you should call Allen yourself. Head this thing off at the pass."

"You're right. OK. Christ. I just need a few minutes to get my story straight and figure out how I want to tell it."

"Sure boss, I…"

Oliver had long since ordered SAR alarms piped to her stateroom, and she heard it chime now, followed by Baskins' weirdly calm voice.

"Foreign-flagged vessel, unlawful entry. LSST scramble. SAR-1 launch. I say again, SAR-1 launch."

Oliver jumped to her feet, ran to the ready room. Ho puffed along behind her. "You sure you don't want to sit this one out, and–"

"I said I needed time," Oliver said. "May as well take it on the road."

The team was blinking up at the monitor when she arrived. A foreign-flagged vessel penetrating US territory unlawfully was troubling enough, but the scrambling of the Lunar Safety and Security Team made her blood run cold. They were SPACETACLET's heavy-hand, the pipe-hitters and steel-eyed killers that rolled out when the Coast Guard had to confront a heavily-armed and intractable enemy, dug in and fighting to the last. That Baskins was sending out SAR-1 while they waited for the LSST to gear up meant that whatever this foreign-flagged vessel was doing, the COTP considered it an immediate threat to American lives.

These thoughts were doubtless registering in the minds of her crew as they slowly stood, their eyes flashing to the monitor, back to her. Oliver moved quickly to break the paralysis. "OK! Hats and bats! Let's get on the road!" She chucked McGrath's shoulder as she raced to her locker, "How's the knee?"

McGrath shrugged. "Last run was a cakewalk."

"Last run you didn't have to do anything. XO! Get up on the control floor!"

She could hear the tone of command, felt it reverberate, saw her people react instinctively. They raced into their gear, Chief already running boat checks by the time Ho was sealing Oliver into her hardshell. "You sure you want me to sit this one out?"

"Absolutely," Oliver said as the seal indicators flashed green. "I love Baskins to death, but this could get serious. I can't have us high and dry out there. I want someone I trust riding herd in the control room. I also want you to run interference in case Allen calls before we have this job buttoned up. Run down the LSST and make damn sure they're lighting a fire under this. We'll intercept, but I don't want us fighting this fight alone. Get us backup and get it to us fast."

"I won't let you down, boss."

"I know you won't," she said, and ducked into the longhorn's hatch. Chief had already radioed control and gotten permission to launch. Pervez was firing the belly thrusters just as soon as Oliver sealed the hatch. Scott's arrest hovered in the back of Oliver's mind, and she knew it would be weighing on the crew as well. The Navy would doubtless drop the charges, but there was no way the slight would be ignored. Oliver tried to put the event out of her mind to focus on the task ahead.

"SAR-1 launch." Oliver felt chills crawl up her spine at the words, the thrill more intense for the urgency of the mission. *It never gets old. It will never get old.* Joy was an odd thing to feel at the prospect of launching on a likely dangerous mission against a violent enemy, but she'd have been lying to say she felt anything else. She thought she detected the same emotion in the voices of her crew as they completed their internal radio checks and SAR-1 lifted off into the Moon's wisp thin exosphere.

Chief punched up the plotter and tapped a finger on the screen. "They just belted out of the Chinese EEZ and are running the edge. Twenty bucks says they're fleeing Chinese pursuit. Probably organized crime." Oliver glanced at the assignment log at the screens' top. Sure enough, the words she expected were flashing there – INTEL DRVN. Control was basing the urgency on intelligence, probably secret. "Maybe it's a triad."

"That's my guess," Chief said. "Not good."

"For them," Oliver finished for him. "Get on that throttle, BM1."

"Aye aye, ma'am," Pervez said and punched the aft thruster. The longhorn lurched and spun as Pervez set the course, and the Moon's surface began to blur beneath them.

"I need us on top of them *before* they decide they want back in the EEZ. We don't need another confrontation with China today, thanks."

"On it, ma'am," Pervez said.

"XO," Oliver radioed back to control, "what's the status of the LSST?"

"Still spinning up, boss, but they're not dragging ass. They should be launching in ten minutes tops."

"Can you give us a line on the intel popping this off?"

"Baskins says it's a possible Shui Fong arms shipment gone pear-shaped."

"It's a whose-what?"

"Organized crime. Bad news, boss."

"Is the PLAN in pursuit?"

"I'm trying to get a line on comms for them now. There's a lot of traffic this close to the border, ma'am. Hard to tell if any of it is specifically CBDR with our bad guys. They're sticking close to the EEZ, so I don't think they intend a run deeper into our space. You have hot pursuit authority."

"Level with me, Wen. How bad are these guys? How worried do I need to be?"

"I have a call in with the two, and they're scrambling to get me briefed, but just from my knowledge? I'd be pretty damn worried."

"Yeah, that's my thought too. We'll intercept and board. Pin them for the LSST. Get them running, XO!"

"All over it, ma'am."

"Got a visual," Pervez said. "Half a nautical mile, port bow. Man, she is hauling ass."

Oliver leaned forward and squinted out the longhorn's front window. She could see the vessel now, a squat, lozenge shaped monster at least twice the size of a six-pack. She could make out the orange and yellow striped tow fenders, two of them, fore and aft. It was in the process of folding back its solar sails, stripped bare of their ablative coating. Its aft thrusters were firing now, probably at the sight of SAR-1 on an intercept course. Without waiting to be told, Chief hit the blue lights.

"OK," Oliver said, "you all heard my conversation with XO. We are boarding this beast. I want to keep these… whoever they are, busy long enough for the LSST to get into position and do their thing. No heroics. We're the anchor around their neck, nothing more."

"Aye aye, ma'am," the crew answered in unison.

"McGrath, try not to get shot again."

"Aye aye, ma'am," McGrath answered.

"Man, that's big," Oliver said. "That's a twelve-pack?"

"It is indeed," Pervez answered. "Double the crew."

"XO," Oliver toggled back to control. "We got anything approaching a count on the crew?"

"That would be nice, wouldn't it?" Ho responded immediately. "On the bright side, LSST is suited up and running boat checks."

"Go kick the two in the ass, XO."

"I'd have to pull my foot out to take another swing, boss."

Oliver silently cursed as the twelve-pack grew in SAR-1's front window. The vessel had more thrust, but it needed to propel its greater mass, and SAR-1 steadily gained. Pervez tapped the joystick and the longhorn juked perfectly to port, sliding onto a course that would settle it on the aft tow-fender. "Here we go," she said.

"Gun!" McGrath shouted as a hatch popped open on the twelve-pack's aft and an autocannon thrust up through it, swiveling to lock on the longhorn.

"Got it!" Pervez's voice was even as she tapped the joystick again and the longhorn shuddered, dancing left and right, never deviating from the direct course to the twelve-pack's tow-fender.

"XO! Are you seeing this?" Oliver radioed Ho.

"Got it, boss. LSST is launching. Your call whether to wave off."

"What the hell is an autocannon doing on a hauler? Do the Chinese build these things differently?"

"Nope. But bad guys do. COTP wants to know what your play is."

"We're boarding. Do not let the Navy–"

"Too late, boss. I'm sorry. They were already in the water, so to speak. Not sure if they heard about you collaring Scott or not, yet."

"I'm sure everyone in 11th Fleet knows already. They're going to be ornery as hell. Wen, find a goddamn way to wave those fuckers off. This is going to be bad enough without them shooting up the place. You get Donahugh on the horn and remind her that no matter what happened with Scott, the Coast Guard is the *supported* command on this op."

"Already trying. It won't work. Be careful, boss."

"Worry about the bad guys. You don't point a gun at the United States–"

The muzzle of the autocannon flashed, and Pervez slapped the joystick. The longhorn dove to one side, shuddered with an intensity that Oliver knew meant they'd been hit. An instant later, Pervez had them back on course, blasting the aft thrusters hard in an effort to close the distance they'd lost.

"Damage?" Oliver said.

Chief was toggling through systems diagnostics. "We're good. Clipped the sail housing. I wouldn't risk deploying it, but we don't need it now anyway."

The longhorn's bow gun tracked as McGrath worked the controls. "Request SNO, ma'am. Let me light these fuckers up."

"Denied," Oliver said. "We just staved off a shooting war with China, and we're not going to start one now. Can we…"

"I've got this, ma'am," Pervez said, raising the longhorn's nose and exposing their belly to give the nipple a chance to latch on. She punched the aft and roof thrusters in time, and the longhorn swept in.

"Back off, BM1!" Chief said.

"No way, Chief," Pervez answered, "that'll just put us in range longer. I am getting us in close. Once we're on the tow-fender, we'll be under that gun."

"If that turret can decline you'll get us all killed!" Chief shouted.

Pervez turned in her seat, letting Oliver see her face through her hardshell's visor. "Ma'am, please. I can do this. I need you to trust me."

She was already turning back to the controls as Chief raised his hands. "Your call, ma'am."

That autocannon has a lock on us for sure. That round is in our sail housing instead of our cabin because they are trying to get us to wave off and don't want to hurt anyone.

She swallowed the sick worry in her throat. "Get us to soft dock, BM1."

"All over it, ma'am," Pervez said and raised the bow higher. The gun disappeared from view, and Oliver struggled with the panic coursing through her, the itching certainty that any minute 23mm rounds would come ripping through their hull.

I need you to trust me.

Christ, BM1.

"MK3!" Pervez was shouting.

"I'm on it!" Okonkwo had already dropped into the nipple gangway, cutting torch over his shoulder.

"Long guns up!" McGrath raced after him. "Stack on me!"

Oliver knew it was only the space of a few seconds before she felt the gentle nudge as the nipple grabbed hold of the twelve-pack's tow fender, but it felt like an eternity. "Soft dock!" Okonkwo called. His voice was tenser than Oliver would have liked, but in his defense, this was scaring the shit out of her too.

Chief dropped down into the gangway as she tapped Pervez on the shoulder. "BM1, I need you with us. I want all guns in the fight."

She toggled to the crew wide channel. "Cleared hot, everybody! We've already taken fire, so we are going in ready to stop the threat!

Suppressing fire! I want that vessel disabled and its crew pinned down until the LSST gets here. Roger up down the chain! Sound off!"

She listened as each member of the crew acknowledged her order, then toggled back to Ho. "XO, you got all this? Where's my LSST? We're about to get into a fight and I'd prefer it to be as short as possible."

"Roger all, boss. They've launched and are inbound. Just keep them from jetting off until they arrive."

Oliver paused, let herself feel the longhorn trembling through her spider boots. Sure enough, the twelve-pack was still firing its aft thrusters, dragging the longhorn along. "Okonkwo! Can we fire the longhorn's thrusters to arrest our movement?"

"Negative, ma'am. Belly thrusters shut down when we cover the tow-fender. Attitude thrusters would just set us spinning."

"Damnit. OK, I need you thinking about a way to kill these engines."

"I already know ma'am," he radioed back. "There's an access panel inside where I can cut the propellant, but that's not going to stop our inertia. We'll need to fire the bow thrusters for that."

"Can you do that without us having to fight our way to the helm?"

"Never tried on a Chinese-made twelve-pack, ma'am, but I bet I can figure it out."

"Damn right you can, start cutting."

"Cutting, aye, ma'am." She heard a clunk as he retracted the nipple, hugging the two vessels tight together. "Hard dock! Venting atmosphere!" She saw sparks beginning to fly up the nipple gangway below her. "Exterior hatch is sealed," Okonkwo radioed. "I think I can cut the... Got it!" She heard his panting as he raced the few feet into the airlock to the interior hatch. "*Now* I'm cutting!"

She toggled back over to Ho. "Any sign of pursuit?"

"Looks like it boss," Ho answered. "Two Chinese-flagged government vessels CBDR with your position. They look like they're going to arrive before the LSST."

"Well, if they're PLAN, hopefully they'll thank us for stopping criminals."

"Hope's a dangerous strategy, ma'am. And that's not your biggest problem."

"Jesus, XO."

"Yeah, well. The Navy is going to beat everyone else, including the LSST."

"Fucking Christ. Make damn sure they know we're already cutting in. I need them to keep it in their pants long enough for the LSST to arrive. Make sure they know that we've possibly got two PLAN boats inbound. I do not want a shooting war over our fucking heads. Christ, twice in one day."

"Already on it," Ho said. "Be careful, ma'am."

She toggled back to the crew channel as she prepared to drop into the nipple gangway, but before she could speak the deck lurched under her feet, throwing her against her seat. A moment later the ship stabilized and she pushed herself off, dropping down into the gangway. "What the hell just happened?" she radioed her crew.

"They just cut hard to port and then burned the aft thrusters again," Chief answered. "We're heading back into the Chinese EEZ."

Oliver's stomach sank. "Why the hell would they do that?"

"Because something on this side of the border scared them, ma'am," Chief replied. "Anything you want to tell us?"

"Navy's here, aren't they, ma'am?" Pervez asked.

"Not yet," Oliver answered.

"They're coming?" Okonkwo asked. "Who's coming?"

"Everybody!" Oliver said. "Find a way to fire those bow thrusters before we wind up in Beijing. How's that cut coming?"

"Almost there." Okonkwo grunted.

"Chief, please tell me you hailed them," Oliver said.

"Three times," Chief answered. "No reply."

"I also tried them in Mandarin," Ho broke into the channel, "so we're covered there. Sent them two text cables too, in English and Chinese. No replies. Might be they've had enough of talking to the Coast Guard for one day, but I'll keep after it."

Oliver swallowed. "Thank God for you, Wen, seriously."

She dropped into the gangway and took up the anchor position behind Chief. Okonkwo had just finished his cut, dropped his torch, lifted his duster and faded back behind McGrath. The boarding officer lifted his hand, crossed his first and second fingers in the air, then spread them. *Crisscross by twos.* He then made a fist followed by spreading his fingers. *Deploying explosive munition, get ready.*

Okonkwo gave a nod that was nearly imperceptible through his hardshell, moved up alongside the cut plate.

"These are likely bad hombres," Oliver radioed. "Get ready to fight."

The stacked line trembled as each member nodded, edged a little further out of the fatal funnel that would be opened once Okonkwo knocked the plate aside.

"Here we go!" Okonkwo said, then slammed the butt of his duster into the cut section of the plate.

The blast of metal dust exploded through the opening just as soon as the plate fell inward, followed by a second, and then a hornet round that punched through the cladding at the back of the nipple gangway.

"XO! Taking fire!" Oliver radioed Ho, "Where the fuck is my LSST?"

"Jesus Christ, boss. Navy boats practically shouldered them to beat them out. They're still on course, but the Navy's blaming them for a near-collision, and telling them to wave off."

Oliver fought against the sick rage bubbling up her throat. "Are you fucking kidding me?" *No, you cannot worry about this now. For now, you keep your head down and your crew safe.*

Ho echoed the thought a moment later. "Don't think about it now, boss. Either way, cavalry's coming. Don't get shot."

"Working on it."

"Fire in the hole!" McGrath radioed, tossed a grenade through the opening. The team rolled aside as the flash, eerily silent without atmosphere, was followed by a third cloud of dust.

"Go! Go! Go!" McGrath shouted and high-stepped through the hole, racing through the twelve-pack's compromised airlock and into the cargo bay.

Oliver took up the rear, squinting to peer through the cloud of smoke, metal dust and drifting plastic particles. The twelve-pack's interior was a tunnel of silver-white fog, slowly clearing as it was bulled aside by the passage of the crew's charging bodies. One moment, there was only Chief's plunging back, and the next she blinked and realized just how much trouble they were in.

Most six-packs stored their cargo in port and starboard bays, leaving the aft clear as a gangway to load machinery, or to give teamsters space to work. This twelve-pack had converted that space to storage, packed to the ceiling with gray plastic crates now scored and abraded by explosions of dust, lids peeled back and knocked askew, yellow Chinese lettering so badly scored it was well-past readable. They had been tied-down against the micro-gravity, but the sharp metal particles of the dust clouds had turned the nylon strapping to tattered ribbons. The crates towered to either side of the team, extending the fatal funnel from the entry point all the way into the twelve-pack's interior, tall solid walls of materiel to either side of them, pinning them into a straight-line shooting gallery with no way to get out of the line of fire.

"Shit," McGrath muttered, and Oliver could see him begin pumping off rounds from his duster, not worrying about hitting anything, desperate to simply keep the unseen enemy's heads down, to blind them before they could get their wits about them enough to return fire down a passageway where they literally could not miss.

Oliver leaned back, craned her neck to look out the top of her hardshell's visor. Was that a gap she saw between the top of the stacked crates and the ceiling? No time to think on it, she would have to pray it was. She dropped her duster to hang in its sling and pushed off Chief's shoulders, sending herself shooting up until her hardshell helmet knocked against the ceiling. She turned to her right and nearly cried out with relief at the sight of a space just big enough for her to scramble on her back.

"Everybody, back it up!" she called into the radio.

"Ma'am, I..." McGrath was grunting as he racked the slide and fired again and again.

"Back it up right now! I'm about to get you cover!"

The team jostled each other as they performed the difficult maneuver of moving the stack backward, bounding in the micro-g, timing their hops to use the momentum of the person in front of them to propel them in the right direction. *Guess the simulator training wasn't for nothing.*

The cloud of dust was settling at the far end of the passageway where it widened into the twelve-pack's cabin. Oliver could see dark shapes moving beyond it.

A hornet round streaked out of it, blazing down the passageway and colliding with McGrath. "I'm hit!"

"Hang on!" Oliver scuttled backward on her backside, got her feet braced behind the first tower of stacked crates, and shoved. McGrath had just cleared the way, driven backward by the momentum of the hornet round as the stack tumbled across the passageway, tops popping off, dumping a stream of plastic packing pellets, dotted with the slender, insectile shapes of guns across the deck. The crates tumbled on their sides, choking the passageway, creating a low barrier that Oliver knew wouldn't offer real cover, but would at least obscure the line of fire.

The crew turned and began to scramble into the tiny alcove she'd created, out of the fatal funnel. Oliver immediately scooted to her right and toppled the next stack of crates as Pervez took a knee and pumped three more rounds from her duster up the passageway before scrambling after her shipmates into the rapidly growing safe-zone.

After the third stack of crates was down, the team had a large enough area to squat out of the line of fire, and Oliver dropped down off the stack and observed her handiwork. The pile of guns, packing pellets, and crates was roughly three feet high, and thick enough that Oliver felt confident it might give them some protection from dust, at least.

Chief had drawn a hornet pistol and was stacked on the edge of their enclosure, covering in case the enemy decided to rush their position. Oliver squatted in front of McGrath. "You OK?"

She could see through his visor that his emergency seal had activated, swept her eyes down until she located the small black hole in the left side of his hardshell's torso.

"Yeah," his answer was pained. "It got meat this time, but I don't feel like a bone's broken. Doesn't hurt when I breath."

"What's your HUD saying?"

"There's liquid. I'm definitely bleeding, but I think I've got time. Hornet round's propellant probably cauterized when it went through."

"XO? What are you seeing on your end?"

"Just like the man said," Ho answered. "He'll make it. I think."

"Jesus fucking Christ, ME3," Oliver said, "you have got to stop getting shot."

"Sorry, skipper." McGrath winced.

"XO, what's our position?" Oliver asked.

"You're still hauling into the Chinese EEZ," she could hear Ho tapping keys in the background. "We can follow under hot pursuit, but this is about to go seriously dynamic. It would help if you could stop the boat, or get it turned around."

"Chief! How many contacts downrange?"

"Uh, I count ten, boss. Give or take one or two," Chief said.

"I'm putting you in remedial math class when we get back to Pico, Chief."

"With all due respect, boss," Chief ducked back as another hornet round streaked past, "you come up here and count moving targets through a dust cloud."

"MK3, can you get this boat stopped?" Oliver radioed Okonkwo.

Okonkwo was already scrambling his way up a stack of crates, leap frogging his way up by pushing off the opposite stacks in the micro-g. "Should be an access hatch somewhere back here."

He crawled his way aft, crate lids toppling in his wake.

"Dude!" Oliver radioed. "Do not put debris in our egress route!"

"You want the bow thrusters fired or not, skipper? I'm following the propellant lines. There'll be an access panel."

"You sure it's the same on a Chinese hauler?" Pervez asked.

"Chinese need to clear their propellant lines same as anyone else," Okonkwo answered. "Got it!"

Oliver turned to look, saw Okonkwo had crawled all the way to the vessel's stern, where a plastic pipe was penetrating the bulkhead. He reached out, ripped a panel away, sending it drifting down into the passageway, and thrust his head into the dark void beyond, his helmet lights turning on.

"Shit!" Chief muttered, leaning out and firing at someone Oliver couldn't see. "BM1, give me some dust!"

Pervez rolled out, her long gun flashing, before rolling back. "They're coming, skipper."

"Well, don't let them!" Oliver radioed back.

"They don't seem interested in my opinion," Pervez said as she rolled out again, firing before jerking back. "Fuck! Got singed on that one!"

"Look at me!" Oliver raced to Pervez, turning her so she could see her visor. The plastic was badly scored by metal dust, but the seal indicators were still green, and the failsafe didn't appear to have fired.

"Fuck, skipper. I can't shoot like this," Pervez said.

"It's a duster," Chief said, "just point in a vague direction and you'll be fine."

"Okonkwo!" Oliver said.

"Almost…" The engineer's voice was taut with effort. "Hope this is the right one."

"What do you mean you hope this is the right one?" Oliver demanded.

"I can't read Chinese, ma'am! Everybody hold on to something."

"There's nothing to hold on to!" Oliver called back.

The ship lurched to one side, and Oliver felt the sudden stability of centrifugal force as she slammed into a stack of crates. They were spinning.

"Guess that was starboard thrusters," Okonkwo grunted. "Sorry."

A moment later, the vessel shuddered, stabilized. "Was that you?"

"No," Okonkwo said, "that came from the helm. OK, I've got it now. Hang on… again."

Oliver felt the ship lurch again, her body pitching forward and slamming into the stack of crates before her. "XO?"

"You're moving backward now, ma'am," Ho said. "Unfortunately, post spin, it's got you moving laterally to the border. You're not going any deeper in, at least."

"Well, that's something."

"Yeah, well, the Chinese pursuit is making contact as we speak, so fingers crossed they're in a good mood."

"No response to your hails? What's the Navy–" She was cut off as the ship shuddered, and she felt the deck slow under her feet. "XO? What's happening?"

"You've got a Chinese vessel on the opposite tow-fender," Ho said. "They're at soft dock already. My guess is that they're cutting now."

"They are," Okonkwo said. "I can see sparks from the conduit."

"XO, got a read on their transponder? Who is it exactly?"

"Ma'am, do you have good cover?" Ho asked.

"Not great, but enough to hold what we've got until rescue."

"Do me a favor and stay in it?"

"This dance of a thousand veils shit is seriously pissing me off, XO." Oliver said.

"It's PLAN naval infantry, ma'am," Oliver could tell Ho was desperately struggling to stay calm. "Stand by for the Chinese marine corps."

Oliver managed to toggle her radio off just before she spoke. "Jesus fucking Christ."

Okonkwo dropped down next to her. "They're in, ma'am."

Chief ducked back as a hail of hornet rounds blazed past, followed by a sizzle of smoke from further down the nipple gangway. "Jesus Christ, ma'am. Plasma railgun fire. The nipple is shearing. We're gonna lose the longhorn."

"What's the status in the cabin?" Oliver asked.

"I think the first crop of bad guys are down, ma'am," Chief said, "but we've got a new crop of bad guys now. They're putting a mobile barricade into the p-way."

"Tell me they're not advancing. I do *not* want to get into a gunfight with the PLAN."

Chief ducked out into the passageway, rolled back as several crackling plasma balls whipped past. "Momma taught me that lies make baby Jesus cry, ma'am. Looks like we're already in a gunfight."

"XO! What's the status on rescue? PLAN is advancing on our position and we're about three ticks away from being overrun."

"LSST is on scene, but the Navy's keeping them back. Navy small boats are on top of you, but both tow-fenders are covered. They'll have to cut through the hull."

"MK3! How long will that take?"

Okonkwo had braced himself against a stack of crates, his duster ready for the first PLAN marine to round the corner. "Too long, skipper." Before he toggled off his radio, Oliver could hear him whispering a prayer.

"OK, Chief!" Oliver looped a gauntleted hand into McGrath's armpit. "Help me get McGrath up."

"Where are we going, boss?" Chief asked.

"Up on top of the stacks, and from there, into the propellant access hatch. Okonkwo! How many can we fit in there?"

"If we go one at a time? Maybe three." Okonkwo answered.

"OK, get your ass back in there and get ready to receive McGrath."

"Ma'am," McGrath said, "I can fight, put someone else…"

"Are you fucking kidding me? You're shot. Get your ass up there before I get truly pissed."

McGrath gave no answer other than a grunt of pain as Chief helped Oliver boost him up the stack. He crested the top and began wriggling out of sight as Pervez rolled out, firing her duster. She rolled back and dove to the farthest side of the tiny enclosure the crew occupied.

An instant later, three crates in the stack closest to the passageway vaporized as a plasma ball enveloped them. The crates above them hung suspended in the air, then slowly began to drift their way down.

Holy shit, we are actually going to die. The thought was oddly liberating. Her memories sparked, played back in a rush across the backs of her eyes, moment after moment – her promotion to captain, Ho and his family applauding in the front row of the auditorium. Adam teaching her how to work her smartphone, his face lighting with one of his rare displays of genuine affection, standing on the deck of the cutter Ibis in the Hudson River on the Fourth of July, the ash from the fireworks exploding overhead dusting her shoulders. Tom, always Tom, his face filling her vision, his thumb tracing the line of her mouth. *I swear, Jane. I have never loved a human being in my life like I love you.*

At least I'll see you again, Tom. At least I'll see you again real soon. Tom's face dissolved into Alice, a crystal-clear picture of her daughter curled up on a mod couch in her hab, smiling contentedly as she surveyed her mining drones on her smartphone. There was sadness, sure, but mostly Oliver felt lighter. Boarding Action, the threat of a war, Fraser and Donahugh and Allen and the Commandant himself, all disappeared. They couldn't touch her now.

Alice. The thought of her daughter jolted her. She couldn't die. Alice needed her. She had promised she would get through this and join her, help her find her feet and get her stake running right. That thought had kept her going throughout this whole thing, and she would be damned if she would give up on that now. *Stay alive. Save your team. Then save your daughter.*

Oliver took a breath, rolled out into the passageway, raised her duster. She did not want to shoot at the PLAN, but they were clearly already shooting at her. She had to slow them down long enough for help to arrive.

The mobile barrier had been pushed to less than five feet away. Oliver could see the rubber wheels supporting the ballistic sheeting, the clear plexiglass at the top, slits cut for the PLAN marines behind it to thrust the barrels of their plasma railguns through. Their skintight biosuits were patterned with an obtuse blue and white digital camouflage pattern that made them stick out like sore thumbs.

She could see them freeze, hesitating, clearly stunned that a single person would actually engage them. It gave her a moment to raise the duster and pump off three blasts in rapid succession. The mobile barrier would make short work of the actual munition, but she could see the marines flinch back instinctively regardless. She saw a flash of orange erupt past her head and knew a plasma round had nearly decapitated her. *The next one won't miss.*

And then she was knocked to her side, bouncing against the stacked crates, the ship shuddering around her. The ship shook again, and Oliver almost imagined she could hear it groaning despite the lack of atmosphere. The shooting had stopped, and she found that her legs still worked, glanced down at her body in amazement, still struggling to process the miraculous fact that she was still alive.

She wrenched herself out of the passageway, back behind the remaining crates, sawing her head to her left, looking down toward her longhorn's nipple gangway.

And realized who had saved her.

A Navy small boat's nipple had replaced her longhorn's. She recognized the digital camouflage pattern of a US Marine boarding team as they raced down the gangway, pushing a mobile barrier of their own.

Her own longhorn was nowhere to be seen. *They must have just rammed it out of the way, and docked in its place.* She caught her breath at the skill necessary to execute a maneuver like that. Pervez could have done it, she felt sure, or… *or Gunnery Sergeant Fujimori. It can't be them. What are the odds?*

Her question was resolved an instant later as the mobile barrier was shoved forward by the biggest marine she'd ever seen up close.

Farah Abadi.

She could see Koenig beside her now, his lieutenant's bars thin black lines on the shoulders of his hardshell, leveling a hornet gun, popping off two of the rockets in rapid succession. Beside him, Slomowicz pulled the pins on two smoke grenades, tossed them gently down the passageway, enveloping all of them in thick, viscous pink fog, blossoming like dandelion balls, perfectly symmetrical, gradually expanding out from their containers in the micro-gravity.

More marines were coming down the gangway, Oliver scanned for Fujimori, guessed the gunnery sergeant was up in the boat's cockpit, firing the thrusters to keep the vessel locked in place. The sheared remains of the longhorn's nipple prevented the Navy boat from extending their own nipple to get hard dock with the Chinese vessel. But Fujimori managed to pilot the Navy boat perfectly, thrusters keeping it moving in perfect concert with the twelve-pack.

The marines were toppling crates, setting up firing positions behind the mobile barricade. Oliver counted at least ten hornet guns pointed down range. Oliver waited, not daring to look out into the fatal funnel for fear of getting shot. Ten seconds. Thirty. No more rounds fired either way. It appeared to be a standoff.

She radioed Okonkwo. "Can you see anything from up there?"

"Only a lot of people pointing guns at each other but not shooting. Which is… good?" Okonkwo replied.

"Jesus, XO. Are you seeing this?" Oliver asked after toggling back to Ho.

"I am," Ho radioed back. "You've got eight marines there."

"That's eight marines blowing this vessel apart if this détente breaks."

"I don't think it's going to break, boss," Ho said.

"Why not?"

"Can you get a view out the starboard side windows?"

Oliver turned, glanced up toward the low windows spanning the sides of the hold. She could just make out the long, gun-studded keel of a Perry Class frigate coming out of orbit and burning to station keep alongside them.

"Cavalry's here," Oliver said.

"Theirs too, boss. There's a Chinese Type-054B frigate off your port beam. But from what I can hear on the radio neither side wants to start a war here. I guess if shooting starts, Donahugh wants it on her terms."

"I'm relieved to hear that."

"Admiral Oliver," Lieutenant Koenig had bridged to her radio, come to stand before her in the half-melted remains of their enclosure of crates. "General Fraser has asked that you allow my coxs'un to escort you and your crew to the *Gibbs*, ma'am. My apologies for your longhorn, but its drift trajectory is sending it back toward SPACETACLET. I'll send a salvage team as soon as we get the situation stabilized here."

"That won't be necessary, lieutenant, thank you." Koenig's cool professionalism added insult to injury. Of course this was the team that had saved her. A part of her wondered if Fraser had planned it that way. She toggled back to control. "XO..."

"I've already launched a UTB, ma'am. They'll recover the longhorn," Ho replied.

She glanced back at Koenig, radioed Ho. "So, I guess we're not the only Boarding Action team that feels it's more effective to do the work than stick to the simulator."

"I guess great minds think alike, ma'am," Ho said.

"Thank you, lieutenant," Oliver said to Koenig. "I know I speak for my entire command when I say how grateful I am for the assistance."

Koenig's mouth twitched inside his helmet. "It's our pleasure, ma'am. You know how it is out here. One team, one fight." *That is the complete and polar opposite of how it is out here.* "Are any of your people injured?"

"My boarding officer took a hornet round, I haven't had a chance to see how bad it is." She toggled to her team's channel. "Everybody out! We're getting off this thing."

A part of her wanted to contest Koenig's assumption of command of the situation. Her team had intercepted the vessel, she was the supported command. But she looked at her team clambering down off the stacks – Pervez with her visor abraded beyond use, McGrath with his failsafe shrink-wrapping visible through his visor – and she knew the truth: they had bitten off way more than they could chew, and the marines had saved their asses. She wasn't going to pretend it was different. And, even if it was, SAR-1 was not in a position to negotiate with hostile PLAN naval infantry.

The team dropped back down from the crates and followed her up the nipple gangway and into the Navy small boat. Fujimori sat at the controls, turning to regard McGrath as he winced his way on board. "Are you all right?"

"I'm good," McGrath heaved his bulk onto the boat's casualty crash bench. "Just got shot up a little, is all."

"He does that," Pervez explained. "Thinks it makes him tough."

"I'll make sure corpsmen are waiting on the *Gibbs*," Fujimori said, firing the starboard thrusters to push them off. Oliver looked out the starboard windows to see another Navy small boat, its cabin crammed with more marines, maneuvering to dock in place the moment Fujimori pushed off. Behind it, she could see three PLAN boats, and the massive, sleek bulk of the Chinese frigate beyond. Like the Chinese biosuits, it was more compact and streamlined than American manufacture, its four hundred feet shaped somewhere between a cigar and a bullet, the smooth lines broken by regularly studded ball-turrets, bristling with ordnance trained past the Navy boats where Oliver knew the *Gibbs* awaited them.

Past that, she could see the LSST's rhino, blue-light flashing, firing attitude thrusters to keep it alongside the twelve-pack. Oliver could see one of the Navy boats matching its position, interposing itself between the LSST boat and the twelve-pack. She bit back rage and radioed Ho again. "Tell the LSST to RTB. They can't do anything out here. Make sure they understand they have my gratitude and that I will get this worked out."

"Aye aye, ma'am," Ho radioed back.

Fujimori glanced sideways, caught Pervez watching her, looked back to her controls. When a second glance revealed that Pervez was still staring, she turned. "What?"

"Sorry," Pervez said. "It's just that I watched you the last three years, and I'm just a huge fan of the way you fly."

Fujimori smiled, nodded. "From what I hear, you're going to be getting up close and personal with everything my team does real soon."

Pervez's smile vanished, and she looked studiously out the front window for the rest of the trip.

In a development that surprised no one, Fraser was waiting for them when they exited the airlock, accompanied by two marine security guards and two hospital corpsman who swarmed McGrath, breaking the seals on his suit and getting him loaded onto a gurney Oliver assumed would be rushed off to sickbay. "I'll go with him," Okonkwo said, "if that's OK."

"I'm fine," McGrath said.

"I'm not," Oliver said. "You like catching rounds so much, I'm worried that you'll do it again if you're not supervised. Whole team is going with you."

"You'll be all right," Fraser put a hand on McGrath's boot just before one of the corpsmen whisked it off. "I'm glad you all made it out in one piece."

"Us too," Oliver said. "Thanks."

Fraser shook his head. "You can thank me by coming to speak with the Commanding Officer of 11th fleet. The *Obama* is about to drop in out of orbit to assess the situation. Admiral Donahugh is on board, and she is going to want my report on… this. She's also… concerned about your arrest of one of her JGs. I think you should speak with her personally."

"I think that would be best," Oliver said. "I need to discuss with her why the Navy nearly provoked hostilities a stone's throw from my faculty, and then practically shouldered my rapid response force in their rush to respond to this incident."

"Perhaps we should discuss this in private, admiral?" Fraser asked.

Oliver looked back at her crew and turned back to him. "Do you know what a contubernium is, general?"

Fraser smiled. "Of course I do."

"We're a contubernium. If you have something to say to me, you can say it to them, too."

"Look," Fraser said, "Donahugh's going to make a… request directly to Admiral Allen. This is your chance to speak your piece to her. That is," Fraser turned to Pervez and Chief, "if your coxs'un and ranking NCO will permit it."

Chief smiled and Pervez laughed out loud. Oliver was amazed at how charming the marine general could be. "Just have her back before 21:00, sir," Pervez said.

"Aye aye, BM1," Fraser said, gesturing to the adjacent launch bay where another small boat waited.

The Navy boat had barely gone five hundred meters from the *Gibbs* when a huge shadow swept over and the coxswain angled their bow upward to meet it. Oliver looked up to see the massive thousand-foot length of the USS *Obama*, 11th Fleet's flagship, and the largest spacegoing warship in any American service. Small boats clustered around it like pollenating insects, the groups of its antennae arrays, solar collectors, and gun batteries making it look like some dark coral reef.

"Man, that is awful big." Oliver tried to keep the awe out of her voice, failed.

"It's not the size," Fraser said, "it's the ordnance. That monster can launch seventy-five boats in a pinch, can put over two thousand marines anywhere on the surface in just a few hours. The Chinese can't match it. Not even close."

"They're working on it, surely."

"They surely are, but it's the same game as it is back on Earth. We've got the better gear and training. They've got the numbers. The *Obama's* badass, to be sure, but it's just one. The Chinese Type-003 is three quarters the size, and they can throw five of them at us. I don't like those odds."

"All the more reason not to ever test them."

Fraser turned, regarded her through his visor. "I'm sure Vice Admiral Donahugh will be interested in your perspective on the matter."

Oliver ignored him, watching as one of the *Obama*'s six docking bays on this side of the ship grew in her vision. A tethered traffic controller drifting in the micro gravity waved their boat into place with lighted wands. Oliver swallowed her admiration and her sense of vertigo as they disembarked into a loading bay that could have easily accommodated most of the Coast Guard's spacegoing vessels all on its own. Huge cranes and robotic arms were at work all around them, hauling small boats into dry dock, or even fixing larger ships in place while Navy crews swarmed their exteriors, welding torches blazing.

Inside the airlock, the ship's spin gravity took over, and Oliver leaned gratefully into it as her stomach settled. A sole adjutant, white uniform crisp and gleaming with gold braid, waited patiently for them to remove their hardshells. Fraser, at least, was wearing his duty uniform underneath, and she watched as he reached under his blouse, adjusting his shirt stays until most of the wrinkles were smoothed out. Oliver had to make do with her suit's base-layer –technically a uniform, complete with her name, service and rank – but the contrast between their appearance was marked. Fraser made no offer to give her a chance to freshen up before the adjutant led them down a maze of passageways, getting Oliver quite lost before ending at a hatch with a brass plaque reading: COMMANDING OFFICER, beside 11th Fleet's logo – an owl clutching a trident, soaring up into the black of space on a trail of blazing stars.

Fraser caught Oliver's eyes, gave a sympathetic look, and knocked.

"Come!" Donahugh's voice was the rasp of someone who had quit a bad smoking habit many years back, running just beneath the even tone of command that Oliver instinctively recognized in the most powerful leaders. Donahugh was a woman who didn't yell, and this was because she didn't have to.

Oliver followed Fraser through the door, into a modest office perfectly balanced to blend the cramped military efficiency of shipboard life on the 16th Watch with the trappings of authority. The reflective-surfaced cherry-wood desk was small, the stars-and-stripes and US Navy flags taut on plastic spreaders that ensured they would remain perfectly smooth even if the spin gravity switched off. A hardshell stood stacked on top of its case in one corner, conspicuously in a state of readiness. Vice Admiral Donahugh was every bit the woman from the recruiting ad Elias had shown her back on Earth. Her smile was warm, her eyes alert, and her presence commanding and regal as royalty. "Demetrius, great to see you! Admiral Oliver, it's a pleasure to finally put a face to a name."

Oliver knew it was most assuredly *not* a pleasure to put a face to a name in her case, but she was grateful for the diplomacy regardless. She shook Donahugh's hand, the grip firm, not the insecure crushing handshake of someone attempting to intimidate, but not the dead fish Fullweiler had given her either. Donahugh was a pro. "Great to finally meet you too, ma'am," Oliver said.

Donahugh sat down, motioned for them to take their seats. Oliver noted her seat put her head lower than Donahugh's, in a tactic that was well familiar.

"Can I offer either of you something to drink?" Donahugh asked.

"We're fine, ma'am," Oliver said, smiling toward Fraser, who inclined his head.

"All right," Donahugh said. "Thanks for coming on such short notice. I hope you don't mind if I ask my adjutant and JAG to join us."

Oliver felt a chill lance through her belly. The handshake wasn't an attempt to intimidate, but this surely was. She wished like hell that she'd had Ho by her side. She considered asking for him, but it would take far too long for him to arrive. Still, it wouldn't do to object on Donahugh's own flagship. "Of course."

Donahugh pushed a button on her phone, and a few minutes later the adjutant entered with another officer, with the crossed sword and quill pen on his lapel that marked him as a JAG officer. Both took their seats off to one side, silent, but conspicuously visible. Donahugh steepled her fingers. "I want you to know that my corpsmen are going to take good care of your man. As soon as I have a report, I'll let you know."

"That's much appreciated, ma'am," Oliver said. "So, how's it lay now?"

"The Chinese don't want to make an issue out of this anymore than we do. It's not going to be another Lacus Doloris. From what I can gather from Admiral Sheng, they've been trying to keep the Shui Fong from spreading to the Moon since they got here, and they're embarrassed that they've failed. They don't want this going public, and I'm inclined to let them have that."

"As am I," Oliver agreed.

Donahugh met her gaze silently, her expression reading *I didn't ask,* so loudly she may as well have yelled it. "Anyway, the PLAN is taking custody of the ship and the prisoners. General Fraser's team is already back aboard the *Obama*. This won't make the press as more than a routine boarding."

"That's good," Oliver said.

"But we have two matters to discuss, admiral. Firstly, you arrested an officer carrying out orders assigned from this very office."

"I arrested him under proper authority for breaking international law."

"I've reviewed the logs from our launch. Lieutenant Junior Grade Scott was outside the Chinese EEZ."

"With all due respect, ma'am, I am confident in my own instrumentation and that assessment is incorrect. Your team was a half-klick inside the EEZ, and Scott's arrest staved off what I am certain would have been a dynamic and potentially lethal situation."

"I wonder what kind of tune you'll sing when word of this hits the press, Admiral Oliver. Face matters in standoffs like these. It affects the delicate political calculus. We looked like fools, thanks to your intervention."

Oliver shrugged. "I guess. You're the politician. I'm just here to enforce the law."

Donahugh's face colored, but she didn't take the bait. "I appreciate your transferring Lieutenant Scott to my command. I am having the charges dropped. I will not prosecute a man for following orders."

Oliver shrugged again. "That's your call. It's my intent to enforce the law to the utmost of my ability. Orders or no orders, one of your people breaks it, they're getting collared. End of story. I will report this incident accurately up my chain."

Donahugh said nothing, and the silence dragged on. At last, she inhaled and said, "That's just the first incident. The second is this… confused interception. This could have gone a lot worse if we hadn't arrived on scene. And the PLAN sure as hell isn't happy about your intercept. This is twice in a single day they've gone guns up with the Coast Guard. You've certainly caused quite a stir."

Oliver was conscious of her shabby underlayer, the sweat still not fully dried, surrounded as she was by Fraser with his shirt stays and the Navy officers in their crisp whites. "I prefer to think of this as a logical evolution of the Coast Guard's expanding mission in protecting lunar traffic. And the fact remains that while we are grateful for the Navy's assistance here, the Coast Guard had a rapid response force inbound that was practically shouldered by your team."

Donahugh's smile reminded Oliver of the way she would look at Alice and Adam when they talked back to her. "That's not the story I'm hearing from Lieutenant Koenig and his team. As with the arrest, this intercept underscores that you fail to appreciate international relationships are based largely on rapport built over a long period of time. The PLAN knows me and my people. They had no idea who they were dealing with when they rolled up to find a bright orange small boat tied up to one of their national's vessels."

"Sounds like a great opportunity for us to get acquainted."

"I have the Commander of the People's Liberation Army Navy on the line in my CIC. Also, the Commandant of Coastal Troops of the Russian Federation. As soon as we're done here, I have a call with the Secretary of the US Navy. This could go very badly for you."

Oliver gave an exaggerated shrug. "I'm breathing, those thugs are in custody, and that arms shipment didn't make it to Earth. I'm feeling pretty good about today."

"Those thugs are in the custody of the PLAN, admiral. And one of your people is in my sickbay with a hornet round wound."

That made her gut clench. If McGrath was seriously injured, she would never forgive herself. *No. Don't let her get to you. McGrath was doing his job. He knew what he'd signed up for.* She pushed the worry off her face. "Yeah, well. He gets shot a lot. Seems to me you should be taking that up with the asshole who pulled the trigger."

Donahugh leaned forward, putting on a conspiratorial smile. "Look, I know what you're trying to do here, but you have to realize that we have the same goals. We both want to see settlements on the Moon stabilize without any deterioration of relations between the United States and China. Russia also has a dog in this fight. And you have to realize that the approach you're taking is undermining that."

"I believe I'm speaking for my Commandant," Oliver said, "when I say that I don't believe a warfighting agency is best positioned to meet that goal."

Donahugh's cheeks colored. "Need I remind you, that without General Fraser's task force, this could have gone a lot worse?"

General Fraser looked at Oliver and raised an eyebrow.

It was meant to lighten the mood, but Oliver's voice went serious. "I want you to know how incredibly grateful I am for General Fraser's support, and I intend to highlight his role when I return to Mons Pico and write my report. I will also be sure to highlight that his support would not have been necessary if my own team was permitted to respond. It also wouldn't be necessary if your instrumentation errors didn't result in you stationing military units inside foreign territory. I'll add, ma'am, you're not going to secure peace through superior firepower here. It's the Commandant's view that deescalation is needed, and the Coast Guard is in the best position to deescalate. Look, I'm thrilled the Navy showed up when you did. You saved our butts and no mistake. But this was a high seas pursuit, and under that doctrine, we could have held out for our LSST. The Coast Guard is the right authority for this incident."

"Admiral Oliver, the Coast Guard is a warfighting branch of the military, same as the Navy. You think that just because you also have a SAR mission you're somehow better equipped to take on China?"

"Be fair, ma'am. We do lots of other things. Break ice, scrub decks."

Admiral Donahugh's cheeks reddened. *There. Finally got to her.* She glared, but said nothing.

Oliver smiled, spread her hands. "What can I say? We're awesome."

"I find it ironic," Admiral Donahugh sighed, "that we rescued the great deescalators from a full-on gunfight."

"I don't share your sense of irony, ma'am," Oliver said. "You stepped into your appropriate role once that role became appropriate, but if my LSST had been permitted to deploy, perhaps they could have resolved the issue before the PLAN arrived. Gunfights with foreign powers is your job. Catching quarantine-runners is ours. Now, respectfully, ma'am, if you have nothing further, I hope that, in the future, we can arrange a more coordinated effort, so that the Coast Guard, as the supported command in this instance, can call on support when we're overwhelmed in the future, *after* we've exhausted all of our own measures to resolve the problem. And I'll remind you to have your technicians triple-check your instruments before deploying troops close to the EEZ. I catch *anyone* in there without hot pursuit authority, they are going to jail. End of story."

Fraser did his level best to control his expression, but Donahugh went pale as she caught the ghost of his smile before he locked it down. "I'm going to ask the Secretary of the Navy to speak with the Secretary of Homeland Security when I return to my ops floor," she said, standing up. Fraser immediately followed suit, but Oliver remained seated, holding the vice admiral's gaze. Donahugh stared at her, and Oliver imagined she could at least feel the struggle to control her temper that didn't reach her expression. "I suggest you prepare your response," Donahugh finally said. "I hope we can find a way to coordinate operations more effectively in the future."

Now Oliver stood. "Thanks for looking after my ME3. If you don't mind, I'd like to remain aboard until he's discharged."

Donahugh looked like she'd swallowed sour milk. "Of course."

The adjutant who escorted them in conspicuously made no move to escort them out. Fraser waited until they'd walked out of the office, and several feet down the passageway back toward sickbay before he burst out laughing. It was a rich sound, deep and genuine, and Oliver felt the tension of her exchange with Donahugh unknot in her gut as she waited for him to finish. "You've finally lost it."

"No," Fraser clapped her on the shoulder. "I'll make it, I think. Man. I like you."

Oliver blinked. "You do? I thought I was making your life miserable."

Fraser laughed again. "You don't have the power to make my life miserable. I like that you stuck to your guns in there. You'd have made a good marine."

"That... that's high praise."

"It is. Heartfelt, too. You're a straight shooter, and it's clear that you give a damn about your people. That's rare among the political animals that usually become flag officers."

"Does this mean that Donahugh thinks I'm a straight shooter, too? That she secretly admires me and wishes I were Navy?"

"Hell, no," Fraser laughed again, "that woman is sharpening her knives as we speak. You have made a very powerful enemy."

"Meh. I was almost turned into a pile of bubbling lipids and superheated plasma an hour ago. It's gonna be tough to rustle up fear of a kind old lady in an ice cream truck driver's uniform."

"Jesus, you've got brass balls, Jane. That woman is going to pull your legs off."

"But you like me."

"I do."

"So, what's your professional advice?"

Fraser paused, stroked his chin. At last, he turned to her. "Let me show you something."

Without waiting to see if she would follow, he turned and made his way down another passageway, Oliver followed as he moved abaft, and then through another zigzag of passageways that she realized was crossing the *Obama*'s keel. After a few minutes, he paused at a long bay window that Oliver could tell overlooked the launch bays on the opposite side of the ship. He leaned against it, grinning like the cat who swallowed the canary, arms folded across his chest. As she approached, he jerked his chin toward the scene below. "See for yourself."

Oliver joined him, looked down.

The launch bay had been cleared and recommissioned as a training range. One side was lined with popup targets, pinned to posts rigged to blade or move at the instructor's command. The range was backstopped by the open void of space outside the launch bay's open doors. Three small boats were up on pylons further along, the hulls in various states of perforation where teams had practiced cutting, shooting and setting charges. Tether pegs were set at regular intervals on the floor, the walls, the ceiling. Oliver could tell the bay was kept open at all times and never spinning, ensuring the occupants were constantly combating the rigors of micro-gravity.

She could see the Marine Corps team drifting in as she looked down, unmistakable by PFC Abadi's massive bulk. They locked their tethers in place, testing the slack, then turned to face Koenig, who was gesturing to one of the dummy small boats as he doubtless radioed them on their private channel. Oliver doubted they'd had time to strip out of their hardshells and shower, or even grab a meal. They'd probably come straight from the fight to the training bay, unwilling to miss a second.

"That's my crew," Fraser said. "I didn't tell them to get back on the stick after that fight. This is how they do it, all day, every day. They live for this."

"You must be very proud." Oliver's throat was dry. She thought she'd been pushing her people hard, thought she'd been working through the issues, making the smart bet on getting them out into the field, that it would somehow give them an advantage over dedicated professionals. But she looked down on the team in that bay, already running gear checks on gear that had just been in an actual firefight, and realized with a final heave of her gut that these were more than professionals. These were prodigies, these were talents, these were singular beings.

Oliver knew that any enemy could be beaten, but watching the unflagging energy the marines below her showed as they bounded to their armory table to load up gear, she began to wonder how. She knew that kind of doubt was poison, that letting it reign even for a moment would erode her ability to lead the team to victory. Poor morale was as airborne as a flux. Everyone around you could feel it, and if they could feel it, it could infect them. She felt the twinges of despair, tried to step on its head and kill it before it could breed, failed utterly. Her gut coiled in on itself, and she could feel Fraser standing beside her, watching her reaction. He could feel it. She knew he could.

"This is your crew for Boarding Action again this year? You don't think maybe they could do with a break? They look a little worn out to me." She was grateful Fraser didn't laugh, let her have her feeble attempt to hold the line of her flagging morale.

But she could see Fraser's grin out of the corner of her eye. "Oh, I'd say they've got another run in them yet. Not sure they'd do too well back out in the regular fleet anyway, what with them being big time media celebrities and all."

"Wait," Oliver tore her eyes away from the MARSOC16 team and looked back at Fraser, "you said they train in a separate facility on the far side of the Moon!"

Fraser smiled. "I lied. Why would the corps shell out all that money for a top flight orbital training center when we can just use the Navy's flagship?"

"A marine, lying. I'm going to have to adjust my world view."

"Pretty sure it's authorized under certain circumstances in the Drill and Ceremony Manual. I'll have to check the chapter on dealing with troublesome coast guards."

They watched in silence as the MARSOC16 crew below finished gearing up and Koenig ran through the mission brief. They stood, heads together, helmets touching. The radio made it unnecessary, but Oliver could tell the bonds ran deep enough that they drew strength from it.

"They're impressive, aren't they?" Fraser asked, as the crew finally pounded fists and stacked on the entry for one of the dummy boats.

"You know they are," Oliver replied. "What's the point to all this?"

"Navy has six times our budget and almost double our personnel. Worse, they're more connected in Washington. Eight US Presidents served in the Navy. You know how many served in the marines?"

"None. Same as the guard."

Fraser nodded, "It would be beyond easy for them to sideline us if they wanted to, put the SEALs in instead."

"So? Why don't they?"

Fraser gestured at the marines training below them. "Because we're the best at what we do. Not the close second, not pretty good, not even great. The absolute best."

Oliver nodded, taking his meaning. She tried to focus on the team below, gathering intel she could relay to her own people, but it was impossible to concentrate over the pit yawning in her stomach, the voice whispering in the back of her mind, over and over again, that McGrath's injury aside, there was no way in hell her team would ever be able to win.

CHAPTER 13

For science fiction fans, and finally the public at large, the colonization of the Moon was supposed to be a second chance. It was humanity's opportunity to start with a blank slate, to transcend the mess we'd made of earthbound geopolitics. It was difficult to describe the heady optimism of just a decade ago when the SpaceX purse reached the tipping point that sparked the Space Race. In just a few short years, that optimism is hard to remember. The slog on the Moon mirrors the slog on Earth. The same environmental degradation. The same power dynamics. The same pall of fear drifting down from rattling sabers in constant orbit over the lunar surface. The Moon may have been a blank slate, but human experience is millennia old, and we bring that baggage with us no matter where we go.

MEET THE NEW WORLD, SAME AS THE OLD WORLD
OP-ED IN THE *NEW YORK TIMES*

It took another Earth day for the *Obama*'s medical team to clear McGrath and discharge him. Oliver tried to send the rest of the crew back to Pico, and was not remotely surprised when they refused. Ho practically begged to be allowed to come out and join her on the *Obama*, but Oliver insisted he remain to make sure she had a reliable set of eyes at SPACETACLET in case there was fallout from her meeting with Donahugh.

As she sat in one of the *Obama*'s two MWRs, watching her crew relax, she tried to put the conversation with Donahugh out of her mind. It was difficult at first, but she found she could manage it by focusing on what SAR-1 was doing. *They're safe. Whatever happened yesterday, your people are OK.*

Pervez remained parked in front of a video game console the entire time, completely absorbed in muscle-car racing games while Okonkwo sat in a corner, knees drawn up to his chest, leafing through a well worn copy of the King James Bible. When Oliver checked in on McGrath, she found Chief at his bedside, the two of them sitting, mirror images of one another with arms folded across their broad chests, listening to the Irish punk rock McGrath favored. "I will never," Elgin shook his head in disbelief, "understand what the hell it is you like about this shit, ME3."

"One more song, Chief," McGrath smiled, scratched at the sutures beneath the bandage over his ribs. "This is the one that'll convert you." It wasn't, of course. Nor was the next one, or the one after that, and the two were still arguing about the definition of punk by the time the shuttle arrived from SPACETACLET to take them home.

McGrath had gotten lucky again. The Chinese hornet round had punched through a gap between two of his ribs, far enough out to clear the lung, the propellant from the motor cauterizing the wound as it went through. An inch to the right and there was no question he would be dead. As it was, there was little to do. Oliver stood uselessly beside his bed, trying to find a way to apologize. But in the end she knew how the conversation would go, with an embarrassed McGrath saying it was the job, and her feeling no better for having made him do it. He would be back on the line quickly, of that she had no doubt, and he would insist on reporting for duty as soon as he was able.

But she stood next to that bed and endured the uncomfortable silence as Chief and McGrath respectfully waited for her to leave. *I can't protect you. I can't protect anybody.* The thought repeated itself in her mind over and over on the shuttle ride back to SPACETACLET.

Ho greeted her as they shuffled into the squad room, moving gratefully through to their lockers to finally change out of their suits. "Hey, boss. Glad you're back safe."

"Thanks, XO. It's good to be back in one piece."

"Yeah, look, could I get a word?"

Oliver froze, all the dread she'd managed to vent watching her people safe and unwinding came crowding back. Ho knew Oliver better than anyone, and he certainly understood her contubernium ethic. If he wanted a word alone, it was bad. "Sure," she managed with a mouth suddenly gone dry.

Ho's look was sympathetic. "In your stateroom, boss."

She turned to head to her quarters off the squad room, stopped as Ho touched her elbow. "Your official stateroom, boss."

Oliver followed him down the passageway to the stateroom, desperately trying to conquer the sense of dread, to stop herself from pumping Ho for information, to find her military bearing for whatever was about to happen. Her XO paused at the entrance to her stateroom. "This will be OK, boss. Just remember that."

"You're not coming in with me?"

"Not this time, boss, but I'll be right out here to meet you when it's over."

"Jesus, Wen. I feel like I'm about to have a kidney harvested."

Ho smiled at that, which took some of the edge off the dread. "Good luck, boss."

Oliver wasn't exactly surprised to find Admiral Allen sitting on her rack as she entered. He was wearing his utilities and a grave expression. He didn't get up. "Jane, glad to see you're OK," he gestured to the chair behind the desk. "Have a seat."

Oliver sat in the chair as straight backed as she could manage. "Good to see you too, sir. To what do I owe the pleasure of a personal visit?"

Allen ran a hand over the back of his head, ruffling the spikes of his thinning hair. "I don't how to say this, Jane, so I'll just say it. You're relieved."

She blinked, her mind unable to process the word. "Relieved?"

"Of command, Jane. Avitable will continue as acting CO of SPACETACLET until we can find a replacement. I'm sure you'll agree he's been doing fine so far."

"Relieved," Oliver repeated. A weird sensation of burning cold was crawling up the back of her neck to tingle beneath her scalp.

"I'm not going to make a big deal out of it, or a formal announcement," Allen went on. "Neither you, nor the guard needs that embarrassment. You're already focused on training SAR-1, and that's what you'll continue to do through to Boarding Action, but you won't be assuming command of SPACETACLET when it's done. You'll head back to Earth and retire. I'm sure you'll agree that changing their coach this close to the competition is a bad call."

Allen's words were a buzzing in her ears, hearing the words, her brain refusing to process them.

"Jane," Allen said, and Oliver realized she'd been staring at her own reflection in the surface of her desk, jerked her eyes up to him.

"Are you reading me?" Allen asked.

"Yes... yes, sir."

"OK," Allen stood.

Enough of the shock wore off for the questions to start flooding in. "Sir, may I ask why?"

Allen sighed again. "Look, Jane, I appreciate what you tried to do here. For what it's worth, the old man was impressed by the innovative line you took. But when you risk a lot, you pay a lot when it doesn't work out. If it were up to me, this wouldn't be happening. I'm sure if it were even up to the old man, this wouldn't be happening. But this is coming from the Secretary of Homeland Security, Jane. I guess you tweaked the Navy's nose hard enough for them to go as high and hard as they could. This is the result. I'm sorry, Jane. For what it's worth, we're not demoting you. You'll retire as a rear admiral. As far as I'm concerned, you earned those shoulder boards, and you'll hang them in your shadow box with pride. I hope that's something."

The shock and dread began to boil away, the anger surging in its place. "So, that's how it goes, sir? You sent me out here to do the job my way, and when my way becomes inconvenient, you hang me out to dry?"

"We sent you out here to train this team to win Boarding Action, Jane. We didn't send you out here to try to win this jurisdiction fight with the Navy all by your lonesome. I tried to tell you before that this fight is bigger than just you, that you had a team around you, that you could trust *us* to be doing our jobs in the head-shed. I get why you hit it the way you did, and I'm as impressed by your guts as anyone, but there are some things in the world that are bigger than one person, Jane, and this time, it bit you. Even if we had no doubts about your methods, it's out of our hands now."

Oliver's mouth worked, a thousand retorts forming and vanishing, the churn of rage and hurt and humiliation and despair utterly disarming her. *Oh God, Tom. I really fucked this one up.*

Allen waited another moment, giving her a chance to respond. At last, he shook his head, placed a hand on her shoulder. "Jane, I hope that, whatever you do after this, you give yourself some peace. Kariawasm and Flecha. Tom. They weren't your fault, Jane. Skipper or no, you were *one* person at Lacus Doloris that day. You were one piece of a big and incredibly complex machine that was breaking down under equally big and complex stressors. If there's one lesson I'd take from this, it's that it isn't just you. You don't have to carry everything yourself. I hope you'll remember that in your retirement. For once in your life, Jane. I hope you'll give yourself a break."

He went to the stateroom hatch, paused again. "You've still got another two weeks to Boarding Action. I know I can count on you to continue training the team with the same intensity and passion you've exhibited so far. But you got to do it your way, and it has nearly gotten one of your star players killed *twice*. That is over. SAR-1 is *off* alert status. No more radio calls. You will stick to the simulator, the range, and exercise evolutions until show time. And I do *not* want you sitting in the boat with them. You direct from a distance."

"It was the MARSOC16 team that saved our bacon in that dustup, sir. They've got their people out there doing the job, too! They're not sticking to the simulators!"

"We are not talking about MARSOC16, Jane. We're talking about SAR-1. SAR-1 is done running radio calls, and you are damn sure done riding herd with them when they get underway. Is that clear?"

The rage fled, leaving Oliver only with a drifting numbness. "Crystal, sir."

"OK, good. We'll talk again after Boarding Action and figure out how best to get you retired. You never did a headquarters tour, so I think it makes more sense to do it at Yorktown, or even…"

"Yorktown! What about my waiver to retire here? Alice needs me to help out with her operation."

"That waiver was granted before…" Allen waved an arm as if to indicate some invisible pile of wreckage, "…this, Jane. The old man isn't inclined to be doing you any more favors right now. You know the regs. Nobody retires on the 16th Watch. You'll head back to Earth. If you want to come out here to be with Alice, you'll have to buy a berth on a rocket."

Oliver felt her stomach clench. "Sir, you know damn well that I'll never be able to afford that."

"Alice managed."

"Alice was staked by a financier for her mining operation, won the space elevator lottery, *and* she came out here during the H3 rush years ago. You know damn well I won't be able to do any of that now."

Allen only shrugged. "Thanks again for all you've done, Jane. It was a demanding assignment, and you gave it your all."

Oliver stood, staring at the stateroom hatch after it closed behind him, battling the numbness and confusion. It took Ho a full five minutes waiting in the passageway before he finally came in.

He took in the expression on Oliver's face, the fact that she was standing, staring at the hatch. "That bad, huh?"

The familiar sarcasm of Ho's tone allowed some of her humanity to return, and Oliver collapsed into her chair, the breath whooshing out of her. She felt tears track from the corners of her eyes, blinked them away. "How much did you know?"

"Only that Allen was here, that he was going to be speaking with you alone, and that I was not to let you give any additional commands until after that conversation had occurred. I kind of put two and two together from that. What's the damage?"

"I'm relieved, Wen."

Now it was Ho's turn to slump. He sat on the rack, hunched over, his shoulders hooped forward as if his tall frame had been deflated. "Fuck. When do we leave?"

"Not until after Boarding Action. Avitable is going to continue running things, I'll finish training the team. We're off alert status. Simulation only. And once we finish Boarding Action, then I go home."

"Jesus, boss. I'm sorry."

"*I'm* sorry, Wen. I dragged you all the way out here…"

Ho waved a hand. "Stop that. I was honored to come, and I'm still honored. I'm guessing this is because of the arrest and that last run?"

"Not sure. He said it was out of his hands. It came down from the Secretary of Homeland Security. Donahugh must have pulled strings with the Secretary of the Navy and I guess they did some horse-trading. Jesus Christ, Wen, how could I have been so stupid?"

"Don't do this to yourself, boss. You weren't stupid. You saw a shot and you took it. They sent you out here to do an impossible job and you tried your best. That's not a thing you have to apologize for."

Oliver punched her desk. "I got McGrath shot. Twice."

"McGrath signed up to get shot. He's ME rated. That's literally their job. You think he'd have been happier attacking a plywood six-pack? Or playing laser-tag with a video screen? He's OK. They all are. You are too."

"Allen said it was because I tried to fight the Navy all by myself. He said that I… that it was because of…" Her throat closed, and all she could get out was a choked gurgle.

Ho pursed his lips. "Yeah, well. There might be something to that, boss. I know you never really let yourself off the hook for what happened at Lacus Doloris."

"You knew? Why didn't you say something?"

"Look, you're my friend, but you're my boss first. There have to be boundaries, even with us. You let me get away with too much as it is."

"Yeah, I guess I do. Fuck! I can't believe I fucked this up."

"Boss, just because your decision to put the team on real radio calls instead of the simulator was driven by your personal demons doesn't mean it was *wrong*. Allen, the old man, the Secretary of DHS, whoever made this call is making the *wrong* call. You were given a New York minute to get a demoralized and fractious team whipped into shape to go out and win one of the most demanding competitions against the toughest opponent this side of the Moon or Earth. You were faced with an extreme task, and so you took extreme measures to achieve it. And that bit you on the ass, sure. But that doesn't mean that you made the wrong call. It just means that you missed the target this time."

"At least he's going to keep it quiet. He's talking to Avitable now, but they won't tell the command. I'll finish out the training, take the team to Boarding Action, then quietly head home."

"Home?"

Oliver bit back tears. "They're sending me back to Earth to retire. Regs. Nobody can retire out here."

"They can make an exception."

"Allen says they won't."

"Jesus Christ, boss. How are you going to get back out here to help Alice?"

Oliver put her head in her hands. "I won't."

Ho started to stand. "Boss, I'm so…"

Oliver felt the tears gathering behind her brow, didn't want to cry in front of him. "Let's not talk about it, please. I just… I can't right now. Tell me what you'll do, Wen?"

"Nothing for now. I'm not saying a thing to Ting-Wei until after Boarding Action. Then I'll turn in a dream sheet to the detailer and see where they want me."

"God, Wen, I hope this doesn't reflect badly…"

Ho stopped her with a wave. "Don't be dramatic. You're a flag officer who got caught up on the wrong end of a political scrap. You're not a virus. You can't infect my career."

"God, and now I have to walk back into that ready room like nothing happened and try to keep on training these people. What am I doing, Wen? Every time I follow my gut, things go pear-shaped."

"I've got news for you boss, every time anyone does anything things go pear-shaped. I know you outrank me, and you have more time on the job, but I've learned a thing or two in my day. Nobody ever knows what they're doing. You remember when Alice came along?"

"Of course I do."

"I remember when Lillie was born. I thought I had it all figured out with Hui-Yin, but I somehow managed to screw things up just as much. The only difference was that I screwed them up more confidently."

As he spoke, Oliver rummaged around in the desk's top drawer, grateful when she found that the bottle of Widow Jane was still there, and still a quarter full. She pulled it out, uncorked it and took a slug, not even bothering with a glass.

"Look, boss," Ho went on, "if turning out top-tier sailors was easy, they could have grabbed some middle-of-the-road-just-follow-orders officer out here to get the job done. But training great people and making them work together as a great team doesn't work like that. If it did, I'm sure someone would have written a manual on it."

"There are manuals written on it. Lots of manuals."

Ho waved a dismissive hand. "Not good ones. There's a reason they brought you out here, boss. There's a reason they picked you for this impossible job."

"For the life of me, I can't figure out what it is."

"Because they trusted that gut you keep following." He stood, put a hand on her shoulder. "Now, you just need to learn to do the same."

CHAPTER 14

When you act on your gut, you're unpredictable. Mercurial. Authentic. You make leaps of logic and see connections others miss. Gut instinct lets you see beyond where your business is today to what it could be tomorrow. That's why it's such an important part of what I call the Rare Breed. Don't get me wrong – instinct isn't always right. Brain science tells us that useful gut instinct depends on having plenty of knowledge and experience about your field. And as powerful as intuition is, if you don't follow it with planning, skill and strong management, all you've got is a cool idea on a whiteboard.

SUNNY BONNELL,

4 LEADERS WHO WON BY FOLLOWING THEIR INSTINCTS (DESPITE BEING TOLD THEY WERE CRAZY)

Oliver felt barren, stripped of hope. She hadn't realized how much she'd been counting on a future with Alice until the option had been taken from her. The grief was so powerful that it approached physical numbness, in her face, in her fingertips. *How could you have been so stupid. How could you have let this happen.* She tried to recall Ho's comforting words in her stateroom after Allen had left, but she couldn't conjure them now. All she could do was take numb step after step back to where SAR-1 waited. The further future sprawled before her in a gray, hopeless wash. She could only focus on the minute by minute in front of her nose.

The crew was waiting for her when she came into the ready room. They weren't in their hardshell undersuits, which could only mean that they'd gotten word somehow, probably from the monitor that no longer listed them as the duty crew.

They looked up at her, strange in their utility uniforms, so long unworn that they looked brand new. She reached the table, braced herself on her knuckles, paused, suddenly unsure of how to begin. The silence stretched uncomfortably long, and her stomach clenched at the thought that Ho might try to break it to them himself, but her XO only gave her the silence and room she needed to get her bearings. It was Chief who finally cleared his throat. "How are you doing, ma'am?"

"Not so good," she admitted. She felt her grief over the loss of her life with Alice rising in her gut, pushed it back down with an effort. *God. I have to call her. Later. I'll deal with it later.* "I take it you know we're off alert status. It's back in the simulator."

"Says 'crew rest' on the monitor, ma'am," Pervez jerked a thumb at the screen, but Oliver held her eyes, only taking her at her word.

"Oh no," Oliver somehow mustered a smile. "There will be no rest. We're back to training starting tomorrow. We are still going to win Boarding Action."

The expressions on the faces of the crew told her attempts at shoring up their egos had fallen flat. "I don't get it," she said, "when I first suggested taking you off the training regimen and putting you on the job, you all looked at me like I was nuts."

"Yeah, well," Pervez said. "I guess we kinda got used to it, ma'am."

Oliver surprised herself by chuckling. "Yeah, kinda gets under your skin, doesn't it."

"Literally," McGrath tapped his bandaged side, which got a smile from everyone, even Chief.

"Firing those thrusters," Okonkwo said, "that's the toughest thing

I've ever done as an engineer, ma'am. Never would have happened in a simulator."

"Look," Oliver said, "this is on me, not you. Those MARSOC bubbas couldn't have done better than you did had they been the first boat on scene back there. I picked a political fight and I lost. Me. Not you. That's why this is coming down from on high."

Chief arched his eyebrows. "You going to be OK, ma'am?"

Oliver waved a hand. "I'll be fine. What you need to remember is that you went after that mission like it owed you money, and that's all any commander can ever ask. Boarding Action is a stupid contest. It doesn't mean anything. The mission is what matters, and no matter what happens when we finally get out there for the actual exercise, you should know that you ran that *mission* like no other SAR operators I've ever launched with, and I've pretty much launched with them all."

Oliver could feel emotions around the table running high, but she was shocked to hear big, near-silent McGrath biting back a sob. "I'm sorry, ma'am," he said, paused to make sure of his composure before continuing, "we wanted to... we wanted to..."

"If you're about to say that you wanted to make up for Tom's death," Oliver said, "or Kariawasm's, or Flecha's, you know you can't. That's not how these things work, it's not your job, and there's no need. But I hope you can take some comfort in knowing that this is exactly what all of them would have wanted. All of you working together. All of you fighting to do the job."

The silence that followed was nearly as long as when she'd first come in, and Oliver looked at each of the crew's faces, trying to see if her words were helping, unable to tell. At last Chief sighed, shook his head. "So, what do we do now, skipper?" *Not your skipper,* Oliver thought, *not anymore.*

She pushed the thought away. If she wasn't technically their skipper, she still had a job left to do. "What do you think we do?" she asked.

"We get back in the simulator, out on the range. We train our asses off, and we win this thing."

Oliver spent a solid ten minutes staring at the receiver that night before returning it to its cradle without calling Alice. She couldn't face the horror of admitting to her daughter that she had failed, both in her mission and in securing a future where they could be together. She lay on her side instead, her mind doing endless self-recriminating loops that banished all hope of sleep.

When she reported the next morning, the crew was already performing boat checks. Without the need to wait for an alarm call, they could get underway for training evolutions just as soon as Oliver launched a boat for them to target. They nodded at her, smiling the smiles of kids who'd just gotten away with something, and Oliver spent a solid ten minutes looking around for anything different before settling on it with a start.

Someone had taken the longhorn out to the pad and put it back into the fleet. They were performing checks on a sparkling new rhino.

"Well," Oliver breathed. "This is certainly surprising. You sure this won't throw you off? Kind of late in the game to be switching horses."

"Yeah, well," Chief said, "I figure there's different ways to honor legacy. The truth is that Flecha would have loved the new thrusters. And there's…" he turned to Okonkwo, "you'd say double the room?"

"At least," Okonkwo smiled.

"At least double the room under the cowling to work. She'd have really dug that. And Kariawasm would have appreciated the more responsive control." Chief looked at his hands. "So. It's still honoring them, really."

"I'd say so," Oliver swallowed the lump in her throat. "Not going to be too much of a lift for you, BM1?"

Pervez shrugged. "Be cool to fly the latest and greatest."

"I thought you didn't need all those 'bells and whistles.'"

"I don't," Pervez agreed. "It's still skill in the end. And sure, it's late in the game to be introducing a new element. But," she looked up, locked eyes with Oliver, "we just took on the PLAN twice in one day and lived to talk about it, the five of us. What's one more impossible thing?"

"You're not suiting up, boss?" Chief asked.

Oliver shook her head. She thought of telling them Allen had ordered her not to, decided against it. Her own morale was shattered, but she could still preserve theirs. "Nope. I think you've had enough executive supervision for one tour. Time for me to fade back and let you roll on your own. I won't be able to be with you on your runs at Boarding Action. Just cheering from the sidelines like everyone else. With a week to go, best start getting used to that, I think."

"Aye aye, ma'am," Chief said, turned to help Okonkwo seal his helmet. Okonkwo tried to do the same for Pervez, but fumbled the thumb tabs, knocking her helmet askew. Oliver saw the tremor of annoyance ripple across her features, dissolve just as quickly.

"Sorry," Okonkwo said, trying again.

"No worries," Pervez's voice was barely above a whisper, but Oliver still heard it.

Through the window, Oliver saw Ho and his crew of roleplayers launch, their longhorn rising up off the pad before engaging aft thrusters and heading out past the cutter launches. A moment later, SAR-1 followed. She settled herself behind one of the terminals and watched the mission logs scroll by, trying to figure out a way to get back to the Moon post-retirement. She could take out a personal loan? Start her own mining stake? Maybe Alice had made enough money to… All the thoughts came to the same dead end. Individual berths on the space elevator were the province of the super rich. Heavy lift rockets were even more expensive. Without government-backing, getting to the Moon would be impossible.

She needed something else to think about, so she picked up the receiver and radioed Ho on his private channel.

"What's up, boss? We're almost in position to start the evolution."

"This is going to sound weird, but... they're all acting... nice."

"Nice." Ho sounded skeptical. "Nice, how?"

"Like, they're treating one another... like I always hoped they would. Back when I first got here."

"Okaaaayyyyy," Ho drawled.

"I'm serious, Wen. It's like someone flipped a switch. What the hell happened?"

"Can't you tell? They're trying to win, boss. They want it because they know you want it. And they don't want to let you down."

It was a moment before Oliver could speak. "But why now? I wanted it from the moment I got here."

Ho was quiet for a while before radioing back. "I guess, when you first got here, they wanted to make up for Tom, for the shipmates they lost. They wanted to do that for you and you told them they couldn't, and they finally know you're right.

"So, now they're doing this for you, instead."

Boarding Action's ground facility was housed, in a development that surprised absolutely no one, at 11th Fleet headquarters on the edge of the Kepler Crater. The *Obama* was decked out in red, white and blue bunting that Oliver thought made it look like some kind of oblong Fourth of July picnic table. Its bays had been cleared of small boats to make room for the various competitors crowding in for docking, each one freshly cleaned, waxed and flying service flags from their mastheads. Oliver spotted the other four armed services, at least a half-dozen local police departments, and a host of other federal agencies with "close-quarters" missions – the ATF, FBI, State Department

Diplomatic Security, Department of Energy Security Forces, she even saw a Postal Service boat.

"What they heck are they doing here?" she asked Ho.

"You know, mail fraud. Sometimes the bad guys make a run for it and don't consent to a boarding."

"Man," Oliver breathed. "Everyone's in on the action."

"They made it through qualifiers, ma'am," Chief said. "We should take them seriously."

"We absolutely should," Oliver agreed.

A flashing light made Oliver wince, but a quick glance confirmed it was just another camera crew. They swarmed around the *Obama*, darting in and out between the boats, shooting every team from every angle. Okonkwo gave a salute that turned into a wave as the camera's spotlight swept across his helmet.

"Well, I guess we're famous now." She was grateful she couldn't hear the roaring crowd or the announcers she knew were in the temporary sound stage they'd built at 11th Fleet, no doubt already predicting MARSOC16's imminent victory.

Still, it was a stirring sight. The camera lights played across the hulls of the gathered regatta, dancing on the waving flags, the glowing running lights, the bright orbs of the mastheads. Oliver felt the same stirring in her heart that she'd felt when she'd participated in the parade of ships into New York harbor during Fleet Week, standing behind the bow gun on one of the Defiance Class boats escorting the Coast Guard cutters in, underway bow to stern down the channel, flags fluttering in the May breeze. "A fleet underway sure is a sight, isn't it?" she whispered into the radio.

"It sure is, ma'am," her crew came back.

Ho put a gauntleted hand on her shoulder, radioed her on a private channel. "Well, boss, we made it. What do you think?"

"I think," Oliver said, "that I've never missed Tom or my kids so much in my entire life."

"Have you told Alice yet?"

"I just… I can't bring myself to make the call, Wen."

"It's OK," Ho radioed back. "Don't think about it now. I know she'll understand when you're ready to talk to her."

Oliver's throat closed, and she couldn't respond.

"So," Ho deftly changed the subject and gestured to the team, who were running through system checks yet again as they prepared for clearance to dock with the *Obama*, "what's the verdict, boss? Can they win?"

Oliver was surprised to feel herself smiling. "I don't think it matters anymore."

"Maybe they'll surprise you."

The small boat in front of them dipped its bow, fired its aft thrusters, and began to drop down toward the open bay. "We're on deck, everybody," Chief radioed. "I know the actual competition hasn't started yet, but you can bet your asses the cameras will be all over us as we tie up, so everyone look smart, and we do it by the numbers. Save the edgy stuff for when we need it. Don't let the attention make you squirly."

"Aye aye, Chief," the crew replied.

The *Obama*'s open flight bay looked like a giant roll-top desk, its accordioned bay doors lifted all the way up, the long teeth of the boat jetties sticking out like a collection of loose pens. Nearly every one of them had a small boat tied up, the crews in their hardshells going over their post-mooring checks with a seriousness and alacrity she was certain they never showed any other time. The reason was apparent. The space swarmed with camera launches, the spotlights sweeping and intersecting and splitting apart until the bay looked as if it were in the midst of a sparkling snowstorm.

Pervez sighed. "Christ. No pressure."

"We're good," Chief said, "just pretend they're not there."

The bay shimmered with camera lights. Oliver could see where most of the *Obama*'s crew off duty had come to crowd the railings to watch the boats come in. Pervez turned to look at Chief. "How do you propose I do that, Chief?"

Chief laughed. "Imagine they're all naked."

"I didn't think it was possible to make it worse," Pervez said, "but I guess that's why you're the Chief."

The laughter went on for a while, but when it finally ran itself out, Oliver noticed they were still in a holding pattern. "Did we miss the signal to tie up? I feel like we've been here forever."

"No, ma'am," Pervez said. "We'd have seen one of the controllers waving us in." She pointed at the controllers, floating in their hardshells in the micro-g, EVA maneuvering packs around their waists. They held lighted wands to guide the boats to their jetties, but these were currently still.

"I don't get it," Oliver said. "It looks like everyone in front of us is tied up. What are they waiting for?"

"Dunno, ma'am," Chief said. "That is kinda weird."

"How's the line behind us?" Oliver asked.

Chief looked at the radar. "Long enough that they shouldn't be wasting this much time. I wonder what's…"

Oliver saw three Navy small boats streak past them, guns out. They weren't flying their flags and their aft thrusters were burning, pushing them hard down to the surface. "Where'd they come from?" Oliver asked.

"Next bay over, ma'am," Okonkwo said.

"That's got to be their ops bay," Chief said. "They probably keep that one up for alert status while all of us are tying up here."

Oliver felt pinpricks of worry blossom in her lower back and slowly work their way up her spine. "But wouldn't they be on alert status to guard the event?"

"I'd imagine so, ma'am," Chief said. "This is definitely a security concern. Bigger than the Super Bowl."

"What the hell is…" Oliver began, then froze.

She could see the MARSOC16 boat, the first into the bay, an honor reserved for the returning champions, and tied up front and center at the jetty closest to the airlock that led into the *Obama* and the impromptu press room beyond. The MARSOC16 team was racing down the launch, hardshells on. Fujimori opened the hatch, and Koenig rushed inside. Slomowicz jogged behind them, tapping a plastic tablet that probably was their boat check sheet.

Pre-launch boat checks. They were getting underway.

Two more Navy boats streaked past them, heading down to the lunar surface. Then two more.

Oliver toggled the channel to the *Obama's* control center, keeping the channel open for the crew to hear. "Control, control, this is US Coast Guard SAR-1. What's going on?"

No response.

She toggled to SPACETACLET, called the ops center. She didn't know if Avitable or Allen had sent the word down yet that she was relieved, but Allen had said he wanted to keep it quiet until after Boarding Action, so it was worth a shot. They might still obey her.

"Ops," Oliver recognized Baskin's voice.

"Baskin! It's skipper," she lied, "we're trying to dock with the *Obama* and suddenly everything is on its head. Is there something going on?"

"Yes, ma'am. There's fighting on the surface."

"Fighting? What kind of fighting? Where?"

"We're not sure ma'am, but it sounds like…"

"Baskin! Where!?"

"Sinus Medii, ma'am."

Sinus Medii.

Alice.

"Baskin, I need coordinates. SAR-1 is inbound." Oliver worked to keep the panic from her voice, "Who is the alert crew right now?"

"SAR-3 is already patrolling…"

"Send them my transponder signal and have them meet me on the surface."

"Ma'am, I…"

"Coordinates in my plotter right now!"

"Aye aye, ma'am."

"Boss," Ho radioed her on a private channel. "You know you can't…"

"Yes, Wen, I know. And you know I'm damn well doing it anyway."

"I know you are," Ho said. "Aaaaand, it's Admiral Allen on encrypted. Seems like he knows you as well as I do."

"Fuck," Oliver said. "Hang on." She chin toggled over to the encrypted channel.

"Jane," Allen was already half-way through saying the syllable of her name when she picked up. "I know what you're thinking, and you are to stand down, do you hear me?"

"Sir, it's–"

"Jane, I don't give a flying fuck what it is. You want to help, and you can, but right now, this is an international incident and weapons are hot and that is *not* your job."

"Sir, it *is* our j–"

"No, Jane, it is not, because I have two more stars on my shoulder than you do and I am *telling* you it is not. Do you fucking read me?"

Oliver swallowed. The images of Alice's face, of her hab burning. Of Tom's boat dancing in gunfire swamped her, making her feel faint. "Yes, sir," she managed.

"Good," Allen's voice softened. "Now, I need you over Sinus Medii with all the other SPACETACLET boats which are launching right now. Once this evolution plays out, you will do SAR and be on standby to provide a force multiplier if required by the Marines. The 32nd

Marine Expeditionary Unit is the *supported* command for this, and you are the *supporting*, is that clear, admiral?"

"Yes, sir. But can you please tell me what the hell is going on?"

"It's Doloris all over again, just in a different spot. Flare up between American and Chinese miners. I have no idea over what."

"Sir, we're not interrupting Boarding Action over a flare up."

"We're not, the People's Armed Police responded, and the Medii police responded to their response. There was a shootout and the Navy got involved. It's spiraling. Right now it's a hab-to-hab fight in the mining camp."

"Holy shit, sir. Is it war?"

"Let's hope not. But if it is, it's starting with the best. General Fraser is leading the team personally, it's the best the Marines has to offer. Hopefully, we won't be needed, but just in case we are, get down there and standby for orders. I'm on the SPACETACLET control floor. Commander Avitable is with me, but I will be commanding this operation personally. I, and not you. Remember that. You can reach me here."

"Aye aye, sir," Oliver said, her stomach settling somewhat now that she had a plan of action.

"Ma'am," Pervez radioed, "I've got coordinates in my plotter from SPACETACLET control. It's coded as a–"

"Hot war, yes," Oliver said. "We're fighting the Chinese in Sinus Medii. Get us down there, BM1. McGrath, guns up."

"Aye aye, ma'am," they said at the same time. The silence was thick as Pervez fired attitude thrusters and shifted the boat to starboard, angling the bow before firing the aft thrusters and setting them moving. No one said a word, but then again nobody needed to. Everyone knew where Alice lived.

"Wen..." she radioed him privately, "Christ I know this is unprofessional but..."

"I've already tried calling her twice, boss. No answer. Don't freak, that could mean anything."

"OK, thanks. Keep trying."

"Switching magazines," McGrath radioed, and the autocannon shuddered as its feed belt rotated out the simulation rounds they would have used for Boarding Action, replacing them with the live rounds they were required to carry. "We're at half-capacity because of the competition."

"Well, shoot straight," Oliver said, trying to force some humor into her tone and failing miserably. "How far out are we?"

"Shouldn't be much longer, ma'am," Pervez said.

"We're getting a live feed from 11th Fleet, ma'am," Ho radioed. "I'll put it on the monitor."

The crew leaned in around the popup screen normally reserved for their own camera. It showed the view of one of the Navy boats station keeping just above the hot zone, probably as a hedge against any of its arriving Chinese counterparts. Below it, Oliver could see Sinus Medii's flat gray surface, broken here and there by tire tracks, footprints, or the lip of a shallow crater. The mining district rose up out of the bare expanse without preamble, the habs higher at the center where they'd still been constructed on the surface in the old style, heat exchanger piping ribbing their sides until they looked like bubbles of veined star fruit. Further out, the newer models were buried deeper and deeper below the regolith, using the Moon's natural convection for heat exchange, the small circles of the habs' radiation-shielding breaking the lunar soil like a scattering of coins. Interspersed between them were the Helium-3 furnaces, their long conveyor belt ramps silent and still for now, the tracked drones sitting idle, their bucket arms curled over the motors like scorpion tails. Oliver scanned the habitations wildly, as if she could somehow pick out Alice's operation by sight alone. The gardeners 3D-printed for functionality, not decorative variety, and the structures were only differentiated by their age.

The fighting was worse than she'd imagined.

The SMPD officers were taking cover behind overturned police buggies, huge, thick-tracked tires sticking up into the air. She could see them in their hardshells, sheltering behind the engine blocks, most of them cradling dusters useless at long range, waiting for their tactical teams with hornet guns to give them enough covering fire to close. No more than a hundred yards away, Chinese People's Armed Police were adopting a similar posture behind a makeshift barricade of heat exchange piping, hab debris, and a crashed six-pack. Corpses littered the space between them, Chinese and American both, judging by their suits. Oliver saw one or two bodies down on the barricades, too, fresh wounds still venting oxygen fast enough to be visible to 11th Fleet's camera. As Oliver watched, one of the SMPD officers rolled out from cover, fired their hornet gun wildly, making no real effort to aim. The round streaked above the barricade and disappeared into the lunar sky. *Who knows where that will stop*, Oliver thought. One of the Chinese PAP officers stooped, picked up a chunk of hab debris nearly the size of a car and heaved it up over their head, sending it hurtling toward the SMPD position in the lunar gravity. The American officers dove aside as it collided with one of their overturned buggies, sending it tumbling.

It's Lacus Doloris. It's Lacus Doloris all over again. Oliver tasted sick panic, fought against the vertigo that threatened to swamp her. *No. Get your bearings. You will not make the same mistakes twice. This time, you will do it right.* But she could already tell it was different from Lacus Doloris. There, the fight had all been civilians, miners and mining hands fighting hand-to-hand with chunks of debris, pipe conduit and flagpoles. The fighting here was entirely between law enforcement. The civilians were nowhere to be seen. Ho noticed at the same time, leaning over the monitor. "I don't see any civilians down there at all."

"They're hiding," Oliver managed despite a mouth that had gone completely dry. "This is a shooting fight. They won't risk it."

"Our side's losing," Chief said, pointing. With their barricade of

buggies smashed open, the SMPD were falling back. The PAP saw
their advantage and pressed it, moving out from behind their barricade.
Oliver could see a squad of PAP officers bounding forward to get into
duster range. A flash from one of the Chinese hornet guns and an
SMPD officer went down, then another.

"No, they're... It looks like they're just trying to establish a
perimeter," Oliver said, pointing as the feed showed the PAP slowing to
a jog, spreading out, seeking cover where it was available, or dropping
prone and sighting down across the regolith. She felt the knot in her
stomach unclench a fraction. "I think they're just trying to protect the
Chinese habs."

The SMPD rallied as the pressure eased, covering behind one of the
furnace conveyer belts. Oliver could see them gesturing to one another,
coming up with a plan of attack. "If those fuckers would just stay put,
I think this could be over."

"They've got," Chief paused to count. "That looks like seven people
down at least. No way they're staying put, ma'am."

Oliver turned to Ho. "I need a channel to SMPD ops."

"Boss, there's no way," Ho said. "We'd have to get a relay through
SPACETACLET, and Allen's there."

Oliver chin-toggled through to SPACETACLET control, and was
surprised when Allen answered immediately. "Jane, sit tight."

"Sir, the PAP are holding position, if we don't..."

"There are things you're not seeing, Jane. Let it unfold."

Ho put his hand on her shoulder, radioed her on a private channel.
"Alice is fine, Jane. Her hab is nowhere near the fighting."

"Are you sure? Can you promise me that?"

"No," he said, "but I can promise you that if you lose focus, you'll
have less of a chance of helping her once they do let us go in."

Pushing back against the urge to act took every ounce of her. Oliver
could feel herself vibrating inside her hardshell's undersuit, could see

her heart rate spiking on the vitals monitor in her helmet's HUD.

"Cavalry's here, ma'am," Chief tapped the radar. Oliver had seen the Navy small boats on the screen, but they had finally completed their recon or planning, and were touching down now. 11th Fleet moved their camera angle, and Oliver could see the hatches opening, disgorging teams of marines who bounded out toward the flanks of the SMPD officers, moving and covering by squads. Only one charged straight up the center. "That has to be MARSOC16."

Oliver nodded. "They only make one marine in that size," she tapped the screen to indicate what could only be PFC Abadi. She was carrying a hive – a massive, repeating hornet gun mounted to her body on a stabilizing gimbal arm. "Jesus," she whispered. "What's the rate of fire on that monster?"

"Sixty rounds a minute at max," McGrath answered instantly, "About forty rounds sustained."

Oliver looked at the ammunition belt snaking around Abadi's waist, up over her shoulder and into the compartment mounted on her hardshell's back. It looked like it could sustain for quite a while. She thought of what she'd seen a single hornet round do.

"Hey, McGrath," Pervez said with forced joviality. "If we go down there, stay the hell away from that thing."

McGrath didn't answer, and Oliver privately radioed Ho. "That monster is going to turn this thing on its head. I guess these are conditions Donahugh wants to start a war."

"Not this time, boss," Ho answered. "Look." He tapped the radar and Oliver suddenly realized why the Navy was committing so much firepower.

A Chinese Type-054B was dropping in, the lowest Oliver had ever seen a frigate of that size come to the surface. Small boats were launching from its bays so quickly that Oliver wasn't able to count them, but she guessed it was the full complement. PLAN naval infantry were disgorging from the boats' open hatches even as the vessels were in motion, descending using only their belly thrusters, avoiding lateral burns to keep the line of travel clear for their marines to reach the ground.

"Fuck," Oliver said. "This is not good."

The shooting began before the PLAN marines even reached the surface. Oliver watched in horror as Abadi took cover behind one of the overturned buggies and opened up. The hornet rounds fanned out in a white-orange flash, leaving globe shaped flowers in their wake, before streaking out to punch holes in small boat and marine alike. Abadi was every bit as skilled as she was big. Oliver could see Koenig bounding out from his team, seeking to outflank the Chinese position. He raised a hornet gun with some thick secondary device mounted beneath the barrel, and fired. The round streaked out, its propellant contrail at least twice the size of a standard hornet round. The reason why made itself apparent when it blossomed into an explosion that sent one of the PLAN boats spinning end over end to crash smoking into the regolith.

Slomowicz and Fujimori were bounding in the opposite direction. Oliver could see Fujimori aiming for the wreckage of a Helium-3 furnace. Slomowicz carried a long anti-materiel gun and a stabilizing tripod. "They're setting up a firing position."

"Probably going to act as FOs too," McGrath added. "Call in covering fire."

Rounds were flashing further out on the battlefield where the other marines were engaging. The Chinese appeared to have been caught flat-footed, were being driven back. Their small boats had finally reached the surface, at least six, and were beginning to get their bearings and engage, but the US Marines seemed to have initially won command of the battlefield, and Oliver felt her stomach unclench a fraction. Her mind still churned, seeking a way this could still be deescalated, searching for an off-ramp. *I know it looks bad, but this is still just a skirmish. It's not much worse than Lacus Doloris. If we can just...*

"Holy shit!" Okonkwo said.

The Chinese frigate had fired its port thrusters, spun its massive bulk sideways to the approaching marines. A moment later, it burned to starboard, and pushed itself forward but turned-sideways over the battlefield. "It's coming broadside!" McGrath's voice was uncharacteristically intense.

"Jesus Christ, don't..."

Oliver could see Abadi look up. Koenig was pointing, raising his weapon. She could imagine him shouting frantically into his radio.

The Type-054B ignited. One moment, it was a sleek, black lozenge, silent and dark, marked only by the blue-white plumes of propellant appearing over its hull from the controlled burns. The next, it was hidden behind the muzzle flashes and tube-ignition of its entire port side batteries, as every autocannon and missile pod let loose.

The screen feeding SAR-1 their view of the battlefield turned white as it sought to grapple with the flash of the explosion. Oliver stared at the screen, fists clenched, as if the force of her gaze could make the camera's thermal dampeners resolve the image. It seemed an eternity, but at last the image flashed again, went black, then flickered back into life.

There was nothing left. The line of buggies was scattered rubble. Huge furrows had been plowed in the regolith, piling it up into what looked like pitted gray snow banks, swirled and mixed with the wreckage of habs, furnaces, pipes and vehicles. Oliver couldn't see a single marine. She squinted, made out a Navy small boat on its side, its bow sheared off. Three bodies in hardshells were visible draped across its broken hardpoint, one missing an arm.

The camera began to pan rapidly, sweeping for survivors. Oliver made out a few US Marines now, and two more Navy small boats, still up and moving, but they were specks in a field of wreckage. The camera swung back over, and Oliver could see the PLAN troops surging forward. They didn't deploy out on the flanks as the US Marines had, but instead stayed close to their small boats, who were beginning to sweep the field with autocannon fire.

Oliver looked back to the cluster of US Marines, running now, desperate for cover in the wreckage. She scanned the transponder, looking for inbound Navy contacts, looked back to the field. Abadi was a giant. If she was down, surely Oliver would be able to pick out her hardshell from the others? *Fraser.* She thought of his smile, his singer's bass. *You should have been a marine.*

Before she knew what she was doing, she'd chin-toggled back to SPACETACLET. "Sir, request permission to engage."

Again, Allen answered instantly. "Damn it, Jane, I told you that…"

"Sir, are you and I watching the same feed? They're getting slaughtered down there! They need relief!"

"The Navy will relieve them."

"The Navy has three small boats down there already, and I don't see any inbound on radar. I have no transponder codes."

"They're scrambling them now."

"That will take time! We're right here!"

"Just hold what you've got and…" But Allen's voice was receding, washed away by the blood pounding in Oliver's ears. Her mind was a split screen – half replaying Tom's death over and over again, the other half allowing her to see the fleeing US Marines bounding through the wreckage. As she watched, a PLAN boat fired an anti-materiel kinetic round that churned the regolith into a ball of blinding dust around the feet of three Marines. When it settled, there was nothing left but pieces. The Navy small boats were returning fire, but Oliver could tell that their crews were addled, and they were targeting the frigate above, unable to spare attention to the greater threat of the mop-up crew coming for them.

Oliver began to pick out more survivors. They must have lost radio contact, because they were waving frantically now, desperately trying to catch the Navy gunner's attention, pointing back in the direction of the PLAN small boats.

They were going to be slaughtered.

No. I will not let this happen again.

She toggled to the crew's channel. "SAR-1. Boarding stations for surface action. Go on my mark. Mark!"

Her crew reacted instantly, and Oliver realized with a wash of relief that she wasn't the only one who had been feeling the same helpless tension. Her stomach took a sickening dive as Pervez punched the throttle and SAR-1 dipped her bow and tore through the lunar sky, rocketing toward the Chinese marines. "BM1, put us on that PLAN troop transport," Oliver tapped the radar. It was twelve-pack sized, about a hundred meters behind the majority of the PLAN boats. "Maybe we can cause some chaos in their backfield and get them to turn their head."

McGrath looked at her. "But it's on the surface, boss."

"Yup," Oliver said. "Which means it's not moving. Piece of cake."

"Ma'am," Ho said, "Admiral Allen on encrypted. I'm not answering it."

"Good man."

"Getting us there," Pervez said. Under Pervez's control, the rhino gave the lie to its name. It was faster and more maneuverable than the old longhorn, and Pervez pushed it to its limit – forcing Oliver back in her seat under hard thrust, then flinging her forward again as she fired the bow thrusters to stop them hard, and rotated around to center over the Chinese boat's tow-fender. The world around them vanished into a blur as they moved, punctuated by flashes that Oliver assumed were the PLAN boats firing on them. The flashes stopped a moment later and Oliver knew that Pervez had them over the PLAN boat, too close for their comrades to risk opening fire.

A moment later, the boat shuddered, and Okonkwo dropped down into the nipple gangway. "Soft dock!"

"Everybody in the stack!" Oliver said. "Nobody stays on board. McGrath! Call it!"

"On me!" McGrath called, punching out of his restraints and dropping down into the gangway. He cradled SAR-1's sole hornet gun. "Guns up!"

"Hard dock!" Okonkwo called. "Cutting exterior hatch."

Oliver dropped down into the gangway just as Okonkwo completed his cut. An instant later, the PLAN boat's exterior hatch exploded outward, tumbling toward her. Oliver rolled aside, watched as the thick metal spun through her field of vision, tearing through the nipple cladding and opening them to the lunar environment outside. It was followed by a burst of hornet rounds, Oliver counted at least three contrails whisking past her visor. It was happening too quickly for her to register it, but Oliver's body reacted as if she were going for a casual stroll. She was a veteran of enough ops to know that the knee-shaking, gut-churning bill would come due when this was all over and she had a moment to reflect.

"Welp," Okonkwo dropped his torch, brought his duster up, "guess I don't have to cut the inner hatch."

McGrath didn't bother to call the entry, shouting "fire in the hole!" instead, and throwing two dust grenades into the hatch, rolling aside. Oliver flattened herself against the side of the gangway as the explosions sent columns of dust bursting past them and out through the shredded cladding. Beyond the spreading dust, she could see a crowd of PLAN Marines bounding toward them, two of their boats firing thrusters behind them, turning to counter the sudden threat to their rear.

"Gogogo!" McGrath was through the hatch, firing off a hornet round. The rest of the crew jumped through behind him.

"Hope we don't die," she radioed Ho, moved to follow.

Ho grunted as he followed. "Allen hasn't stopped calling this entire time. Maybe it'll be better if we do."

Oliver cleared the hole where the exterior hatch had been, and stepped into what was clearly a troop transport. Long benches, little more than a fabric seat held out by an aluminum rod, stretched the length of the passageway, empty restraints dangling over them. Ahead, a short passage led to the boat's cockpit, a small yellow ladder disappearing up into what Oliver assumed was the boat's ball turret. A Chinese sailor lay motionless beneath it, his biosuit shredded by what Oliver assumed was McGrath's dust grenade. The sight made Oliver's heart race. *You've killed a foreign national. If this is a war, then it's your war as much as anyone's now.*

McGrath was bounding down the passage, his chin accidentally toggling his radio on and off, treating the team to his war cry, a long incoherent bellow. His hornet gun imparted no recoil, and he fired as he ran, the flashes of the munition propellant visible beneath his armpits as they sped down the intervening distance. The team ran behind him, and Oliver paused long enough to turn to Ho and jerk a thumb up the ladder. Her XO nodded and launched himself up it. "Turret's clear!" He radioed a moment later.

Oliver burst into the cockpit, shocked to find how much it resembled one of her own rhinos. Apart from the Chinese writing on the hatches and instruments, Oliver was fairly certain she could have flown the thing herself in a pinch. McGrath was standing over the corpse of another sailor, his helmet shattered by what Oliver guessed was his hornet gun's butt. A second was backing into the bulkhead, his hands in the air. Okonkwo kept him covered with his duster while Pervez pulled the restraints off her belt, adjusted them to fit the biosuit's narrower wrists, and moved to secure him.

"That's it?" Oliver radioed the team.

"Looks like it," Chief said. "They were here to deliver troops to the battlefield. Skeleton crew was all that was left."

Pervez looked out the window, jerked away. "Boss! We're about to have company!"

Oliver raced to what she assumed was the fire control system. She tapped what she hoped were the right buttons, pulled back in frustration. "Jesus Christ, it's all in Chinese!"

Ho pushed her gently aside. "I'm shocked, absolutely shocked, to find Chinese writing on a Chinese vessel," he said. "What do you need?"

"I want control of the ball turret on top of this monster."

Ho scanned the controls. "Uh, this is... simplified Chinese. I can't read it."

"What, at all?"

"Hang on!" He hit a button. "I think I just put it on manual control?"

"Good enough," she said. "McGrath, get up there on that... whatever fucking gun they have up there."

McGrath nodded, turned toward the ladder to the turret, stopped. "What do I do with it?"

"What do you think you do with it? Shoot the enemy!"

A moment later, Oliver could see the streaking tracer fire rushing past the port side windows, the PLAN Marines there scattering as their own boat's weapon was turned on them. One of the other PLAN boats had completed its turn and Oliver could see its own autocannon turret swiveling to direct fire on them now that the Chinese knew their vessel was taken.

"McGrath!" Oliver radioed. "PLAN 12-pack port beam one hundred yards. They've got a bead on us!" The tracer fire ceased, and then a moment later started again, arcing into the PLAN boat, the rounds punching through the windows and the starboard side bulkhead, flipping the vessel onto its side and sending it rolling. It tumbled into one of the PAP's surface-rovers, knocking that vehicle on its side, its massive knobbed tires spinning uselessly up at the lunar sky.

A less competent gunner might have tried to target the boat's turret, but McGrath knew that if he wanted to stop the threat, that meant he had to stop the people. Oliver watched as he put a few rounds into the rover for good measure.

"Nice shooting!" she radioed him. But she could see more PLAN boats detaching from the assault, turning toward them.

"I dropped the emergency inner hatch seal!" Okonkwo radioed, backing away from it. "I'll go see what the propellant situation looks like. Might be we can drive this thing too… aaaaand they're already cutting."

Oliver turned to see the sparks and bright blue flame of a PLAN cutting torch as their marines started to cut their way in. "McGrath! Keep that turret working! Everybody else, cover down on that hatch!"

"Boss!" Ho said. "That's not…"

There was a flash and one of the front windows fell inward. Ho shouted before cutting his radio, tumbled backward, smoke rising from his hardshell.

Oliver turned to see two PLAN Marines on the boat's bow, already making their way inside. Oliver raced to her XO, raising her duster, afraid to fire for fear of catching him in the wide-pattern blast. One of the PLAN Marines raised a slim gray tube and Oliver threw herself down as she saw another flash, rose, scrambling to get her duster into her hands. Ho was already up, moving stiffly. *Stiffly means he's in pain. Pain means he's been hit.* Oliver went feral; not even bothering to fire her weapon, she ripped it off its sling and charged the remaining distance, clubbing it down on the PLAN Marine. He raised his weapon to parry and she hammered it aside, bringing it back up to crunch into his face plate. His failsafe fired, and she could see the shrink-wrapping tighten behind his cracked visor as he tumbled off the boat's bow.

Ho was grappling with the second. Oliver could see him snarling through his visor as they wrestled. The marine was trying to pull free, but Ho's arms were longer, and the wound had made him desperately strong, he yanked backward and the two toppled inward, the PLAN Marine flipping over Ho's head and skidding face first along the deck. Pervez followed behind, clubbing him with her duster until he went still.

Three more marines were climbing their way up the bow. One fired a hornet pistol, and Oliver rolled aside yet again, then swept back, raising her duster. The three marines froze as she locked her spider boots in place and leaned in to compensate for the recoil. The weapon boomed silent, the dust pattern wide enough to sweep all three of them back and out, sending them tumbling in the lunar gravity. She didn't watch to see how badly hurt they were, and a hornet round zipped in past her face to remind her that trying wasn't a good idea. She crouched to the deck, pulling Ho into the corner beside the Chinese prisoner, racking the slide on her duster to cover the window. They were out of the line of fire of both the hatch and the window, and she'd get a shot off on whomever came through either.

"How bad is it?" she radioed Ho.

Her XO had pulled himself into a sitting position, was looking at the singed, black dimple in his hardshell exterior. "I don't believe this, it self-sealed. My failsafe didn't fire."

"What? Are you hit or aren't you?"

"I am, boss, but it was an old carbon-dioxide laser. Cauterized me. Hurts like hell, and I feel a little dizzy, but I think it self-sealed the hardshell as it went through. Everything is cooked."

"Ho, do not die, do you hear me?"

"I'll do my best."

McGrath dropped out of the ladderwell, came racing into the cabin, followed by the rest of the crew. They took cover in the opposite corner. "What's up with the turret?" Oliver asked.

"It's gone," McGrath said. "I got out just in time."

"Thrusters are shot to pieces too, ma'am," Okonkwo added. "This boat's not going anywhere."

He glanced back down toward the boat's aft. "They're coming through the hatch now," he added.

Oliver saw the barrel of a weapon pushing through where the quartz-glass of the window had been. "Through the bow, too. Get ready to fight."

She raised her duster, waiting for the gun's wielder to make themselves visible. They'd have to if they wanted to get a shot off of their own. *Unless they get smart and throw a grenade in.* Her mind spun, searching for a way to counter that threat, but there was nothing. Her team was crammed into the only spaces on the vessel not visible from the bow window or the rear hatch. There was simply no cover to be had. If a grenade came through that window, she would have to dive on it in the hope of giving the rest of the team shelter from the blast. *Well, jackass, you wanted to be in the fight. Now you're damn well in it, aren't you?*

The gun barrel dipped a fraction, steadied. Pumped out two hornet rounds in quick succession, sending the munitions streaking aft, toward the hatch Okonkwo said the Chinese had just cut through. *Why would they…*

A moment later, the weapon's holder pushed through the window – their hardshell patterned with the blue and gray digital camouflage of SPACETACLET's LSST.

Oliver slumped in her corner, suddenly weak with relief. The sailor fired again, thumped down onto the deck, followed by two more LSST operators, hornet guns up and trained on the rear hatch. They advanced slowly, followed by another handful of LSST sailors and two US Marines. Oliver recognized their faces instantly – Koenig and Fujimori.

"Admiral Oliver," Koenig said, extending a hand to help her to her feet. "We seem to keep rescuing you."

"Looks like my LSST rescued me," she said. "My XO is hit. Do you have corpsmen handy?"

"No, ma'am," Koenig said. "He'll have to shelter in place until we can get the battlespace stabilized."

"I can fight, ma'am," Ho said, trying to rise, wincing.

"The fuck you can," Oliver said, "but you can't stay here either. Do your best to keep up, but I want you to keep your head down."

"I have to admit, ma'am, you certainly split their attention," Fujimori said. "Took some pressure off us. Really appreciate it."

Koenig gave her a look, but kept his peace. "Still could go either way, ma'am. If your team is fit to fight, we could use you."

"We are absolutely fit to fight," she said. "Point us at them and pull the trigger."

"Outstanding," Koenig said. "We lost the rest of the squad, but I think they're back by our lead boat. We want to fight our way through, if you'd care to join us."

"General Fraser's there?"

Koenig nodded. "We lost radio contact when the Chinese frigate engaged."

"Ma'am," one of the LSST operators approached her. "Admiral Allen's orders are for us to tie up with you here and hold this position in the enemy rear."

Oliver glanced out the window at the PLAN Marines moving to find cover among the debris. Another two small boats were gliding toward them. "Absolutely not. It's a miracle this position hasn't been overrun already. We stay here and we're just going to wind up shot full of holes. This is going to be a running fight."

"Ma'am," the LSST operator said, "my orders come directly from Admiral Allen."

"Good for you," Oliver said, "you can testify at my court marital. I am taking my team and we are going right now. Come with us or stay, your call."

Oliver turned back to Koenig. "Lead the way, lieutenant."

Koenig nodded and scrambled back out the missing window, Fujimori following. "Let's go!" Oliver radioed her team. "The marines need our help!"

She glanced to ensure the team was following after her, even Ho, limping along with one hand clamped over the sealed black spot in his hardshell. Okonkwo reached his side and gripped one of his elbows, pushing him along. Oliver dropped out through the window, slid down across the boat's bow, letting her weight take her the rest of the way until her boots crunched down in the regolith. She turned as she slid, saw the ragged ruin of the boat's turret, the autocannon sheared neatly in half.

She turned back to the battle behind her and froze.

The Chinese frigate was under thrust, rising and withdrawing from the surface. Oliver turned and saw the reason why: a Perry Class frigate burning hard toward it, turning itself broadside as it came. Its open bays were still launching Navy small boats, racing toward the Chinese positions beneath their rising frigate. Oliver turned to look behind her and saw the Coast Guard touching down. In addition to the LSST, two SAR boats had landed, blue-lights flashing ill-advisedly; further out and up Oliver could see a growing white dot that she knew was a cutter.

The Chinese, caught in the middle and abandoned by their frigate, were milling in confusion. A body of the PLAN troops seemed dug in around the base of a large, partially ruined structure, a Navy boat crashed into its domed roof. The rest were turning to track the coast guards deploying in their backfield. Oliver noted with satisfaction that the LSST had emerged from the disabled PLAN boat and were making their way toward the Chinese position. *Well, they're not stupid, at least.* The Chinese fired a few desultory shots toward them before turning to track the fresh Navy boats touching down on both their flanks.

"That Fraser's boat?" Oliver pointed to the Navy boat crashed into the structure's roof.

"That's it," said Koenig.

"Where's the rest of your team?"

"We're hoping they're with the boat," Fujimori said. "Lost comms."

Oliver looked at the US Marines deploying from the Navy small boats. "They'll help with the main fight, but they're not going to get to whoever is trapped on that roof in time."

"No, ma'am," Koenig said. "Don't see how we can get through to them in time either without going through the worst of the fighting."

"Not on foot," Oliver said. "We won't stand a chance. We have to run the perimeter as quickly as possible. Wish that Chinese boat was still operable. Okonkwo, are you sure you can't get it running?"

"No way, ma'am," Okonkwo said. "Propellant lines are comprised." He scanned around them. "There's the ground rover that McGrath shot up."

"Can you get *that* running?"

But Okonkwo was already bounding toward the six-wheeled machine, moving around to its side, heaving it back up onto its wheels, assisted by the weak lunar gravity. A hornet round streaked past him, answered by three more from the LSST, advancing toward them. Okonkwo flinched, but kept working, dusting regolith off the controls, pulling on a cable, pushing some buttons. A moment later, he waved to them.

Koenig shrugged and bounded toward him, followed by Oliver and her team. "MK3, this vehicle has no helm." Oliver gestured to the ragged hole where the steering column was visible through the broken dashboard.

"No, ma'am," Okonkwo said, "but the throttle still works, and I can sort of steer with this," he gently tugged a metal cable, and Oliver watched the big wheels turn in response.

"That's just one cable, Okonkwo," Pervez radioed.

"Yeah, we can only turn left. But it'll go."

"That seems… unreliable," Koenig said.

"I'm sure your guy could build an entire surface rover out of coconuts, sir, but you're stuck with me for now," Okonkwo said, "If you've got another ride. I'm all ears."

Koenig scanned the battlefield again. "OK, I guess we start angled to the right a little bit."

"A lot," Okonkwo said, settling himself behind the broken steering column. "Everybody hop on, I guess I'm driving."

Pervez clapped his shoulder. "I'll sign off your coxs'un sheet for this."

"Little different from a boat helm, BM1," Okonkwo said, "but I think I can keep us from flipping over."

"I can't believe we're driving on a buggy that can only turn left."

"NASCAR!" Chief and McGrath said at the same time.

"Hold on," Okonkwo said, and the rover shuddered to life, lurched forward. Okonkwo drove it straight, angling away from the enemy for a few yards.

"MK3," Oliver radioed. "We need to go that way."

"I know, boss," Okonkwo said, "just one more second to get lined up right."

Something detonated off to their left, spraying them with regolith, and Okonkwo pulled the cable. The rover turned, leaned, its right wheels coming up off the surface. "We're unbalanced! Everybody over to the…"

But they were already scrambling to the other side, and the wheels bumped back down into the soil, gripped, and the rover jumped forward, bouncing off a pile of regolith and losing contact with the surface for a moment before thudding back down. Oliver felt her weight shift, scrambled to grip something, and found herself clinging to Ho. Her XO began to slide off the rover, flailed his own arms, and finally grabbed onto the low railing that ringed the vehicle. "Ow, boss," he grunted, "can you cling to life for someone else? I just got shot."

"Sorry," she radioed as she balanced, reached out for the railing, and held on.

The rover picked up speed, and Oliver could see some of the PLAN Marines moving to track it. "Christ," McGrath said, wedging one boot under the railing and trying to steady his hornet gun across his raised knee. "I can't shoot bouncing around like this."

"Sure you can," Fujimori said, snapping off two rounds in the direction of a PLAN boat moving toward them. One of the rounds sparked off the bow, and the other missed, but the Chinese coxswain jerked the vessel out of the line of fire, and the boat lurched away from them.

Koenig imitated McGrath's posture, locking himself in place for a short moment before he flinched to one side as a hornet round streaked past him. He turned, leveling his weapon at a squad of PLAN Marines bounding to cut the rover off, and the airburst launcher beneath his gun barrel spat a thick contrail that detonated right at their feet. The PLAN Marines disappeared in the cloud of regolith the blast kicked up, and then Oliver was turning away as her suit was pounded by debris. She heard someone cry out as their radio accidentally chin toggled. When she looked up again, everyone appeared to still be holding on, the rover bumping along steadily.

"Jesus, lieutenant," she radioed. "How about a little warning."

Koenig never came off his weapon sights. "That or those fuckers would have run us down, ma'am. Just assume a general fire-in-the-hole until we're done here."

The rover jumped along, rattling them around like ball bearings in a can, and Oliver didn't even bother to raise her weapon, opting instead to hold on for dear life. The PLAN boats flashed by to either side of them. She could see their barrels tracking the vehicle, and could feel her muscles clenching in anticipation of the blast. But the Chinese guns stayed silent, and looking over her shoulder, she could see why. They were in middle of the Chinese troops now, and any fire ran the risk of hitting other Chinese positions opposite them. Oliver looked behind them, their tracks snaking back along the open regolith toward the advancing LSST, who were also holding fire for the same reason. They were safe for now, but the moment the Chinese circled around to their rear, they could fire on them without risking hitting their own people, and then they'd be done.

"MK3, we've got about a minute before we get our asses lit up," Oliver said.

Okonkwo said nothing, but the rover sped up and Oliver watched the boat crashed into the structure's roof growing closer. McGrath and Koenig realized they were in no danger of hitting their own people, and they fired as the rover bounced along, hornet rounds slinging into targets packed so densely it was difficult to miss. She could see PLAN Marines hitting the deck, boats veering out of the way, turrets tracking them as they went. "They are not going to put up with this for long."

"Nope!" Pervez pointed.

Another rover, its flatbed crowded with troops, was careering toward them. "Contact starboard bow, two hundred…"

But two hundred yards was already one hundred. Koenig turned and fired an airburst round that missed the rover by at least fifteen feet, detonating over an empty patch of ground fifty yards beyond. Fujimori managed to get a hornet round off that sparked against the rover's railing but did nothing to deter its course. Okonkwo hauled on the cable and their rover lurched to the left, wheels losing contact with the ground briefly before slamming back down. The Chinese rover sped past, so close that Oliver could see the faces of the shouting enemy through their visors. Like Oliver and her people, they were clinging to their railing for dear life, and none raised their weapons to fire.

Oliver looked up, now they were moving at an angle toward the crashed Navy boat, getting closer still, but not for long. "MK3, what can we do to get back on course?"

"Get out and push the nose of this thing around," Okonkwo said. "Unless you want me to cut a big circle right now."

Oliver looked at the Chinese troops moving around them, decided she didn't want to risk heading back toward them.

"That's not gonna happen," Chief agreed with her thought. "We'll have to keep going until we're as close as we can get, and then bail."

"Man, I don't like our odds on foot," Okonkwo said.

"We'll be OK," Oliver said, "we just have to make sure we're backstopped by other Chinese troops." *Christ, this is risky.* She silently prayed for LSST or the US Marine reinforcements to break through. She could see hornet rounds zipping past behind them, guessed they came from American troops on the flanks unaware of their position.

"We're not going to get the chance!" Pervez pointed again.

Oliver turned and cursed.

One of the PLAN boats had broken away from the fighting, was barreling straight toward them. They weren't willing to risk firing on the rover while they were backstopped by other Chinese troops, but they could ram them. "MK3!" Oliver radioed. "Now's the time for your circle! Loop around that thing!"

It would have to be timed perfectly, and while Okonkwo was a gifted engineer, he lacked the instinct for handling a moving vessel that Pervez had. Oliver could see him turn in his seat, trying to gauge distance and speed as the PLAN boat arrowed toward them. *Jesus, Everistus, don't wait too damn long.* She could see the PLAN boat's window growing in her vision, its autocannon bouncing in the empty ball turret. The coxswain and lookout beside the helm were holding onto the railings on the helm chair, steadying themselves for impact.

"Here we go!" Okonkwo shouted, yanked the cable again. The rover jerked to the left as if it had been kicked, shuddered as it tipped up on its left tires, the right lifting so high that Oliver doubted even the weight of the crew would be able to right the thing again. The horizon tipped sideways. Regolith spraying up from the rover's left side. They turned as if on a dime, the vehicle's nose sweeping so close to the PLAN boat's hull that Oliver doubted she could have slipped her hand down between them. One of the Chinese sailors threw open the port side hatch, clung to the railing, aiming a duster one-handed, desperately trying to get a shot off while the two vehicles were so close. But the looping dance was far too bumpy for the sailor to even attempt it, and boat and rover pirouetted like dancers, whipping around one another. *My God,* Oliver thought, *he's doing it. He's really fucking doing it. I can't bel—*

There was a jolt as if some giant hand swatted the rover's rear end and suddenly everything was upside down. Oliver felt herself tumbling, the lunar sky and ground switching places, bodies flipping all around her, the rover tumbling, one of its tires burst where the PLAN boat's collar had struck it. The lunar gravity made her tumble a slow, almost languid thing, her body expecting her to impact the ground long before she actually did. She found herself growing impatient by the time she struck the surface, a sliding impact that was so soft it was almost disappointing. She tried to scramble to her feet too quickly, before her momentum was truly spent, and sent herself into another tumbling roll. She caught herself on her shoulder, let the momentum carry her to her feet. Her hands fumbled for her duster, patted the broken clasps of its sling and realized the weapon was gone. She could see Pervez, getting to up twenty feet away. Her duster miraculously still hung by its sling from the crook of her elbow, currently tangled between her knees. There were figures moving further out, and Oliver couldn't tell amidst the swirling dust kicked up by the tumbling rover whether they were friend or foe. Of the rover itself there was no sign, though Oliver could guess by the thickness of the billowing dust which way it had tumbled. She scanned wildly for the PLAN boat that had struck them, couldn't find it.

She raced to Pervez, grabbed her elbow. The coxswain spun, cocking a fist before realizing it was Oliver and bridging to her radio. "Jesus, skipper! I almost clocked you."

"Are you OK?"

"I think so. I think I bit through my fucking tongue," Pervez said wetly, "but you fall light out here."

"Yeah, we need to get moving yesterday. As soon as this dust clears, we're going to get jumped by the entire goddamn PLAN."

"Which way?" Pervez asked.

"Any way. Let's get off the X," Oliver turned and began bounding away from the dust cloud. *If it were me, I'd start looking right around the crash site.* She wanted to be as far from there as she could as quickly as she could. She scanned the horizon, made out the crashed boat and the sloping roof beneath it. As she watched, a hornet gun barrel emerged from the shattered front window and sent a round blazing down into a squad of PLAN Marines scattering at the building's base.

"There," Oliver pointed, started bounding without checking to see if Pervez was following.

"Why there?" Pervez asked. Oliver could tell from her breathing that she was moving behind her.

"There's at least one American in that boat. That's more than I see anywhere else right now."

"That's… that's not a great plan, boss."

"Nope, and if you come up with a better one, sing out."

Pervez didn't answer, and Oliver checked the radio display on her HUD looking for the signals of any of her crew. There was nothing.

"I've got nobody on radio," Oliver said.

"Me neither, boss. Christ, I hope they're OK."

"Probably just dust interference, or maybe they broke their antennae when they tumbled," Oliver said with a conviction she didn't feel. "They're fine. I know they're fine." *They have to be fine.*

"Christ, skipper. You don't even have a weapon," Pervez said. "You better let me go first."

"I am a United States Coast Guard," Oliver said, forcing humor into her voice while she swallowed the thick panic roiling her stomach. "I am a living weapon. Just trying to keep things fair."

The hab had originally been surrounded by a series of Helium-3 storage tanks. They must have been ruptured when the boat crashed into the roof, and their detonated remains had churned the surrounding regolith into a series of low dunes. A squad of the PLAN Marines had taken cover behind one, were gesturing to one another as they planned to rush up the hab's side to reach the boat on the roof. The hornet gun emerged from the front window again, but the PLAN troops had moved far enough around the side of the structure to be out of the gun's range. A moment later, the autocannon on the boat's ball turret swiveled and declined, but it also couldn't get a line of fire on the PLAN position. It belted off a few rounds to chew up the regolith over the PLAN troops' shoulders.

"That's a warning," Oliver pointed. "The gunner's letting them know what'll happen if they try to come up the sides."

"OK, ma'am," Pervez said. "Let's go around, if we come up the other side we can… I got Chief!"

"You do?" Oliver scanned her own radio. "I don't have anyone! Where is he?"

"Less than a quarter-klick out. He's got us and McGrath. They're coming."

"Outstanding. Make sure you tell him…"

"Already on it, ma'am," Pervez said. "God that is such… Uh, ma'am?"

She pointed at two of the PLAN Marines, bounding away from the rest of their squad, moving around toward the vessel's bow – and toward Oliver and Pervez.

"Shit," Oliver grabbed Pervez's elbow, and dragged the two of them into the wreckage of a Helium-3 furnace, pulling them down into the scraps of twisted 3D-printed regolith. "Ma'am," Pervez whispered out of instinct, even though no one could hear them outside the radio channel, "what the hell are we doing?"

"We are playing dead," Oliver said, "and hoping they're too busy with the boat to worry about us."

Pervez cursed, but held still, and Oliver waited as long as she could stand, her body crying out to get up and get moving, to do *something*, anything other than lying there waiting for the PLAN troops to find them and deliver the coup de grâce.

The moments stretched out, and her only view was of the lunar sky above them. Dark shapes were gathering there now, long and narrow, studded with weaponry and clouded by swarms of launching small boats. "There's got to be at least three frigates overhead BM1. This is heating up fast." *Why aren't they firing? Is it a standoff?*

"That's... not super encouraging, ma'am," Pervez said.

"Well, I guess those PLAN bubbas aren't going to kill us. Can you see where they went?"

"Yes, ma'am, I'm looking right at them. They're setting up a crew-served gun behind one of those dunes. Hornet gun just took a shot, but they're covered."

Oliver sat up, looked over at the squad of PLAN Marines at the base of the hab. They were pressed flat against the side of the structure, well below the incline of the boat's ball turret. Their heads were turned to their right, watching the other two PLAN Marines setting up their tripod behind the shelter of their dune off the crashed boat's bow.

"That's not good," Oliver said.

"No, ma'am," Pervez said. "That boat's toast."

"How far out are Chief and McGrath?"

Pervez paused as she checked her suit's HUD. "Too far, ma'am. We need to make a decision."

Oliver watched as one of the PLAN Marines steadied the tripod, opening the locking clamps. The other settled a long, heavy-looking weapon over it, its barrel flaring at the far end.

An anti-materiel gun. The same weapon that had started Oliver down this road what seemed a lifetime ago. And as at Lacus Doloris, it was swiveling to target a Navy small boat, helpless to respond.

Oliver's heart raced, her mouth went dry. *Not again. I can't let this happen again.*

She was up before she knew it, bounding toward them, launching herself through the wisp thin lunar exosphere that suddenly felt thick as molasses. "Boss!" Pervez shouted after her, "what the hell are you doing?"

Oliver didn't answer. The world had shrunk to the PLAN gun crew, pausing in their assembly of the weapon, staring in frank shock at the American in the day-glo orange, bounding toward them, unarmed. "Ma'am! I am not getting myself killed!"

That's OK, Oliver thought. *You don't have to.* Pervez was yelling something more into her radio, a chattering that receded into a buzz, buried beneath the roaring blood in her ears, the hammering of her heart. The flared muzzle of the anti-materiel gun was pointed up at the hab's roof, blocked by the lip of the regolith dune. It would take the PLAN crew just a couple of nudges to point it out over the top and fire. Tom's boat, the *same* boat, danced in her vision, shredded over and over again before her eyes. *No. Not this time. Not if I can stop it.*

Time slowed in the tunnel that connected her to the gun crew, the edges gone to a gray blur of the passing regolith, hab-debris, distant boats. She watched as if from outside her body as the crew swung the gun toward her, the flared barrel blooming in her vision like some metal flower. She remembered the last time she'd looked down the barrel of an anti-materiel gun, the spinning world-erasure, the awakening in the wreckage of her longhorn, Flecha and Kariawasm dead in their seats beside her, watching helplessly as Tom's boat danced itself to pieces. *Not this time*, her mind repeated over and over and over again, *not this time not this time not this time.*

But it would be this time. Even as the distance closed, Oliver knew there was no way she was fast enough. There was no burst of speed she could put on, hindered by the hardshell's cumbersome articulation. The timing was off, she had given them more than enough to sight the huge weapon in and fire. She had seen what an anti-materiel gun had done to a small boat. It would turn her, hardshell and all, into red mist. And yet she couldn't turn aside. She barely even saw the crew now, the flared gun barrel fixed in her vision – the sight of it alone a time machine, the scene around it Lacus Doloris and the chaos that Oliver only now realized had effectively ended her life. The woman charging them now was someone else, someone who had risen from the ashes of that conflagration. Someone who didn't care if she lived or died.

And just as when she had tumbled from the overturned rover, she found herself waiting for the impact, for the muzzle flash, for the jerk of the stock, for the split second that would presage her end. But it didn't come. The barrel only grew and grew, and at last her focus shifted and she saw the crew again, the two PLAN Marines frozen behind their weapon, staring at her in amazement, their faces close enough to be visible through their biosuit visors.

Why aren't they firing? She saw one of them gesture to the other and realized with a start, *the other PLAN Marines. They're my backstop. They don't want to hit their own people.*

But neither were they going to sit idle and let this unarmed old woman tackle them. One of them lifted the weapon, tripod and all, began to crabstep up the dune, changing the angle of fire to put empty space behind his target. The second drew a hornet pistol from his thigh rig and sighted in. Oliver had closed the gap considerably, but not nearly enough. She might be spared the obliteration of the impact of the anti-materiel gun, but the hornet round would certainly do the trick.

Oliver pushed down with her heels and launched herself forward. The last feet between them shrank, the hornet pistol barrel rising to track her progress.

Then two things happened.

The PLAN Marine dropped his hornet pistol, his head exploding sideways, the hornet round fired from the small boat's front window driving through the dune's peak and punching straight through his ear. The second PLAN Marine had finally found his position and raised the giant anti-materiel gun to his hip. He'd be firing without aiming, but Oliver was so close that it wouldn't matter. In the next instant, he was tumbling across the regolith in a cloud of his own blood and metal dust, the anti-materiel gun dropping back down onto its tripod as gently as if it had been set there.

Oliver landed on her hands and knees, skidding forward in the regolith, blinking in astonishment. Somehow, both PLAN Marines were dead. Somehow, she was alive. *Jesus Christ.*

"Boss!" Pervez shouted as she leapt over Oliver, landing behind the anti-materiel gun, dropping the duster she'd just used to kill the PLAN Marine, and propping herself up behind the anti-materiel gun's sights. "Not a good time to take a break! Clear the lane!"

Oliver realized she was still in front of the weapon that Pervez was now trying to aim. *Aim at what...* and then she remembered the squad of PLAN Marines behind her. She threw herself to the side, just in time to catch the first flash of the anti-materiel gun, its contrail raking up regolith as it exited the barrel, shrouding her in a wreath of dust. Through it, she could glimpse the PLAN Marines diving to the side as the kinetic round splintered their debris pile into exploding fragments. She saw one of them shredded, limbs flying in separate directions, another launched into the lunar sky so far that Oliver doubted he would survive the fall even in the weak gravity.

One of them turned, raised his hornet gun, but then Pervez had put another round downrange, blowing up the ground a foot to his left. It was nowhere near his body, but the explosion of regolith and hab debris was enough to send him rolling, the hornet gun tumbling from his hands.

And then the PLAN troops were clear of their dune, and the ball turret on the small boat opened up, the rounds chewing the regolith around the marines up into a funnel of plastic, metal and fist-sized chunks of lunar soil. There was no way anyone could have survived it.

Pervez left nothing to chance. As soon as she saw that the marines had dispersed, she rotated the anti-materiel gun, sighting back down into the battlefield. Oliver waited for a moment, expecting her to open fire again, but she only lifted her head. "Boss."

Oliver turned.

Overhead, three Perry Class frigates were station keeping at broadsides, their batteries trained across the space at a matching number of Type-054Bs. Beneath them, she could see the PLAN boats withdrawing, burning short bursts from their bow thrusters to move them under the cover of their own capital ships' guns. The Navy small boats on their flanks were fanning out to form a skirmish line, guns trained across the battlefield, but silent for now.

"I think..." Pervez breathed, "...I think it's over."

"Jesus," Oliver straightened, stared at the sheer enormity of the firepower all around her. "This whole thing could go pear-shaped if somebody sneezes."

Pervez stood, lifting the anti-materiel gun by its carry handle. "Guess we better not sneeze."

"Where's Chief? I still can't see him on my radio nodes display."

"Maybe five minutes out, ma'am. Jesus Christ, what the hell were you thinking? You have some kind of death wish?"

"I couldn't let them shoot up that boat, Naeemah. Not if I could have stopped it."

Pervez blinked at her. "What were you planning on doing when you got to them? Play patty-cake?"

"I figured maybe they needed a hug." Oliver felt light. The sense of slowed-time didn't abate, but she could see everything – the swirling dust, the outlines of the ships above her, the spray of stars overheard, in crystal clarity. She could feel her heart and her lungs and the pumping of her blood, slowing now as she processed that the immediate danger had passed. Lunar gravity always made her feel somewhat like floating, but this was different, as if a single step would send her rising up to the frigates station keeping above her.

"Come on," she said, her own voice bright and resonant in her ears. "Let's go see how they're doing up there."

Pervez bounded up after her as she ascended the hab's side, straddling the dented and pockmarked coolant pipe, until she came level with the boat's shattered front windows. She kept her hands up, thankful for the day-glo orange of her hardshell. A twitchy gunner might pop her without thinking, but if she had survived charging two PLAN Marines unarmed, she figured whatever force was watching over her would have to have one hell of a sense of humor to end her now. Still, she scanned her HUD for the boat's radio net, and breathed a sigh of relief when she found it was still active and bridged in. "Admiral Oliver, United States Coast Guard. I'm unarmed. Permission to come aboard?"

"Holy shit, Jane," came a deep singer's base. "I should have figured the guard would come to the rescue."

She crouched her way up the bow and through the window, Pervez following, dragging the Chinese anti-materiel gun behind her. The inside of the small boat was completely destroyed. The binnacle had clearly caught fire and been put out with foam retardant, which had frozen solid in the freezing lunar atmosphere. The cabin interior was so holed with hornet-rounds that it looked like some kind of metallic cheese. Two dead sailors and a marine had been lain on their backs in the fan tail. A single remaining sailor cradled the hornet gun that had probably saved Oliver's life. She knelt beside a man in a marine hardshell that had clearly been compromised. Looking through the visor, Oliver could see the failsafe mechanism had fired, shrinkwrapping General Fraser. She could still make out his face through the clouding of the emergency oxygen, smiling up at her. "Guess we're one and two now, Jane. You still have to save me one more time."

"Are you OK?" Oliver knelt beside him, scanning the hard shell for an entry wound.

"I'll make it," Fraser said. "Round came in through the back, didn't exit. Must have come a long way and spent some of its force tearing through the hull. Damn, Jane. It's good to see you. I really thought we were done here."

"Hey there," Chief's voice sounded on the radio as he and McGrath ducked through the front window. "You OK, sir?"

"I'll pull through," Fraser said. "How are my marines?"

"Sorry, sir," Chief said. "We were with Lieutenant Koenig and Gunny Fujimori, but we lost them when our rover took a roll. Couldn't find their radios after. Still missing two of our own, too."

Fraser grunted. "We'll find them. What's going on out there?"

"Well," Chief looked up at the lunar sky over his shoulder, back to Fraser. "We've got the making of the second Battle of Trafalgar overhead, sir. So far, it seems like neither side wants to write the page just yet."

"OK," Fraser said. "Jane, help me up. We should probably get ourselves somewhere out of the hot zone in case this whole thing decides to touch off."

Oliver leaned down, got a shoulder under Fraser's armpit, levered him to his feet. He grunted, swayed. Oliver froze, but Fraser blinked, shook his head, straightened. He looked at her, saw the concern in her eyes and chuckled. "Lemme guess, you disobeyed orders when they told you to stay put."

Oliver shrugged, but not with enough force for the motion to show through her hardshell. "You sure you're OK?"

"I am now. Thanks for saving our bacon, Jane."

"Ah," Oliver looked at her feet, "figured I owed you."

They limped their way toward the front window. The sailor joined them, taking most of Fraser's weight. Oliver let him go, felt a sudden surge run through her. She had almost died. They both had. There were so many things she would have said to Tom, if only she'd known. She wasn't going to miss the chance now. She was never going to miss the chance again. "I'm… I'm really glad you're OK," she blurted out.

"Me too," said Fraser. "I suppose we're at war with China now, huh?"

"I guess we won't know until we get back on the *Obama*."

"Reckon we better get about it."

"Not me," Oliver said, "I gotta take care of something."

"Jesus, Jane. You're in enough trouble as it is."

She beckoned to her crew, turned, started crouching her way through the window. "So? They can fire me. SAR-1, on me."

CHAPTER 15

You are my rainbow to keep. My eyes will always be watching you; never will I lose sight of you.

VESNA BAILEY, *NOTES TO MY DAUGHTER BEFORE YOU GO*

They found Ho and Okonkwo sheltering under a pile of rubber belting and plastic hose. "I have no idea where the hell it all came from," Okonkwo radioed after Pervez picked up his radio signature and bounded over to dig him out. "Storage container must have taken a round and went up in the air. One second, XO and I were getting our bearings, the next we were underneath all this crap."

"Well, it looks like it kept you out of sight," Oliver said once she got close enough to bridge to his radio. It turned out her antennae was intact, but its range was shot. She lost Pervez every time she moved more than a few feet away, even with line of sight; after a few frustrating attempts to maintain the correct distance, she gave up and held her coxswain's hand. "How's XO?"

"XO is fine," Ho's voice crackled in her ears, "but he doesn't want to risk aggravating his laser burn, so if you kind souls wouldn't mind digging me out from underneath this heap that would be awful swell."

"Christ," Oliver said as she knelt beside Chief and began throwing debris over her shoulder. "That shot sure as hell didn't knock the whining out of you."

"Is it over, boss?" Ho asked as they reached him and helped him wincing to his feet.

"For now it is," Oliver said, "but this is one hell of a standoff. Someone blinks wrong and they're going to start shooting again. We had capital ships engaged, at least fifty dead, I'd bet. No way we can just sweep this one under the rug. Let's get you into atmosphere, Wen. I don't like the thought of just that compromised suit between you and the exosphere."

"Sure, boss," Ho said, "Okonkwo can get me to one of the boats."

"I'll take you, Wen." Oliver bent to sling his arm over her shoulder.

"No, boss, I think you've got something else to take care of not far from here."

Oliver froze. It was a long time before she could speak, but at last she managed a brief swallow and, "Where?"

Ho pointed to a hab on the horizon. A line of Helium-3 furnaces had gone down like dominoes beside it, tumbled over one another to sever the heat-exchange piping that ran up its scarred sides. "I couldn't get a good look, boss, but it seems like it might have taken some fire."

"And you're sure it's hers?"

"Absolutely sure. Had some time to connect to the chamber of commerce intranet while I was lying there. Alice was very careful to file all her paperwork and keep it up to date. I even saw the deed. That's her mining stake and her residence. You go check it out, I'll get to atmosphere and see how bad I got cooked."

"Thank you, Wen," Oliver was already up and bounding toward the lopsided bubble on the horizon.

"Don't sweat it boss," Ho radioed back. "Just do me a favor, huh? Let me know when you've confirmed she's OK?"

"You know I will–" but then she was out of range and the radio signal dropped.

The hab grew in her vision as the PLAN Marines she'd charged just a short while ago had, and just as with them, she could feel her life hanging in the balance. Oliver knew if she found her daughter's body, she'd be lost. There would be nothing left, no coming back from a void as black and as complete as that which swirled above her. No. Alice had to be alive. Because if she wasn't, then Oliver surely would die with her.

As she bounded around the hab's edge she could see the massive crack that had been ripped in its side where a hatch cover from some unlucky small boat had been blown off and flown into the wall. The inside was exposed to the vacuum of the lunar surface and Oliver could see papers and houseplants, throw pillows and broken crockery all rimed with gray ice. She was finally getting what she now realized was a dearly held wish – to see the inside of her daughter's home, flash frozen. Oliver shimmied her way up the crack until it widened enough to admit her, then let herself drop down through it and into the living room. It had been neat before the hatch had ripped it open, but now her daughter's sparse décor – ultra-modern plastic chairs, a wide-screen projection monitor dominating one entire wall across from what looked like a foam combination couch-bed – was all coated with a thin sparkling layer of regolith dust. Oliver could see Alice's desk, smashed in half beneath a chunk of the hab's roof. Peeking out from beneath it, glass covering shattered, was the same photograph of her daughter's wedding day that Oliver had kept with her every day since it had been taken.

A moment later her radio crackled, and Chief and Pervez came through the hatch. "You could have just used the door, boss."

Oliver looked up at them, amazed they existed, that other human beings could somehow come into the sacred bubble that was her investigation of the ruins of her daughter's house. "I figured it wouldn't work."

"Power's still on," Chief said. He looked around. "I take it you didn't find her?"

"Haven't really started looking yet."

"I'll look around the grounds and the furnaces," Chief said, heading back toward the door.

Pervez headed for the spiral staircase winding its way down to the subsurface level. "I'll check the hold, ma'am."

Oliver caught Chief's eye as he stepped out the door, felt her throat close. "Thank you."

Chief nodded, embarrassed, then met her gaze. "Alice is alive, boss. We're going to find her."

And then Oliver couldn't speak, so she turned from him, and made her way inch by inch through her daughter's house, opening drawers, closets and cupboards, as if her daughter would somehow be hiding in them as she had when she was a little girl.

After what felt like an hour she felt Pervez taking her by the shoulder, gently steering her around to face her. "Ma'am," she said.

"Just let me do another round," Oliver said. "Maybe I missed…"

"Ma'am," Pervez shook her head. "We've been over it again and again. Your daughter isn't here."

Alice is gone, Oliver's mind repeated to her again and again. *Alice is gone.* And though she knew that until she saw her daughter's body, that meant she could still be alive, she wept just the same.

Oliver slipped into a fog. She was dimly aware of sailors ushering her onto a Navy small boat, of that boat lifting them up into a huge blot of shadow, of hands gently steering her out of the *Obama*'s launch bay and through a maze of passages into a room. Somewhere along the way she had been stripped out of her hardshell, and she had no idea how much time had passed before she looked up and saw Ho leaning against the opposite wall, arms folded across his chest. He was wearing a blue hospital gown and a medical bracelet. Oliver could see a lump underneath the gown where a broad bandage swathed his abdomen.

Oliver looked down at her palms, blazing like a coal was cupped between them. Someone had given her a mug of tea. "Peppermint," she said.

"Supposed to relax you," Wen said. "At least that's what it says on the bag."

"How are you?" she asked.

"I'm OK," he said. "If you have to get shot, CO_2 laser is a pretty good thing to get shot with. I'm probably going to be down a kidney but we won't know for sure for a few days."

She knew she should be focused on him, his wound. But her mouth moved on its own, blurting out what mattered most to her. "I can't find Alice," she said to her reflection in the surface of the hot water.

"I know," Ho said. "I've already put her name and description in with the ground crews. They're looking for her as we speak. Chief and Pervez are out there too. Okonkwo went to help them and McGrath wanted to go too, but I ordered him to stay. Guy's been banged up enough for one tour."

"Thanks, Wen," Oliver said. "I'll finish this and then I'll suit up and head out too."

"Sorry, boss," Ho said. "That's not going to happen."

She looked up at him, frustration began to tug at the back of her throat. "What do you mean?"

"I mean you're confined to quarters for now. That comes down from the top. Thought it would be better if you heard it from me."

Oliver stood, her legs beginning to shake. "Wen, did you not hear what I just fucking said to you: I can't find my goddamn *daughter*–"

"I know," Ho said, "and it doesn't matter. There are multiple teams of professional search-and-rescue operators down there right now doing that very thing."

"They need my–"

"No, boss, they don't. What they need for once is for you to stay the fuck out of the way and let them do their jobs. You're a goddamn admiral. And I know this is the hardest thing I've ever asked you to do, but you are going to have to act like it, at least for now."

Oliver looked back down at her tea, fought to keep the tears from coming, but saw her reflection ripple as the drops fell and broke the surface. "I can't. Wen, I can't anymore."

"Yes, you can." Ho had crossed the room, placed a hand on her shoulder. "Take as much time as you need here, and when you're done, call Allen. He's still on the control floor at SPACETACLET, and it will come as no surprise that he wants to talk to you."

"I can't, Wen," Oliver looked up at him pleading. "Not without Alice. Not without Tom and Alice. I can't do it."

"You don't have to do anything," Ho reached down and pulled her into his arms, cradling her head against his chest. Oliver realized that it was the first time he'd ever hugged her. "You don't have to do anything but wait here, and finish your tea, and then make a phone call. Just one phone call, and then it's over and you can go."

"Go where?" Oliver asked. "Without Alice, where will I go?"

But Ho didn't answer. He only disengaged from her and touched her cheek. "You're not alone," he said. "While I draw breath, while my wife and children draw breath, you will always have a home."

And then he was gone, leaving Oliver with the tea cooling between her slick palms, and the shaking of her shoulders, heaving under the weight of sobs she only now realized had been building for so very long.

When, at long last, she was done, Oliver made her way to the terminal and receiver set into the wall of the medical bay where'd she'd been set to cool her heels. An orderly answered as soon as she picked it up. "*Obama* medical."

"This is Admiral Oliver, I need a line to–"

"Yes, admiral, I'll put you through now." Oliver's stomach clenched. However bad this was, they'd been very careful to order the admin staff to put her through without delay. *Whatever they do to me, they have to find my daughter. They can court martial me. They can lock me up and throw away the key. But they have to find my daughter.*

A moment later, the receiver crackled, "Jane."

"Admiral Allen, sir, I just want you to know that I–"

"Jane," Oliver realized with a start that the familiar voice was not Allen's, "your XO told me about your daughter. I want you to know we're doing everything we can to find her."

It took Oliver's mind another moment of stumbling through surreal fog to place the voice. Zhukov. The Commandant. The old man.

"Sir…" she managed.

If Zhukov noticed the tremor in her voice, he gave no sign. "How are you doing, Jane?"

"I'm all right, sir," she lied. "Are we at war with China?"

"Not yet. If we were, I'd probably be radioactive vapor. But, then again, so would a lot of people in Beijing. Nobody wants that," he paused, sighed, "so right now they're calling it a standoff."

"People died, sir, that's hardly a standoff."

"If you've got a better word that the news can run with that won't get everybody on the Moon killed, I'm all ears."

"You make a good point, sir."

"I know it. And that brings me to the reason for my call."

He paused again, and Oliver was surprised to find herself calm. He could court-martial her. He could demote her. Hell, he could have her flogged and publicly executed. It wouldn't touch her. Alice was missing. And until Oliver found her, nothing else would ever matter again.

"It's a good segue, actually," the old man finally found the words. "We could call this a battle with lives lost on both sides. A complete breakdown of diplomacy and law, and the seeds of the first war in space, and that would be accurate, right?"

"Dark, but accurate, sir," Oliver said.

"But you could also say that there was a standoff at Sinus Medii, and that tempers flared, and that both sides are rattling sabers and making dire threats, but that all it looks like is another Cold War, and that both sides, being nuclear-armed, don't want to press forward into open conflict, terrified as to where that might lead. That would be equally accurate, wouldn't you say?"

"That's the story I like better, sir."

"Me too," said Zhukov, "and so that's the one I'm sticking with. Let's just hope the PLAN is spinning the same yarn on their end."

"You got an over-under on that, sir?"

"Don't look at me, Jane. It's not like I'm the head of an entire branch of the United States military."

She stifled a laugh, was surprised that there was humor down there after the wreckage of Alice's hab, but there it was. *You're alive. You're alive and Alice might be, too.*

"Now, there's another story that could be told two ways, Jane, and it's a story about you," the old man went on. "In one version of the story, you refused a direct order from the Vice Admiral in charge of Operations for the entire service, and took your SAR boat into a firefight, resulting in the serious wounding of your Executive Officer. And that would be accurate, wouldn't it?"

"Yes, sir." Oliver's stomach tightened after the admonition after all, more evidence she was still Jane Oliver, deep down beneath the shock and grief. "It would, but I won't apolog–"

"But the other version of the story," Zhukov cut her off, "is here in this citation that was put in by one Brigadier General Demetrius Fraser, telling how your bravery and initiative was responsible for turning the tide of that battle when you distracted the enemy by landing in their backfield, granting the marine force time to regroup and dig in, and that, had it not been for your quick-thinking and selfless disregard for your own safety, every American in Sinus Medii would be dead right now. He credits you with saving his life and that of his precious MARSOC16 squad, and has put you up for the Navy-Marine Corps Commendation Medal with combat 'V.' Do you think that General Fraser's story is also accurate?"

Oliver's head spun. The events of the battle flashed through her mind, too bright and too fast to make sense of. Had she truly done those things? She was only sure of one of them. "It was my team, sir."

"I know that, Jane. It's always the team. But the fact remains that we have two versions of the same story regarding your conduct during the Sinus Medii incident. And we are agreed that both of them are credible. So, let me ask you, admiral, which one do you like better?"

"The true one, sir."

The old man laughed. "Me, too. Tom would be so unspeakably proud of you, Jane. I know that I am. Commander Ho is in good hands. I want you back on Medii to oversee the cleanup, and I want you to lead the personnel recovery effort there. I know Alice's hab was damaged. You must be worried sick."

And now, the tears returned. Even though this was the Commandant of the service. Even though now she needed to shore up his confidence in her ability to command the personnel recovery, to give her the personal chance to make sure Alice was found. But as she grasped for military bearing, it only slipped further from her grasp, and she choked out her next words between sobs. "I am, sir," she said. "I really am."

If her lapse of composure bothered him, he gave no sign. "I know it. So, go do something about it with my blessing. We'll pin that medal on you when you're back on Pico. I'm flying out as soon as I get off this call."

EPILOGUE

Despite your best efforts, people are going to be hurt when it's time for them to be hurt.

HARUKI MURAKAMI. *NORWEGIAN WOOD.*

Vice Admiral Donahugh sent Oliver back to the surface in her own executive shuttle, the Navy crew silent and deferential the whole way. Oliver knew that only social lepers and heroes got this kind of treatment. Rumors of her conduct in the battle were surely spreading, and she wondered what kind.

But the minute the shuttle touched down and she walked down the ramp to where her crew waited amid the stacked plastic cases packed with medical supplies, spare parts for the numerous construction vehicles, and ammunition in case things went hot again, her mind shifted gears. Sick worry about Alice was a new emotion, a task that she had no training for. But ops planning for a recovery effort she could do. She began surveying the pocked wreckage of the landscape, saw the civilians picking their way through it, trying to assess the damage to their homes and businesses, still under the guns of the distant PLAN boats, holding position just at the limit of the naked eye.

"Hey Chief," Oliver said, "what's the SITREP?"

"Still getting set up here, ma'am. Waiting for the on-site commander to get assigned."

"Yeah, that's me," Oliver said. "What's the plan?"

"Well, the first thing we need to be doing if you ask me," Chief said, "is dig through this rubble for survivors. Can't imagine we'll find many, but I'm willing to bet there's one or two trapped and kept alive by their suits. That should be priority one."

"Concur," Oliver said. "But first I want all the ambulatory civilians cleared out of here. You got casualty tents?"

"Yes, ma'am," Okonkwo said, gesturing at a stack of long, low boxes two sailors were lifting off a rover.

"Get them set up about two klicks that way," she pointed behind her. "Then muster everyone there. Nobody in the battlespace, under threat of arrest."

"They won't like that, ma'am," Chief said.

"They'll like it even less if this zone goes hot again and they start getting shot to pieces. And that's likely exactly what's going to happen if we let American and Chinese civvies mix right now and tempers flare. Get 'em separated, Chief. First order of business."

"Aye aye, ma'am," Chief said. "Where's Commander Ho?"

"He's got an extra crispy hole in him," Oliver said, "and he has to lie down until it cools off. You'll have to be my XO for now. You like that idea?"

Chief arched an eyebrow. "No, ma'am."

"Welp," Oliver said, "if you wanted options, you wouldn't have joined the military. Let's get this show on the road, XO!"

"Aye aye, ma'am," Chief said, and turned to where the LSST was unloading more crates to relay Oliver's orders.

Oliver scanned the splintered remains of what had once been a thriving mining community and shook her head. So much work, undone in an instant. The Moon represented everything ambitious and noble about mankind. The constant reaching for more, the refusal to be satisfied, the unquenchable hope. But the shattered habs and toppled furnaces reminded her of the darker side of each one of those coins. She caught movement out of her peripheral vision and looked down to see Pervez, her hand on Oliver's forearm.

"I'm glad you're back with us, ma'am," she said.

Oliver nodded, looked up. Overhead, the capital ships held position. Oliver counted three American and five Chinese frigates, attitude thrusters firing to keep them in position over the battlefield, broadside-to, a dark, slender canopy of weapons hanging over the rescue effort. Dry tinder ready to go up at any moment.

Oliver wrenched her gaze away. There was nothing for her up there. Alice was down here on the surface. "I'm sorry you didn't get to compete," Oliver said.

"Ah, you know," Pervez smiled, "just like the marines, isn't it? So scared they started a shooting war with China rather than risk losing to us on TV."

Oliver laughed, and Pervez matched her, loud and long, leaving echoes on the radio link that buzzed pleasantly in her ears.

When Oliver opened her eyes, Pervez was still looking at her, serious now. "We'll find your daughter, ma'am. She's alive and we're going to find her."

"I believe you," Oliver said.

And when she checked her gut against her words, she realized it was true.

GLOSSARY

0600 – 6AM.

16th Watch – A colloquial term to refer to any military duty anywhere in space. It refers to the 16 sunrises seen on the old International Space Station (ISS) in a single Earth day.

1LT – First Lieutenant.

72 COLREGS – 1972 International Regulations for Preventing Collisions at Sea.

Actual – Radio argot indicating the commander of a given unit is speaking.

Acceleration Gravity – Artificial gravity induced by rapid acceleration.

Abaft – In or behind the stern of a ship.

Aft – The rear of a vessel.

AIS – Automatic Identification System.

Anti-Materiel Gun – A large gun designed to penetrate vehicle armor.

ASAP – As soon as possible.

ATF – Bureau of Alcohol, Tobacco, and Firearms.

Autocannon – A large, fully automatic, rapid-fire projectile weapon that fires armor-piercing or explosive shells.

Binnacle – Standing panel for nautical instruments such as the radar and plotter.

BIV – Body in Vacuum.

BO – Boarding Officer.

BM1 – Boatswain's Mate 1st Class. An enlisted rank (E6) in maritime service.

BM3 – Boatswain's Mate 3rd Class. An enlisted rank (E4) in maritime service.

BMF – Boat Maintenance Facility.

Beam – The widest part of a vessel, usually the direct center.

Bow – The front of a vessel.

Bridge – The elevated, enclosed platform on a ship from which the captain and officers direct operations.

Bulkhead – A dividing wall or barrier between compartments in a vessel.

Bunny Suit – The second layer of American spacesuits, worn under the hardshell. The bunny suit is a soft, insulated layer much like a snowsuit.

Captain – The sixth highest commissioned officer rank (O6) in maritime service.

CBDR – Constant Bearing Decreasing Range. Indicates that a vessel or object is on a collision course with the speaker.

Cert – Certification.

CGMS – Coast Guard Messaging System.

Charlie Status – Indicates a vessel is undergoing significant maintenance and is not available for operations.

Chief – A colloquial term for a Chief Petty Officer.

Chief Petty Officer – The seventh highest enlisted rank (E7) in maritime service. Chiefs are the heart and soul of maritime service, and the achievement of this rank is a considerable badge of honor among the enlisted corps.

Cleared Hot – Authorized to open fire at your own discretion.

Coastie – A member of the United States Coast Guard.

Commander – The fifth highest commissioned officer rank (O5) in maritime service.

Crew Served Weapon – A gun large enough that it takes multiple people to operate it.

CO – Commanding Officer.

Coords – Coordinates.

Conn – The act of controlling a vessel's movements at sea or in space. The person said to "have the conn" is also known as the "conning officer." Conning officers are usually not physically steering, a job reserved for the helmsman, to whom the conning officer gives orders.

Coxswain – A boat's steersman. On a Coast Guard boat underway, the coxswain is considered the operational commander, and their voice carries the most weight regardless of actual rank.

Cox'sun – Colloquial pronunciation of coxswain.

COTP – Captain of the Port.

Cover – Military parlance for a hat.

Cutter – Any United States Coast Guard vessel over 65 feet in length.

DC3 – Damage Controlman 3rd Class. An enlisted rank (E4) in maritime service.

DHS – Department of Homeland Security.

DIPSEC – Diplomatic Security.

DIW – Dead in the Water. A vessel that is not moving. On the 16th Watch, this term is also used for vessels that are not moving in space.

DOA – Dead on Arrival.

Dust – Metal dust packed into a shotgun shell. In lunar or micro gravity, the particles are lethal at close range, but disperse quickly enough so as not to compromise a ship's hull.

Duster – A large bore shotgun design to fire dust, primarily in boarding actions.

EEZ – Exclusive Economic Zone. An area in which a single nation has exclusive rights for economic exploitation.

ENDEX – End of Exercise.

EVA – Extravehicular Activity. Any action taken in space outside the confines of a vessel.

FBI – Federal Bureau of Investigation.

Flag Grade – A commissioned officer of the highest rank. In maritime services, this is a Rear Admiral and higher. In land and air services, this is a Brigadier General and higher.

Field Grade – A commissioned officer senior in rank to a company officer but junior to a general officer. In the United States Coast

Guard, this corresponds to the ranks of Commander (O5) and Captain (O6).

FITREP – Fitness Report.

FO – Forward Observer.

GAR – Green, Amber, Red. A vessel's fitness score for launch.

Gardener – A tracked, robotic 3D-printer. It uses the lunar regolith to autonomously 3D print structures on the Moons' surface.

Gunnery Sergeant – The seventh highest enlisted rank (E7) in the United States Marine Corps. As with Navy and Coast Guard Chiefs, Gunnery Sergeants are the heart and soul of the Marines, and the achievement of this rank is a considerable badge of honor among the enlisted corps.

Gunny – Colloquial term for a Gunnery Sergeant.

Guns Up – Command to raise weapons to the ready and prepare to fire.

GYSGT – Gunnery Sergeant.

H3 – Helium-3

Hab – Short for "habitat." A dome shaped structure built for human residency on the Moon. Older models are constructed on the surface and use a series of heat exchange piping for heating and cooling. Newer models are built mostly below the surface.

Hard Dock – Describes the suction process after the nipple is engaged with a vessel in soft dock. Hard dock locks the vessels together and creates a stable connection between the two.

Hardpoint – A location on a vessel designed to carry a load, usually a fixed weapon.

Hardshell – A rigid, articulated spacesuit worn by American service members and civilians alike. The hardshell is the outermost of three layers worn.

Hatch – Any door on a vessel. In maritime service, all doors, even those on fixed buildings, are referred to as hatches.

Helium-3 – A non-radioactive isotope of Helium found in lunar regolith. During fusion, the isotope can be used as a source of electricity, making it a potential clean source of energy.

Helm – A vessel's steering apparatus.

Helmsman – The person physically steering a vessel.

Hornet Gun – A specialized gun that fires hornet rounds.

Hornet Round – A specialized munition intended to compensate for recoil in space-based combat. The munition has a weak charge that pushes the round out of the hornet gun's barrel. An instant later, the munition's own rocket-propelled motor ignites, launching it at the target at lethal speed. Since the round is fully exited from the hornet gun before igniting, it does not impart recoil to the shooter.

HS3 – Health Services Technician 3rd Class. An enlisted rank (E4) in maritime service.

HUD – Heads Up Display.

JAG – Judge Advocate General. Military lawyers.

Jaw Jacking – Engaging in useless talk.

KIA – Killed in Action.

Klick – Kilometer.

Knot – A maritime unit of speed equivalent to approximately 1.15 miles per hour.

LADAR – A portmanteau of "light" and "radar." LADAR measures distance to a target by illuminating the target with a pulsing laser and then measures their reflection.

Lagrange Point – The points near two large bodies in orbit where a smaller object will maintain its position relative to the large orbiting bodies.

LED – Light Emitting Diode.

Longhorn – An older model of spacegoing small response boat.

LDPD – Lacus Doloris Police Department.

Lift-Point – Portion of a vessel where a tow cable or crane hook attaches.

LMGRS – Lunar Military Grid Reference System.

Logs – Logistics.

LSST – Lunar Safety and Security Team.

LT – Lieutenant.

MARSOC – Marine Special Operations Command.

MARSOC16 – Marine Special Operations Command, 16th Watch.

Maser – Microwave Amplification by Stimulated Emission of Radiation. Sometimes colloquially called a "microwave laser."

Master Chief – A colloquial term for a Master Chief Petty Officer.

Master Chief Petty Officer – The 2nd to highest enlisted rank in maritime service (E9). Master Chiefs usually occupy senior administrative roles, in charge of advocating for enlisted needs, and advising commissioned officers in their duties.

MGRS – Military Grid Reference System.

Micro-g – Micro gravity. Used interchangeably with zero gravity.

ME3 – Maritime Enforcement Specialist 3rd Class. An enlisted rank (E4) in maritime service.

MK3 – Machinery Technician 3rd Class. An enlisted rank (E4) in maritime service.

MPPD – Mons Pico Police Department.

MWR – Morale, Welfare, and Recreation center.

NASCAR – The National Association for Stock Car Auto Racing.

Nautical Mile – A unit of distance measurement used by maritime services. Equal to 1.151 miles.

Naval Infantry – A term used by China and Russia to describe marines.

NCD/0G – Non-Cooperative Docking/Zero-Gravity training. The basic school all spacegoing boarding teams must graduate to qualify in their discipline.

NCO – Non-Commissioned Officer.

Nipple – A grasping device, the size and shape of a man-sized hatch, mounted to the end of a flexible, extendible gangway. The nipple extends from a vessel's belly and attaches to the tow fender of another vessel, creating a connection between the two vessels to facilitate boarding.

NJP – Non Judicial Punishment.

Non-Cooperative Docking – A contested boarding of a vessel against hostile crew.

Non-Rate – An enlisted sailor of the lowest ranks (E2-E3) who has not yet attended an "A-school" to obtain a rate – their job in the service.

PAX – Passenger.

Perp – Perpetrator.

PIV – Person in Vacuum.

PQS – Personnel Qualification Standard.

O6 – The sixth highest grade of officer in the US military. In maritime service, this is a Captain. In air and land service, this is a Colonel.

O-Country – The portion of a ship or building reserved for officers' quarters.

OCS – Officer Candidate School.

Off to See the Wizard – Colloquial term for consulting a mental health professional.

Ops – A colloquial term used to refer to the senior operations officer involved in any given event. Also refers to the operations center, and operations in general.

OTRACEN – Orbital Training Center.

PFC – Private First Class.

P-Way – Passageway.

PA – Public Address system.

PAP – The Chinese People's Armed Police.

PCS – Permanent Change of Station.

Petty Officer – In maritime service, a non-commissioned officer. Encompasses all enlisted ranks from the fourth highest (E4) to the highest (E10).

PLAN – The Chinese People's Liberation Army Navy.

PO – Petty Officer.

Port – The left side of a vessel.

PT – Physical Training.

PTs – Colloquial term for the clothing worn to engage in PT.

Regolith – The layer of loose rocky soil over bedrock.

Rhino – A newer model of spacegoing small response boat.

RTB – Return to Base.

SAR – Search and Rescue.

SASC – Senate Armed Service Committee.

SEALs – Sea, Air, and Land Teams. The US Navy's primary special operations force.

Skipper – Technically the person in charge of a ship, but in maritime service the colloquial term used for anyone in charge of anything. The equivalent of "boss."

SITREP – Situation Report.

Six-Pack – A vessel rated for a maximum of six passengers and crew.

SMPD – Sinus Medii Police Department.

Small Boat – A colloquial term used by the Coast Guard to refer to vessels less than 65 feet in length.

SNO – Statement of No Objection.

Soft Dock – Describes the initial stable contact between two vessels in preparation for boarding.

Solar Sail – Devices that propel spacecraft using radiation pressure exerted by sunlight on large mirrored surfaces. In this book, smaller sails have been developed that use a coating that provides propulsion as it ablates.

Space Elevator – A planet-to-space transportation system consisting of a cable anchored to the surface and extending into space. A car transports passengers and cargo directly to low-Earth orbit.

SPACETACLET – Space Tactical Law Enforcement Detachment.

Spider Boots – Boots used to adhere the wearer to surfaces in a micro gravity environment. The boots rely on setules in the sole and the

Van der Waals force to provide adhesion that the wearer can control through their movements.

Spin Gravity – Artificial gravity generated by a rotating toroidal chamber on ship, station or other structure.

Starboard – The right side of a vessel.

STARTEX – Start of Exercise.

Station Keeping – Holding position in any vessel.

Stem to Stern – The entirety of a matter.

Stern – The rear of a vessel.

Tow Fender – The exterior fender on a spacegoing vessel where rescue vessels may attach for purposes of towing, or to board. The tow fender leads to the vessel's airlock.

TTPs – Tactics, Techniques, and Procedures.

Twelve-Pack – A vessel rated for a maximum of twelve passengers and crew.

The Two – The designation for the intelligence shop in any military organization.

USAF – United States Air Force.

USMC – United States Marine Corps.

USN – United States Navy.

VBSS – Vessel Boarding Search and Seizure.

Voluntold – When a subordinate is asked to volunteer to perform a task or attend a function by their superior. The implication is that, even though compliance is technically voluntary, they are expected to comply.

Watchstander – A person on a ship who is standing watch. Watches come in many forms and may include lookout duty, manning a radio station, or serving as a guard to a restricted area.

XO – Executive Officer.

Zoomie – A member of the United States Air Force.

ABOUT THE AUTHOR

MYKE COLE is a devoted comic fan and voracious fantasy reader who never misses his weekly game night. His fandoms range from Star Wars to military history. He's a former kendo champion and heavy weapons fighter in the Society for Creative Anachronism. At the D&D table, he always plays paladins. After a career hunting people in the military, police, and intelligence services, Cole put these skills to good use on CBS's hit show *Hunted*, and on Discovery and Science Channel's show *Contact*. Myke is the author of The Sacred Throne Trilogy, which begins with *The Armored Saint*. He's also the author of the contemporary military fantasy Shadow Ops series, and its prequel Reawakening trilogy. His first work of nonfiction, the ancient military history *Legion Versus Phalanx* will be followed by *The Bronze Lie* in 2021. Myke lives in Brooklyn, New York.

Looking for another action-heavy read?
Take a look at the first chapter of
The Rise of Io by Wesley Chu

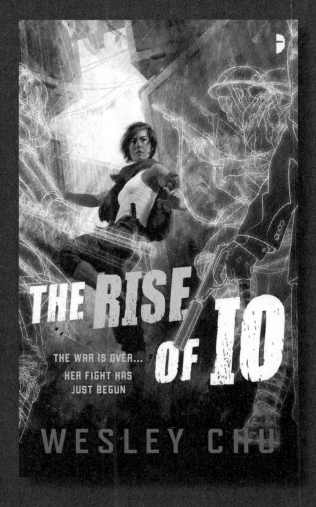

Out now from Angry Robot Books

CHAPTER ONE
The Con Job

They call every major world war "the war to end all wars." The day we actually get a war that deserves the title is the day the world ends.

Baji, Prophus Keeper, two days before the Alien World
War, the war that almost ended all wars

Ella Patel loved metal briefcases. When she was a little girl, her appa used to take her to the cinema, and anything that was shiny and expensive and worth stealing was always kept in metal briefcases. She had learned that obtaining these sleek, silver boxes was the key to success, riches and good-looking, tall Australian men with muscular arms and etched cheeks.

Today, Ella's dreams had come true. In bunches. The Australian men part was the notable exception.

Purple smoke drifted into the air out of the many cracks and rust holes of the Cage, a local bar welded together from twenty-three shipping containers stacked across three levels. The smoke was followed by a string of loud bangs from a fool blindly shooting his assault rifle in a small metal-enclosed room. The results weren't pretty. Dazed bar patrons, eyes burning and ears concussed, stumbled out, some rushing away while others collapsed onto the muddy ground, too disoriented to walk.

Ella, a generous head shorter than the shortest patron, hid herself within the crowd as it spilled into the streets. She wore a set of swimming goggles she had permanently borrowed from an unsuspecting tourist and lime earmuffs bartered for with a pack of cigarettes. In her hands, she half-dragged two metal briefcases, each nearly as heavy as she was.

She waddled down to the bottom of the ramp leading to the bar's entrance and dropped the briefcases. She raised the goggles to her forehead, hung the earmuffs around her neck, and looked back at the Cage. People were still streaming out, and she could hear curses coming from inside. Just for good measure, she took out another canister, pulled the pin, and lobbed it into the entrance. This time, the smoke was yellow. So pretty. Satisfied, she picked up the two briefcases, grimacing as she plodded down the busy street.

By now, she had revised her opinion of metal briefcases. Like that mythical fat man who was supposed to give her presents every year, this particular childhood fantasy fell far short of the painful reality. Metal briefcases sucked. They were big, unwieldy, and their sharp corners kept scraping against her legs.

Ella passed a vendor pushing a cart filled with scrap. The two made eye contact, just briefly, and then she continued waddling, one small step at a time, down the street. She was about to turn the corner when four men in military fatigues ran out of the Cage. One of them carried an assault rifle. He must have been the idiot who thought it was a good idea to open fire blind in a cramped smoke-filled room with metal walls.

They saw the big, shiny, sun-reflecting metal briefcases right away and gave chase. Just as they reached the bottom of the ramp, the vendor pushing the cart plowed into them, knocking all four into the mud. Ella suppressed a grin; she wasn't out of danger yet. She continued down the side street and made four more quick turns, moving deeper into the Rubber Market near the center of the slum.

By now, word had spread that someone had discharged a gun. Several in the crowd eyed her as she passed, first staring at those blasted shiny briefcases, then at her. A few glanced at the commotion behind her. Violence was just an unwanted neighbor who always lingered close by. Most of the residents ignored the ruckus and continued their day.

Ella could hear the gangsters behind her, yelling at people to clear out of their way as they barreled through the streets like raging oxen. She looked back and saw the lead man waving his assault rifle in the air as if it were a magical stick that would part the people before them. She grinned; that was the exact thing not to do in Crate Town. The good inhabitants of this large slum on the far southwestern edge of Surat didn't take kindly to being bullied. In fact, she watched as the main street suddenly became more crowded as the people – vendors, children and passersby – all went out of their way to block these outsiders.

By all indications, Crate Town's name was as appropriate as it was appealing. Located at the front line between Pakistan and India during the Alien World War, it had grown from the shattered remnants of several broken countries' armies. Without governments to serve or enemies they cared to kill, and no means of returning home, the soldiers became more concerned with feeding their bellies and finding roofs over their heads than fighting. The thousands of cargo containers at the now-abandoned military port proved the perfect solution for their infrastructure woes.

Four years later, Crate Town was a blight of poverty on the

western edge of India as the shattered country struggled to rebuild after a decade of devastation. Ella wouldn't have it any other way. She called this hellhole home, and she loved it.

She grinned from ear to ear as she turned another corner, confident that she had lost the gangsters. She carried the briefcases another three blocks and walked into Fab's Art Gallery, halfway down a narrow street on the border between the Rubber Market and Twine Alley.

Fab's Art Gallery was the only one of its kind in all of Crate Town. There wasn't much need for commercial art when most of the residents lived in poverty. The gallery was long and thin, with perhaps nine or ten hideous paintings. A person didn't have to be an art critic to think that the owner of this gallery had awful, awful taste. One of the pieces was actually painted by Fab's six year-old son. It showed three stick figure hunters throwing pink spears at a stick figure elephant or giraffe or something. Ella didn't have the heart to ask Tiny Fab what the creature actually was. Big Fab, the owner, likely wouldn't have been offended by this, because the whole hideous art gallery front was his idea.

Ella walked behind the counter in the gallery and dropped the briefcases onto the floor. She collapsed, huffing and puffing. A pair of eyes blinked through a beaded curtain off to the side, and she saw the ends of a machete poking through it slowly retract.

"Was it everything you hoped it would be?" the crackly voice asked from behind the curtain.

"These things suck," she snapped, kicking one of the briefcases. That was a bad idea, since hard steel easily beat toes in rubber sandals. "I was a stupid kid."

A yellow-stained smile appeared beneath the eyes, and the machete pointed at the back door. Ella picked herself up and grabbed several strips of sweet salmon, ignoring the blade shaking at her threateningly as she passed by the beaded curtain. She wolfed down the strips as she entered a narrow alleyway and turned toward home.

Those gangsters would need the gods' own luck to find her during early evening at the market in Crate Town. They might as well try to pick a kernel of rice from a pile of pebbles. All she had to do was wait out the day and keep an ear to the ground. Eventually, the foreigners would learn why the slum she called home was nicknamed the dirty black hole. Not only was it admittedly and almost proudly filthy, once you lost something in Crate Town, you weren't going to find it.

That included people.

Once the coast was clear, she would fence the goods she had conned from the Pakistani gangsters, and she'd be living good and easy for at least the next few months, if not the rest of the year. It all depended on how many people were going to get sick this season, but from what she could gather from Bogna the Polish midwife, it was a great market right now for those with medical supplies.

Whistling, Ella rounded the corner and cursed the gods, all three hundred and thirty million of them. There, standing just out of arm's reach, with their backs turned to her, were three of the gangsters, including the one with the rifle. She froze and slowly took a step back. And then another. One more step would have cleared her from the intersection, but today one of the three hundred and thirty million gods hadn't taken kindly to being cursed at.

Just as she was about to retreat around the corner, something hard bumped into her from behind and, with a loud squawk, she found herself flying headfirst into the middle of the intersection then face down halfway in the soft ground. Sputtering, she looked up out of the mud. All three gangsters were staring directly at her. She froze. With just a little luck, they wouldn't recognize her covered in all this grime.

"Is that the translator who just robbed us?" one of the big ugly guys asked.

So much for luck.

"Grab her!"

Ella slipped trying to get to her feet and one of the other gangsters, even bigger and uglier than the one who had spoken, got hold of her. Rough hands grabbed her by the shirt and easily picked up her scrawny body. Ella flailed in the air as the man squinted at her face.

He turned back to the others. "I think this is the right bit—"

One of the few advantages Ella had as a small girl was that no one ever thought her dangerous. That was a mistake. She grabbed a shank strapped to the back of her pants, and right as the uglier guy looked away, jammed it into his armpit. The man stiffened and looked down at her, and then both of them went crashing into the ground. Ella scrambled to her feet and ran for dear life.

There were several loud cracks and the ground nearby spit up mud in a straight line. She careened to the left and barged into a stall, and then bounced off it, overturning a passing wagon. She turned down a side street, then another, hoping to throw off her pursuers. Unfortunately, once they had caught sight of her, it was easy for the bigger men with their longer legs to stay on her tail.

Crate Town was Ella's home though, her playground. She knew all the nooks and crannies like she knew her knuckles. She veered onto a narrow path between two rows of tents facing outward and sprinted as hard as her short legs could drive her down the divide, hurdling over the crisscrossing tent lines as if she were in one of those track and field races. Behind her, the tents began to collapse one after another as the two gangsters giving chase uprooted the stakes tying the lines down. Eventually, one of the men tripped and fell in a heap of tangled rope.

That was Ella's cue. She cut to the right and made her way into a refuse dump at the end of an alley behind a warehouse. This wasn't her favorite part of the plan, but one that almost always succeeded in emergencies. She found a small opening in the garbage heap and burrowed until there was only a small gap, just large enough for her to see the evening sky. Ella pursed her lips so tight her teeth cut into her flesh, and then she listened, and waited, breathing as shallowly as she could, both to avoid moving the garbage and to avoid smelling it.

Footsteps grew louder and faded. Men shouted nearby, and then they too were gone. Far away, a foghorn from a ship docked at the port blew, and then nothing. Few people came by this part of Crate Town except to dump their garbage, and most did so early in the morning. Once she thought the coast was finally clear, she stretched her hand out of the heap until it touched the air, and began to claw her way to the surface.

Just as she was about to poke her head out, she heard footsteps again. This time, it sounded like an army, far too many for it to be those gangsters. Ella pulled her arm back into the trash heap and waited.

Two figures ran by. There was something strange about the way they were dressed, as if they had thrown on their clothes hastily in the wrong way. The first figure, a man, reached the end of the alley and beat a fist on the brick wall. He was covered with a long dark jacket that seemed far too warm for Crate Town's early summer weather. He went to the adjacent wall and tried the doorknob.

"It's locked." His eyes darted around the alley. "We're trapped."

He was speaking English, not like the mushy version she'd seen in American movies, but more like how Ella had learned the language when she first attended school in Singapore. Her knowledge of the language had come mostly from cinema though. The man turned to his companion, giving Ella a clear look at his face. He was a tall Caucasian with a receding hairline, high cheekbones, and a face so white, light seemed to reflect off it. His eyes were huge, but that seemed more from terror than genes.

The other figure, a woman by the looks of it, pulled back her headscarf, and a mass of long blonde hair fell out. A quick appraisal of the woman's plain but finely-woven dark anarkali salwar told Ella she was well off. There were easily a dozen items on her person that Ella could fence.

The woman scanned her surroundings and Ella saw the glint of something shiny appear in her hand. "I guess we do it my way after all," she said.

Ella immediately liked her. There was something about the way she composed herself. She held her hands in front of her and leaned in a way that suggested she were about to pounce on something, or someone. Her posture felt confident, intimidating.

Most of all, there was something attractive about her face. Ella couldn't stop staring at it. It wasn't really a pretty face or anything out of the ordinary; Ella had seen much better in the magazines. Nor was it scarred or ugly. It had no unique features. It was just how the woman wore it. There was something so determined and confident about her. It was the way she set her jaw and that aggressive, determined look in her eye.

New footsteps approached, and then Ella saw shadows, two hands' worth at least. They surrounded the man and woman.

Someone barked out words. There were sounds of machetes sliding out of their scabbards, and then the night became silent as all the players in that small alleyway froze.

And then chaos erupted.

Ella pitied the two. Two versus what looked like eight was terribly unfair. In the slums, numbers were all that mattered in a fight. She kept her eyes trained on the woman as the group of dark figures converged.

The woman attacked, swinging what looked like a metal stick in her hand. Her movements were a blur as she danced through them, flashes of silver slicing the air in the dim light. There was a beautiful violence to her, lyrical, fluid, deadly. Every time it seemed the shadows were about to envelop her, she would dance to safety, leaving a trail of falling bodies in her wake.

Ella had never seen anything like that outside of the movies, and she knew those kinds of fights were fake. This, however, was the real thing. In Crate Town, men got their way by being the biggest, strongest or meanest. There were few women here who could stand up to them. Maybe Wiry Madras by way of sheer meanness, but few others. Most resorted to cunning, cajoling or subterfuge. But this woman – this woman was something else.

Ella was so mesmerized, she forgot to keep her lips squeezed together. Her jaw dropped, and she took in a mouthful of garbage. She gagged and spit, then went back to staring at the woman.

Every so often, a random blow or cut would nick her, and she'd retaliate. A few more blows began to wear the woman down. She slowed, and the enemy attacks got closer, and soon she was getting struck more and more.

Ella held her breath, badly wanting to do something, to help, to fight alongside her. However, living on the streets, she knew the rules of Crate Town. She should not get involved. To her left, she noticed the man pressed against the wall. He had a silver stick in his hand, but he didn't fight. He just stood there, frozen, wearing a look of indecisive panic on his face.

This guy was leaving her to fight all these thugs by herself. This hit Ella right in the gut. He should be doing something! It was so unfair. Being smaller and scrawnier than most kids, she had often been bullied as a little girl. A righteous rage twisted and burned inside her.

She looked back at the woman. By now, more than half of her attackers were lying unmoving on the ground. However, the remaining three or four were beating her up pretty badly. Her movements were no longer beautiful; she was staggering from each blow. One of the men took a bat and jammed it into her stomach, doubling her over. Another punched her in the face, and she crashed into the pile of garbage not far from where Ella was hiding. The woman's eyes were glazed over and unfocused. Yet she continued fighting, struggling to her feet.

One of the men approached from the side, wielding a stick with two hands, ready to bash in her head. Ella watched the end of the stick hover in the air, about to end the woman's life. She looked down at the woman's face, and saw the determination still around her cheeks and mouth, even as the life in her eyes faded. Ella noticed the trinket around her neck and the expensive-looking watch around her wrist.

Something in Ella snapped. In a split second, she calculated the possible reward to risk for doing something. The woman was wealthy and there were only a few of those men left. Ella bet there would be a massive reward for saving her life. That, and honestly, it felt like the right thing to do, since that ass of a friend of hers was just standing there letting her die.

Ella jumped out of the garbage heap, shank in hand, and

stabbed the guy behind the knee. He screamed and toppled over, and then the woman finished him off with a knife that magically appeared in her hand. She struggled to her feet and limped toward the remaining three thugs. She glanced over at Ella once, and then, without a word, focused on her assailants.

The three attackers weren't taking Ella lightly. They were clearly puzzled by this scrawny little girl holding a bloody object in her hand, and they maneuvered accordingly, trying to stay in front of both Ella and the other woman.

The woman attacked, baton in one hand and knife in the other. She swung them in wide arcs, and the sounds of clashing metal hung in the evening air. She ducked under a swing and jammed the knife into the sternum of one of the attackers. Another thug got behind her and was about to strike when Ella jumped on his back and jammed her shank into the side of his neck.

The woman turned to face him just as blood spewed from his mouth. She shot a side kick to his chest that sent both him and Ella crashing to the ground. Ella just managed to jump clear and roll away to avoid getting crushed. The woman nodded at her and, for an instant, smiled.

"Look out!" Ella cried.

The woman stiffened as the point of a blade suddenly appeared through her abdomen. She lashed out in a circle with her baton and struck the side of her attacker's head. Both bodies crumpled to the ground. Ella was on the man in an instant, her shank stabbing him in the chest over and over. She didn't know how many times she thrust downward but when sanity returned, she realized that her hands were covered in blood, and his eyes were staring off into nothing.

Ella looked at her hands and fell onto her back. She had never killed anyone before. At least, none she was aware of. She had stabbed dozens of people in her short nineteen years. Most of them had even deserved it. It was one of the occupational hazards of living on the streets, but she had never actually stuck around long enough to see someone die from injuries she had inflicted. Until now.

The woman next to her coughed, and her labored breathing snapped Ella back from her daze. She crawled over to the woman and checked her wounds. There was blood everywhere, and Ella could sense her life slipping from her body with every second. Ella hovered over the woman, frantic. She looked up at the man, still frozen in place near the back wall.

"Help me!" she screamed. "Do something! Save her!" She picked up a rock as big as her fist and chucked it at him.

It brought him out of his stupor and he rushed over. He checked her wounds and paled. He turned to Ella. "Where's the nearest hospital?"

"There's no hospital in Crate Town."

The two of them tried to lift the woman but the instant they moved her, blood gushed from the wound in her stomach. Her eyes rolled back and she grasped the man's arm. "Make sure," she gasped. "The news... Seth... reaches..."

And then she was gone.

Ella had seen enough death in her life for it not to affect her any more. Growing up during a war and then in the slums, she had seen terrible things. People beaten and robbed, their bodies left on the streets. The ravages of sickness and famine and starvation.

But for this death, Ella felt a terrible sadness. The feeling aggravated her. She lashed out at the closest person. She stood up and scowled at the man. "I saw you stand there doing nothing. Coward!" She was about to give him a swift kick to vent her frustration when she stopped.

The woman was glowing. A strange fog with sparkling lights was slinking out of her body until it formed a cloud hovering in the air. The tiny lights, thousands of them, blinked as if alive. The cloud began to float toward the man. And then it stopped, and then it moved toward Ella.

Ella yelped and retreated, taking several steps backward and tripping over one of the bodies. She fell onto her butt and began to crawl on all fours, trying to get away from this weird, supernatural demon stalking her.

The light floated directly above her and hovered. At first, Ella shielded her face, but then she peeked. First, one eye between her fingers, then both. Up close, the cloud with its thousands of swirling lights was beautiful. If this was a demon, it was an awfully pretty one. She reached an arm out toward it.

"You want her to be your host? You can't be serious," the man said. "You, get away from the Quasing."

Quasing? Ella had heard that name mentioned before in passing every once in a while. They had something to do with the war that had raged across the world for most of the past ten years. Is this what everyone was fighting over?

"She doesn't deserve you."

Ella had no idea who the man was talking to. However, being told she didn't deserve something grated on her. She had already experienced a lifetime of ridicule, of being denied and demeaned. She didn't need this feeble man to pile onto it.

"Shut it, coward," she snapped.

She reached for the living cloud, and then tiny bursts of light moved directly into her. Ella felt a jolt and a hard jab in the back of her skull. Her entire body clenched. She thought she heard a strange gravelly voice in her head that definitely wasn't her own.

This is probably a mistake.

Blinding pain punched her in the brain and Ella felt her stomach crawl up her throat. She opened her mouth to scream, but all that came out were the regurgitated chewed up strips of sweet salmon. The last thing Ella felt was the sensation of flying, or falling, or the world being pulled from beneath her feet as she hit the ground.

Like what you read? Good news!
There's a sequel available too...

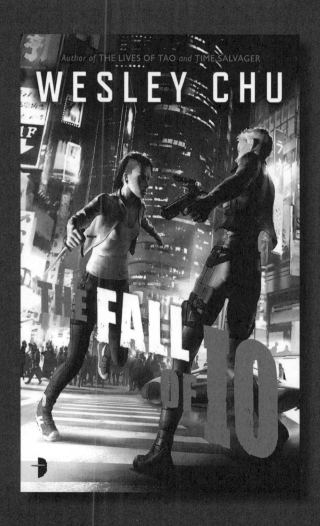

Author of THE LIVES OF TAO and TIME SALVAGER

WESLEY CHU

THE FALL OF IO

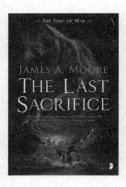
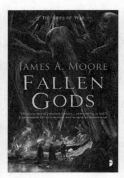
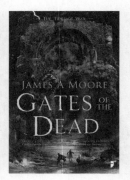

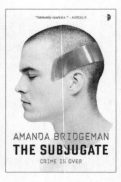

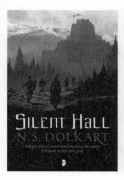
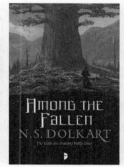

Science Fiction, Fantasy and WTF?!

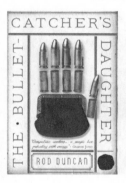

@angryrobotbooks

We are Angry Robot

angryrobotbooks.com